A FLAG FOR SUNRISE

"POWERFUL STUFF...

AT ONCE A TOPICAL THRILLER,
A POLITICAL TRACT, A NOVEL OF IDEAS,
A RELIGIOUS PARABLE. IT'S SPLASHED WITH CLASHES:
GRINGOS AGAINST LATINS, LATINS AGAINST INDIANS,
MARXISTS AGAINST CHRISTIANS, SPIES AGAINST INNOCENTS,
WOMEN AGAINST MEN, MEN AGAINST WOMEN, ALL STRUGGLING
IN AN OILY WHIRLPOOL OF BETRAYAL...
THEY MAKE *A FLAG FOR SUNRISE*...
IMPOSSIBLE TO FORGET."
CHICAGO SUN-TIMES

"STONE'S FORCE IS UNDENIABLE... ONE KNEELS IN AWE."
THE VILLAGE VOICE

Also by Robert Stone
Published by Ballantine Books:

A Hall of Mirrors

Dog Soldiers

A FLAG FOR SUNRISE

ROBERT STONE

BALLANTINE BOOKS • NEW YORK

Portions of this book have been previously published in *American Review #26* (November 1977, published by Bantam Books, Inc.), *Harper's*, and *TriQuarterly*.

Library of Congress Catalog Card Number: 81–47507

ISBN 0–345–30650–3

This edition published by arrangement with Alfred A. Knopf, Inc.

Manufactured in the United States of America

First Ballantine Books Edition: December 1982

for Deidre

Father Egan left off writing, rose from his chair and made his way—a little unsteadily—to the bottle of Flor de Cana which he had placed across the room from his desk. The study in which he worked was lit by a Coleman lamp; he had turned the mission generators off to save kerosene. The shutters were open to receive the sea breeze and the room was cool and pleasant. At Freddy's Chicken Shack up the road a wedding party was in progress and the revelers were singing along with the radio from Puerto Alvarado, marking the reggae beat with their own steel drums and crockery.

As Egan drank his rum, his inward eye filled with a vision of the Beguinage at Bruges, the great sculptured vault overhead, the windows inlaid with St. Ursula and her virgins, the columns gilded with imperial red and gold. It had been many, many years since he had seen it.

The Coleman lamp cast the shadow of his desk crucifix across the piles of books, bills and invoices that cluttered the space around his typewriter. He took a second drink of rum and considered the cruciform shadow, indulging the notion that his office space suggested the study of some heterodox doctor of the Renaissance, a man condemned by his times but sustained by faith in God and the Spirit among men.

The work on which Father Egan was engaged would fail of imprimatur, would be publishable only by a secular house. When it appeared he would be adjured to silence. He would resist, appeal to Rome if only to gain a wider hearing. When Rome thundered condemnation, he would turn to the Spir-

1

itual Church, the masses so hungry for comfort in a violently
dying world.

It was the composition of this work that had led to Father
Egan's intemperance in drink. For over thirty years as a Devotionist Father he had been a moderate man in that regard—
but writing was hard for him and the cultural deprivations
of his voluntary mission posting had rendered his life difficult
by the day. He had rewritten the work six times and had
reached the point where he could no longer endure it without
alcohol. Yet without the work, he had found, life itself was
not endurable. As for his faith—it was in a state of tension,
the dark of his soul's night was such that he could not bring it
to bear. And if that faith seemed moribund, he could only
hope that it had returned to the seed to grow, to be trans-
mogrified, dried and hardened in the tropical sun, destined to
rise like a brilliant Tecanecan phoenix from Pascal's fire.

He had put by him the thought of a third slug and was
halfway back to his desk when he heard the sound of a jeep's
engine on the beach below the mission buildings; he stopped
to listen as the jeep drew closer. At length, he heard the
brakes squeal and the engine die, and then a man's ascending
step on the stairs that led from the beach to his veranda.

"Oh my fucking word," Father Egan said aloud.

He quickly took the bottle of Flor de Cana, put it in his
shower stall and drew the curtain that closed off the bath.
Then, popping a mint candy in his mouth, he stepped outside
to the veranda.

It was the night of the full moon and the ocean before him
was aglow. The tips of coral along the reef, the wind-driven
whitecaps beyond were edged in silver shadow, the very grains
of sand on the beach sparkled faintly. In the dispensary wing,
an oil lamp burned behind Sister Justin Feeney's bamboo
shade.

At the foot of the steps a jeep had been parked, and a man
was climbing toward the main house, humming along with the
music from Freddy's. He climbed very slowly, putting both
feet on each step and shuffling to the reggae beat. On the last
step, he raised both hands above his shoulders in a little flutter
of stylized ecstasy and lurched onto the veranda. When he
saw Father Egan in the moon-swept darkness, he stepped
back, startled.

The man wore a white *guayabera* and dark trousers. There

was a holstered pistol on his hip, hanging from a webbed guard belt which he had buckled casually over his loose shirt. His hair was combed slickly across his skull; he was not a man of the coast, but a mestizo from the interior. Egan saw that it was Lieutenant Campos, social agent of the Guardia Nacional, uncharacteristically out of uniform and thoroughly drunk. Recognizing Campos, he drew his breath in fear.

"Holy Father," Lieutenant Campos said. He crossed himself and kissed his fingers as though Egan were an object of veneration. "Bless me, Father," he said in Spanish. "Bless me, for I have sinned."

Egan, having coiled a sentence of greeting, released it without enthusiasm.

"Good evening, Lieutenant, my friend. How may we help you?"

"Yes," Lieutenant Campos said. "And now you have to come with me."

Father Egan recoiled, in spite of himself. The words froze his heart. Campos was staring at Sister Justin Feeney's lighted window. The two men stood bathed in the unrelenting moonlight, both of them swaying slightly with drink. At Freddy's Chicken Shack, the beat went on.

"Where is the nun?" the lieutenant asked with distaste. "The earnest nun?"

"Gone to bed, I would suppose," Father Egan said cheerily. God save us, he thought. We're being arrested.

"No no," Campos said. "Because, see, her light is on. She's staying awake. And who knows what she's thinking?" The lieutenant had raised his voice over the distant music but from Sister Justin Feeney's room there was no sound or stirring. Campos belched sadly and turned his attention back to the priest.

"Come with me," he said in his policeman's voice. "We're going."

"It's so late," the priest said. "Does it have to be now?" He was aware of the lieutenant's insane intelligent eyes smoldering in the moonlight.

Campos laid a hand on his arm.

"Come!"

"Lieutenant," Egan said, "please. A moment." He went inside to get his stole and breviary, in case there might be some emergency.

They went down the steps to the beach in silence. Campos stood by the side of his jeep and held the door open for the priest.

The road, such as it was, followed the packed sand of the beach, descending now and then into a sea-flooded hollow that splashed phosphorescence as they forded it. Egan sat with the stole in his teeth, the missal between his legs, holding fast to the sidebar of the jeep. The lieutenant drove as fast as the vehicle would move; now and then he muttered something in a low voice which the priest could not understand.

He did not brake for animals. If a cow, transfixed in the headlights, was too slow in heaving its flyblown bulk from the roadway, the lieutenant would unhesitatingly ram it bellowing into a ditch, throw the jeep into reverse and charge forward.

In twenty minutes or so they came to the peninsula on which the lieutenant maintained his residence. In a country of frenetically gregarious people, Lieutenant Campos lived alone, without family or servants. The turnoff that led to his compound was barred by a chain link fence, its gate secured with a padlock. Campos kept his jeep motor running as he opened it; when they were inside he got out again and locked it behind them.

Breathing deeply, Father Egan followed Campos from the jeep and stood by while he unlocked his front door. The lieutenant used more locks than one was used to seeing along the coast.

Egan went in first; the presence of Campos, entering behind him in the darkness, touched the priest with terror.

The lieutenant had electric light and his bungalow was very neat. There was a picture of the President of the Republic on one wall—the president appearing as the apotheosis of the nation-state, his full cheeks in pink with retouching, his uniform inked in pastels, his peculiar ears unobserved—the whole swathed in the furled colors of Tecan. Beside it was a framed copy of the lieutenant's commission, then a framed shot of a younger—perhaps a more reasonable—Lieutenant Campos, posing with his buddies at Guardia school.

Below the pictures were two bookcases. One held bound logs and law books; the shelves of the other were stacked with American detective magazines arranged by name. *True, Startling, Inside, Master* and *Underground Detective*—Egan thought there must be a thousand magazines in the stacks. On the other wall was a picture of John Kennedy, below it was what appeared to be an electric freezer and next to that the only glassed window between Puerto Alvarado and the frontier, overlooking the moonlit ocean. In an alcove near it was the Guardia's Hallstadt radio transmitter. The circuit was open, now and then picking up a Caribbean voice.

". . . up in Belize, mon."

". . . well, you know . . . dat de British port, mon . . . dey goin' to come down haard . . ."

Egan turned toward his host and saw that the lieutenant had produced a bottle of Flor de Cana and was offering him a drink. He accepted with gratitude but the rum did little for him. Campos sat down in a wicker chair by the transmitter and asked him in strained English if he required another.

"Yes, please," Father Egan said, ashamed.

Campos poured it slowly and as he proffered it, Egan had the sense that he might suddenly snatch it away again to torment him. Just as he was imagining the dreadful smile that might appear on Campos' face if he did in fact snatch the glass away—the smile appeared.

Egan polished off his rum.

"You . . ." the lieutenant asked, "you are a queer? A *maricón?*"

Egan was jolted stone sober. He stared at the lieutenant in outrage. He had been in the country for ten years and never—never had anyone, not even a drunken Baptist—addressed him in that manner.

Yet the horrible word brought to his recollection a desperate sodden night. He had been in town, in Alvarado, and he had gotten tight. Something had happened in the bar of the Gran Atlántico hotel; he remembered the lights of the bar and the lights of the street outside—a boy in a death's-head motorcycle cap, a European-looking boy with greasy long hair falling to his shoulders and the boy shouting at him scornfully —*Maricón! Eres maricón!*

Was it memory? Had such a thing happened? Egan was not clear.

"Lieutenant," he asked humbly, "why are you speaking to me like that?"

"I know what I know," Campos said. "I know you're good. You're O.K. I want to confess to you."

Father Egan tried to clear his head.

"Now, Lieutenant. . . . Is this the time? When you've been drinking?" He attempted a sympathetic chuckle. "I think you should reflect a little."

Lieutenant Campos raised his hand in a slow gesture that indicated the frivolousness of further conversation.

"No," he said. "I want to confess to you. It will be under the seal."

"I can't . . ." Father Egan began. He had been going to tell the lieutenant that he could not give absolution to a man who was drunk. Contrition and resolve would be questionable. He took another drink.

Lieutenant Campos was standing up; he was staring at Egan with a dreadful intensity. He walked to the red freezer by the window and lifted its top door open. With a slight raising of his chin, he signaled Father Egan to draw near. The priest advanced slowly, his eyes fixed on Campos' face. The lieutenant looked down into the open freezer with an expression of stoic grief.

Fearfully, Egan followed the lieutenant's gaze and saw that the freezer contained an unplucked turkey and a great many bottles of Germania beer. Beneath them was a bolt of green cloth. Puzzled, he turned to Campos but the lieutenant had closed his eyes and was biting his lip, as though to control his emotions. Egan reached down, moved a few of the bottles of frozen beer and his eye fell on the maple-leaf flag of Canada. Father Egan was a native of Windsor, Ontario, and for the briefest moment he entertained the idea that Lieutenant Campos had devised some drunken ceremony of appreciation for him, some naïve filial gesture of esteem that might one day be the basis of a pleasant story. He glanced at the lieutenant and was confronted with the extreme unlikeliness of so innocent a notion.

He scanned the surface contents of the chest, amorphous cubes of ice, the enormous turkey, the bottles of beer with their peeling labels, and saw at last—in one corner, partially concealed by ice—a human foot. Looking more closely, he saw that it curved downward from a turned ankle on which there was a small cut gone black. The outer side of the foot was visible, its callused edge pressed against the top of a South American sandal. The thong of the sandal divided the darkly veined front of the foot; caught between two of the toes was a tiny cotton pompon of bright red. Father Egan looked down at the foot and understood only its beautiful symmetry, its functional wholeness, the sublime engineering that had appended its five longish toes. The top of it, he saw, was suntanned.

Then his knees buckled under him. As he reached out to steady himself, his hand clawed across the ice cubes and revealed a moist matting of yellow hair, then a tanned forehead. Then below, the freckled bridge of a nose and an eye—blue with a foliate iris—the whites gone dark, an eye so dull, so dead with sheer animal death that Egan received the sight of it as a spiritual shock.

He staggered back from the ice chest.

"Oh my God," he said. He reeled to the wall and leaned under the picture of the President, trembling with disgust and fear.

A sad smile had appeared on the lieutenant's face. He turned to Egan and the smile broadened until his features quivered to contain it. Looking back at him, Egan had the sense that he was in the presence of a man who, though obviously mad, understood him thoroughly.

"Father," the lieutenant said, "do your duty. You have to be cool and brave. You have to have mercy." He moved closer to Egan. "The power of Christ commands."

Father Egan realized that he had no idea what the power of Christ was. Christ, it seemed to him, had no more power than he himself did and he had hardly the power to stand up. Panic rose in him like a sudden fever and he fought for his reason.

"What happened?" he heard himself ask.

Lieutenant Campos raised his eyes, yielding the question to heaven. Egan made himself go to the freezer. With a gentleness that he realized was only a studied part of his priestcraft, he moved some of the ice and beer from over the corpse.

It was a young blond girl in khaki shorts and a Boy Scout shirt with the maple-leaf flag sewn to the back of it. Jackknifed into the chest.

Egan's revulsion was tempered by sorrow. He supposed she had been dead for a long time. Far from the lakes, he thought, trying to master his trembling, the tamaracks, the elm-lined streets.

"How did she die, Lieutenant?"

"I'll tell you that," the lieutenant said. "You'll find out how." He poured himself another glass of rum and extended the bottle toward Egan.

"No, thank you," the priest said.

He saw his stole and breviary on a bookcase where he had set them and absently picked them up, and sat down in the rocking chair, clasping his forehead.

"Who was she?"

"She was a hippie," Lieutenant Campos said solemnly. "Drugs. Whoring."

You swine, Father Egan thought.

"But I mean her name, Lieutenant. Didn't she have a passport? Surely you realize that she has a family?"

Campos went to his desk beside the transmitter, sat down at it and began to write. When he was done, he handed Egan a yellow message form with block letters on it.

JANET FOGARTY ALBERTA, the paper read.

The lieutenant pronounced the words with difficulty.

Egan fingered the edges of his stole. From her name the girl might well be Catholic. Yet first, he thought, glancing again at Campos, it would be necessary to minister to the living. He kissed the stole and put it around his neck.

"All right then, Lieutenant. Make your confession."

To his embarrassment, Lieutenant Campos came and knelt on the floor at his feet. The lieutenant crossed himself and clasped his heavy hands prayerfully. Egan looked away.

"She was a hippie," Lieutenant Campos declared, his hands clasped.

"I see," Egan said in a quavering voice. The dreadful question lay squarely before him. Asking it, he was sure, would eventually cost him his life.

"Did you kill her?"

"No!" Campos shouted, startling the priest utterly. He climbed from his knees, brushed them off and began to pace the floor of his office.

"She was spearing fish, understand? That's not allowed. Everyone knows it's not allowed."

"Of course," Father Egan said.

"Listen," the lieutenant said, setting his chair beside Egan's, "listen to this! She hid the spear gun under the dock at Playa Tate. The mayor there told us. We went out and we saw her. She had the spear."

"Yes," the priest said.

"We called her to come in. She pretended to be afraid. She teased us like a little whore. We said O.K., if she's going to act like that we'll tease her back a little."

Egan could see the scene quite clearly—the frightened girl in the water trying to ease over the inshore coral to the narrow shelf of sandy bottom, the drunken Guardia along the beach with their M-16's unslung, Campos standing on the rotting pier, laughing at her.

"And she drowned?"

"She died," Campos said vaguely.

"I see."

"So I took command," the lieutenant said. "It was my responsibility. I dismissed them. You see—I dressed her. These little clothes, they're all she ever wore. I preserved her for ceremony."

"What ceremony?" No ceremony else, he thought. Her death was doubtful.

Campos only laughed quietly, tears coming to his eyes.

"How long ago was this?" Egan asked, feeling that he had wasted a question.

"The winter."

"It was certainly wrong of you," Egan said, "to keep her here like this. Her family has no knowledge of her, so think how they must feel. As a policeman and especially as a social agent, you should reflect on the violation of your responsibilities involved."

He looked into the warning that was composing itself in Campos' eyes.

"Don't believe," the lieutenant said, "it was easy for me to have her here. It was hard. Listen—it was very hard to have her in there all the time."

Egan found himself listening to the steady hum of Campos' generator.

"Why did you keep her, then?" He felt that it was important to put the question correctly, reluctant though he was to impute to Lieutenant Campos any further suggestion of weakness or dereliction. "Was it loneliness?"

The delicacy of the priest's question was lost on Campos. His features went cold.

"What do you know about it?"

Egan only nodded.

"When I ask you a question, Father, I require you to answer it. What do you know about it?"

While Father Egan was reflecting on what he knew about loneliness he saw Campos stagger toward him.

"You—you *maricón*, you know nothing about it! You *maricón*! How can you question me?"

"You've asked me to hear your confession," Egan said mildly. "It's necessary that I ask questions."

"Confession is right," Campos said. "It's under the seal, understand? That means you keep your mouth shut. You keep it shut, understand me?"

"The law is plain," Egan assured him. "What you tell me is privileged."

"And don't," Campos said, "think I care a shit about priests and religion. I'm a man—not a woman or a *maricón*. You keep your mouth shut."

"You can be certain of that," Egan said. It occurred to him that the promise was a rash one.

"Look," the lieutenant said, gentling. "I think it's wrong for me to keep her here."

"I agree," Egan said.

"Very well," Campos told him. "You can take her then."

"What?"

"You can take her. Take her away."

"I take her? But, my dear Lieutenant, how can I . . ."

"That's the duty of the church!" Campos shouted at him. "That's the duty of priests to take the dead!"

"Well, it's the duty of the police . . ." Egan began, but the lieutenant cut him off.

"Don't tell me my duty. You think I don't know what goes on? That nun—she's not a true nun. You think I'm stupid?"

"I don't know what you're talking about."

Campos suddenly smiled.

"Come on," he said, touching the priest's sleeve in an attitude of merry conspiracy, "we'll give her to you. You're the priest. You take her for me—that's what's right."

Egan watched him bring a nylon sleeping bag from one corner of the room and drag it to the freezer.

"Come now," Campos said. "We'll get her out."

"Look here," Egan said, "I'm leaving."

He stood up and marched out the front door into the

moonlight. He was halfway down the steps when the lieutenant caught him.

"Get back inside," the lieutenant said. "I'm telling you officially."

Egan went back up the steps.

"For heaven's sake," he said pleadingly as Campos marched
him inside, "you can dispose of a body better than I can. I
mean, if you're determined to keep the whole thing hid-
den. . . . I wouldn't tell anyone."

"I am not an animal," Campos said. "I believe there is a
spiritual force. I believe in life after death."

"Yes, yes, of course," Egan said.

"All right. For the relief of my heart—I give her to you."
He walked to the freezer and picked up an end of the bag.
"And don't try to run away again."

Father Egan had collapsed in a chair. He listened with his
eyes averted while Lieutenant Campos struggled cursing with
the bag in the freezer.

"Very well," he heard the lieutenant say, "now come and
help."

Turning, he saw the floor littered with ice and beer bottles.
The sleeping bag was half out of the chest, looking like a
squat brown serpent that had swallowed a lamb. The body,
its fetal outline unmistakable under the quilted cloth, was
propped against the metal edge while the twisted ends dangled
fore and aft.

Egan walked toward it, a man in a dream.

Lieutenant Campos wiped the sweat from his eyes.

"Pick up the end."

But the priest could not.

"Pick up the end!" Campos shouted. "You coward! You
maricón!"

Egan stopped tugging at the limp end and put his hands
under the human shape in the center. Through the ticking, it
felt like a block of ice.

Together, they lifted the bag and carried it out—down the
steps and into the back seat of the lieutenant's jeep. Egan was
so overcome that he thought he would faint at any moment.
Besides, he was unused to exercise.

As they drove back along the moonlit beach road, he clung
to the jeep rack in despair. The wind caught the stole around
his neck and blew its strands taut behind him.

"I just can't believe this is happening," he said aloud to himself.

Lieutenant Campos heard him.

"Then," the lieutenant said, "you shouldn't be a priest."

At the foot of the mission stpes, they hauled the bag out and set it down on the hard sand. Freddy's Chicken Shack was still wailing, the mellow barrel drums telling out life's time, getting down.

Swaying a little, Lieutenant Campos put his hand on Egan's arm.

"Do your duty," he said. "Everyone must."

Father Egan watched the jeep drive off; the bag at his feet was a dark shape on the luminous sand.

Down the beach from the mission steps was a gear shack with a small dock extending out over the ocean where the station's fiberglass whaler hung at moor. Looking over his shoulder, Egan hurried to the landing and saw that the boat was secured to its customary piling and the outboard attached to the stern, the screws hauled up above the waterline. He went back to the bag, seized its ends and began to pull with the resolution of despair. It was a fearsome business of inches —the drums from Freddy's mocked his panting breaths. When he had pulled the bag halfway to the boat, he looked up the beach and saw that two late-departing wedding guests had staggered out of Freddy's and were approaching the dock. Quickly, he crouched down beside his horrid burden and stretched out beside it, his body pressed against the sand and rotting palm fronds.

The two men walked in step, carrying their shoes in their hands. Both of them wore dark suits with dress shirts and ties and as they walked they hummed softly in counterpoint. Passing the pier, perhaps a hundred feet from where Father Egan lay with the stuffed sleeping bag, one of the two stepped out on the pine slats and began to dance. With one hand, he waved the shoes he held in an arc over his head while the other snaked out at a right angle from his body gliding against the background of the moonlit ocean as his knees swayed. With his bare feet, he stamped the wooden surface of the pier to the beat of the barrel drums and at each stomp the water beneath the pier erupted in small bursts of glowing phosphorescence. When he had finished his dance, the man and his companion fell into step again and moved off toward the darkened clapboards of French Harbor.

Egan lay still until they were out of sight, then rose stiffly and hauled the corpse the rest of the way.

The gear shack was kept unlocked, according to the custom of the coast; from a shelf inside he took two heavy fish-head anchors and a coil of wire line. He dropped the anchors and the line into the boat, climbed in and set the outboard in the water. With a final effort, he dragged the sleeping bag off the pier—it fell into the boat at his feet with such force that for a moment he was afraid that it had stove the bottom in. Then he cast off the line and let the movement of the water carry the boat free.

Gritting his teeth, he pulled the cord to prime the engine and—not daring to look behind him—set a course for the outer reef. Five hundred yards from shore, he wheeled north to skirt the first wall of coral—he was grateful for the moonlight now—then turned north again until the boat had cleared the second reef. When he cut the engines, the whaler picked up the swell of open ocean and began to roll back toward the beach. After the second reef, the bottom fell away abruptly; the water beneath his keel was hundreds of fathoms deep.

Wide-eyed, Father Egan forced open the bag's zipper and dropped both anchors inside, then looped the wire line around both ends of the bag, leaving the rest of the coil in snarled dangling confusion.

A short distance from the boat, two bonito jumped, their bodies glinting silver, avoiding a shark.

He put the light end over first, and then kneeling in the scuppers, with his hands as a scoop he eased the frozen mass of the girl's body over the side. His great fear had been that the bag would not sink—but it sank quite readily, sliding down under the hull and disappearing utterly with hardly a bubble to mark its descent into darkness. The deck of the boat and the ocean's surface held no trace of what they had borne a few seconds before.

Father Egan was amazed at the ease with which it had been done. He felt as though he had gained a thoroughly new insight into the processes of the world.

When he started the engine again, an impulse seized him to head for open sea, to let the sunrise find him miles from the mission landing and the coast of the Republic. But he mastered himself and headed the whaler for shore at trolling speed. Once the engine stalled on him, but he got it turning again without much difficulty. As he passed the inshore reef, he began to cry.

As the beach grew nearer, a moment of lucidity and calm hovered before him like a holy apparition and he gripped it desperately. Within the calm moment sounded his own voice, the voice of Christian humanist witness in a vicious world. Somewhere, in some reasonable, wood-paneled overheated room, he heard himself recounting what had happened and explaining it thoroughly. He made his voice repeat the explanation over and over lest it be lost and his reason overthrown.

I buried her myself, Father Egan heard himself explain. Of course, I couldn't tell anyone.

On the day Holliwell left for Central America, his wife had volunteered to arrange the weekend outing of a brilliant young paranoid. Holliwell's wife was a Master of Social Work at the state hospital. Before seven, she drove the girls to school and went on to the facility to pick up the paranoid and conduct him home to his nervous parents in the suburbs of Wilmington.

Holliwell finished his packing alone; he and his wife had taken leave of each other during the night. When his bag was locked and standing by the front door, he went into the kitchen and made himself a strong bloody mary. He drank it by the living-room window, looking out at the front yard where his magnolia hung snowbound and his mountain ash stood tortured and skeletal in an envelope of ice.

She was a little bit in love with this one, Holliwell thought —and the man was unquestionably dangerous. But she would almost certainly be all right. She was very sensible.

His plane left from Kennedy the following morning and he planned to pass the day in New York, first lunching with Marty Nolan, then checking into his favorite hotel to see what the evening might bring. He no longer knew anyone who lived in the city. At four or so, he would phone his wife to make sure that everything had gone well.

He finished the first drink and then had another, not bothering with breakfast. By the time he put his suitcase in the back of the Volvo, he was high enough to stop at the smoke shop in town and buy his first pack of cigarettes in a month. Driving to the turnpike, he smoked one cigarette after another.

The road to the pike—like the road his wife would drive to Wilmington—ran through pine forest and swamp. Each time he passed over a culvert, or the frozen course of a creek dividing one stand of pine from another, the picture would come into his mind of his wife lying dead in the woods, her red and white scarf knotted round her neck in a thin line, her bloodied fingers stiffening across a log.

After the turnpike entrance, he hit the radio and in a mile or two WWVA eased down from space, selling lucky crosses and Christian good fortune. Holliwell tuned it in carefully and between commercials heard a singular musical recitation, delivered in up-country dialect, about a young football player.

The youth on the record was his high school's star quarterback; it was the Big Game against the school in the next hollow and at half time the home team was a couple of touchdowns behind. During the half-time break, the boy disappeared from the locker room and he was late returning for the third quarter.

"Where in the hell you been?" demanded the anxious hometown coach, who was decent but hard. He swore at the boy and shoved him toward the line of scrimmage.

There then commenced an astonishing display of unforgettable schoolboy ball. The kid played like a young man possessed, and the fans in the little country-and-Western town had never seen the like of him. The opposition was devastated, the coach awestruck and penitent. Amid the jubilation outside the showers, he drew the young quarterback quietly aside.

"Coach," the youth explained, "my father was blind."

The boy's father had been blind and for a week had lain upon his deathbed. The boy had been phoning the hospital regularly and during half time had learned of his father's death.

The coach cleared his throat. How then to explain the spectacle only just witnessed—the sixty-yard touchdown passes, the seventy-yard scoring runs?

"You see, coach," the boy said quietly, "it's the first time he's ever seen me play."

By the time WWVA faded out, Holliwell was aware of the tears streaming down his face, staining his tie, wetting his moustache and the stub of his cigarette. He eased the Volvo into the next turnoff, and sat, with the motor running, staring through the windshield at a row of green refuse cans until he had stopped sobbing.

So much for morning drinking. An hour and a half from home and he already had an anecdote for his wife, one that would engage her sympathy and attention, one to save for his return home—providing, of course, that both of them returned alive.

We're getting pretty shaky, he told himself, wiping the foolish tears from his face with a Kleenex. It was being forty, marriage, soft suburban living.

She gets tougher and smarter, he thought, and I get shaky —a pattern of class and culture. Perhaps he might tell her about the country song but not about his breaking up at the wheel.

In the snowy woods beyond the paved rest area and the green garbage cans, a young black man in city clothes was carrying a paper parcel toward the road. He saw the parked Volvo with Holliwell at the wheel and turned quickly back into the maze of pines. Holliwell sighed, put the car in gear and rolled back onto the turnpike, headed for lunch and New York.

An hour later, he was crossing the Narrows bridge; the harbor and the Manhattan skyline were bright with January sunshine. Holliwell's spirits had lifted in the wastes of Bayonne; except for a palpable desire for more alcohol, he felt that he was doing fairly well. It would be a drinking day—the morning stirrup cup had set off an old mechanism. But his habits had become so generally temperate that it seemed to him he could afford some reasonable indulgence in the field.

He took the Belt Parkway northward and fought his way into the traffic around the King's County Courthouse. He had not been to Brooklyn for years and being there gave him the mild elation that came with a new and unfamiliar town. The restaurant was on Court Street; it had valet parking and a few sumac trees out back and he found it on the first pass. He brushed the cigarette ashes from his jacket, put his suitcase in the trunk and handed the keys to a uniformed Puerto Rican attendant.

McDermott's was the name of the place, three huge rooms of cut glass, oak and dusty ceiling fans. McDermott's, Holliwell decided, was great fun—and when he thought back on the business later, it seemed to him that it was largely the prospect of dining in downtown Brooklyn that had persuaded him to lunch with Marty Nolan in the first place.

A captain in a tuxedo escorted him among the seated landlords and deputy inspectors, leading him to a round table on which reposed a half-finished martini and a rumpled paisley napkin. He ordered a martini for himself and admired the huge mirrors on the paneled walls. The drink had arrived and Holliwell was taking his first sip when he saw Marty Nolan step out of the gents' in the next salon and proceed nearsightedly across the hall.

As Marty walked, his left hand absently brushed an area below the belt of his double-knit trousers; he was checking to see if his fly was unzipped. When he saw Holliwell, his round face brightened. Holliwell stood up to shake hands with him.

"Herr Professor," Marty Nolan said.

His hand was damp, his thick horn-rimmed glasses seemed almost about to steam and although it was not at all hot in McDermott's there was a band of perspiration below the line of his fair curly hair.

"Good to see you, Marty," Holliwell said.

It would be possible, he thought, to describe Nolan as fastidious—yet there was always something faintly gross about the man, the suggestion of unwholesome secrets.

Nolan raised his glass and they drank.

"I'm delighted that you made the time for lunch. I'm honored."

"Not at all," Holliwell said. "I looked forward to it."

He was privy to a few of Marty Nolan's secrets. One was that during the Tet offensive, the Viet Cong forces who overran Hue had buried him alive—and he had lain in the earth half conscious for six hours until a party of German medical missionaries dug him out.

And on one occasion, Holliwell, visiting from the Central

Highlands, had found a manuscript sheet in Nolan's portable typewriter with a single sentence at the top of the page and the sentence had read: "The Jew is at home in the modern world." Whether or not this was a libel depended entirely upon one's sense and experience of the modern world—but the business about "the Jew" was distinctly sinister. Can of worms there, Holliwell had thought.

But his ties to Nolan were old and strong. They had both gone to Regis in the fifties—it was a Jesuit high school that took in the smartest kids from the city's parochial grade schools. They had both been released into the nineteen sixties from prestigious secular universities. They had both been to Vietnam on their government's service.

Marty was peering over his glasses at the room in which they sat.

"I'm in transports of Brooklyn nostalgia," he told Holliwell. "I come from Bay Ridge, you remember."

"Of course I remember. What brings you up here? I thought you worked down in Washington."

"Oh yeah," Marty said, "in the Washington area. I'm visiting my mother."

Holliwell inquired after Marty Nolan's mother, wondering if he had ever married and whether or not to ask.

"Mom's O.K. She gets around."

"Well, it's a great place, this," Holliwell said. "It's really old Brooklyn."

They ordered more martinis, a bottle of Barbarousse. Holliwell asked for a steak and salad, Nolan the veal piccata.

"Did you know," Nolan asked as a waiter opened the wine, "that Paul Robeson died this morning?"

"I thought he died in Russia about ten years ago."

"This morning," Nolan said. His eyes flashed a thick whimsy which Holliwell remembered very clearly from the past. "It was on the radio."

"Well," Holliwell said, cutting his steak, "I hardly know how to react."

"I wasn't trying to goad you to malicious satisfaction, Frank. After all, everybody dies. It just brings back old times. I'd like to go to his funeral."

"You mean officially?"

"Don't be ridiculous. I'd just like to go. To see it."

"Think the FBI will be there? Taking everybody's picture?"

"I wouldn't think so. But who knows with those guys?"

Holliwell, chewing his steak, became aware of Marty's eyes on him again.

"How's your life, Frank? Quiet desperation? Self-fulfillment?"

Holliwell nodded and finished chewing.

"Last month," he told Nolan, "my oldest daughter burned herself slightly. It was the winter solstice and she was jumping over a flaming log with her boyfriend."

"Is that the way they get married now?"

Holliwell poured them both some Barbarousse.

"How about you, Marty? Ever get married?"

"I was married in Nam, didn't you know that? In the Saigon cathedral."

"It must have been after I left," Holliwell said. "What's the lady like?"

"Neat," Marty said.

Holliwell found himself touched. "Is she Vietnamese?"

"From Worcester. We're separated now. We don't have any kids."

Holliwell nodded to convey comprehension, sympathy, whatever might be called for.

"And you," Nolan said. "You're off to Compostela for a little something different."

"I fiddled it. I invited my friends at the university down there to invite me. How did you come to hear about it?"

"I had a letter from Oscar Ocampo. He said you'd be coming down."

Holliwell realized then that there would be a pitch. He must, he thought, have realized all along that there would be one. But it would not disturb him, he decided; it was part of a game, an artifact of his friendship with Nolan, a little fencing between gentlemen. Neither of them would take it too seriously.

"How come Oscar's writing to you? I thought he was a leftist."

"Sure he's a leftist. But we're not enemies. We have a dialogue going."

Ocampo was a government anthropologist with a sinecure in the university at Compostela, a gambler and a great womanizer. Holliwell had always known him to be a passionate sympathizer with revolution.

"Oscar and I used to have some great arguments," Holliwell said. Apparently Oscar had stopped arguing. They had turned him—either with money or with the offer of a job in the States. It was a shame, Holliwell thought, and Oscar must feel very bad about it.

"I suppose," Holliwell said, "that in a couple of years, you'll be asking me to get him a job up here."

"Frank—how about doing us a favor while you're down there?"

Holliwell buttered some French bread and said what he had decided he would say.

"If you approach me with something like that, Marty, I'm supposed to publicize the approach. My professional association passed a resolution against doing favors for you guys."

"Your professional association," Marty Nolan said humorously, "is a bunch of long-haired disorderly persons. Pinkos, Frank. Red rats."

"All anthropologists are brothers," Holliwell said.

"Suppose I ask how you voted on that resolution?"

Holliwell put his bread down and set his fork beside it.

"I abstained. I was in favor of the resolution but I felt compromised. Because of what I did in Nam. The favors."

"God," Marty said soberly. "You're an honest man, Frank."

"Well," Holliwell told him, "there it is. As they used to say. What do you hear from Ho Chi Minh City?"

Marty looked at him for a moment and finished his wine.

"Not much. They arrested the Hoa Hao. A lot of them were friends of ours and nobody bothered to get them out. Look—what can I say? You want to know if I'm bitter? I'm not. Neither am I repentant. The other guys fought hard, they earned it."

"If you were bitter I wouldn't blame you. You really came through the whole thing damn well."

Nolan put his own fork down. They had both stopped eating.

"What should I do—run for Congress? Get myself a tent show in Orange County—I Know the Red Terror Firsthand? I'll tell you something, Frank—the night they dug me out I was in a hospital compound with this old Spanish priest. The guy was walking up and down chain smoking and they'd had him under the ground longer than I was. He said to me—

Hombre, this was nothing. They buried me alive in Murcia in thirty-eight and it was a lot harder."

Holliwell laughed and shook his head.

"Frank," Marty Nolan said, "let me tell you about what's going on down south. I guarantee, you'll love it."

Holliwell shrugged; Nolan was leaning across the table at him, his eyes shining with good-natured intrigue.

"Down in Tecan, on the east coast, even as we sit here— some of our countrymen find themselves in a state of social and spiritual crisis."

"Let's let them work it out for themselves," Holliwell said.

"All I want to know, Frank, is what they're really up to."

"Ask Oscar what they're up to—he's on the payroll, right? Speaking as an American taxpayer, I don't give a shit."

"Oh, Frank," Marty said. He sat back in his chair as though scandalized. "Information is a positive force. It furthers communication. It reduces isolation and clarifies motives. The more everybody knows about what everybody else is doing, the less misunderstanding there is in the world."

"I'm going to Compostela. I'm not setting foot in fucking Tecan. It's a rathole and it gets on my conscience."

"Nonsense," Marty said, "it's a wonderful place. They have American-style hardware stores and the President speaks English just like we do here on Court Street."

"And he's wonderful too."

"He certainly is," Marty said. "He's a Rotarian."

"Marty," Holliwell said, looking around for the waiter, "get off my back. I'm not going there and I'm not doing you any favors."

When the waiter came near, Nolan ordered them both a stinger. A busboy took their unfinished lunches away.

"On the Caribbean coast of Tecan there's a little place the locals call French Harbor. A couple of clicks down from Puerto Alvarado. For the last thirty years the American Devotionists have had a mission there but they're on their last legs now and they want to close it down. The only people left there are a priest in his sixties and an American nursing nun. Now the Devotionists have been asked about this and their provincial in New Orleans is being very cagey—but it seems that these characters won't come back."

The drinks arrived; Marty raised his glass in salute.

"There's a lot of medieval church diplomacy going on. The provincial says he'll cut off their funds but he hasn't. The priest and nun say they'll come back presently but they won't. Also the Tecanecan government has become aware of their presence and the Tecanecan government is extremely paranoid."

"And extremely murderous," Holliwell said.

"O.K.," Marty said, "they're murderous troglodytes and we put them in. But there it is. The Tecanecans suspect that the two of them are somehow mixed up in subversive activities but it hasn't got a line on them and it doesn't want a hassle with the church."

"And what do your sources say?"

"That these people are wrongos, Commies et cetera. That's what they always say. You know, Tecan is a special situation —it's still the fifties there. Our ambassador is a Birchite moron. The cops lock you up for reading Voltaire."

"Another corner of the free world."

"Don't give me clichés, Frank. Save them for the meetings of your professional association and someday they'll make you their president."

He finished his drink looking pained.

"Listen, old chap—I want to know what these people are up to. They're my compatriots and erstwhile co-religionists and they're fucking with El Toro down there. Somebody may have to bail them out."

"I'm not going down there to spy on them."

"Spy on them? Are you crazy? They're already being spied on seven ways from sundown by people who'd love nothing more than to mess with their private parts."

Holliwell signaled for another pair of stingers.

"You're going to Compostela. It would be the easiest thing in the world for you to get a Tecanecan visa and check out French Harbor. Go diving, go bonefishing. There's even an Old Empire ruin a few miles from there for you to scramble around. The thing is," he went on, before Holliwell could protest, "it's me that wants to know about these people. Not so much the outfit as just me. And I'd like to get it not from some informer or right-wing spook—but from somebody with some sensitivity. Somebody who could give me a real insight into what they think they're doing down there. You might be in a position to help *everybody* out."

"The last time I thought I was in that position things didn't work out very well."

"So what do you want? A perfect world? Tell me something, Professor, have you stopped believing that people have to take sides?"

"No," Holliwell said. "People have to take sides."

"What side are you on then? Do you really think the other guys are going to resolve social contradictions and make everything O.K.? Worker in the morning, hunter in the afternoon, scholar in the evening—do you really believe that's on, Frank?"

"No," Holliwell said.

"Well, it's them or us, chum. Like always. They make absolute claims, we make relative ones. That's why our side is better in the end."

"Is that what *you* believe?"

Marty shrugged. "Sure I believe it. You believe it too. Anyway I'm not recruiting you and it's not some kind of hostile operation. I told you what I wanted—just a little insight. It could be that we have something to learn from these two people in Tecan."

"Why don't you just write them a letter. Ask them what it is they want down there."

Nolan exhaled slowly and let his narrow shoulders sag.

"Give me a brandy," he told the waiter. "Two brandies." He turned from Holliwell to look around the room, at the wainscoted ceilings and the dwindling crowd of heavy-faced, hard-eyed diners.

"Jesus, I picked this place because I thought the atmosphere might discourage moral posturing."

"It must be you and me, Marty. We're spoiling the atmosphere."

Nolan took his brandy without ceremony.

"This conversation depresses me," he said, "because it reminds me that we live in the land of total vindication. T.V. T.V. or nothing. I mean twenty years ago we had the total vindication of William Jennings Bryan, and Father Flanagan and apple pie. Secularism"—he made a little equals sign in the air with his fingers—"was Communism. Modernism was godlessness. Bolshevism . . . All the eggheads were Commie stooges and you had to go to Fordham or Darlington, South Carolina, to find a loyal American. Then we get fucked up in

Nam and Saigon falls and the whole card's reversed. Hiss didn't do it, the Rosenbergs didn't do it, nobody fucking did it and Truman started the cold war. Total vindication."

"Well," Holliwell said, "there's nothing like total vindication."

"Exactly. See, it's all a movie in this country and if you wait long enough you get your happy ending. Until somebody else's movie starts. In many ways it's a very stupid country."

"Is this the patriotic approach?"

"Hell, no," Nolan said, "the patriotic approach is out of date."

They sat drinking in silence for a while. When the check came, Holliwell moved it to his own side of the table and kept it there.

"We're at a very primitive stage of mankind," Nolan declared, "that's what people don't understand. Just pick up the *Times* on any given day and you've got a catalogue of ape behavior. Strip away the slogans and excuses and verbiage, the so-called ideology, and you're reading about what one pack of chimpanzees did to another."

Holliwell paid the check with his BankAmericard and Nolan did not move to prevent him.

"Sorry," Holliwell said. "Not this time."

They walked to the front door together and stood beside the parking-lot fence. The brisk wind raised whirls of dust from the sidewalk and Nolan shielded his eyes with his right hand.

"When you're down there you may feel differently. So if I may, I'll ask you again through a third party."

Holliwell only smiled and they shook hands. It was not until he was halfway across the Brooklyn Bridge that the suggestion of a threat in Nolan's final words struck him, making him think of the man entombed beside the Perfume River, the involved observer of the modern world. A chill touched his inward loneliness. He was, he knew at that moment, really without beliefs, without hope—either for himself or for the world. Almost without friends, certainly without allies. Alone.

He drove toward Manhattan facing the squat brutality of the new buildings that had gone up around the bridge; he was depressed and too drunk for safety. The drive uptown left him tired and anxious. Gratefully, he turned the Volvo keys over to the hotel doorman and once upstairs ordered a bottle of scotch from room service. When the drink arrived, he sat with his feet on the windowsill looking out over the midtown rooftops. On a day in May, he and Marty Nolan had once walked from the library on East Seventy-ninth Street all the way down Second Avenue to the bridge and then across it, ending up in a bar on Clark Street. It would have been about 1955. Hour after hour, block after block of talk.

After a while, he moved over to the double bed, propped a pillow up behind him and dialed his home number. When he heard his wife's voice on the line, he lit a cigarette.

"So you're O.K.," he said. "You got back all right."

"I told you not to worry. He had his medicine at the hospital. He was half zonked."

"So he didn't rave and carry on?"

"He slept. When we got to his house he didn't know where he was."

"Does he ever?"

"Sure. He's very aware."

"What were his parents like?"

"Very middle-class. Quite well off, fancy house. They asked me in but I didn't go. They'll drive him back."

"So that's that."

"Yep," she said.

"I had my lunch with Marty. We drank a lot."

"You sound like you've been drinking. What are you going to do with yourself now?"

Holliwell poured himself a little scotch and ice water. In the blue sky beyond his window, fleecy January clouds were speeding over Manhattan.

"Maybe I'll walk over to Eighth Avenue. For some twenty-dollar fellatio."

"You're kidding, aren't you?"

"Yes," he said. "Of course."

"Well, I wish I was up there with you. And I wish I could go along."

"Marty told me that Paul Robeson just died."

"My God, was he gloating about it?"

"He was sort of gloating."

"Listen," she said. "Did he ask you to do any work for them?"

"He had something up his sleeve. I turned him down cold."

"Did you let him know you were mad at him?"

"I wasn't mad at him."

"I think they have a hell of a lot of nerve," she said.

"I love you," Holliwell told her. "Take care."

"I love you too. You take care too."

He sat on the edge of the bed, drinking still more whiskey and thinking about his conversation with Nolan. Shortly he began to wonder what Marty had been writing in that hootch outside of Hue, what he had meant by the modern world and by being at home in it. And by "the Jew."

A great deal of profoundly fractured cerebration had gone down in Vietnam. People had been by turns Fascist mystics, Communist revolutionaries and junkies; at certain times, certain people had managed to be all three at once. It was the nature of the time—the most specious lunacy had been conceived, written and enacted on both sides of the Pacific. Most of the survivors were themselves again, for what it was worth. No one could be held totally responsible for his utterances during that time.

The Jew was presumably the one who squatted on the estaminet, blistered in Brussels, patched and peeled in Antwerp. Holliwell knew him; his name was Sy, he had once run a newspaper stand on the corner of Dyckman Street and Broadway. Sy had lived almost across the hall from Holliwell and his mother in a cheap hotel in Washington Heights for ten years and Holliwell still half suspected that Sy had been his mother's lover. He had never asked.

For years, he had worked for Sy at the paper stand and they had conducted a running discourse on the state of the world at midcentury. Holliwell had learned the words of the "Internationale" from Sy but whenever Holliwell mentioned church or churchly things Sy would smile with lupine contempt.

"They pound that shit into your head. At that school you go to."

Sy was a Communist, he had been an organizer in the merchant marine during the war. Holliwell had found Sy's being a Communist appalling. He would bait Sy with the Hitler-Stalin pact, the Katyn massacre, forced-labor camps, the NKVD.

When the trucks brought bound stacked papers to the curb, Sy would cut the twine from them with a sharpened knuckle-duster, baring his teeth at the red banner of Hearst's *Journal-American*.

"That school—they pound that shit into your head."

They would stand hunched over the stacks, in ink-stained aprons full of sweaty change, their backs to the ice-cold sour wind from the Bronx breweries.

"What do you know about the Soviet Union?" Sy would ask. "You ever been there?"

Stung, Holliwell would play his trump.

"What do I know about Germany and Auschwitz and like that? I never been there either."

Sy would stick his hands in his pea-coat pockets with the same wolfish grimace.

"Go ahead—be a Fascist. Be an anti-Semite. They pound that shit into your head."

But he was not at home in the modern world.

On one of his last visits to New York—it had been a few years before—Holliwell had gotten drunk to the point of riotous indulgence and he had undertaken a sentimental journey uptown. He had found himself walking around Fort Tyron Park in the fading light, feeling perfectly safe, and everywhere he turned he had seen vistas that were part of his interior landscape, all the scenes of his early adventures imaginary and real. Immediately, he had realized that the neighborhood had nothing for him anymore.

Then he had seen Sy on a bench along Broadway in a black overcoat too warm for the weather and a cloth cap out of *The Grapes of Wrath*.

Sy had asked after his mother. "Alive?"

She was dead, Holliwell had told him. She had gone back to Glasgow on her Social Security and died there.

He had said to Sy: "I thought you'd be in Florida."

And Sy had said forget Florida. The fucking animals, they hunt me on the street. They want to break down my door and put a rope around my neck. The scumbags, they ruined the neighborhood, they ruined the city. Fucking Lindsay.

His broken nose was sprouting gray whiskers. He was old unto death.

Then Sy had told him the story of Press who ran the drugstore on Manhattan Avenue.

Press the druggist. Retired, closed the store—he was robbed so often. Visiting his brother on the Concourse. In a car—he wouldn't dare walk. And the animals got him in his car. Just bang—fuck you, he's dead. The cops stop the car, they catch the animals, one animal confesses. But Press, they put him in the city dump at Mott Haven—they don't remember where. The cops can't find him. The city says we can't find him, the dump's too big. A needle in a haystack. He's there now, under the garbage. A religious Jew. Nice for his family. A fucking dog you bury in the ground.

While he told the story of Press, Sy looked across Broadway where a Hispanic woman in red boots was leaning against a squad car, talking to the cops inside. Holliwell's last view of him was walking along behind the woman in the direction of the river, hurrying until he caught up in mid-block and they turned the corner together.

The hotel where Sy and Holliwell and his mother had lived was still standing. It was a welfare hotel now and the junkies were lined up on a metal rail outside, resting their scarred hams on the pigeon spikes, blowing their noses into Orange Julius napkins.

This time he would refrain from sentimental journeys and gestures. Sy would be dead now, like his mother.

He took his drink to the window to look down at the patch of Central Park that was visible from his room. The lights were going on; the lawns darkening. It was remotely possible, he thought, the depression and the war years being what they were, his mother being who she was—that Sy was his father. But it was unlikely. There had once existed, at least legally, a person called Michael J. Holliwell who was his father of record.

The thought of Sy made him feel like mourning, really like weeping. Drunk again, boozy ripe, ready to sniffle with promiscuous fervor over lost fathers and hillbilly songs. He put the glass down. The juice was turning on him altogether, softening him up; it was all catching up with him. His past was dead and his present doing poorly. In his briefcase was an unfinished address to the Autonomous University of Compostela but he was too far gone, he decided, to even look at it.

Hunger made him feel ashamed; he experienced it as further evidence of his frail sensuality. He ate from room service and nearly finished the bottle.

When he had put the empty tray outside his door, he dutifully took up the briefcase and opened it on his night table. After a moment, he took out the address and set it aside face down. Beneath it in the case were his air tickets and a yellow file folder in which he kept a changing collection of notes and clippings, drawn from the long hours he spent in idle reading. At any one time, Holliwell's file might contain bits from the *Times* and the news magazines, religious pamphlets, anything which seemed to him when he read it to have some relevance to the proper study of mankind. Often, when he reread the pieces in his file, he experienced difficulty in recalling why he had clipped them in the first place. If, after a while, he could not use the pieces in an article or introduce them into one of his classes, he would throw the entire stack away.

The file which Holliwell was bringing with him to Compostela contained only two items—a *National Geographic* article on Port Moresby and a letter that had appeared in his local alternative newspaper.

Holliwell took the printed letter from the file and set it before him. "Dear Editor," it began.

> Now it is evening again and the metal bars that separate we poor shadows from the outside world have slammed shut with a soul chilling echo. Before me lies another night in which moon and stars are only a phantom memory on the ceiling of my cell. During the night I shall experience many things. Some will be the faces of those I have loved and lost, others will be the memories of hatred and violence. And during the long night ahead I will cling to my dreams, hoping to find in the peace of slumber a surcease from the rage that gnaws inwardly at my heart.
>
> My convict's world is a lonely one and I would be bold enough to ask if there is a reader (woman, race not important) who would share my lonely hours with me by writing and speaking to me of the outside world from which the so-called justice of our society has banished me.

> Yours truly,
>
> Arch Rudiger
> # 197–46
> Box 56 G.F.
> Farmingdale, Wash.

Holliwell had found the clipping in his daughter's room. It had lain for something like a year between her book of the films of Rita Hayworth and her copy of *The Last Unicorn* until he had finally snatched it up and incorporated it into his collage.

Once he had read the letter aloud to his wife; she had looked at him closely, suspecting mockery.

"I hope she answered it," his wife had said. She had helped to fashion Margaret's sense of social and moral responsibility. Holliwell was quite certain that she had not.

He lay back on the bed, holding the clipping between his fingers, indulging Arch Rudiger with the pity he felt for himself. It reminded him of a few nights of his own.

Holliwell had ended by feeling guilty about Arch and he had assuaged his guilt by fantasizing the ideal response.

Dear Arch 197–46,
  I know that you are a young community male while I am a student at a privileged and elitist woman's college in the East. My family's immense wealth and status fill me with shame when I consider the cruel injustice which you have suffered. . . .

Holliwell threw the clipping into the wastepaper basket and then tossed the Port Moresby article in after it. He turned on the television set to watch the first part of a World War II movie and fell asleep in the flickering light of burning Germans.

"Well," Sister Mary Joseph said, "I don't believe for a minute that it all ends in the old grave."

She and Sister Justin Feeney were sitting in the shade on the mission veranda drinking iced tea. Sister Justin frowned at the sunlit ocean. Mary Joe's Bronxy certainties drove her to fury.

"Let's not talk theology," she said.

"Who's talking theology?"

"You," Sister Justin said. "Pie in the sky."

Sister Mary Joseph had come down from the mountains around Lake Tapa to talk sense to Justin. Her own situation was very different; her order was strong and adaptable, her dispensary could measure its effectiveness in lives preserved. Arriving at French Harbor she had quickly surmised that the local people were staying away, that something was seriously wrong with Father Charlie Egan and the stories she had heard about the state of the Devotionists on the coast were at least partly true.

"You gotta have an element of pie in the sky, kiddo," she told Sister Justin. "That's part of the basics."

Justin shaded her pale blue eyes from the glare of sky and ocean and leaned her chin on her fist.

Sister Mary Joe stood up and took their tea glasses.

"You want to talk pragmatism—O.K. we'll do that." Holding the glasses between her thumb and fingers, she waved them before Justin's averted face. "You're accomplishing nothing. You're not needed. Am I reaching you now?"

These were words as hard as Mary Joe commanded and the satisfaction with which she flung them at poor Justin caused her immediate remorse.

She was rinsing the glasses in the kitchen when Father Egan came in, shuffling toward the icebox, holding a flyswatter absently in his right hand.

"How's things, Father?" Sister Mary asked, looking him up and down.

"My dear Joe," Egan said. "Things are rich." He fixed himself a glass of water and gave her a vague smile. "How nice of you to come and visit us."

"Beats working," she told him. "Still going over your book?"

"Scribble scribble scribble," the priest said, and retreated back to his room.

Mary Joe wiped the glasses and went to the refectory to get a stethoscope from her black bag. Then she rapped once on Father Egan's door and let herself in.

She found him sitting by his window, the shutters thrown open to the green hillside below, a working bottle of Flor de Cana at his feet. Outside chickens picked among the morning glory vines, an old woman chopped at a stand of plantain with her machete.

Sister Mary settled her thick body on the window rail.

"We're old friends, aren't we, Father? We can speak plainly to each other."

"Yes," Egan said, "we're old pals, Joe." His smile faded and he turned his head to look over his shoulder. "And I won't have her tyrannizing you. You don't have to listen to her."

"C'mon," Mary Joseph said, "Justin's O.K. She's a good kid." She opened one of the buttons of his white cotton shirt and pressed the scope over his breastbone. "Let's talk about you."

The beat was feathery and irregular. Egan was in his early sixties; to Mary Joe his heart sounded as though it should belong to a very old man.

"So how about laying off the sauce?"

"Ah," Father Egan said. "You have me there."

"Yeah, I got you there, Charlie. And from where I'm standing you look a little portly to me and what do you bet your liver's enlarged? The right bug would knock you flat on your back."

She bent down, picked up the rum and set it down on Egan's desk beside the crucifix.

"You need to go home, Father. This kind of life—keep it up and it'll be curtains."

Father Egan scratched his ear and looked out of the window.

"I mean, what are you guys doing here anyway?" Sister Mary demanded. "Your instructions are to close this joint. This is the religion where people do what they're told, right?"

"Yes, well," Father Egan said, "you see, I thought I'd finish the book before we struck the flag."

"Boo for that idea," the nun said. "Because if you want to finish that book you better strike your flag or whatever— quick.

"Look," she told him. "I'll leave some pills with Justin for you. Take one every four hours instead of the joy juice. But don't take them both or you're dead."

"Bless you, Joe," Father Egan said. He said it in a far-off manner that Mary Joe found alarming.

"God bless you, Charlie," she said. "Pray for me."

She went back to the refectory, put the stethoscope away and carried her bag out to the veranda. Sister Justin was still in her chair, staring sadly out to sea, and Mary Joseph suspected she had been crying. Mary Joseph was not very sympathetic.

From time to time, up at Lake Tapa, Sister Mary had found herself with the obligation to comfort some of the younger and tenderer agents of the Peace Corps. She forgave them for their tears—Tecan was a hard place and they were young and American. First time away from their skateboards, she liked to say.

But the sight of a nursing nun in tears made her feel ashamed and angry. Tears were for the Tecanecan women, who always had plenty to cry about.

"Great day in the morning," she declared, forgetting that she had repented her earlier hardness, "if I lived around here and I needed help I sure wouldn't try to get it from this balled-up operation. I'd go right straight to the Seventh-Day Adventists or the LSA's or to somebody who knows what the heck they're doing."

"The LSA's!" Justin said savagely. "The LSA's are a bunch of right-wing psalm-singing sons of bitches. They've got a picture of the President on their wall, they suck ass with the Guardia and they fink for the CIA."

In spite of herself, Mary Joseph blushed.

"You got a lot of nerve," she said, "to talk like that."

Justin looked down at the veranda deck and shielded her eyes. Mary Joe waited for her to calm down and then sat beside her.

"Look, Justin, the very fact that you have the leisure to sit around and brood should tell you that you're not doing your job. I mean, great guns, kid—it's no time or place for ego trips."

"Am I ego-tripping?" Justin asked. "Isn't it supposed to bother me that people starve so America can have Playboy Clubs and bottomless dancing."

Sister Mary snickered. "Aw, c'mon," she said.

"Maybe I'm putting it stupidly. Doesn't it bother you?"

"If it's true it bothers me. But what do I know? I'm just a pill pusher. So aer you. Nobody elected us. You know," she told Justin, "in many ways you're a typical Devotionist. You all tend to be very bright and high-strung and short on horse sense."

Sister Justin brushed the windblown hair under her checkered bandana.

"I've had it with the order and I've had it with my sister of mercy number."

"Then it's time you went home," Sister Mary said. Justin's words made her shudder. "Justin—something special is happening now. The church is really turning back to Jesus. It's gonna be great and it would be a shame to miss out on it."

Justin put her hand across her eyes.

"If I told you," Sister Mary went on, "that you need to pray—that you need to ask God's help—would you say I was talking pie in the sky again?"

Sister Justin had turned her face away and was pursing her lips to make her tears stop. Mary Joseph watched her young friend cry; she no longer felt it in her to be outraged.

"Doesn't it mean anything to you anymore?"

Justin only shook her head.

She was a real beauty, Mary Joseph thought, the genuine article. In her own order they would never have let one so pretty and headstrong take final vows. But it was hindsight—Justin had soldiered on for six years, cheerful and strong, the wisest of catechists, a cool competent nurse. A little too good to be true in the end.

"This is no place for a personal crisis," Mary told her.

"I know," Justin said. She patted her cheek with a folded handkerchief.

"On the practical level—the fruit company repurchased the property—you can't stall them forever. And there's really a lot of negative talk. The Archbishop is starting to get upset."

"That old creep," Justin said. "He's not even a Christian. He's a cross between a Grand Inquisitor and an Olmec priest."

Sister Mary sat stiffly for a moment and then dissolved in guilty laughter.

"Justin—you're such a smart aleck."

Even distraught Justin could not help smiling back at her.

"Well, he ain't Bing Crosby," Sister Mary said in a low-comedy mutter. "But he represents the church here and that means plenty. And believe it or not he's protecting you from a government investigation."

Justin Feeney rose from her chair and walked to the edge of the veranda.

"Give me a few days before you speak to anyone. I have to make some plans of my own."

Mary Joseph frowned. She did not believe that one could plan in idleness.

"Now I want to hear from you in a week and I want to hear a date of departure. If you need extra help maybe I can sneak you some Peace Corps kiddos to pull and tote."

"Thanks, Joe. Thanks for giving a damn."

Mary Joseph picked up her black bag and went to the top of the steps. She had mastered an impulse to touch Justin on the cheek or to give her a hug. Such demonstrations were contrary to her training.

"Hey, listen, you did an A-1 job here for a long time. Don't go feeling like a complete flop. Don't let yourself get morbid. Just get busy and pack up."

Justin nodded briskly.

"God loves you, Justin. You're his special lady. He'll help you."

"O.K., Joe."

On the first step down Sister Mary Joseph was smitten with dread. In Justin's impatient goodbye smile she read the word "lost"—and the word sounded in her scrubbed soldierly soul with a grim resonance.

"Hey," she said, turning around, "I got a thing for Charlie Egan, know what I mean? I really want to see him get home alive. Can you take care of it for me?"

"You bet," Justin said.

Walking to her jeep, Sister Mary caught sight of another vehicle rounding the palm grove between Freddy's Chicken Shack and the water's edge. It was a four-wheel-drive Toyota and the driver she recognized as Father Godoy, a Tecanecan priest from Puerto Alvarado. She waited beside her Willys as he pulled up.

Father Godoy wore creased chino pants, a blue plaid shirt and expensive sunglasses. He was out of his Toyota shaking her hand and breathing English pleasantries before she could utter a greeting.

His long face lengthened further in a bony yellow smile; he was tall and angular, a tragical Spaniard of a man.

"Well, it's going great, Father," Sister Mary heard herself declare. "We have an OB now and some new hardware and God willing we're going to have a real good year."

He bobbed his head before her in hypothalamic agreement with everything in sight. Very sexy, she thought. She distrusted intellectual priests and the native clergy she generally regarded as soft, spoiled and unprogressive.

"Terrific," he was saying, in the racy Stateside which he affected for people of her sort, "really great! What would they do without you up there?"

"Looking in on our friends here, Father?"

"Right, right," he said, as though he had not understood her question.

"I hear," she said, "you have a nut loose down the coast. Somebody killing little kids."

"It seems that way," Godoy told her. "The people think it's a foreigner."

"Yeah," the nun said, "I'd want to think that too. I hope the word's out to be careful."

"Everyone knows," Godoy said. "That's how we are here."

"Well, so long," she said, climbing into her jeep. "Keep us posted."

"All the best," Godoy called to her. "All the best to everybody."

When she had driven as far as the palm grove, she stopped the jeep with the engine idling and bent into the lee of the dashboard to light a cigarette. Inhaling, she glanced over her shoulder and saw Godoy at the top of the steps beside Sister Justin. Both of them were looking out to sea.

"Oh, boy," she said to herself as she put the jeep in gear, "a couple of stars."

Father Godoy was complimenting Sister Justin on the beauty of the ocean and her good fortune in living beside it. His doing so made her feel guilty.

"Would you like some tea?" she asked.

"No, no, please." He looked about him cheerfully, further embarrassing Justin with the station's lack of activity.

"How's Himself," Godoy asked in a low voice.

She smiled at the missionary Irishism.

"Not well, I'm afraid. He's rather crushed and not always rational. A while ago he had the boat out in the middle of the night. I can't imagine why."

"Strange," the priest said. "A little worrying, eh?"

"Please have some tea."

"I have to go. It's the day of the procession in town."

"Oh drat," Justin said. "It just got away from me. I haven't missed it once since I've been here and today I forgot." She shrugged sadly.

"I can take you in tonight," he said. "For the festival afterwards. You see, I'm coming back to take some children from the company school. So we'll stop for you if you like."

"That'd be great. Would you?"

"Yes, of course. Of course. In fact I came now to ask you."

"Well," Justin said, laughing, "yes, please."

"Great," the priest said. "I'll go now and then after six we'll pick you up."

"Wonderful."

"Well, until then," he said, and went down the steps, leaving the image of his shy smile behind him.

"Wonderful," she said.

Wonderful. "Wonderful wonderful," she repeated dully under her breath. "Goddamnit, what a fool I'm becoming."

As she watched Godoy get into his jeep, she felt mortified and panic-stricken. She hurried from the veranda before he could turn and see her.

For a while she busied herself with sweeping out the empty dispensary, spraying the stacked linens for mildew, poking in the corners for centipedes or scorpions. Within the hour a man came from the village with a red snapper and a basket of shrimp; Justin went down the steps to pay him. The man brought a message from the Herreras, a mother and daughter who did cooking and cleaning for the station, that they would not be coming for several days. They had not come for some time before—nor had the young women who worked as nurse's aides, two girls from the offshore islands whom Justin herself had taught to read and write, her barefoot doctors. It was just as well since there was no work for them.

Somewhat later Lieutenant Campos drove by to give Sister Justin a quick glimpse of herself in his silvered sunglasses.

She cleaned and scaled the snapper, washed the shrimp and showered in her own quarters. Changing, she put on a cool khaki skirt, a red checked skirt, an engineer's red scarf over her hair. When she went back into the kitchen, she found Father Egan mixing cold well water into his rum.

"Are we friends today?" she asked him.

"There's a level, Justin, on which we're always friends. Then there's a level on which we can't be."

Justin received this response in silence. Mystical as ever,

she thought. She picked up the cleaned fish, stood holding it for a few moments, then set it down again.

"Sister Mary Joseph is after us to close. You probably know that."

"Yes," the priest said. "Of course it's up to you."

"Why is everything up to me?" she asked, wiping her hands on a towel. "I mean, what's happening with you? It's very worrying."

"Don't reproach me," Father Egan said. "I'm reinforcing this mutiny with my frail presence. It's up to you because you're a sensible girl."

"Must you keep drinking?"

"Never mind that," Father Egan said.

She walked over to the kitchen table and leaned on her fist, watching him.

"You've been so darn irrational I can't cope. And I know you've been worse since that night you had the boat out. I wish I knew what *that* was about."

"Under the seal," Egan said. "The rest is silence."

Sister Justin shook her head to clear it of his madness.

"I don't feel very sensible now," she said. "I feel like a complete idiot."

"Not at all," Egan said. "Do you want to know what I think?"

"Yes, please."

"I think you're very intelligent and moral and all good nunnish things. You had an attack of self-righteousness and you decided to try the impossible. Nothing wrong with that, Justin. Fine tradition behind it."

"You encouraged me."

"Yes. Well, I wanted to stay too. And I respect you, you see. Believe it or not."

"I thought I could pull it off."

"Because you were always made much of by the order. They want to keep you. You've had things your own way. You've been spoiled, dear."

"Oh, Lord," Justin said. "Spoiled hell." She folded her arms angrily and went to stand in the doorway with her back to him. "I've been on my hands and knees since college. I mean —I work for a living. I wouldn't call this a cloistered life, would you?"

She heard his dry sickly laughter and turned.

"Is what I'm saying ridiculous?"

"You've been morally spoiled. There's always been some-one around to take your good intentions seriously—and if that isn't being spoiled I don't know what is." He sniffed at his rum and drank it. "Religious women are always a good deal younger than their ages—Mary Joe's an example. Religious men are worse. One's always a kid. The life is childish." He shrugged. "Believing *at all* is childish, isn't it?"

Justin looked at him surprised. Perhaps, she thought, he was snapping a paradox. They were all great Chestertonians in his generation.

"You haven't been saying your office," she said, realizing it for the first time. "You haven't said it for ages."

"I consider it wrongly written down."

She smiled, watching him polish off the rum.

"Are you serious?"

"I will—if called upon—say Mass. I will administer the sacraments. But my office is strictly between myself and God and I won't say it their way. It's all wrong, you know," he said, fixing her with an unsettling stare. "They have it all wrong. The whole thing."

"I give up," Justin said.

"Interesting my orthodoxy should make any difference to you. Surely you don't believe?"

"I can't answer that question."

"Well," Egan said, "you're supposed to answer it every day."

At the kitchen counter, she took up the fish again. The right thing would be to broil it, to make a sauce with peppers and onions and greens. But he would be more likely to eat it if she simply shredded it into the soup with some shrimp. It was such a shame. Red snapper.

It went into the soup and Egan faded back toward his quarters.

Justin found herself on the veranda again. Her hands were clenched on the rail as she leaned out toward the ocean, the ebbing tide. The sea's surface was soft blue; the sun had withdrawn beyond the green saw-toothed hills above the station.

Utter total foolishness, she repeated silently.

Her soul extended along this meditation as it might in prayer. There was nothing. Only the sea, shadowed deeps, predatory eyes. Her heart beat quietly alone, its panicked quickening like a signal to the void, unanswered, uncomforted. It beat only for her, to no larger measure, a futile rounding of blood. The desire for death made her dizzy; it felt almost like joy.

She was still leaning over the rail, half stunned with despair, when she saw a young man walking along the beach from the direction of the village. He was barefoot and full-bearded, extraordinarily blond; he wore a white shirt of the sort that required a detachable collar, and faded bib overalls. When he drew closer she could see the filthy condition of his shirt and the dirt and dried blood that soiled his hands. His appearance bespoke need and for this reason she was vaguely glad to see him there. She assumed he was one of the North American kids who drifted up and down the Isthmus following the beach. They had first appeared in numbers the previous spring. Some of them were far gone with dope or alcohol. Her ready impulse was to have him come in and see if there was anything that might be done—before Campos and his men or the local *ratones* caught scent of him.

Justin had gone as far as the top step when the odd cut of his hair registered on her. It was crude cropping that one did not see on even the weirdest passing gringos, almost medieval, monkish. As she started down to the beach, he turned toward her and his face stopped her cold.

Although the man's walk and carriage were youthful, his face was like an old man's, the skin not tanned but reddened and weathered, deeply seamed around the features. The massiveness of his brows and cheekbones made his upper face as square as a box; his nose was long, thin and altogether outsized, upturned toward the tip. Elfin, she thought, staring at him, gnomish—but suggestive of carving like some sort of puppet, a malignant Pinocchio.

Two things about his small blue eyes impressed her—one was that they were not, she was sure, the eyes of an English speaker, another that they were the most hating eyes she had ever seen.

Justin had to remind herself that she was in lay clothes. But even people who thought nuns bad luck had never looked at her so.

Fascinated, she watched the man's mouth open and she braced herself for a threat or an obscenity. His shout, though when it came it contorted his face, was absolutely silent.

It seemed that one of the words he mouthed at her was *Schwein*—the bared teeth savaging the lower lip. There were other words. *Du* was one. She had only known German as a tourist in Austria but she felt certain that German was his language. *Schwein, Du*.

"Beast" was the word that came to her. She was quite frightened.

Then the youth walked on, toward Puerto Alvarado. He was very big. His shoulders under the stained white shirt looked broad as an ox yoke.

She went back into the kitchen, lifted the pot lid and stirred her red snapper and vegetable soup. The young man, she realized, must be a Mennonite—there were a few of their settlements in the south, inland. They were not numerous in Tecan and it was years since she had seen a band of them in the capital, in the central bus station there. They had seemed shy, cheerful people, very clean and friendly.

It was the time of late afternoon when the color drained out of the day. Sky and ocean gentled to temperate pastels and the jungle on the hillsides was a paler green. Wandering to the doorway, she savored the breeze.

Along the beach, from the grove at Freddy's to the point southward, there was no one to be seen. Vanished, the passing youth seemed to be a creature compounded of her fears; the hatred, the Germanness were the stuff of nightmare and bad history. Somehow her despair had summoned him.

When Godoy and his jeepload of small boys pulled up at the foot of the station steps, she ran down gratefully to join them. The boys were black Caribs and there were six of them crowded into the jeep, some with the Indian cast of eye or the shock of coarse straight hair that marked the Caribs among the black people of the coast.

"*Buenas*," she called to them and to Godoy.

"*Buenas*," the boys said, and made room for her. Some of the younger boys smiled, the two oldest ogled her with grim elaborateness. She sat down next to the priest.

"We're off," he declared.

"Right on," Sister Justin said gaily.

Along the roadside, plantation hands walked homeward
cradling their machetes against their shoulders; children
struggled along under loads of firewood for the evening meal.
At every fresh creek there were women gathering up laundry
from the rocks on which it had been drying in the last of the
daylight, and other women were hurrying along balancing
ocher jugs on their heads filled with cooking water from the
public well. But most of the people on the road were walking
toward Puerto Alvarado and what remained of the day's fiesta.

Each time they passed a settlement of sticks and palm
thatch Godoy would sound his horn, a child would wave and
the boys in the jeep display their privilege as passengers in a
private vehicle.

The road led them inland through banana and then pine-
apple, to the top of Pico Hill, where they could see the ocean
again and the wharves of the distant port, then down again
past acres of yellow-painted, numbered company houses, finally to the tin-and-crate-wood shacks on the edge of town.
From the town center they could hear the report of exploding
firecrackers and the blare of the sound truck the Syrian store-
keeper had hired to publicize his holiday specials.

There was a block of paved street where the houses had
carports and painted fences, then the Gran hotel, the Texaco
station—and they turned into the crowded plaza. Godoy
eased the jeep through the crowds and parked against the
church wall, behind a barrier of bicycle stands. As soon as the
jeep was stopped, the six Carib boys leaped out and disappeared among the crowd.

Godoy watched them go and looked at his watch.

"Now," he told Justin with a sad smile, "the trick will be to
get them back."

The two of them went past a line of helmeted Guardia and
along the edge of the church steps.

In the center of the square, a ceiba tree had been hung
with paper garlands and an elderly band in black uniforms
was ranged beneath its branches. There were Japanese lanterns strung between trees at two sides of the plaza and the
square itself was jammed with people. Men of property stood
with transistor radios pressed against their ears, teen-aged
parents in cheap cotton dress-up clothes clung to their several
tiny children—and lone children by the hundreds puzzled

their way through the crowd's legs. The shoeshine boys had given over their space by the fountain and sat together with their boxes at the park edge, watching for flung cigarette butts, fallen change, loose wallets.

The sailors' girls had marched uptown from the waterfront brothels and occupied their own space on one lawn where they sat on open newspapers, singing along to the music of the nearest radio and trading comic books with each other.

Along the fountain there were teen-agers, arranged according to social class—the boys watching the prostitutes and the girls, more or less demurely, watching the boys.

There were girls in hip-huggers and "Kiss Me, Stupid" tee shirts and girls whose fancy dress was their school uniform. There were nearly white boys who wore Italian-style print shirts and looked bored, stiff self-conscious mestizos in starchy white sport shirts, blacks who broke their Spanish phrases with "mon" and "bruddah," practiced karate moves, swayed, danced with themselves in a flurry of loose wrists and flashing palms. Across the street, at the gate of the Municipalidad, a few Guardia leaned against the pillars and watched the crowd. They were given all the space they might require.

A little boy with an inflamed eye chased two smaller girls toward the church.

"*Mono malo, mono malo,*" he shouted after them. "Bad monkey."

It occurred to Justin that she had been hearing children shouting "*mono malo*" at each other for weeks, and calling it also at such of the ragged wandering anglos who were still about. She had never heard an epithet like *mono malo* before.

In the street at the foot of the church steps, a squad of local technicians was struggling with an enormous antiaircraft searchlight, adjusting the dogs and swivels, playing out the wire that led up the steps and into the church interior. Nearby there were men and boys in the purple hoods and cassocks of the Holy Brotherhood, those who had carried the images in the afternoon's procession.

Justin and Father Godoy stood together near the ceiba tree, facing the church. The air smelled of frangipani, of perfume and hair oil, above all of the raw cane liquor, barely rum, that was being passed in Coke bottles among the sports in the crowd.

At the stroke of darkness, the band broke into a reedy *paso doble* and the great searchlight sent forth an overpowering light. The light broke up the foremost ranks of the crowd, sending the people there reeling back, forcing them to turn away, hands to their eyes. Then it swept around the square, ascending until the beam was pointed straight upward, a pillar of white fire heavenward. A great gasp of joy broke from the crowd.

Spinning again, the column of light descended on the plaza, catching each second a dozen transfixed faces, dazzled the old men in their wicker chairs in the Syrian's shop and the lounging Guardia, electrified the posters of *Death Wish* in front of the cinema. It made the whores' beads sparkle, shone on the balloons and patent-leather shoes of the better-off children and on the slick flesh of the banana plants. As it whirled, the crowd screamed and applauded.

The beam came finally to rest on the steps of the church, centering on a glass-and-mahogany coffin which four men in the purple robes of the Brotherhood had carried out during the display. Prone in the coffin was the figure of Christ, which was the occasion of Puerto Alvarado's rejoicing.

Christ wore a burial shift of waxy linen and worn lace; his hands, clutching a lily, were folded across his chest. Around his brow was a crown of thorns and his long hair was matted with blood. Both the hair and the blood had the appearance of reality and Sister Justin, who had seen the figure many times before, had always wondered about them. The eyelids were also quite authentic; one felt they might be pulled back to show dark dead eyes beneath.

A hush settled as the light fell on the dead Christ—but only for a moment. As the plaza beheld its murdered redeemer, a murmur rose from the crowd that grew louder until it drowned out the dirge of the band, swelled into moans and cries of women, hoarse *Viva el Cristos*, drunken whoops of devotion.

As he lay under the light in his glass box, he looked for all the world as though he had died the same day, in Tecan, of meningitis like the overseer's daughter who went at Christmas, of an infected scorpion bite, of undulant fever, of a knife on the docks. So the crowd began to cheer, the children of the early dead, the parents of perished *angelitos*, secure in their own and their children's resurrection—cheering the sharer and comforter of death.

Around Justin there were people on their knees. Some steps away, a woman holding a balloon in one hand and her infant daughter's hand in the other was weeping for the deceased—out of courtesy perhaps, or habit.

Justin turned to Godoy and in the shadowy light saw a look of patient detachment on his face. When he realized that she was looking at him, he said: "See, it's all done with light. Like the movies."

She thought that it was something very like what she might say, although what she felt at the moment was very different. It made her wonder whether he said it only for her benefit, from embarrassment for his country.

After a few minutes, the searchlight was turned off and the encoffined savior carried inside and placed at the side altar where he reposed except during procession days and Holy Week. A number of people stood chatting in the church doorway, and among them Justin recognized Father Schleicher, an Oblate Missionary from the Midwest. The other clerics there were two Tecanecans, or rather Spaniards—one the vicar of the cathedral and the other a monsignor from the capital, a representative of the Archbishop.

"We should go up there," Father Godoy said, when they had done a round of the square. "I have to at least."

Together, they climbed the church steps, and while Godoy made his obeisances to the senior clergy, Justin endeavored to converse with Schleicher and a young Tecanecan woman who was with him.

Father Schleicher was young, and was said to be politically engaged. Sister Justin had heard also that he had unofficially purchased a colonial press edition of the *Quixote* from a clerk at the Catholic university in the capital and that he paid plantation workers to bring him such pre-Columbian artifacts as they might find. Although none of this was quite illegal, although it was practically innocent hobbyism and a mark of his cultivation, Justin held what she heard against Schleicher's account. She disliked him; he was chubby and blond, and it seemed to her that his face was set continually in an expression of thick-lipped self-satisfaction. A creep, was what she called him.

They talked for a while about American politics and Schleicher introduced the girl with him as a community planner. When their conversation ran thin, they all turned toward the interior of the church to look for more to talk about.

Inside, a great many people were crowded in a semicircle around the dead Cristo, kneeling on the floor.

"It's an incredible statue," Justin said. "Isn't it strange to see him presented like that—I mean *laid out*?"

"When I first saw it," Schleicher said, "it reminded me of Che. You know, the picture taken after he was killed? It still makes me think of him."

The Tecanecan girl smiled slightly and nodded.

"I wonder what it's made of," Justin said.

The Tecanecan girl laughed, a bit too merrily for Justin, and turned to Schleicher.

"It's such a North American question," the girl said. "What's it made of?"

Schleicher laughed as though he thought it was such a North American question too.

"I'm like that," Sister Justin said. "When I saw Notre Dame Cathedral I wondered what it weighed. We're all like that where I come from."

The girl's laughter was a little less assured. Father Schleicher hastened to ask her where it was that she came from, but Justin ignored him. She had told him often enough before.

"Did you study in the States?" Justin asked the Tecanecan girl.

"Yes. Yes, in New Orleans. At Loyola."

"That must have been fun," Justin said. "Community planning."

"Yes," the girl said warily.

Godoy disengaged himself from the old Spaniards and joined them for a moment's stiff exchange of pleasantries. Then he and Justin said their goodbyes and went back down the steps to the square. Justin found herself wondering whether the hip Father Schleicher might be sleeping with his young community planner. She sighed, despising her own petty malice. That night she was against anyone with a purpose to declare, anyone less lonely and beaten than herself.

The plaza was emptying as she and Godoy walked across it. Men approached them in the shadow of the trees, begging, calling for a blessing against bad visions from the cane alcohol. A youth warbled a birdcall after them and a woman laughed.

The crowds, the lights and the music were on the other side of the church now, where they had set up a market and a fun fair for the children. The trees had been stripped of garlands and lanterns by the crowd and the central street ran deserted toward the harsh bright lights of the company piers.

"Hungry?" Godoy asked.

Justin was not at all hungry but she supposed that he must be. She nodded pleasantly.

"We'll give the kids some time at the games," the priest said, "before we go and arrest them. Now we can go to the Chino's if you like."

The Chino's was a restaurant that called itself the Gran Mura de China. It had a small balcony section with two tables that overlooked the harbor.

The lower floor of the Gran Mura de China was empty when they arrived; the Chino's wife and daughter sat at a table stringing firecrackers. Justin and Godoy smiled at them and went upstairs to the balcony. They sat down and Godoy lighted a Winston.

"Do you know what Father Schleicher said about the image?" Justin asked Godoy. "He said he thought it looked like Che."

Godoy looked at her evenly, unsmiling.

"Father Schleicher said that? Was he joking?"

"Not exactly joking. I think he had a point to make."

"Iconography," Godoy said vaguely, tapping his ash and looking out over the pier lights at the dark ocean.

After a minute the Chino's daughter came up to serve them. Under her apron, the child wore a white party dress; she had been up to the plaza.

Godoy asked for shrimp and rice; Justin a bottle of Germania.

"You may have heard about our troubles," Justin said, when they had ordered. She found the puzzled look Godoy gave her disingenuous. It was impossible, she thought, that he had not heard.

"I'm going to close us down and go home. I'm tired of arguing with the order and I don't believe we're getting anything done."

"It's a shame you had no support. It must be difficult."

"Yes, it's difficult to make a fool of yourself to no good purpose. But of course it's a lesson." She was beginning to grow quite irritated with Godoy. "Yet another goddamn valuable lesson."

"I have to tell you," the priest said as he watched the little girl serve his dinner and their beer, "that I'm very sorry to hear that you're closing."

"Really?" Justin said impatiently. "Why, thank you."

He's downright super-serviceable, she thought.

"Please excuse me," Godoy said. "I haven't yet eaten today."

"Please go ahead," Justin said. She decided that he was dandified and vain. Frightened of, and therefore hostile to, women. For a long time it had seemed to her that Godoy had a difficulty in comprehending plain English that went beyond any unfamiliarity with the language.

"You know," Godoy said, tasting his shrimp, "I think you stayed this long because I wanted you to."

"Are you kidding?" Justin demanded.

"Just a superstition of mine."

"If you wanted us to stay you were very subtle."

"It wasn't only because I like you," the priest said. "And not because I thought you were the very model of a Yankee missionary. Obviously you are not that."

The bluntness of his language startled her. "Then why?" she asked.

"Because I know how you think. I know your attitudes. I even know the books you own."

Justin watched him delicately take his shrimp.

"Then everyone must," she said. "So I'm probably in trouble."

He shrugged.

"You are North American and that protects you. The Archbishop in his way protects you."

"Campos," she said.

"Don't worry about Campos for now." He kept his eyes on his plate as he said it.

"Really," Justin said, "it was stupid of me to try to keep the station open."

"Godoy gave her a quick amused glance.

"I don't know what you were thinking of. But I admire you for it. And I sympathize."

"I was being naïve as usual."

He looked up from his plate again and held her with the look.

"You were never as naïve as I was," he said, "and I was born here. You think you've failed? Of course you failed. There's nothing but failure here. The country is a failure. A disaster of history."

"That's very hopeless talk," Justin said.

"It's where we begin," Godoy said. "We start from this assumption."

His meal finished, the priest took a sip of beer and lit another Winston. The beer seemed to bring a faint rosiness to his pale pitted cheek.

"When I was in the Jesuit college here I wrote a letter of which I was very proud. I wrote to your President Eisenhower."

"Good Lord," Justin said. "To dear old Ike."

"Yes, to Ike himself. And I sent the same letter to the leader of our opposition—his name was Enrique Matos, of the great Liberal Party. In this letter—which I covered with tears—I told them that if the free world was to conquer Communism it must not follow the way of greed and narrow self-interest but the way of the Great Redemptor. He whom we saw dead tonight."

Godoy crushed his Winston out in an ashtray and put another in his mouth.

"I told Ike and Matos—I was only a kid, you understand— that their leadership must be spiritual. Also that they were overlooking the evils of our country, that we were suffering because of the government and the rich and the North American attitude.

"In the same week my father disappeared. Not for long and he came back alive. You see, he was a watchmaker in the capital, an immigrant from Spain. He wasn't hurt badly but he was very frightened. He told me not to write any more letters.

"A little later there arrived a message from the White House in Washington. I can tell you that it was an occasion of terror in my house, my parents were quite unsophisticated in some ways. It was a perfectly amiable letter. It thanked me. It was signed by an assistant. A typical letter."

"A form letter," Justin corrected him.

"Yes, a form letter." He lit his Winston and blew the smoke upward. "Under that government people often disappeared. When our great hope Matos became President it was the same. It's the same now. When Matos was President there was a man from your country in the capital—he was the head of your intelligence here and Matos' great friend. Last year his name was in the papers a little because of the scandals in Washington. We believe now that he knew a great deal about who disappeared and why. It was strange to read about him in the newspapers. He seemed a foolish, trivial man, almost likable."

Justin said nothing.

"I'll call you Justin," Godoy said.

"It's been my name so long," she said, "I guess it's my name."

"If you tell your superiors that you agree to leave—how long can you keep the mission station?"

"Well," Justin said, "it's company property to start with and they'll take it right back. There are medicines there and furniture, so I guess they'll reoccupy it and we can be out in a week."

Godoy shook his head in exasperation.

"No good," he said. Before she could ask what he meant he asked her: "What will you do in the States?"

"I don't know. I'm going to laicize anyway. I suppose I'll look for a job." She touched her hair in confusion. "I'm afraid to think about it."

"I want you to keep the station open. For a month anyway. You can stall. Say that Father Egan is too ill to travel."

"Father Egan will die if he stays."

"All right then, send Egan back. But keep open any way you can. I'll help you to keep open."

"But why?" she asked him.

"Because," Godoy said, "I have friends who are doing illegal work. They are going to make a *foco* in the mountains. They need a place on the coast for a while."

"They're going to fight?"

"Not here. But not so far away. You see, for years it's all been smoke." He permitted himself a quick smile. "But it's time now."

"Oh, my gosh," Justin said. Her heart soared.

"So we need you if you can help us. If you want to."

"Thank you for asking me," Justin said. "For trusting me."

"I have good reasons to trust you," Godoy said, "and it's easy to ask." He watched her, and she knew that he was measuring her hesitation.

"It's not only for the use of the station. We need you too if you think you can help. If you feel you can't—well, I understand."

"I will," Justin heard herself say. "I'll help you any way I can. Not only with the station. There's nothing I want more."

"I don't try to seduce you in this," Godoy said. "You have to make your own decision."

"I have no family," Justin told him, smiling. "No special home. Where people need me that's where I go. See, I'm lucky that way."

She could not read his look. Suddenly she wanted him to reach out and touch her in some way, clap her on the shoulder, shake her hand, give some human token of what they had entered into. But he did not move and neither did she.

"This is work of armed struggle, so people may get killed. I won't deceive you."

"I don't come from a pacifist tradition," she said. Immediately it struck her as a cold and pedantic thing to say. She kept wondering how she must appear to him. That he would ask, that he would say that she herself could help—it meant he must esteem her. Surely, she thought, he must.

Godoy looked at his watch.

"We'll go," he said.

She walked beside him toward the dark square; somewhere beyond it there was music, uncertainly amplified, and the noise of a crowd.

"Maybe," he said as they walked, "we can arrange your status within the church if you stay. It would be better."

"Whatever you think."

"We won't talk about it anymore now. During the week— we can meet and talk further."

Justin nodded; she felt lonely again, and frightened.

As they started across the plaza, Godoy stopped and turned to her.

"In the work we're doing," he said, "one has to change a

little. You develop and you become a slightly different person.
It's hard on the ego but it's for the best."

"I understand," she said. She understood thoroughly. His
message was the one she had been receiving all her adult life,
the one she had always lived by.

I'll be right at home in this outfit, she thought. It would
have cheered her up to say it aloud to him but she did not—
because it would be boastful and presumptuous and because
he would not have understood her. As far as she could tell, he
was without humor.

Immediately, she reproached herself for reflecting on his
lack of humor. It was judgmental and perhaps a little racist.
Look to your own seriousness, she told herself.

They found the little fun fair on the far side of the church,
behind the ruined eighteenth-century wall. In the space between the old church wall and the river, a traveling carnival
from the capital had parked its bright machines. There were
two carousels, a small loop-the-loop with pink and purple
cockpits and a whirly ride called the Carretera de Fortuna. Two
ice-cream sellers had brought their wagons up from the square,
there was a man with balloons, a man with a fortune-telling
parrot and an Oriental in a kimono demonstrating karate
strokes to an audience of teen-agers and cane cutters. A stand
sold soda and beer and black or white rum.

The Syrian's sound truck was parked beside a mobile generator with its sale signs still aloft but it was empty and silent.
The carnival machines made their own music as they turned,
music as peeled and rusted at the seams as the machines
themselves. The fairground was surrounded by colored lights
and around each bulb was a little cloud of insects drawn from
the riverbank.

As Justin and Godoy walked toward the fair, beggars crept
out of the shadow of the church wall to intercept them. In the
darkness, they were tiny, barely human figures, small wads of
cloth appended to upturned palms, uttering soft wails. Justin
handed out some ten- and twenty-centavo pieces, Father
Godoy gave them nothing.

One of the machines played "*La Cumparsita*" as the two of
them strolled out on the little midway. The light there was
fantastical, compounded of rainbow colors. Children's faces
were unearthly shades, the grass underfoot looked painted.

The men in the crowd were drunk and somber but there were mainly women and children about. A few groups of teenagers huddled beyond the light like predators around a camp, some of them smoking marijuana. In the darkness by the river, a drunk or a madman was screaming but his cries were drowned by the music.

People greeted Father Godoy as he passed among them; stony Indian faces softened toward him, there was some quick whisking off and clutching of straw sombreros. Both he and Justin towered over the crowds.

"A fair was a great thing once," Godoy said. "There were a great many tents and tricks. Today it's not so much because the movies come here now."

"It's still a great thing," Justin said.

Four of Godoy's schoolboys were waiting in line by the larger carousel. Justin watched him apprehend them and point to his watch. The boys waved little red ticket stubs up at him. He shrugged and then stood looking about him over the heads of the crowd. Justin thought of having a beer but decided it would not be right for her to approach the stand and the drunken men there.

"I'm missing two," Godoy said to her. "It's a nuisance."

"It's fine," Justin said. "I'll wait by the merry-go-round."

While Godoy combed the shadows, Justin found herself some space by the rail to watch the carousel. Around her were women whose children rode and women who stood with their children around them, watching the others.

He sees me as a fool, Justin thought fearfully. He sees my foolishness.

Under the lights, her face fixed on the whirl before her, she contemplated her inward place. It was a foolish place, of course, but orderly. Like a corridor in some worthwhile institution, the walls and floors all spotless, the suffering and the flesh behind white screens. A virgin's place, a bit of a whited sepulcher.

It was dim and Lenten, its saints were shrouded and if it held any tabernacles they were open and empty. It was very far away.

The notion frightened her. Far, she thought—far from where?

It was fearful and a prison and so was the world. She

looked at the crowd across the lights from where she stood;
she and they were separated by miles.

But she had been in prison before and she had been afraid.
Marched through the cicada din of a Mississippi night, to a
place where the cotton fields were ringed with hooded watch
lights and barbed wire under a million stars, to a blockhouse
smelling of drains and urine. And then they turned out the
lights in the block and the matron came out to tell ghost
stories in the dark. It was the torment reserved for outside
agitators that night, the treatment the guards had smirked
about all the way to Parchman. No prods, no bucket across
the skull, not that night—but darkness and ghost stories.

Somebody said boy, if Folkways Records was here. They
were in a black block because the white girls would kill them.
In the dorm outside their jammed segregation cell, the black
girls laughed or moaned and cried; some of them were sisterly,
some insane and armed with razors.

The matron's dusty little voice demanded "Who Got Mah
Golden Ahm?"

The jughead innocence had its own horror. And nuns
were bad luck there.

Goddamn it, Justin said to herself, I'm not a fool. He must
know that.

She had seen the guns and the dogs; she knew well enough
the difference between real wounds and painted martyrdoms.
She had courage—her parents had it and she had it from
them. All her life she had worked and soldiered with the best;
wherever work and soldiering were required she could pay her
way. We are not afraid today, she thought. What am I getting
myself into? She shivered.

Then she looked up and saw that Father Godoy had taken
a place opposite her along the carousel rail and, with the
lights behind her, she felt that she could look at him unem-
barrassed. The two older boys whom he had sought stood,
looking annoyed and drunk, behind him. Godoy was watching
the children on the carousel.

The machine was playing a march from an old operetta;
the children, with their eyes full of lights, were reaching out
to snatch the brass ring that was suspended by a strap from a
stanchion beside where Godoy stood. They circled past his
gaze, undersized, rickety, plenty of them dwarfed or scabrous,

the sixty-five percent, the survivors of birth and infancy in Tecan—on their painted horses. He looked at them as no father she had ever seen looked at his own children. His gray eyes shone like theirs, with such fierce love that she trembled to see him.

She felt then that all the companionship, all the moral recognition she had ever required from the universe reposed in the eyes of this priest. Between them the children went round and round, children of the *campesinos, rojos, jíbaros*— the wretched, the *probrecitos*. She could not take her eyes from his face as he watched them.

At 0401 Pablo Tabor signed himself off the circuit and put out the last cigarette of his watch. On his way through Search and Rescue to the Coke machine, he saw the sky through the Operations Room window, it was alight and clear, pale yellow.

"Ah me," he said softly.

Breedlove, the Operations yeoman, was watching him.

"Ol' Pablo must have smoked about a thousand cigarettes tonight," Breedlove told his yeoman striker. "I been watchin' him and he's smokin' the shit out over there."

"Leave me alone, Breedlove," Tabor said. "I already told you."

"Air," Breedlove said, winking at the striker. "Ay-er—that's what you need, Tabor."

"Give him air," the striker said busily.

Pablo was listening to his change rattle in the machine, to the bottle zip down its tin track. He picked it up, icy in his hot hand, and opened it.

"You know, you're just a couple of fucking noises in my head."

The striker smiled.

"That's all you are."

"We're all a deck of cards," Breedlove said.

"Hey, good night, Tabor," he called down the corridor when Tabor walked out. "Sleep well, hear?" He leaned over the Operations desk to see that Tabor was out of hearing and addressed himself to the striker.

"Don't think he ain't scoffin' those pills again. Tell by the little tiny eyes." He narrowed his own eyes to a squint. "Speed-freak sparky. When he moves—it's jit jit jit." He moved the flat of his hand in little jits.

"Jitters," the striker said.

"Don't think they won't nail him," Breedlove said complacently.

"With this old man? Shit sure they'll nail him."

Some morning, Tabor thought, walking into the locker room, I'll kill that skinny prick. Except he wants me to so much, I won't.

He changed out of the dungaree uniform in which he had stood his watch and into civilian clothes. That morning he had brought a silky Western shirt, twill pants, a leather-like jacket and seven-stitch fancy boots. In the pocket of the jacket was a large aspirin bottle of Dexedrine and when he had changed he set the aspirin bottle beside his Coke and sat down on the wooden bench with his head in his hands.

Lord, he said to himself, the shit I sit still for. Make you weep, Jesus. He stood up suddenly and hit the tin grill of his locker with his left elbow and followed through with the palm of his right hand.

Just anybody calls me anything and I sit still for it. I don't know the fucking difference. He sat down again, unscrewed the cap on the aspirin bottle and tucked two Dex tabs in the pocket of his shirt. He swallowed two more with his Coke.

Now Breedlove, he thought, I'll tell him again and that'll be it. Breedlove's old lady worked in the supermarket, a good-looking head.

Gimme a break, God, Tabor prayed going out. Gimme a rush and ease my mind. A little good feeling.

On his way to sign out with JOD, he remembered the Coke bottle in his hand, so he went back around to Search and Rescue to stack it in the rack that held empties. When he left the bottle off, he saw Breedlove watching him.

He walked over and leaned on the Operations counter until Breedlove came over.

"I want to tell you something, Breedlove," he said, leaning close to the counter and speaking so softly that Breedlove had to incline his own head to hear him. "I want to tell you get off my case, man. Now if you don't do it I'm gonna transport your ass over to Gulfstream Plaza and I'm gonna beat the living shit out of you in front of that big old supermarket window. So your old lady can watch from the cash register."

Breedlove walked away pale, shaking his head.

Tabor checked out and went down the magnolia-lined walk that led to the gate and the parking lot. The lemon light was spreading across the sky, coloring the flat waters of the Gulf and the white hull of the fishery protection cutter that was tied up at the end of the pier. Eastward, night lights burned on the steel coils of the Escondido refinery and in the highway distance beyond it westbound headlights glowed snake eyes against the dawn.

"Gimme a rush, Jesus," Tabor said. He walked to his Chevy with the keys in his hand. He put the key in the door lock, smiled and licked his lips. One of these times, he thought, I'll have a car where you don't turn the key upside down. "Contact," he said. He was getting off a little and he turned to look at the sky over his shoulder.

"Gimme a rush, Jesus." He put the car in gear and rolled to the edge of the highway. "If you want me for a sunbeam."

A truck full of melons went by the gate and he smiled after it.

Gimme a rush if you truly want me for your personal sunbeam.

Once out of the gate, he ran in front of the drug, passing the melon truck with a grin.

Good morning, boys. What nice watermelons, yes indeed.

He cooled it at the town line, drove past the line of shrimp boats at the commercial pier, the fish market, the ceviche restaurant. First light hit the wide oily sidewalks of the main drag; a few Mexican women in tailored jeans walked toward the cannery.

He parked his Chevy just down the block from the Sullivan hotel. The Sullivan was a three-story building with rounded corners of frosted glass and a sign beside the door that said "Locker Club, Servicemen Welcome." Tabor went in and across the small dusty lobby to the lounge out back. In the lounge there was a bar on rollers and a few plastic tables and chairs but the jukebox was the treasure of the Sullivan; it dated from World War II like the "Locker Club" sign by the street door. Linda Ronstadt's "Heart Like a Wheel" was spinning on it.

At one of the tables Mert McPhail, the station's chief radio-man, was sitting with two girls in pants suits. The girls were drinking Jax; McPhail had a bottle of bourbon and a card-board cup of ice beside his glass. They all looked up when Tabor walked in.

The older of the two girls with McPhail was named Nancy.

"Haayy, Pablo," she called as he walked toward them, "how're you keepin', keed?"

"Hey," Pablo said.

"You want a drink, honey? Want a whiskey? A cocktail?"

"Just a beer be nice. Why don't everybody have a beer?"

"*Gracias, amigo,*" Nancy said, and went to the cooler, Tabor pulled up a chair and sat down beside McPhail.

"What say, McPhail?"

McPhail had been in the hotel most of the night. He was tired and drunk, a huge balding man with a brown, lined face—sloped-shouldered, six-six or -seven. He glanced at Tabor with distaste. The girl with him watched them both with a spacy smile.

"Real good," Tabor said. "Hey, you know," he told them after a minute, "it's such a nice morning I might just go after some birds. I got my Remington in the car. I might just go up back of the airport and get me a turk."

The girl at the table looked down at Tabor's feet.

"Gonna stomp through that old swamp with them pretty stitch boots on? Just get'em all muddied up."

"I don't mind," Tabor said.

Nancy brought the beers to the table and set them out.

"Don't know about turkeys," she said. "But I bet you could get you a alligator back there."

"If I meet one I'll rassle with him. Hey, you think I could rassle a alligator, McPhail?"

McPhail had been studying the bare wall beside him.

"How the hell would I know?" he said.

"You could bring me back a pocketbook," Nancy said quickly. "But that's against the law now, ain't it? Alligator pocketbooks, they're against the law now."

"Ain't no more against the law than what's doin' in here," the younger girl said.

After a moment, McPhail stood up heavily and walked into the john. Tabor picked up his beer and drank half of it at a draw.

"Dry," he said.

The girls laughed as though he had told a joke.

"Hey, Pablo," Nancy said, "you goin' hunting right away or you gonna hang around a while?"

"I don't know," Tabor said. He picked up his beer and walked into the men's room after McPhail.

In the men's room, he found McPhail flat-footed before the urinal, pissing contentedly. Holding the bottle in his hand, Tabor took up a position directly behind him and leaned against the wall.

"So I'm on report, huh, Chief?"

McPhail had turned his head as far to the side as he could, trying to see Tabor behind him.

"I did put you on report," he said as though he had just remembered it. "Chit's still on my desk. Straighten it out Monday."

He left off pissing and hastened to zipper his fly.

"Sure," Tabor said. "I'd really like to straighten it out, know what I mean, Chief?"

McPhail left quickly. When Tabor went back out, he found the chief radioman sitting on a barstool near the movable bar combing his thin black hair. Tabor watched him with what appeared to be good humor.

"What are you combing that with, McPhail? You combing it with piss? You didn't wash your hands in there."

The younger girl stood up at her place and walked straight out of the lounge into the lobby. McPhail struggled off his stool. His legs were trembling.

"I had just enough of you, you crazy son of a bitch," McPhail said, advancing on Tabor. "You damn psycho."

Tabor stood his ground, his hands by his sides.

"Don't let nothing hold you back but fear, McPhail."

Nancy moved between them, looking as though she were ready to duck.

"C'mon, now," she said. "C'mon, you all."

"What the hell's the matter with you, Tabor?" McPhail demanded. "You lost your goddamn marbles or something?"

"Maybe a lot the matter from your point of view, Chief," Tabor said. "But I don't appreciate your point of view. You don't even wash your hands when you go to the toilet."

McPhail stared at him, blank-eyed, silent, a head taller than Tabor.

"You're just nuts," the chief said finally. He took a step toward the door and lumbered on out, like an oversized old man. "You better see a doctor," he said.

Nancy fixed Pablo Tabor with a wise little mother look.

"Everybody's gonna be pissed at you, Pablo. Not just the Coast Guard but everybody."

"Well, that'll be too bad," Pablo said, and drank the rest of his beer. "I don't give a shit. I'm getting out here. Got to."

"You gonna request a transfer?"

"I'm gonna transfer myself," Tabor said. "This damn station is draggin' me down."

"Where would you go if you had a choice?"

"I'd wait for a message. When I got that message—goodbye. Could be any time. Maybe today."

"Well," Nancy said, "I hope you work it out O.K." She lowered her voice a little and glanced toward the door that led to the lobby. "Hey, Pablo—you wouldn't have any extra speed around, would you?"

"Nope," Pablo said, and went out.

He drove to the inshore end of Main Street and turned west, through a neighborhood of old frame houses with peeling shutters and unfenced gardens gagged with kudzu. After a few blocks the houses and the paving ended and the road ran a course of sandy islands in the mud and saw grass that stretched to a distant line of pines. At the end of the roadway was a small square bungalow with some wooden dog pens beside it. Tabor parked in the muddy yard by the pens; as soon as he was out of his car, the dogs set up a barking.

"Hello, dogs," he said. His own two shorthairs were in the nearest pen, beside themselves at the sight of him, pressing their noses against the chicken wire, rearing and scratching against the boards of the pen gate.

"Wait a minute, wait a minute," Tabor said.

He took his twelve-gauge Remington from its cardboard box in the trunk, assembled it and stuffed his pockets with shells. The disc of the sun was over the horizon; he put his sunglasses on.

Freed, the shorthairs made a lightning circuit of the yard and hurried back to Tabor, bounding at his shoulders, climbing his legs until he put a knee up to force them down.

"Get down, fuckers," he told them. "What you think you're doin'? What you think you're doin', huh?"

An old black man came out of the bungalow holding a coffee pot in his hand.

"Gonna take 'em out?" he asked, glancing at Tabor's Saturday night clothes.

"Sure am," Tabor said. He gave the old man three dollars, the dogs' boarding fee. Tabor lived in a trailer court where they didn't allow dogs.

"They been good dogs," the old man said. "Good dogs."

He followed the old man into the kitchen and accepted a half cup of coffee.

"See any birds?" Tabor asked.

"Le'see—I seen one, two up the other side of the airfield. That dry ground. Brush up there. Didn't have my gun at the time."

"Too bad," Tabor said.

The old man watched him take two pills from the aspirin bottle and swallow them with his coffee.

"I might have a shot at one of them airplanes back there," Tabor said. "Piss me off with the noise they make. Scaring the cows. And the dogs."

"Don't do that now."

Tabor set the cup down and picked up his gun.

"I been wasting my time around this place," Tabor told the old man. "Wasting the best years of my life, no shit."

"You got that feelin', huh?" He sat waiting for Tabor to take his dogs and go. "I s'pec' that's 'cause you a young man. Be restless. Nervous in the service, heh-heh."

"Nervous in the service," Tabor repeated in a lifeless voice. "Well, I'll see you."

"Sure enough," said the old man. "You might could get one outen that dry brush."

He set off along a raised trail through the swamp, the dogs running ahead, the sun behind him.

Nervous in the service. O.K., Tabor thought, he didn't mean nothing by it. Just an old nigger, shooting the shit.

The dogs closed over a rabbit scent, their snouts poking into the saw grass, haunches low and quivering, stub tails wagging out of control. Tabor kicked at the male.

"Get along, Trouble. Goddamn, it's a fucking rabbit."

The dogs, who dreaded his anger, took off through the grass, circled back to the trail and ran ahead looking busy.

They had been good dogs to start with but they were too rarely hunted, gone to seed.

"Fucking morning," Tabor said.

From the airport off to his right, a Cherokee rose on a roar of engines and shot over his head toward the Gulf. Bound for the islands or Tampico, maybe Villahermosa, maybe Yucatán. There were clearings back in the swamp where the dope pilots landed their grass or Mexican brown—thousands of bills for a few hours' hauling. The dogs barked after the plane; Tabor watched the sunlight on its bright yellow wings as it gained altitude and settled in southwesterly.

"Very far from God this morning," he said. The second rush of speed began to jangle him. "Very far from you this morning, God."

The morning sun was raising the sweat beneath his shirt but his limbs felt cold and unconnected.

If I were God, Pablo Tabor thought, I wouldn't have mornings like this. The sun up on a swamp, two worthless dogs, a sparky with his blood full of speed and gasoline. No such morning could have a God over it.

If I were God, he thought, if I made mornings I wouldn't have no Pablo Tabor and his dogs in 'em.

"You do this, God?" he asked. "You operate and maintain mornings like this?"

He came to a fork in the raised trail and the dogs ran off to the right, toward the deeper swamp where the game was. Tabor turned left toward the shore. After a few minutes, the puzzled dogs fell in behind him; then, scenting the carrion of the beach, they whipped forward, running together.

The sun was partly in his eyes, his rush came up speckled, buzzing in his brain, old rages rose in his throat. Tasting the anger, he clenched his teeth.

Where the fuck to begin? he thought. But these people—there was hardly any getting at them.

"Usin' me," he sang out, "usin' me usin' me. Turning me and turning me and turning me around."

His mind's eye started flashing him shit—death's-heads, swastikas, the ace of spades. Dumbness. Dime-store badness. His anger rolled along, cooling and sharpening on the Dex. Before long he was standing on the beach, the sunlit Gulf spread out before him, coarse sand clinging to his wet cowboy boots. The dogs nosed along the waterline.

He walked down the beach, away from the sun, then stood with his eyes closed, his shotgun resting on his neck and shoulders, his forearms curled over it. His heart was throbbing in his side, in his temple, under his jaw. He eased the gun down and propped the stock against his thigh; from the jacket pocket he fished out two of the red and gold cartridges, forced them into the magazine of his shotgun, pumped them into place. Then a third—inserted it and pumped it forward.

The dogs had found the shell of a horseshoe crab and were worrying it, trying to lift it from the sand with their soft retriever's teeth. Tabor watched them.

If I moved, he thought, it would be like this.

The anger fell away from him as he raised the gun. He felt as though he were a metal image of himself, cool, without much reality.

Like this.

The charge drove the male dog's head down into wet sand, sent the rest of its body swinging on the pivot of its nearly severed neck to splash in the ebbing of a faint Gulf wave. Blood on the shimmering regular surface of the washed sand.

Tabor pumped the spent shell out. The female stood quivering at the shot, confused at what she saw, almost, it seemed, about to run. His second charge sent her into the air and she fell, still quivering, across a bough of flotsam mangrove.

He pumped the second shell out and licked his dry lips.

You happy now, you fool, you just murdered your dogs?

"I feel fine," Tabor said, "just fine." But it was not true. "They're fucking with my head this morning," he said.

He was walking away from the dogs, making himself not look back, when he caught sudden sight of two heads above the line of saw grass at the edge of the beach.

Stopping, he saw a boy and a girl in the grass not forty feet away from him. They stood in a peculiar crouch as though they had just stood up or were about to duck. He walked over to them.

The boy was blond, with a red bandana tied around his head; the girl almost as tall with shorter, darker hair. Tabor saw that she was crying.

"Had to be done," he told them. "They was sick, know what I mean? They had heartworm, had it real bad."

The young people seemed to relax a little. The girl wiped her sunburned cheek.

"Jeez," the boy said. "They were pretty dogs."

Tabor looked away from him.

"What the hell you know about it?"

He saw the girl's sad blue eyes on his shotgun.

"Don't you be crying over my dogs," he told her. "I'll cry over my own dogs."

They fell silent. The boy swallowed and twisted his mouth slightly.

"You want to chant with me?" Tabor asked them.

"I don't believe we know any chants," the boy said, with something like a smile. The girl clung to his arm.

"You think I'm gonna hurt you, don't you?"

"I hope not," the boy said softly. "We didn't mean any harm. We were just sad about the dogs."

You little bastard, Tabor thought, you got it all figured out. Humor the crazy man with the iron. Be gentle. Save your own and your girl friend's ass. Smart boy, Tabor thought. Smart boy.

"You're good kids," Tabor said. "I can see you are. You go to college, don't you?"

The boy nodded warily.

"Well I ain't gonna hurt you," Tabor told him. He turned from their frightened faces toward the sun. "Go ahead and have a nice day."

He walked off toward the water and they called "You too" in unison after him. As he passed between the corpses of his dogs, he turned back toward them and saw that they had not moved.

Cold to the marrow of his bones, he drove through town again and onto the Interstate, traveling west. The trailer court where he lived was beside an old canal, padded with water hyacinth. Across the highway was a brown slope where a billboard advertised a beach hotel and three derricks stood, their pistons rising and falling in perpetual motion.

Tabor's trailer was in the last row, the one furthest from the road and the most expensive.

He parked beside it, in a little driveway of crushed shell with a sick banana tree at the end of it. He had taken his sunglasses off getting out of the car, and the sun on the streamliner siding of his trailer dazzled his eyes. As he put the glasses back on, he looked toward the sorry little playground that stood fenced between two rows of trailers and saw his son. The boy was lying belly down on one of the rusty miniature slides, his arms dangling to the ground. With one hand he was sifting the surface of shredded shell and dried mud under the slide.

Tabor went to the playground gate.

"Billy."

The little boy started and turned over quickly, guiltily.

"How the hell come you ain't in school? Whatchyou doin' around here?"

Billy walked toward him ready to flinch.

"She didn't get you up, did she?" Tabor shouted. Billy shook his head. Tabor stood tapping his foot, looking at the ground.

"Dumb bitch," he whispered.

Hearing him, the boy wiped his nose, uneasily.

That could just do it, Tabor thought.

"Look here," he told the little boy, "I'm gonna drive you in after a while. Meantime you stay right out here and don't come in, here?"

He went back to the trailer and let himself in. The living room had a sweet stale smell, spilled beer, undone laundry.

And it was just the sort of place you had to keep clean, he thought. Like a ship. You had to keep it clean or pretty soon it was like you were living in the back seat of your car.

Clothes were piled beside an empty laundry bag at one end of the pocket sofa—her blouses, work uniforms, Billy's dungarees. Spread out across the rest of the sofa were the sections of the past Sunday's paper. On the arm was a stack of Jehovah's Witness pamphlets she had let some missionaries give her.

She was asleep in their bedroom, the end compartment.

Tabor went quietly into the kitchen and opened the waist-high refrigerator. There were three shelves in it—the bottom shelf held nothing except cans of Jax beer. On the two top shelves were row upon row of hamburger patties each on its separate waxed-paper square. She brought them home frozen in cardboard boxes from the place she worked.

As he looked at the rows of hamburger, a curious impulse came into his mind. He straightened up and took a breath—

he had the sensation of time running out, of seconds being counted off toward an ending. Finally, he took a can of Jax out, opened it and sat down on the living-room sofa facing the plastic door.

If he allowed himself one more, he thought, he might coax another rush. On the one hand go easy because things were getting fast and bad; on the other hand fuck it. He took a Dex out of the bottle, bit off half and swallowed it with the beer. After a few moments he swallowed the other half.

In the kitchen again, he threw the empty beer can away and stood looking out of the little window above the sink. Miles of bright green grass stretching to the cloudless blue, the horizon broken here and there by bulbous raised gas tanks on steel spider legs, like flying saucer creatures. You could picture them starting to scurry around the swamp and they'd be fast all right, they'd cover ground.

He opened the refrigerator and took one of the hamburger patties out.

"Now that's comical," he said, holding it over the sink. His chest felt hollow.

His hand closed on the hamburger, wadding it together with the waxed paper. A fat, dirty, greasy fucking thing. He couldn't stop squeezing on it. The ice in it melted with the heat of his hand and the liquid ran down the inside of his forearm. He took a couple of deep breaths; his heartbeat was taking off, just taking off on him. He dropped the meat in the sink.

When he had washed his hands, he went into the compartment at the opposite end of the trailer from their bedroom, the place where he kept his own things. Everything there was in good order.

There was a locked drawer under the coat closet where Tabor kept his electronics manuals and his military forty-five automatic. He took the pistol out, inserted a clip and went back into the kitchen.

With the gun in his right hand, he gathered up as many of the hamburgers as he could manage with his left and went to the bedroom.

"Meat trip," he said.

She had the blue curtains drawn against the morning light. The covers were pulled up over her ears; in the space between her pillow and the wall were a rolled magazine and a spilled ashtray that had fouled the sheet with butts. Tabor moved around her bed, delicately setting hamburger patties at neat intervals along the edge.

"Kathy," he called softly.

She stirred.

"I killed the dogs," he said.

"You did what?" she said, and as she came awake she saw the little circle of meat in front of her.

She started to turn over; Tabor let her see the barrel of the gun and forced her back down on the pillow with its weight.

"Pab," she said, in a small broken voice. He held the gun against the ridge of bone beside her eye and let her listen to the tiny click the safety made when he released it.

She had begun to tremble and to cry. Her nose was scarcely two inches from the waxed-paper edge of the hamburger in front of her.

"You want to go out on a meat trip, Kathy? Just you and all those ratburgers all over hell?"

"Oh, God," she whispered. "Oh, Pab."

He was thinking that when he had pressed the safety the thing was as good as done. If I moved, he thought, it would be like the dogs.

"Shall I count off for you? You want to read one of them Jehovah books before you go out?" He reached behind him and pulled a little chair nearer the bed and sat down on it. "No use in getting out of bed, baby, 'Cause it's goodnight time."

He watched her mouth convulse as she tried to breathe, to speak. Like the dogs, he thought.

A fecal smell rose from the covers; he lifted them and saw the bottom sheet soiled with bile. He covered her again.

"You fuckin' little pig," he said wearily.

The voice broke from her trembling body.

"Baby," she said. "Oh, baby, please."

He stood up and put the gun down on the chair. From his wallet he took two singles and dropped them on her covers.

"That there's for all the good times," he told her, and picked up the gun and put it in his pocket.

She was still screaming and sobbing when he went out with

his bag. It was like a dream outside—the traffic on the highway just shooting on by, the derricks across the highway up and down up and down. Craziness. He was weak in the knees; he put the bag in the back seat and walked to the playground to call his son.

"Hey, you gonna drive me now, Daddy?"

"Looks like I ain't today. I gotta go somewhere, so you can just hang out and play."

"Neat," the boy said. "You ain't goin' to sea, are ya, Daddy?"

"Yeah, I am," Tabor said. "The South Sea."

He leaned on the wire fence and took a deep breath.

"You be good to your mother, hear? She needs you to be real good to her."

"Yes, sir," the boy said.

MEANWHILE BACK AT THE

At Miami Airport, Holliwell had a change of planes.

Inside he found the Gateway to the Americas number in full January ripeness. It was not a gloomy scene; the crowds of tourists were cheerful enough. There were *abrazos* and reunions, an unselfconscious flaunting of native pottery and palm straw hats. But under the fluorescent vaults, Holliwell began to sniff out the old curse, to see around him the gathering of a world far from God, a few hours from Miami.

He spied it in small things. A purple jewelry bag lying among butts and spittle in an urn ashtray. A Cuban checking the wall clock against his Rolex. Actual fear in the eyes of a chic South American woman, as she clutched at the sleeve of her plump young son, to the pocket of whose preppy blazer a Parker pen was neatly clasped.

Of course it was all in the mind. He was tired and anxious. But as he made his way through the crowds toward the Aerochac desk, the brightly lit corners began to reek of poverty and revenge, the drawling Spanish in the general din to sound of false-bottomed laughter.

On the wall behind the Aerochac desk was the mask of a Mayan rain god, unsoundly engineered into a pair of wings. The desk was deserted. Holliwell set his bag down and turned to face the passing crowd.

He was seeing the lines go out, past the carved coconuts and the runways, from the Gateway to the lands of stick shack and tin slum, to the small dark man with the hoe, upon whose back, as in a Mayan frieze, Miami Airport rested. To the contrabandist and the grave robber, the mule, the spook, the *esmeraldo*, the agent.

On the edges of the crowd, hippies with yellow eyes passed —and raw-faced contractors, up for toothpaste and the dog races. Beside a litter bin, some sport had dumped his penny-worth of moldering funny money. The soiled notes lay faded red and blue, each one displaying some full-jowled exemplary of the Republican ideal in braided uniform and tricorn hat, on each obverse some arcane fit of Napoleonic heraldry—the National Bird, Aborigine, Volcano. Thirty cents' worth of bad history, waiting for a black man with a broom.

When the Compostelan clerk appeared and confirmed his reservation, Holliwell carried his bag to a changing room off the toilets and changed from his Stateside clothes into a seer-sucker suit and a navy sport shirt. His carry bag repacked, he went to the bar and sat in its midday darkness drinking bloody marys.

The bar he had chosen was filled with Swedes and from such of their conversation as he could make out he surmised that some of them had been to Cuba. They were talking about Havana and Matanzas and sugar. As his eyes became accustomed to the light, he saw that the Swedes sneered a great deal at what was around them—great equine Nordic sneers that distended their fine nostrils. They addressed the Cajun waitress in Spanish and ordered juicy fruit booze concoctions. Holliwell drank beside them until nearly plane time. The drink encouraged him.

His frisk at security made him think of Tecan.

By the time he had settled into his seat in the compartment of Aerochac's hand-me-down DC-8, he was pleased to be under way. The compartment smelled of duty-free perfume and bug spray. The stewardesses fingered their eye makeup and phonetically recited their English greetings and instruc-tions. The other passengers were Compostelan ladies returning from their shopping trips, a few young tourists and bankers—there were always plenty of bankers traveling to Compostela.

Flying out over the Keys, Holliwell had another bloody mary and went to sleep; somewhere between the Gulf and the Belizean coast, he had a dream.

The dream took place in a house that was large and old, a

cold northern house in which there was only one lighted
room. He himself was standing in a shadowy hallway and
beside him was a woman colleague with whom he had once
had an affair and who had killed herself in Martha's Vineyard
nearly five years before. They were whispering together; they
were afraid and guilty as they had been in fact.

In the lighted room was a fireplace where no fire burned
and on the mantelpiece above it a metal letter file full of
opened envelopes and the letters that had been inside.

"What is there to be afraid of?" Holliwell asked the woman
beside him.

"You don't understand," she said.

As they watched from the dark hall, a middle-aged black
man in a postman's uniform walked into the lighted room and
began leafing through the letter file.

Holliwell walked forward; he felt cheerful, amused, almost
high.

"I think that's my mail," he told the postman.

"Is this your house, too?" the man asked him.

Holliwell became annoyed and confused. He denied that it
was, but he felt uncertain.

"Talk to that man," the postman told him.

The man to whom he was directed to talk was not in sight,
but Holliwell knew who it would be. A navy cook he had seen
in Danang; he remembered the man's apron and service hat
but the face was a blank. He had a great reluctance to talk to
that man, or even to see him. He was afraid.

Somewhere in the house a dog began to bark.

"They think I'm a Communist," Holliwell called to his
friend.

"Of course they do," she said. Alive, she had a habit of
smiling in exasperation when people did not understand something she considered obvious.

The dog kept barking.

"If they raid the place," Holliwell said in alarm, "they'll
shoot the dog."

Then he woke up and they were circling Belize City, preparing to land. From the air, the city looked much more
pleasant than it actually was. The sea beside it was a gorgeous
light green; the sparkling beaches down the coast were cres-
cents of summery sunlight.

Holliwell frowned out at the tropical abundance, recalling his dream. It was a variation on one he had been having, intermittently, for several years. It always felt the same.

At the airport, the Union Jack flew over the terminal building; shirtless, red-necked gunners lounged beside emplacements covered with camouflage netting. When the cabin door was opened a warm wet wind sifted through the compartment— and looking out at the palm trees and the guns and the lines of parked deuce-and-a-halfs it was impossible for him not to think back. But of course it was not at all the same, only the comic rumor of a war that would never be found between the Sherwood Foresters and a phantom army of Guatemalan conscripts.

Two men with fishing-rod cases got off at Belize. The DC-8 took off again and the sea fell away behind it; it climbed over a floor of rain forest and cleared the wall of the cordillera— range after range broken by sunless valleys over which the clouds lowered, brown peaks laced with fingers of dark green thrust up from the jungle on the lower slopes. And in less than an hour—in a slender valley refulgent and shimmering— the white city of Compostela, on twin hills, walled in by snow peaks and two spent volcanoes.

From the air, the city was one of the great sights of America, but it was a frightening place to fly into if one knew the stories and the statistics. There was a sign at the airport that marked off the number of days since the last fatal accident. The Compostelans meant it to be somehow reassuring; they were always picking up North American-type public relations notions and getting them slightly wrong. On Holliwell's last trip down the sign had marked off one hundred and eight days.

He stepped off the plane into what felt like June sunlight; the air was clear as sweet water, the sky mountain blue. Three-thirty in the afternoon at seventy degrees.

The customs search, under the guns of young Indian soldiers in blue fatigues, was long and wearying. It reflected the American AID training of the inspectors modified by local conceptions of official dignity and foreign vice. There was a man in his dotage who asked everyone, banker, missionary, elderly tourist, if they had any marijuana. There was a young madman, someone's unemployable relative, who wore ex-

tremely thick glasses, talked to himself during the inspection
and laughed openly at the contents of people's suitcases.

Compostela was an odd place. It enjoyed a reputation for
progressive politics which alarmed conservatives in the United
States. Local malcontents, if they were naïve enough to be
confused by the official rhetoric into any form of organized
activism, were quickly dissuaded, sometimes terminally, by
the police or by mysterious, widely deplored auxiliaries with
names like the Knights of Mary or the Brotherhood of the
Holy Ghost.

Occasionally, the government voted against the United
States at the UN and entertained a Bulgarian vice-premier.
The octogenarian national poet was periodically dispatched to
Havana for cigars. But the Compostelan *honchos* were hustling
arrivistes for whom a buck was a buck; the rest was bullshit
and Bellas Artes. The foreign business community regarded
their government as sound.

Compostela's reserve of international goodwill was funded
mainly by the fact of its contiguity with Tecan, where, as even
the most flint-hearted Compostelan *cacique* would gravely
admit, everything was perfectly dreadful.

The porter who carried Holliwell's bag from customs stood
by while he waited at the currency exchange counter. The
notes in Compostela were yellow and brown and were officially called *grenadas* although the people called them *pesos*,
sometimes *morenos*. The singles carried the picture of a
Negro doctor whom the Compostelans claimed had discovered the quinine treatment for malaria.

Holliwell put one in the porter's hand—they were worth
forty cents. The porter grunted—times had changed—and left
him to carry his own bag through the glass doors of the
terminal and to dismiss the boys who sought to take it from
him.

Oscar Ocampo was leaning against his little Toyota in the
nearest parking row. Walking toward him, Holliwell saw that
he had gone fat. There was a bulge of gut over his belt and
under the green cloth of his tennis shirt. His hard Indian face
was softened and blurred by jowl.

Holliwell threw him a salute, still marveling at how different he looked under the extra weight. Much more European;
with his little pointed beard, like an Italian tenor made up for
Otello.

He was smiling broadly as he reached out for Holliwell's bag; he looked somehow relieved. When the bag was safely in the car, they embraced.

"How does it feel to be here again?"

"Good," Holliwell said. The volcano and the glacial peaks above the town always surprised. They made a man smile to see them. "It always feels good."

"*La dulce cintura de América,*" Oscar said. So Rubén Darío had called Central America, the sweet waist of the joined continents, every schoolchild there knew it, everyone recited it, often without irony. With Oscar it was always a little ironic, always genuinely felt.

"May we speak English?" Oscar asked.

"Sure," Holliwell said. He would have preferred practicing his Spanish on a friend. His address to the university would be in that language.

"How are things?"

"With me," he said, "pretty much the same as always. Everyone's well, thank God."

"Good," Oscar said. "And they gave you tenure?"

Holliwell laughed at his question. In fact, it annoyed him.

"Oh yes. I have tenure in my life too. But I'm not sure it's the right one."

"Don't complain to me," Oscar said, starting up the car. "That's a stylized demurrer. You're very lucky."

"How about with you?"

They drove off down the airport road and turned onto the stretch of the Pan-American Highway that led to the capital. Oscar smiled straight ahead at the road.

"A long story. The moral is that nothing is free."

Holliwell resisted an urge to ask him at once about Marty Nolan.

"Laura and I are split," Oscar told him. "We are pffft."

"That's bad news," Holliwell said. "Am I wrong?"

"I wish I knew," Oscar said.

The Pan-American Highway took them past stock corrals and unfenced fields where lean cattle grazed. After a few miles they passed the steel-rolling mill, the flagship of Compostelan industry; there was a neat, trim government clinic beside it, then a village of square concrete houses and crate shacks.

At the edge of the city there was a floral clock surmounted

by the statue of an Indian chieftain who had resisted the Conquest. Beyond that the *carretera* became the Avenida Morazón, an imitation of the Reforma and Compostela's bright daydream of itself. On one side was the central park with its thousand eucalpytus trees, on the other the public buildings with Buck Rogers ramps and reflecting pools full of papaya rinds and mosquito larvae. Beyond the park was the National University, which had employed Oscar, and the Museum of Anthropology. To the left of the Avenida was a neighborhood of middle-class houses with small lawns enclosed by low cement walls; behind it one could see the shanty towns that climbed the inward slopes of Compostela's twin hills.

A mile or so from the central square stood the Panamerica-Plaza hotel, its fifteen stories of steel and tinted glass defying Compostela's unquiet crust, surrounded by parkland in which there were lawns and ceiba trees and tame parrots.

Oscar eased the car out of the Avenida traffic and into the Panamerica-Plaza's driveway.

"I made a reservation for you here," he told Holliwell. "We don't have the house anymore."

"Well," Holliwell said. He had always disliked the hotel. It was a resort of the high rollers who had battened on the country; the shoeshine boys, the hustlers who lurked at the end of its palm-lined driveway made him feel ashamed. "Well," he said, "I've never stayed here."

When they had parked, Oscar took up Holliwell's suitcase, and shaking off the doorman, advanced aggressively into the lobby with it. Holliwell followed him to the desk, where he was demanding evidence of Holliwell's reservation in a peremptory manner. The reservation was in order.

"Listen," Oscar said, "when you finish here I'll take you over to the apartment for a drink. Would you like that?"

"Sure," Holliwell said. "That'll be fine."

"Good. Then I'll wait down here for you."

Waiting for his key, Holliwell watched Oscar drift across the pale gray lobby. The lobby of the Panamerica-Plaza had a fine banana tree at the foot of its mezzanine stairway and a fetching interior waterfall. Beyond that, it was a spiritual extension of Miami Airport.

Oscar had gone to the desk of a tour agency beside the gift

shop and was in conversation with the man behind it, a tall man in a lightweight Italian suit who appeared to be a European. As Holliwell watched, they both took a quick look at the area around them—and then Oscar slipped a parcel across the desk. The tall man examined its contents beneath his counter. Oscar sauntered off in the direction of the door and lit a cigarette.

While Holliwell and the hotel bellman rode up to the sixth floor, the elevator played the theme from *The Godfather* for them. The bellman smiled unceasingly.

He was shown to a pleasant balconied room over the pool. When the bellman had set his bag down and turned on the air conditioning, Holliwell gave him two grenadas. Two turned out to be enough.

Ocampo was waiting by the elevator.

"I don't like it here," he told Holliwell as they walked to the car. "Not at all."

"Did you think I did? Never mind," he told Oscar, cutting off an apology. "It's comfortable. It's different."

Oscar got behind the wheel. Holliwell gave the hotel lackey who opened the door for him a grenada.

"Look, I'm mortified by this," Oscar said. "My place is small and I'm not alone there."

"Come on, Oscar. It's fine. And you have more important things on your mind."

It was strange, he thought. Laura Ocampo had put up with so much for so many years. Was there female consciousness raising even in Compostela? Had she someone else? It was all so un-Compostelan.

They drove past the cathedral square. Beggars and lottery vendors swept by the car. Holliwell patted his vest pocket, checking his wallet.

"What about the kids?"

"The kids are with Laura. They won't let me see them."

"Who won't?"

"Her family. My brother-in-law threatened to shoot me."

"Obviously they're taking this very badly," Holliwell said.

"*Claro*," Oscar said. "Very badly."

His apartment was in an old and elegant section of the city, on the lake side of the hill called Colucu. It was a neighborhood of cobbled streets and colonial houses with mahogany gates and barred windows. Here and there were new apartment buildings in the California style and Oscar lived in one of these. It was a nice building, three stories of dark wood that blended well with the ancient houses around it. Oscar parked his Toyota in a garage behind the building and they went up the back stairs. In the rear of the building was a garden with fig trees, but it was enclosed by a wall like a prison's.

Inside Oscar's apartment, a stereo was playing Purcell; there was a smell of whiskey about. Everywhere there were stacks of books, some still in boxes. There were also a great many pre-Columbian pieces around the apartment—more than Holliwell had ever seen in Oscar's possession. In the little dining area off the kitchen, clay statuettes from the Pacific coast were lined up like toy soldiers beside rows of jade animals. Against one wall there were bone carvings that appeared to be Mayan, opal grave ornaments and three unbroken chacmools of varying size—the largest a full two feet in length, from the recumbent god's elbows to his toes. The groupings had a businesslike lack of decorativeness that made it unlikely they were reproductions.

In the past, as far as Holliwell knew, Ocampo had always been very scrupulous about the antiquities that passed into his possession. He had never maintained a collection of his own, only kept the odd piece of jade, or a small necklace for his wife or a girlfriend to wear abroad.

Holliwell stood looking at the ranks of artifacts as though by doing so he were being polite. Oscar seemed to be looking for someone in the apartment.

"Frank," he said suddenly, "have a drink."

"With pleasure," Holliwell said.

Oscar went to the kitchen doorway and stood in it for a moment.

"Patrick?" Holliwell heard him call. At first he could make no sense of the word.

When Ocampo came back, he was carrying two glasses full of ice and a bottle of scotch. He made a small circuit of the room and rapped on the bedroom door with the bottom of the bottle.

As Holliwell was taking his filled glass, a tall thin youth came out of the bedroom, brushing long light-colored hair from his face.

"This is my friend Frank Holliwell," Oscar said to him. "And, Frank, this is Patrick Ventura."

Holliwell held out his hand. The boy gave him a soft continental handshake. He was no older than twenty, Holliwell thought, and spaced out—as though he were drunk or on pills.

"Where's mine?" the boy said to Oscar. He looked at both of them in turns with a mannered wariness that Holliwell found distasteful. Oscar handed him the scotch bottle, and he disappeared into the kitchen.

On the wall across from where Holliwell stood was a picture of Oscar and his sons, the boys on ponies, Oscar standing between, holding the bridles.

When Patrick Ventura came back into the room, he held a water glass full of whiskey.

"You're from the States?" Holliwell asked him.

"I've spent a lot of time in Hastings-on-Hudson," the boy said, fixing Holliwell with the same sidereal coyness.

Being suckled by wolves, Holliwell thought. He glanced at Oscar. Oscar was nervous and proprietary.

"My mother's family lives there. But I come from Chile."

"Ah," Holliwell said. "Chile."

"Chile today and hot tamale," Patrick Ventura said. "That's what they say in Hastings-on-Hudson. The South American weather report. Have you heard that, Oscar? Chile today and hot tamale?"

Oscar had never heard it.

"I don't understand," he said. "You were taunted with this?"

"Like, constantly," Patrick Ventura said.

"It's strange," Oscar said brightly to young Ventura. "You and I have never spoken English before."

"Well," Holliwell observed, "Santiago used to be a nice town."

"It's still a nice town," Patrick Ventura said.

"A lot of people have left. Or been arrested."

"Patrick is not political," Oscar said.

"Oscar used to be a Marxist-Leninist," Patrick Ventura told them, "but now he's a hippie."

Holliwell turned away quickly so as not to have to look at Oscar, and walked his drink to the full-length balcony window.

"Well, that's what you said to me, Oscar," Ventura was insisting petulantly.

Then they were in the kitchen, speaking in Spanish, fighting over the bottle. Oscar was cutting Patrick Ventura off. For his part, Holliwell hoped devoutly it could be done without some kind of scene. If there was one—if the kid went into some kind of fit—he would leave at once, he decided. He drank deeply of his drink.

Oscar came into the living room holding the bottle.

"We need this more than he does," Oscar said. "Let's go and sit outside."

The boy was leaning against the back of the sofa, his eyelids fluttering. Holliwell was afraid that he might fall. Oscar turned off the stereo and with the whiskey in his hand led Holliwell outside to the balcony.

When they had settled in the lounge chairs, they heard the sound of glass breaking in the apartment behind them. Oscar did not turn around. The sun was down behind the peaks; edges of shadow softened in the picture-book street below them. Holliwell buttoned his jacket. Sounds of evening traffic drifted up from the distant Avenida Central.

"I'm in a bourgeois crisis," Oscar said. He poured them both another drink.

"Well, you're talking to the right man."

"That's whom I live with now."

"You mean he's your lover?" Holliwell understood that henceforward the ground would be uncertain.

"My wife calls him my 'catamite.'"

Holliwell felt himself closely watched. He drummed on the arm of his chair.

"You're embarrassed," Oscar said.

"No, no. Only . . . you know me, Oscar. I'm a conventional man."

"You? Never!"

"I hope you understand that I don't think badly of you."

Oscar nodded. It had not been quite the right thing to say. Finding the right thing to say now would be difficult and saying too little would be resented.

"And this is why your brother-in-law is threatening you?"

Oscar shrugged and raised his hands.

"What about you, Frank?" Ocampo asked after a moment. "Have you never had a homosexual experience?"

Now he's keeping score, Holliwell thought. In spite of himself, he blushed at the question. He was careful not to laugh.

"Never."

"Never in your life?"

Holliwell began to understand that Oscar would never forgive him for receiving this confidence. He himself hated losing friends. In his regret he veered in the direction of plain candor.

"Look, Oscar—do you want me to tell you I'm homosexual too? I'm not, as far as I know. I haven't had such an experience. I'm sorry."

"There's nothing to be sorry about."

Holliwell finished his drink.

"I guess I could have picked a better time to come down."

"Why?" Oscar asked.

For Christ's sake, Holliwell thought.

"Isn't it a little difficult to try and entertain me while you're dealing with all these upheavals in your life? Don't you need . . . something other than people visiting?"

"I need a friend," Oscar told him.

And so he did. There were few people in that country to be a friend to him now. Everyone knew everything there. Oscar himself, Holliwell thought, in spite of his aestheticism was a thorough Compostelan, a man of the mountains, a cowboy. In his own circle, the most educated circle in the country, he would be surrounded with contempt. In his deepest self, he would share that contempt.

"Then I'm glad to be here," Holliwell said. "I'm proud to be your friend and I'd like to remain your friend."

Oscar's face looked somber and blank to him. It was an Indian face again, and he could not read it. He's off, Holliwell thought, he's closed down on me and gone off to God Seven with our cultural reference point. Instant abyss, veil of centuries. If people are always doing that to us, he thought, surely we are always doing it to them?

He had meant what he had said. Maybe it had been patronizing. Maybe it would have sounded better in Spanish, or in proto-Mayan. In the dim light, he saw that Oscar had begun to cry.

"Thank you, my friend," Oscar said.

"I wish I could help you," Holliwell told him.

"You know, Frank—he's very difficult, my Patrick Ventura. He gets drunk. He takes all kinds of pills. It's very tough on me."

"He's just a kid," Holliwell said. "Christ, he can't be over twenty, right?"

Oscar had not heard the question. He was staring over the opposite rooftops with a fond expression.

"Do you know the German film *Der blaue Engel?*"

"Christ," Holliwell said, writhing. "I mean . . . sure I know it."

He stared down at the tiles of the balcony floor; he was reflecting on the fact that he was about to hear a Central American intellectual compare himself with the professor in *The Blue Angel.* More of the dynamics of contrasting culture.

"Sometimes I feel like the old professor in that film."

"Movies are movies, Oscar. This is your life."

He finished his drink. "This is your life," he had said.

"Because it costs me very much to manifest my love for him. But there is more to it than sexuality, Frank. This boy is very beautiful—not only in the physical sense. But he is also spiritual."

Holliwell shakily reached out for the bottle beside Oscar's chair. When he looked up, he saw that Oscar had closed his eyes.

" *'De que sirve la hermosura,'* " Oscar was reciting.

> " *'cuando lo fuese la mía*
> *si me falta la alegría*
> *si me falta la ventura.'* "

Oscar opened his eyes and there were more tears there.

" *'Si mi falta la ventura,'* " he repeated.

"I don't know it," Holliwell said.

"Calderón," Oscar told him. *"El principe constante."* He lifted his glass and drank from it. "Spoken," he said, smiling sadly, "by the beautiful but melancholy Fénix, spoiled princess of Fez."

Holliwell smiled back and shook his head.

Oscar watched him. "A strange turn of fate, eh? For me?"

"Very strange, Oscar."

"Frank, I want you to see some of the poems he's written. I want you to see that side of him. Will you read them?"

"All right," Holliwell said.

He stood up and went back into the apartment; Holliwell half turned to look inside. Oscar stood for a while over the sofa, leaning on the back of it. Patrick Ventura's bare feet were crossed in repose over the armrest.

Holliwell turned back toward the darkening street. In the downtown distance a red neon sign flashed on. He could see lighted windows in his hotel miles away, on a floodlit hillock.

The extent of Ocampo's ruin became clear to him. He had lost more than even his family—his wife's connections had kept him employed and out of trouble, so that in all likelihood he would presently be out of his job and on the police shit lists. But his political days would probably be over too. Because his self-respect was gone; he saw himself as a *maricón*, *mariposa*, crowing clown and princess of Fez. And no clown, no *mariposa*, could be a true revolutionary.

Holliwell fingered the edges of his whiskey glass. The man was a corresponding associate of Marty Nolan's friends in Compostela. He was destroyed and dangerous. A desperado.

In a few minutes, Ocampo came back to the balcony with a thin sheaf of papers in a tan binder. He switched on the reading light beside Holliwell's chair.

"Here, Frank," he said, thumbing through the sheets. "Read only a few, they're all short. Start with this one."

Holliwell took the binder and looked at the page to which it was opened.

The first poem there was called "Belvedere Fountain."

BELVEDERE FOUNTAIN
Drums of love
And hate
Drive the tambourine man
To spread ebony wings
And my claws too
Clutch
Sweet Puerto Rican bodies
Swing with mango sweetness
The rich weed makes my brain
A slave
To the tom toms beat
And so I dance
Footless Footloose
Eye less in Gaza

There was a second poem.

> ECSTASIS
> Ecstasis isn't static
> It's not advertisements
> And it's not the news
> Ecstasis can be little and
> Bound in a nutshell
> Or big enough to fill even me
> My zodiac, my milky way
> Decans of time imploding

"What do you think, Frank? Publishable?"

Holliwell eased the folder gently down to the floor. He kept his eyes fixed on a potted plant near the sliding door.

" 'Ecstasis isn't static' isn't bad."

"He is creative as can be, Frank. The most thoroughly, the most purely artistic of souls."

Holliwell nodded gravely.

"We can't stay here. If we were in the States everything would be different. He could get himself straightened out. He could get into school. Also it would be better for me. Here it's impossible."

Holliwell felt in his pocket for a cigarette.

"Oscar—before I came down I had a call from a man named Marty Nolan. He mentioned you. He said you were in touch."

Oscar looked past him.

"I know who he is," Oscar said. "But I've never met him."

"That hardly matters, Oscar."

"I've examined my conscience," Ocampo declared. "I don't like them—you know I don't like them. But what choice do I have?"

"What choice?" Holliwell asked. "I don't know."

"They say they can help me. Frank—I must have a job up there. And there are hardly any jobs today—you know it yourself. We've got to get out of here."

"They can't help you as much as you think. They may tell you they can."

"Ah," Oscar said, "you're naïve, Frank. You don't know how your own government works. They can get anything done."

"Even if they got you a job you could never come back. You'd never see your kids again. You'd be compromised everywhere in America. Those guys have no secrets."

"Frank, listen . . ." Oscar put out his hand and closed his fingers over his palm as though he were crumpling a piece of paper. "They have me."

"They're paying you?"

"Yes. Discreetly."

Holliwell lit his cigarette and shook his head.

"I'd ask you what you're doing for them," he said, "but I suppose I don't want to know."

"You worked for them," Oscar said suddenly. "In Vietnam you worked for them."

"You know I worked for them in Vietnam. I know you're working for them here. That's how discreet they are, Oscar." He put the cigarette out and leaned forward to pick up the bottle. "I went to school with Marty Nolan. And Vietnam was a long time ago."

"I can do this without compromising anyone. I can turn it to my advantage and no one will get hurt."

"Allow me to say," Holliwell said, "that this is the logic of desperation."

"I am desperate," Oscar said. "But I can be . . ." He paused to think of the word and when it came to him, he looked pleased. "Shrewd." He pronounced the word as though it had an umlaut. "More shrewd than you believe."

Holliwell turned away from his friend's boyish, unhappy smile.

"You'd do better selling chacmools to tourists."

"I do," Oscar said. "I buy from the *huaqueros* and I sell. Top dollar. I am also available through your hotel as a guide." He stood up, walked to the balcony rail and leaned over the quiet street. "Every weekend I take your compatriots out to the ruins at Uxpan and I present to them Mayans. The wonderful thing about our Mayans is that they can be anything to anybody. I always try to give my gringos the Mayans I think they deserve."

"It'll be you that gets hurt, Oscar."

Oscar shook his head wildly and took up the bottle.

"It's only a dialogue. An exchange of views. Gossip. I can make it up if I like."

Holliwell extended his glass and Oscar poured them both another.

"I'm not judging you," Holliwell said. "I'm afraid for you. The people involved are fighting a war."

"I wish there were no wars on," Oscar said.

"Amen to that."

"You think I'm only an informer for money. But I think that even in war there's room for dialogue. I know my own poor country. I know your country also. If I make communication—what is morally wrong with that?"

Holliwell smiled.

"You're not persuaded?"

"Sure. But I'm easy to persuade."

"We require war," Oscar said. "The advancement of society requires it. Art requires it."

"I'm going back to the hotel," Holliwell said. "I'm out of it."

"They want me to go to Tecan."

Holliwell said nothing.

"For years I've wanted to go down there to photograph the stelae on the north coast. There are very interesting stelae, you see, because they look very Mayan but they aren't. We don't know who the people were. We think they may have spoken Mayan but ethnically they were something else."

"A cover."

Oscar shrugged. "There is a mission there. They want an opinion. A second opinion. You see—they're not all stupid. They're being careful."

"Do you propose to go?"

"Before now I could never get a visa. The Tecanecan police know well my politics. Now the friends of Nolan say they'll get me one." He put his drink down and gripped the balcony rail with both hands. "But it would look all wrong and I told them that. Besides I've always hated priests and nuns. Since school."

Holliwell stood up and rubbed his face.

"You'll be at the lecture?"

"I can't Frank. I can't face them. And it wouldn't be good for you."

"But you set it up."

"I'm sure they've forgotten that," Oscar said.

"Then meet me afterwards at the hotel."

"Yes, I'll try."

Back in the apartment, Holliwell dealt with Oscar's rash offer to drive him back and paced up and down beside the sleeping Patrick Ventura while Oscar telephoned for a taxi. It took quite a long time. Oscar walked him down the back stairs.

At night the rear of the building looked like a fortress. There were tinted lights with wire guards around them along the walkways; floodlights shone on the high back wall.

On the slope behind the house, television sets glowed behind the picture windows of an apartment block. Above, on the higher ground, kerosene lamps flickered among the tin shacks.

They walked across the dry grass to the rear wall and Oscar unlocked a door that led through it to the pitch-black street beyond.

"You condemn me," Oscar said when they were out in the street. "There are things I could say to you that I won't say. You don't know how it works down here."

"I think it works the same everywhere," Holliwell said. "Maybe I know more about that than you."

"Ah, yes," Oscar said. "Vietnam."

A car turned into the street and slowly cruised the wall. As Holliwell stepped forward to hail it, he noticed that Ocampo had moved back from the roadway, as though seeking darkness. But the wall against which he leaned was thoroughly illuminated.

The car was a five-year-old Chevrolet with a taxi sign on the windshield and a plastic Sacred Heart on the dashboard.

"Meester Holawal?" the driver asked.

"Vietnam, no?" Oscar called softly from against the wall.

"Vietnam," he said again, as Holliwell climbed into the cab.

When they pulled out, Holliwell pronounced the name of his hotel. He felt ashamed of it.

The driver repeated the hotel's name with respect.

As the car sped away, Holliwell turned to look behind him. Oscar had disappeared. The lighted wall met the street at a hard empty angle and stretched to the edge of vision. Spotlights shone on the spears of broken glass atop it.

Three blocks from the piers in the port of Vizcaya was an American-style *farmacia* with a green cross over its doorway. Pablo visited it twice to inveigle some speed from the druggist. Twice he was turned away. He concluded that he must be handling it wrong.

At ten o'clock on the morning of his third visit, Pablo found himself aboil with rage and sweat, glaring into the druggist's thick horn-rimmed spectacles in an attempt to engage the dead bug eyes behind them.

"What the fuck's the matter?" Pablo demanded, holding up his Stateside prescription bottle. "I got a script for it back home."

The pharmacist ignored the bottle and gave Pablo not so much as a shrug. Two young female assistants in green smocks watched them over the stacks of medicated shampoo.

"I'm overweight," Pablo said grimly. He was not in the least overweight and in any case the druggist did not understand him. "I'm fucking depressed, dig? How about it?"

When the druggist extended a hand to urge Pablo toward the door, Pablo prepared to belt him. Only at the last minute did he realize that the man's attention was focused on the pink bank note he clutched in his left hand.

The druggist was trying to escort Pablo discreetly outside, an urbane effort which Pablo's nature resisted.

"Tiene que volver a la tarde," the man said softly, trying to speak beneath the hearing of his assistants. *"Más tarde, comprende? Ahorita no."*

By the time they reached the street, Pablo was able to understand that he was being dealt with.

"O.K.," he said. Passers-by were observing his exchange with the pharmacist. Glancing at his reflection in the drugstore window, Pablo saw that if he did not appear particularly fat and low-spirited, he did look rather like a bad-news gringo who might shortly be in jail.

"Más tarde," right?" Pablo asked the druggist. The professional man turned hurriedly inside.

It was hard to be cool. For one thing, the birdcalls were

driving him bananas; they kept sounding like someone making fun of him. Pablo reflected that he had been strung out in some shitty places but that none of them seemed quite so shitty as Vizcaya, where even the birds in the trees weirded you out. He wiped his brow and turned down the Calle Catorce de Mayo, toward the piers and Lana's.

Lana's establishment was called the Pensión Miramar, a little stone barracks of a building that gave two rows of barred windows to the street. It centered on a small interior courtyard with a dying jacaranda tree from which ten low wooden doors led to the girls' apartments. A baby was crying in one of the rooms as Pablo came in; there was always a baby crying somewhere in Miramar. Three dark children, scroungy with gutter dirt, were stalking a cat among the crates and bottles under the tree.

Pablo went to the Coke cooler behind the office and pounded on it with his fist several times. Presently a youth of about fourteen came out, unlocked the cooler and gave him a beer for a fifty-centavo piece. There was no change—there was never any change.

Disgusted and worn, he sat down on a wooden bench near the tree and tried not to let the birdcalls get to him. When I straighten out, he thought, I'll have a plan. The kids in the courtyard began to throw crates at the cat. Pablo drank his beer and watched them irritably. Everything was a trapeze act.

When one of the children kicked a bottle at the cat and smashed it, Lana came out and yelled at the lot of them. One of the kids was hers. She saw Pablo and sat down beside him on the bench.

"You got somethin' to make you feel good?"

"I thought you was gonna get me something," Pablo said. "I can't deal with these people down here."

"Thas all right," Lana assured him. "We take care of you."

"You ain't doing much of a job," Pablo told her.

Lana moved closer to Pablo on the bench and reached over to take a swallow of his beer.

"Don Jorge says you can bring the *maricón* here. If he's got a lot of money we help you take care of him. But it got to be at night, Don Jorge says."

"Who gets his money?"

"Some for everybody," Lana said.

Pablo put the beer bottle down.

"What am I supposed to do—kill him? Is that what I'm supposed to do?"

Lana shrugged. She had lived for two years in Coney Island, she once told Pablo. Off Surf Avenue, by the projects.

"I don't know nothing about it, man. I just tellin' you what Don Jorge says."

"Don Hor-hay says," Pablo said bitterly. "I ain't hustling queers for Don Jorge. And I sure as shit ain't gonna kill nobody for Don Jorge."

Don Jorge was the proprietor of the Miramar and of the bar beside it. A big man with gray wavy hair who always wore dark glasses—you saw him all up and down the waterfront streets bullshitting, doing some kind of bad business.

As far as Pablo could tell, they wanted him to bring the queer down there and kill him. Then they could turn him in.

Gotta get out of here, Pablo thought. Time to walk.

"How about you all give me my passport back?" he said to Lana. "I need it. I can't identify myself without it."

"Baby, I don't have your passport. Maybe Don Jorge has it. Maybe you owe him money—something like that."

"I don't owe him nothing," Pablo said. "If anything, you all owe me."

Lana hastened to say that she knew nothing about it.

"But you can bring that man here tonight," she reminded Pablo. "Then he can't cause you no trouble."

Pablo stood up. "I'm gonna go see him now," he told Lana.

Trucking back up Catorce de Mayo toward the *zócalo,* Pablo noticed a young American couple in backpacks; he wondered immediately about how much money they might have on them. He himself was down to seventy dollars—not counting the local money. His clothes and his passport were in the custody of the Miramar, probably lost to him.

Shoeshine boys harried him across the square, right to the door of the tourist hotel, hissing and whistling like the sinister birds. Inside he dried out in the air conditioning, checked the curio stand and the magazine rack, watching the hotel flunkies for bad eyes or wrong signals. No one seemed to notice him.

Tony Bobbick, the rich *maricón*, was not to be seen. After waiting a few minutes, Pablo sauntered into the poolside restaurant and ordered coffee at the counter.

The question of Tony Bobbick was a difficult one. On the one hand Pablo was a family man; it was degrading to hustle fags and he was a bit old for it. On the other, Tony Bobbick seemed to be Vizcaya's best-known and most popular mark, famous from one end of town to the other for his wealth and the variety of his credit cards. It was a period when credit cards were a popular novelty in Mesoamerica; the locals had acquired the necessary machines and were dispensing rental cars and plane tickets with Yankee dispatch and Old World courtesy on signals which they could barely read, let alone verify. Relatively untouristed, they still relied on the rigor of North American commercial procedures and the Code Napoléon. Pablo—strung out on his trapeze, obsessed with birds and incipient gonorrhea—was lamed by indecision and scruple.

But I got to walk, he thought. Get clear of this Vizcaya.

As he sat hunched over his excellent Compostelan coffee, brooding on Tony Bobbick, the man himself appeared. In blue duck trousers, Adidas, and a Triumph tee shirt, Tony settled himself at a table against the window that looked out on the garden and the pool. He drank greedily of the purified water which the waitress brought and laid out the previous day's Miami *Herald* before him.

Tabor sighed, hesitated for a moment to assume what he hoped might be a pleasant or even desirable aspect and approached Tony's table.

"Hey, guy," Pablo said cheerily. Although he had dealt with many homosexuals in the course of his career, he remained under the impression that they all addressed each other in this fashion. "How you feeling this morning?"

Bobbick looked up wearily and did not invite him to sit down.

"Good morning," he said.

Tabor stood over Tony Bobbick's table with a dreadful smile. Not a grain of good humor was left to him and the very sight of the man's boyish face, drawn and sagging with toxins, caused him to clench his fists. He found it extremely difficult to begin a conversation.

"Say," Pablo said after several despairing moments, "you want to go somewhere and have some fun?"

Bobbick looked up from his paper and shuddered visibly.

"It's been a long time since anybody asked that one," he said. "I think I must have been eleven."

Pablo took a deep breath and sat down in the chair opposite Tony's.

"That's what you asked me last night, man. Do I look like I'm fucking eleven?"

Tony Bobbick rubbed his eyebrows and took another swallow of water.

"If you say I said it maybe I did. But see, Pablo—I've got a friend with me now from the States. We're leaving for the ruins after breakfast."

"Aw shit," Pablo said earnestly.

"You sound really disappointed," Tony said.

"I am," Pablo told him. "You better believe it."

As they spoke, a young American walked into the coffee shop and headed for Tony's table. The American was tall and muscular with thinning blond hair and a broken nose like a fighter's. He nodded stiffly to Bobbick and stood awkwardly beside the table since there were only two chairs. Tony stood up and pulled a chair from another table for him to sit in.

"Bill," Tony said, as the third man sat down, "this is Pablo."

"Pablo?" the man asked Tony in an amused voice. He did not look at Tabor.

"Hi, there," Pablo said. He watched the two of them across the plastic tabletop. He felt angry and sick but also faintly relieved. The hustle was off; instead of one *maricón*, there were two *maricones*.

"Been having a good time?" Bill asked his friend.

"In a manner of speaking," Tony said. "We had a little drinking party last night. And now we have Pablo who proposes to go somewhere and have some fun."

"Really?" Bill said. He turned slowly and looked at Pablo for the first time. "What kind of fun would that be?"

Tabor's desperate bonhomie was disintegrating like an expended spantial. He blew his last pop on a happy smile.

"Any kind you like."

Bill did a stylized double take.

"This man is a complete asshole, am I right? A hustler?"

"Well," Tony said shyly, "I guess so."

"I guess *so*," Bill said. "Take a walk," he told Pablo.

Pablo swallowed. He stared at Bill for a moment and suddenly the confidence, the assurance in the man's face struck him as comical. A dry laugh rose in his throat. Bill smiled patiently back at him.

"You know there's about twenty locals that want a piece of your friend Tony? I already got me a deal to ice him and take his money. That's how he's been coming on since he got here."

Bill gave Tony a quick sidelong glance. Tony sulked in his newspaper.

"Like I don't want to kill nobody," Pablo told them. "I'm broke and I need some money."

"Not from him, good buddy," Bill said. "And certainly not from me. Take a walk."

Pablo leaned forward over the table and spoke in a low voice, meeting Bill's quiet stare.

"This ain't Coconut Grove, faggot. Where you think you gonna get protection from down here?"

"I know all about down here," Bill said.

"He's in the travel business," Tony informed Pablo earnestly.

"I know all about it," Bill went on. "I'm down here a lot and I do a lot of business here. So I'll give you the choice of hitting the street pronto or going straight from that chair to the penal colony. You won't like it there."

"You queer son of a bitch," Pablo said.

Bill raised his eyebrows casually and turned toward the cashier's counter with his hand in the air. Tony touched his arm gently.

"Wait a minute," Tony said, "wait a minute, let it go." Tabor saw that Tony had a bill in his hand. "The poor guy's all fucked up. I'm going to give him something." He slid a U.S. twenty along the table top. Tabor looked down at it.

"Don't you give him a thing," Bill said. "A punk like this?"

"Here," Tony said kindly, "here you go, Pablo. Take it."

"No, you don't, baby," Bill said. He snatched up the bill from under Pablo's eyes and stuffed it in his shirt pocket.

"Look," Tony said. "Maybe I did come on to him. The poor guy's a mess. Let him have it."

Bill sighed, took the twenty out of his pocket and threw it on the floor.

"This is a hell of a way to start out," he said to Tony crossly. He watched Pablo start toward the money on the tile floor. "Pick it up and get out, *Pablo*. We intend to eat here."

Pablo crouched over the bill.

This is it, he thought. I'm gonna have to kill these fuckers.

Bill crossed his bare legs while Pablo reached for the bill. The tip of his expensive hiking boots swung casually in front of Tabor's face.

He pocketed the bill and looked up; Bill was looking down at him with an expression of mild disgust.

"You really wouldn't like the penal colony, Tex."

"He wouldn't," Tony said. "The wind comes howling off the lake and God knows if they ever heard of lobster Newburg."

Tabor stood up and staggered toward the door without turning around.

O.K., he told himself when he was outside, with the shoeshine boys clustered around him. Twenty bills is twenty bills. If I'd have killed them I'd be sorry.

Cursing his way through the beggars and shoeshine boys, he decided on a drink. There was a place by the docks called the Paris where he sometimes stopped by in the vague hope of finding a billet. Wearily he took his hard-earned twenty down there and settled himself at the bar. The place was empty except for a few Compostelan Navy sailors crowded about the new pinball machine. Freddy Fender was on the jukebox, singing "El Rancho Grande." Pablo was on conversational terms with the bartender, a big Belizean, who liked Hawaiian shirts and platform shoes and wore a crucifix around his neck.

"How you doin', mon?" the Belizean asked him.

"I think I'm on a trapeze," Pablo said.

"De darin' young mon," the Belizean said. Pablo ordered a margarita, the one he got came in a little ready-mix bottle, appropriated from the national airline.

"How you mate today? Mister Tony?"

"He ain't my mate. He was buyin' drinks is all. I was drinkin' em."

"Nothin' wrong wi' dat. But now he fren' come."

"Yeah," Tabor said. "His friend come. A couple of cock-suckers."

"Dat put it harshly," the Belizean said. "But he's a bounder, dat Tony. Pretty boys all de time. Mon got no shame."

"He's a fool," Tabor said.

"Dass true, dass true. But he fren' look out for him now."

"How the hell do you know all this?" Tabor demanded. "Everybody knows everything in this fucking place."

"Well," the Belizean said, "das de entertainment, you know. Got to take it like you fin' it, bruddah."

"Shit," Pablo said.

"Hey, bruddah—you a sailin' mon?"

"I do a little of everything," Pablo said cautiously.

"I know where you get a billet, if you de right fella. Mon wid a boat lookin' for crew."

"Yeah?"

Cecil brought him another bottled margarita.

"But he nobody's mark, dis chap. He in business."

"Shit," Tabor said, "send him my way."

"Lemme ask you somethin' di-rectly, bruddah. You a black or a white mon?"

Tabor nearly fell off his stool. He had been asked the same question once before and it had gone badly for everyone.

"What do I look like?"

Cecil kept his easygoing smile.

"I ain't no Yankee, mon. People all de same to me. But dis boat chap, he might see somethin' I wouldn't notice."

"I'm a white man," Pablo said evenly. "Anybody can see that."

"Den you be O.K. wid dis man. Because I suspect he don't want colored for his crew."

He's just sensible, Tabor thought.

"Lemme put dis to you, bruddah. You lay ten bills on me I make arrangements wi' dis chap. I tell him you my old times fren'. Squared away sailin' mon."

"How come he goes to you looking for crew?"

"Because I know everybody, mon. I help him out in de past."

"Ten bills," Tabor said, "that's a hell of a lot. What if he turns me down?"

"Take it or leave it, mon."

Pablo leafed through the bills in his wallet, covering the top with his palm, glancing over his shoulder suspiciously. Cecil watched him with amusement. Pablo found a U.S. ten and handed it over.

"This better not be a rip-off," he told Cecil.

"Put you mind at rest, my fren'," Cecil said with a contemptuous smile. "Come roun' after three o'clock and you be talkin' to de commander."

He went out and sat in the little square across from the navy base where there was a statue of Morazón. Cecil's words stayed in his mind; they savored to him of treachery and double cross.

I already talked to enough commanders, he thought. He suspected Cecil of betraying him to American body snatchers.

They were turning Pablo around again. Within the same hour, he had been humiliated by cocksuckers and practically called a nigger to his face. He doubled up on the bench and ran his hands through his hair. The crazy birds in the trees along the Malecón hooted down at him.

Grim and frantic, Pablo set out through the siesta quiet for the drugstore. The druggist was waiting for him, leaning against the shutters of his shop with a singularly geek-like expression. He had taken off his green smock and was wearing a dark sport coat with three or four ball-point pens in the breast pocket. When Pablo walked by, the druggist fell into step with him. They crossed to the shady side of the street.

"Ritalin?" the druggist asked.

"Uh-uh," Tabor said. "Gotta to be amphetamine, pure and simple."

"Dexamil?"

Pablo nearly snarled with exasperation.

"No downers in it."

"Benzedrin'," said the druggist.

It was the most beautiful Spanish word Pablo had ever heard.

"Benzedrino," he said. "Fuckin-A."

"Twenty dollars," the druggist said as they walked.

"Are you kiddin' me? For how many?"

"For *cincuenta*. Fifty tablets."

"Jesus Christ," Tabor said. "Shit, O.K." He was in no mood to bargain.

They turned into a narrow dirt street bounded on both sides by corrugated-iron fencing on which there were a great many posters celebrating the party in power. The druggist gave Pablo an unmarked bottle with the tablets inside. Pablo handed over the twenty. The morning's financial exchanges were making him dizzy.

All anybody cares about in this fucking country, he thought, is money.

When he opened the bottle to inspect the pills inside, the druggist began to hiss and flap at him to put it away.

"Aw, fuck you," Pablo said, but he stuck the bottle in his trouser pocket.

At the corner, the pharmacist turned away and waddled purposefully back toward his drugstore. There was no one else in sight.

Pablo caught sight of a Coke sign at the end of the next block and trucked on toward it, imagining the rush, hoping to Christ he had not been taken.

The sign stood over a little flyblown *tienda*, where there was a counter with some pastries and a coffee machine. Pablo went inside and whistled between his teeth. After a while a sleepy old woman came out from the back of the shop to sell him a Coke.

He gave her one of the coins with the general on it—five *ratones, gibrones*, whatever—and stared her down in case she decided to fox him out of the change. Nervously, the old woman counted coins into the upturned palm which Pablo held imperiously before her.

Then he went outside, propped the Coke under his arm and took out the bottle the geek had sold him. They were Benzedrino all right, little yellow tablets, three hundred migs.

Hot shit, Tabor thought; he swallowed two of them with his warmish Coke and leaned back in the shade of the corner building.

On his empty stomach, he began to get the rush fairly early on and it felt like the real thing.

"Thank you, Jesus," Tabor said. His being began to come together. When he had rested against the wall for several minutes, a little boy appeared and approached Tabor with his hand out. Tabor happily doled out a handful of *cabrones*. But the boy did not go away—he planted himself before Tabor and pointed at the Coke bottle in his hand.

Just as he was about to hand the boy the bottle, Tabor experienced his true rush. He was moved almost to tears.

As the boy watched him wide-eyed, Pablo wound up like Dizzy Dean and sent the bottle hurtling into the wall of the building across the street—where it smashed magnificently, sending thick shards of bottle glass in all directions.

"Ay," the kid said.

"Ay" Tabor said. "Aye aye aye." He gave the kid a thumbs-up sign and set out for the docks with music in his heart.

"Well, he's gorgeous," the blond woman said to her companion, "but don't you think he's a thug?" Cecil had pointed Pablo out to them at the bar.

The man with her was about fifty, his face deeply tanned and fine-featured. His haircut made him look like a boy in a magazine ad for a military school, gone gray.

He shrugged and lighted a cigarette.

"They're all sort of the same. If you think he's gorgeous that's good enough for me."

"Cecil is doing one of his Cecil numbers on us," the woman said. "He's pissed off because you wouldn't hire his cousin."

"Hell," the man said, "I'm sure he never set eyes on this dude any earlier than last week. I'd just as soon have it that way."

"You know, he thinks it's racial. He heard you make that remark about being born on the dark side of the moon."

"I don't care what Cecil thinks. If I keep hiring those no good *ratones* Cecil says are his cousins I'll really be in trouble."

"Damnit," the woman said. "Whatever happened to the carefree college boy we always dreamed of?"

"I don't want a carefree college boy," the man said. "I want a bad guy I can keep in line."

The woman glanced over at Pablo and worried the lime in her Cuba Libre with a candy-striped straw. "But don't you think this cat looks a little demented?"

"Could be he's high on something," the man said, without looking over. "That could be bad. On the other hand—as long as he can work—it could make him easier to handle."

"Are you sober enough to talk to him? I'd like a closer look."

"Sure," the man said. "Let's run him past."

The woman picked up her straw and waved it languidly until Cecil caught her signal. He walked over to Pablo, who was beginning to fret over his beer, and leaned toward him.

"O.K., bruddah. Front and center for de mon. I tell dem we know each other from New Orleans."

Even being ordered front and center did not stay the surge of optimism that flooded Pablo's heart. He swung off his stool and marched confidently toward the table where the couple sat. He had been watching them, a little greedily. They looked rich and heedless, the lady sexy and loose. They aroused his appetites.

"My name is Callahan," the gray-haired man said when Pablo stood before him. "This is Mrs. Callahan."

"Right pleased to meet you," Pablo said. "Pablo Tabor."

"Well, we're right pleased to meet you too, Pablo," Mrs. Callahan said. "Please have a seat."

Pablo sat down. Mrs. Callahan called for two more rum and Cokes and another beer for Pablo, while he and Mr. Callahan looked at each other blankly.

"So you're a buddy of Cecil's?" Callahan asked.

"No sir, he ain't my buddy. He knows me, though. From New Orleans."

"Salvage diving, wasn't it?" Mrs. Callahan asked brightly.

"Yeah," Pablo said, confused. "There was a little of that."

Mr. and Mrs. Callahan looked at each other quickly. Cecil brought the drinks. He had a smile for everyone.

"Well, the thing is, Pablo," Mr. Callahan said, "that the missus and myself have a boat and we're looking for a crewman. She's a powerboat."

Pablo nodded.

"Do you have any seagoing experience?"

"Well," Pablo said. "I can steer. I'm pretty handy with engines. I can operate and maintain any kind of radio equipment you got. If you got radar I can work with that too."

"You must have been in the service."

"Coast Guard," Pablo told him, taking the chance.

"Good for you," Callahan said. "Can you navigate?"

"Guess I could get a fix on a radio beacon. I never used a sextant much."

"How come they call you Pablo," Mrs. Callahan asked. "Are you part Cuban or something?"

"I ain't part anything," Pablo said. "I'm American."

"Have a passport?" Callahan asked him.

"They got it where I'm staying. I believe they're a bunch of crooks over there."

"I see," Mr. Callahan said. "Now that could be a problem. We might have to work on that."

Pablo chewed his thumbnail. "Where is it you and the lady were going to take your boat?"

"Oh," Callahan said, "up and down the coast. Maybe do a little island hopping. We'd want you for less than a month. You could leave the vessel any number of places."

"Could I ask you about the salary?"

"Well, I usually leave that to my number one. But I can tell you it's higher than customary. Because the work is hard and we have our standards."

"That'd be O.K. with me," Pablo said.

"I'll tell you what," Callahan said. "We have a few things to check out before we can give you the O.K. If you check back here around five—either we'll be here or we'll leave a message with Cecil."

"Jeez," Pablo said. "I was hoping you could tell me one way or the other."

Callahan smiled sympathetically. "Sorry, sailor. No can do. But I'll tell you what"—he slipped Pablo a fist of local notes across the table—"buy yourself a few beers."

Pablo sighed behind his Benzedrine and took the bills. Bank notes had slipped back and forth under his hands all day.

"What's the matter, Pablo?" Callahan asked. "You feeling O.K.?"

"I don't know," Pablo said. "Sometimes you get the idea all anybody's interested in down here is money."

Mr. and Mrs. Callahan looked at him pleasantly.

"Well," Callahan said, "that's because it's such a materialistic society down here. They don't have the same kind of spiritual values we have up home."

"Right," Mrs. Callahan said, "one gets caught up in it."

Pablo smiled and stood up, thinking that he might have trouble with these people. "Hope to see you at five," he said.

On the way out he said so long to Cecil.

When Pablo was on his way, the Callahans drank another round.

"Jesus, it's depressing," Mrs. Callahan said. "They're all such creeps. And what we really need is an extended family."

"The only question these days," Callahan said, "is, will they turn on you? It's sad but that's the way things are."

"I think I've just decided," Mrs. Callahan said, glancing toward the bar, "that I don't like him. I think he's Cecil's idea of a gag."

"He's a deserter," Callahan said. "Those guys are usually a good bet."

"Maybe we're supposed to think he's a deserter. Maybe he's a Fed."

"He's too fucked up to be a Fed. I mean, they're just not that good."

"Maybe we can get by without him?"

"I don't think so," Callahan said.

They sat in silence for a while.

"Look, Deedee, on the level of instinct I go for him. I think he's the best man we've seen. I think he knows how to take orders. I'm sure he doesn't like it much—but I think he takes them."

"I don't like him," Mrs. Callahan said.

"There's three of us and one of him—and he can't really navigate. But I've got to get his passport and check him out. Cecil probably knows where it is."

"It's your decision," the woman said.

"I used to like it," Callahan said, "when the baddest thing around these parts was me. These days I'm just another innocent abroad."

Mrs. Callahan finished her rum and lit a small thin cigar.

"It's really scary," she said. "People are getting to be a disgrace to the planet."

Callahan smiled dreamily.

"We've been lucky, kid. We've met some dingalings but we've met some sweethearts, too."

Mrs. Callahan waved the cigar smoke away from their table. "Don't get me going," she said. "I'll start to cry."

Six stories below Holliwell's window, a French teen-ager and her mother were playing in the swimming pool. The women were fair; their bodies were tanned and charged with the sunlit sensuality of fruit in the softening afternoon light. The daughter was doing laps and even within the confines of the Panamerican's pool it was apparent that she was a fine swimmer. At each length, she performed a racer's turn while her mother watched her with a brown arm resting on the tiles, shading her eyes from the sun and sipping lemonade from a tall iced glass. Tame parrots wandered among the plants before the poolside suites. Beside the wall that divided the hotel pool from the Compostelan street outside, two Indians in braided uniform jackets hosed down the garden, looking neither at the guests nor at each other.

Holliwell was sitting on his pocket balcony watching the Frenchwomen when it occurred to him that, against safety and reason, he felt like going to Tecan after all. The Corazón Islands stood off her Caribbean coast, enemies to winter and the emptiness that awaited him at home. Tecan was what it was, but it was also, like Compostela, the sweet waist of America. A seductress, *la encantada*, a place of pleasure for the likes of him.

Beyond the snow bird's impulse was his mounting curiosity about the Catholics there. It would be strange to see such Catholics, he thought. It would be strange to see people who believed in things, and acted in the world according to what they believed. It would be different. Like old times. He owed nothing to anyone; he could go or not. What he might do and what he might see there would be no one's business but his own.

He put away the thought and drank more and the pool below him surrendered to shade. He had stayed in his room in the expectation that some sort of social invitation would come from the university, that someone there would at least call to welcome him.

No calls came, however, and he suspected that it must be because of Oscar. Perhaps they imagined that they were being preyed on by a faggot cabal.

Fuck them, he thought, pacing the tile floor drink in hand. They would despise his address. Leftists and rightists alike would find it so much gringo decadence.

The women would be puzzled and threatened, they would turn to their husbands for explanation. The husbands would explain about gringo decadence. That professor, they'd say, smacking their lips, he's a friend of Ocampo's, he's a *maricón*. It's no surprise he feels that way.

But hasn't he a wife? the women would ask.

It proves nothing with them, the men would say. Believe it, he has little boyfriends like Ocampo. The wife undoubtedly has lovers.

Then their poor children, the women would say.

And the men—whether of the left or right would say— *Mujer*, the children—you can see them for yourself. They come here all the time. Look at their mouths and their eyes. The boys all look like women. They can't satisfy the girls. All of them are addicted to drugs.

How bitter he had become, Holliwell thought. His own venom startled him.

So be it. If the Autonomous University would not give him dinner, he would come back to the hotel after the lecture and take his dinner there. Perhaps Oscar would join him.

With a drink beside him, he took up his Spanish-English dictionary and worked over the address for a while.

Within the hour there was another bout of hide-and-seek with the hotel phone. He found himself in conversation with a man from the Cultural Affairs section of the American Embassy named Vandenberg. Vandenberg regretted that the Cultural Affairs section had not been able to sponsor his address. He regretted further that he himself would not be able to attend although he understood that there were people from the embassy community who planned to go.

Holliwell explained that it had all been set up very suddenly, through friends; he understood that there had been no time to arrange official sponsorship.

Vandenberg said that everyone was happy all the same. "Keep us in mind," he told Holliwell.

Holliwell assured him that he would indeed.

By six o'clock there were no further calls. Holliwell had a shower to sober himself and then drank more, as though that would further the process. Going along the hallway to the elevator, he observed that his steps were unsteady. On his way across the lobby, he stopped at the bar for a drink, spreading his address out on the polished mahogany before him. He drank two *escosses* and listened to the voices of the men at the table nearest him; there were four, speaking together in accented English. Turning casually in their direction, Holliwell surmised that two of them were Compostelans. The others, from the pitch of their English and their starched white open-necked shirts, he decided must be Israelis. They were too far away and spoke too softly for him to determine what it was they talked about.

Holliwell gathered up his speech and strode out into the gathering darkness, walking the length of the hotel path to stand beside the policemen who stood at the gate to fend off beggars and shoeshine boys. When a taxi pulled up at the curb, he caught it and set off in a peel of rubber for the Autonomous University.

The palm-bordered blocks of the Central Avenue were deserted as Holliwell's taxi sped along them. At one intersection, the cab halted to let a column of youths march across the roadway and at first Holliwell mistook the procession for some sort of demonstration. But as the column emerged from the verdant gloom of the dark traffic island, he saw that it was flanked by policemen with carbines and that the boys and the few girls among them marched ten abreast in a quasi-military step, silent and expressionless. Most of the boys long-haired, the girls in jeans. There were couples among them going hand in hand. The policemen marched them on across the right-hand lanes of the avenue and up a darkened side street.

When the cab was under way again, Holliwell asked his driver who they were.

"*Jipis,*" the driver said. "Youth without morals." The driver seemed to be something of a philosopher, an elderly Spaniard with clerical steel glasses.

"What will be done with them then?"

The driver shrugged. "No harm." Then he turned on his seat and smiled. "Perhaps haircuts *a la policía.*"

At the floral clock, the driver plunged cursing into the maelstrom of rotary traffic. Holliwell held his breath.

"Still," he suggested to the driver when they had cleared the rotary, "it's a free country."

"Claro," the driver said. "Ever since the Reform."

At the edge of the university complex, there was a monument to the Reform that had made Compostela a free country. Once past it, they drove among the floodlit fountains and concrete lawns until they had pulled up before the House of the Study of Mankind.

"So here," Holliwell offered, as he paid and overtipped the driver, "it's not like Tecan."

The driver looked shocked.

"No no no," he said with passion. "It's not free there. And it's very bad for the poor."

The foyer of the House of the Study of Mankind had murals on its walls by a celebrated Compostelan painter, an imitator of Orozco and a habitué of the Brasserie Lipp. The murals contrasted awkwardly with the neo-Florentine design of the building but they did portray mankind in a variety of transcendent postures. The foyer, as Holliwell entered it, was crowded with students who had gathered in conspiratorial groups along the wall. They spoke watchfully and eyed Holliwell as he passed. Many of them appeared to be youth without morals and there were some with the *pistolero* style. There was a great deal of laughing among them, but it was not pleasant to hear. It echoed in the dead space of the windowed Italianate dome high overhead.

There were two exhibit halls at either end of the foyer, both of them closed off behind gates of metal grill. In one was a diorama portraying the history of the Republic with an emphasis on the treachery of her neighbors and her sufferings at the hands of the church. The Catholic university, in another suburb, had one very like it which recounted the Neronian martyrdom to which the church had been periodically subjected by her ungrateful Compostelan children. The hall on the opposite side of the foyer was a museum, a dull affair of feathered rattles in glass cases. Both halls had been secure behind their grill gates for nearly ten years.

Beyond the entrance hall was a patio with native plants and a Spanish fountain; Holliwell displayed his invitation to a university guard in order to pass. It was a pleasant place, the patio, and Holliwell entered it gratefully, seating himself along the fountain's edge to listen to the broken rhythm of the water and student voices in the hall outside. He had not sat for longer than a moment when saw a gray-haired man come down one of the stone stairways from the upper story to approach him. The man was extending his hand but there was a faint posture of disapproval in his manner. The fountains, Holliwell supposed, were not to be sat beside.

"Professor Holliwell?" the gray-haired man inquired.

Holliwell stood up. His stance was unsteady.

"Claudio Nicolay," the man said, taking Holliwell's hand. "Associate rector for the discipline of sociology. Welcome again to Compostela."

Nicolay had the face of the Field Marshal von Paulus, colored in brown.

"I'm very happy to be here," Holliwell told him. "I thank you for inviting me."

"Ah yes," Nicolay said, in what Holliwell thought to be a strangely ambiguous manner. "Will you follow me, please?"

They climbed the stone stairs which Nicolay had descended and walked along a mezzanine lined with open classrooms that exuded a scent of old wood and mold repellent. But the room to which Nicolay finally led him was constructed of bright stainless synthetics and lit with fluorescent ceiling fixtures. There was a podium up front; thirty or so people sat on straight-backed wooden chairs facing it. The audience stirred and turned toward Holliwell as Nicolay conducted him halfway down a side aisle and then leaned against the wall to face him.

"We have expected," Nicolay said, "that you would speak in English. This will be quite O.K. Our group tonight is for the most part English-speaking."

"Well," Holliwell said, "I prepared it in Spanish. I thought . . ."

Nicolay interrupted him.

"You may give your address as you like. My opinion is that English would be preferred."

It was all, Holliwell had come to realize, extremely brusque. Even if Nicolay had decided that he was drunk and was resentful, even if he were trying to be informal and Stateside in manner—the whole business smacked of rudeness. People were not casually rude in Compostela.

Holliwell shrugged. "As you like, Doctor."

"So you will speak and then maybe there will be questions. O.K.?"

"O.K."

"It was thought afterwards to have cocktails on the terrace. We hope you can stay."

"Thank you again," Holliwell said.

"As for your payment—it's been arranged."

"That's fine," Holliwell said. He was determined not to be made uncomfortable.

"Whenever you're ready then, I'll introduce you."

"Go right ahead," he told Nicolay.

The professor doctor conducted him to the dais and he looked over the house. More than half of his audience were women. At least a third appeared to be North American. Their faces were indistinct under the fluorescent lights. Holliwell owned a pair of reading glasses which he used on occasions when innovative lighting or his own intemperance baffled vision; he had left them in his hotel room, beside the scotch.

Nicolay's introduction was as suitable for Holliwell as for anyone else and when it was concluded there was polite applause.

"Ladies and gentlemen," Holliwell declaimed, "esteemed colleagues." Who in hell, he wondered, are these people? He looked helplessly down at his laborious espanished address and paused.

"I see before me," he told them, after an awkward moment had passed, "I see before me, imperfectly, the notes which it had been my purpose to deliver in the language of this country. I must tell you that to put it back in English as I speak seems a very daunting business. I think it is an impossible business."

He looked at Nicolay, who was sitting in the last row and was recognizable to Holliwell only by his dark complexion and iron-gray hair. As he looked, his Compostelan colleague appeared to undergo parthenogenesis; two Dr. Nicolays looked up at him, their grave expressions only to be imagined. In the blurred faces of the audience, he presumed to read geniality and patience.

"Allow me to share, as we say in my country, this experience. The sharing of this experience will constitute an inter-American, intercultural act. In performing together an inter-cultural act, ladies and gentlemen and esteemed colleagues, we may capture the workings of culture in vivo. On the hoof."

There was a little uncertain laughter.

"The address I have here," Holliwell announced, "as I consider retranslating it into English, seems very portentous. Culture, as we know, is very much a matter of language and the language before me seems at the moment to be operatic and mock-Ciceronian and absurd. Looking at it, thinking about speaking it, makes me angry. Not." he hastened to assure them, "that I find Spanish itself mock-Ciceronian and absurd, because I yield to no one in my affection for the tongue of Cervantes and Lorca and the immortal Darío. Only my thoughts, my circulocutions, my artfulness, seem so in that language."

Someone slapped his palm against a leather armrest. There were sighs of obscure significance.

"Another dissatisfaction, friends, another dissatisfaction for me is that the subject of this address was to be Culture and the Family or vice versa or the Family in Culture or some construction of that sort. I tell you in sincerity that I am not the man to speak about such things. I know nothing about families—certainly no more than anyone else here tonight. For a large part of my life I had no family at all. The word, 'father,' for example, was an abstraction to me. I associated it only with God."

A single Spanish word he could not make out echoed against the polished surfaces of the room. It was answered with a guffaw. Holliwell did not look up. A sadness descended on him.

"When I learned about families—The Family, *La Familia* —I found only that it was an instrument of grief. That's all I can tell you about The Family and I assume you already know that much. Moreover, in my culture we are doing away with grief, so the future of the family there is uncertain. As a consequence the topic may not be relevant, and relevance, surely, is what we require here this evening. In this intercultural exercise of ours.

"But seriously . . . seriously, my friends . . ." He paused, stunned for a moment at the wreckage he had piled on himself. "I can certainly talk about culture. It's my bread and butter and I have no hesitation in talking about it. For example, popular culture is particularly fun. In my country we have a saying—Mickey Mouse will see you dead."

There was silence.

"There isn't really such a saying," Holliwell admitted. "My countrymen present can reassure you as to that. I made it up to demonstrate, to dramatize the seriousness with which American popular culture should be regarded. Now American pop culture is often laughed at by snobbish foreigners—as we call them. But let me tell you that we have had the satisfaction of ramming it down their throats. These snobbish foreigners are going to learn to laugh around it or choke to death. It's in their gullets, it's in the air they breathe and in the rich foreign food they eat. They better learn to love it."

Someone called Holliwell by name but he affected not to hear. A party of Americans in one of the forward rows stood up to leave.

"Our popular culture is machine-made and it's for sale to anyone who can raise the cash and the requisite number of semi-literate consumers. Compostela is one of the progressive nations that have been successful in this regard."

People in the back were hissing him.

"Bear with me," Holliwell begged his audience. "I don't mean to sentimentalize the various popular cultures that ours has replaced. You can be sure that in their colorful ways they were equally mean and vulgar and trashy. They simply didn't have what it takes."

He stopped again, dry-throated, to watch the brisk traffic toward the door.

"Yet I would like to take you into my confidence in one regard, ladies and gentlemen and esteemed colleagues—and here I address particularly those of my listeners who are not North Americans—we have quite another culture concealed behind the wooden nutmeg and the flash that we're selling. It's a secret culture. Perhaps you think of us as a nation without secrets—you're wrong. Our secret culture is the one we live by. It's the one we've beaten into wave upon wave of immigrants who have in turn beaten it into their children. It's not for sale—in fact it's none of your business. But because we're involved in this inter-American intercultural exercise I'll tell you a little about it tonight."

A general stir, of hostile ambiance, had taken possession of the room.

"Allow me to recite for you the first poem ever printed in what became the United States of America. It goes like this:

> " 'I at the burial ground may see
> Coffins smaller far than I
> From death's embrace no age is free
> Even little children die.'

"Friends, children in the English-speaking colonies of North America didn't go to heaven to become *angelitos*. What became of them was terrible to ponder. The pondering over what became of them is part of our secret culture. Our secret culture is as frivolous as a willow on a tombstone. It's a wonderful thing—or it was. It was strong and dreadful, it was majestic and ruthless. It was a stranger to pity. And it's not for sale, ladies and gentlemen. Let me tell you now some of the things we believed: We believed we knew more about great unpeopled spaces than any other European nation. We considered spaces unoccupied by us as unpeopled. At the same time, we believed we knew more about guilt. We believed that no one wished and willed as hard as we, and that no one was so able to make wishes true. We believed we were more. More was our secret watchword.

"Now out of all this, in spite of it, because of it, we developed Uncle Sam, the celebrated chiseling factor. And Uncle Sam developed the first leisured, literate masses—to the horror of all civilized men. All civilized men—fascists and leftist intellectuals alike—recoiled and still recoil at Uncle Sam's bizarre creation, working masses with the money and the time to command the resources of their culture, who would not be instructed and who had no idea of their place. Because Uncle Sam thought of nothing but the almighty dollar he then created the machine-made popular culture to pander to them. To reinforce, if you like, their base instincts. He didn't think it was his job to improve them and neither did they. This debasement of polite society is what we are now selling you."

Again Holliwell paused. Voices were being raised but he was not being shouted down. He could make himself heard.

"I have the honor to bring you hope, ladies and gentlemen and esteemed colleagues. Here I speak particularly to the enemies of my country and their representatives present tonight. Underneath it all, our secret culture, the non-exportable one, is dying. It's going sour and we're going to die of it. We'll die of it quietly around our own hearths while our children laugh at us. So, no more Mickey Mouse, *amigos*. The world is free for Latinate ideologies and German ismusisms . . . temples of reason, the Dialectic, you name it . . ."

He became aware of a more substantial disturbance and was compelled to face the room. At the rear, across the heads of those remaining, stood a young man in dark glasses wearing a black shirt and a Richard III haircut. The young man had risen to confront him.

"Is not this facile nihilism, Mr. Holliwell, a screen for Communistic theory?"

A guerrilla of Christ the King, Holliwell thought. The White Hand. He had an instant's inward vision of his corpse rolling from a speeding car onto the lawn of the Panamerican.

"Isn't nihilism, sir, a way of discrediting our Western Christian culture which the Communists seek to displace?"

"You can't be serious," Holliwell said.

"Oh, yes, sir," the young man said, with a hint of unpleasant laughter. "Quite serious."

Stricken by the recklessness of his conduct and reminded of where he was, Holliwell lamely sought a route back toward pedantic convention.

"Do you think that as a replacement for anything lost, I'm proposing Marxism? Do you think that despair leads me to cast envious eyes on Latvia or Kirghizstan?"

"Perhaps you feel for our people," the young man suggested. "Perhaps you feel that *we* should look to Latvia or Kirghizstan."

"What I feel is that I've offended you and you're getting me back. I regard Marxism as analogous to a cargo cult. It's a naïve invocation of a verbal machine."

"But heroic? Perhaps inevitable?"

Idiotic as their exchange was, Holliwell considered, he had had it coming. It would teach him. But he was still drunk enough to be angry.

"Sure," he said. "Perhaps. It's a funny world, son."

Now a middle-aged American was on his feet, encouraged by the young fanatic. Faced with revolt, Holliwell increasingly regretted his folly.

"I'd like to apologize to all the Compostelans here," the American said. "And I want to ask you a question, Holliwell. Did the United States government pay for the display of bad manners you've just treated us to?"

"That's correct," Holliwell said.

"Well, I'm tired of apologizing for all the so-called experts who come down here on the taxpayers' money and give the States a bad name. The only time I hear this kind of garbage is when I come to an event like this."

"Once upon a time," Holliwell told the man, "there was a chartered aircraft carrying American businessmen and their wives over Japan. The businessmen were insulation dealers from the northern Midwest. They were on a cultural tour of the Orient."

"What do you bet," the American asked someone who was with him, "that this little story has an anti-business moral?"

"How can I give your money's worth," Holliwell said, "if you won't listen to me?" The man sat down in disgust.

"Well, sir," Holliwell continued, "these folks were being rewarded with this trip for having sold great quantities of insulation. But just as their plane flew over Mount Fuji it broke apart and all the dealers and their wives fell out. They and their plastic cups and their Kodachrome slides and their wallets full of pictures of the folks back home fell onto Mount Fuji. On the slopes, their bodies were collected by Buddhist monks and the monks laid them out and burned incense over them and that was how their cultural tour of the Far East ended. Now," Holliwell said to the American, "is there a lesson in that or not?"

Dr. Nicolay was approaching him.

"I see no point in continuing," Nicolay said. "I think you should go and rest, eh?"

Before Holliwell could respond, a red-haired woman with broad shoulders and a sad smile rose in the center of the diminished audience. "What about God?" she demanded in an Australian quaver. "Is there a place for God in all this?" Holliwell realized gratefully that she must be as drunk as he.

"There's always a place for God, señora. There is some question as to whether He's in it."

Dr. Nicolay glowed with a smiling revulsion that Holliwell imagined must be Central European. He was at the point of allowing the doctor to supervise his removal when he saw that a honey-haired Compostelan lady had come down along the side aisle and was poised to address him. The lady was striking and her aspect amiable. He waited.

"I could be forgiven, Dr. Holliwell, could I not, if I inferred from your manner and the tone of your remarks that your attitude toward my country is ambiguous?" Her smile was demure, conventual and unthreatening. Holliwell blushed.

"My attitude is friendly," he said. "I'm sincere." He had already set in motion the processes by which he hoped in time to forget utterly the evening behind him. It was not pleasant to be compelled to a defense. "I thought I would improvise. I was after a deeper seriousness that I may not have . . . If my countryman hadn't already done so I'd consider apologizing."

"No need for that, sir," said the smiling young woman. "But isn't this stylized despair an excuse for immorality? Doesn't it explain away all duty? Don't you think your attitude reflects the decadence of your own society?"

"Shall I answer in any particular order?" Holliwell asked.

"The libertine and the Communist are the one hand washing the other!"

It was the young blackshirt, who was lounging by the door in a *pistolero*'s crouch. There were several men with him who also favored dark shirts and tinted glasses.

"I've tried to answer your political objections," Holliwell said evenly. "I'm not a political man."

The *politiques* left looking unhappy. A whiff of Spanish menace, like cordite and jasmine, hung in the air. Holliwell, sobering up, was more and more driven into confrontation with the heedlessness of his demonstration.

The beautiful Compostelan lady in the aisle continued to smile on him.

"You were saying, Doctor?"

Holliwell looked at her blankly for a moment.

"The answer to all your questions is probably yes. Everything that's known is someone's excuse for something."

The woman sat down in a chair that had been vacated. Holliwell was completely taken with her. He permitted himself to wonder if the debacle might not be turned around, if instead of waking up hung over and humiliated in his overpriced hotel room . . . it might be otherwise. Not a chance, he thought. Not this woman, not in this country. And not with him. He became once again aware of Nicolay, who was still beside him.

"I beg you," he said to the doctor, "to accept my remarks as a foreign novelty. Like grand opera."

"You are a master of insult, Professor. You should have made a duelist."

"I understand Caruso sang in Compostela," Holliwell persisted. "In your wonderful opera house. Before the earthquake. That's what I've been told."

"You're told incorrectly," Nicolay said. He was looking into what remained of the audience. The few people who remained could not hear their exchange. The young woman had risen once more.

"I think we should say," she declared, addressing herself to Nicolay, "I would like to say—that if we have been disturbed by what Professor Holliwell has had to say this is all to the good. We must thank him."

But there was no one to applaud. Everyone who had not left was moving toward the table on which the drinks were set.

She was nothing short of marvelous, Holliwell thought. In a few strokes she had rebuked his arrogance and brought him into line, rewarded his gesture or remorse and then practically blanded out the whole affair. He bowed to her and walked unescorted to the scotch. Pouring himself a drink, he found himself across the table from her. Her eyes were gold-spotted. She extended her hand.

"Mariaclara Obregón."

"You're very skillful, Miss Obregón."

"We don't avoid controversy," Mariaclara Obregón told him. "But on the other hand, we don't want to leave a bad feeling either way."

"I'm very glad you were here."

"I am too," she said. "I have what you said on tape. I'll listen to it another time at my leisure."

"I hope it'll make sense."

"I'm sure it will," she said. "Spontaneity is sometimes difficult."

"Yes, indeed," Holliwell said.

"We have political tensions here, I'm sure you know."

"I understand completely." His desire for her made him feel suddenly shabby and absurd. Drunk.

"The academic circles of a country are not the most considerate. I'm sure you know that also."

"The libertine circles are pretty rough too."

He was aware of a young North American couple standing just behind her, waiting as though to speak with him. He was careful to ignore them. Nicolay had produced two attendants in beige uniforms, their heads no higher than his shoulders. He directed them toward the table; they bowed to him and began removing glasses.

"Are you in fact a libertine, Professor?" Miss Obregón asked him playfully.

"Yes, I am," he told her. "In that way I predate the industrial age. I am a man of the enlightenment and a libertine."

"An illuminatus?" she suggested.

"I'm a middle-class professor," he told her. "In every regard. No more than that."

"A leftist?"

"A liberal is what they call people like me."

"Here," the woman said, "to be a liberal you must be a Mason."

Holliwell moved around the table and past the American couple to stand beside her.

"Listen," he said, "is it possible for us to take coffee? If not tonight, then sometime else?"

"I think unfortunately not, Professor. I wanted only to say thank you for speaking to us."

Her hand was in his again; he forced himself to let it feather away.

"But you're not just leaving?"

"It's too bad but I have to go. Please let me thank you again."

And to his dismay she turned away, leaving him with the porters, the two young Americans and Nicolay. He took a step in Nicolay's direction and stumbled.

"Miss Obregón," he demanded of the doctor, "who is she? Is she a member of the faculty here?"

Dr. Nicolay calmly took him by the arm and walked him toward a large soiled window that looked out on the sculpture garden of the university plaza.

"Whether we like each other is not a question, is it, Holliwell?"

"Certainly not," Holliwell said.

"Certainly not. But I hate to see a man, a colleague—a guest, if you like—make a fool of himself. This is fellow feeling. Allow me to tell you that the party is now over and it is time for you to go home. If you require a taxi, we'll see that you get one. Don't embarrass yourself further."

Holliwell looked over his shoulder; she had vanished. He would never see her again. How, he wondered, if he had pursued her down the stairs and into the lobby. Insisted. Dramatically. Romantically. With impetuosity and flair, like a lover. He felt like a lover.

Detaching himself from Nicolay, he returned to the table.

Only the porters remained, removing the tablecloth and folding it like a banner. And the American couple, still loitering awkwardly.

Presently, Dr. Nicolay joined him again.

"One," Nicolay said as though he were declaiming poetry, "for the road."

Nicolay looked over the single bottle of scotch and the several decanters of Spanish brandy that had been set out, and then at his watch.

"Another for the road," Holliwell said, pouring a second drink.

"Another for the road, of course," Nicolay said. "You're our guest. For better or worse."

"Thank you, Doctor," Holliwell said. He moved the bottle across the table toward Nicolay and looked about the room. Oblivious of the little doctor's curled lip.

"I believe," Nicolay said, "that you are a friend of Dr. Ocampo? Is this true?"

"An old friend," Holliwell said. He was hoping that somehow the woman would come back.

"From university, eh? Roommates."

"No," Holliwell said. "Not roommates."

"Companions," Nicolay suggested.

"Asshole buddies," Holliwell told him.

Dr. Nicolay's expression looked strained, as though his hearing were failing him.

"I think it best to prepare more for an address," he told Holliwell. "Even before a small audience. Even in a small country of little importance I myself would not have drunk so much. Perhaps you were nervous."

"Yeah," Holliwell said, without looking at him. "That was it. Take your hand off my arm."

Nicolay withdrew his firm proprietary hand and walked away. It was a low point in inter-American cultural relations.

"The thing to do with embarrassment," he told the young American couple who seemed determined to engage him, "is work it all the way to humiliation."

The Americans looked concerned. They were both dark, small-boned and sharp-featured—the woman indeed could have passed for a Spanish Compostelan but her expression was eastern collegiate.

"Oh, come on," the young man said. "It wasn't that bad. It was stimulating."

"Stimulation," Holliwell said. "That's what I was after."

"Can we give you a ride downtown?" the young woman asked. "We're driving that way."

Holliwell examined them. They seemed good-natured. Educated. Nice.

"Thank you," he said. "That would be very helpful to me."

The Americans conducted him downstairs and across the patio and through the foyer of the House of the Study of Mankind. Nicolay, who had been standing near the door with a group of students, turned his back on them.

Outside it was chilly, a wind off the cordillera blew spray from the illuminated fountain on them. They led him to a four-wheel-drive Honda with Tecanecan plates.

"I'm Tom Zecca," the young man said as he unlocked the car. "Z-e-c-c-a. This is Marie."

Holliwell shook hands with Tom and Marie and settled himself in the back seat.

"Tom always spells it out," Marie explained to him. "People tend to think it's Zecker—you know, with an e-r."

"But we're mountain guineas," Tom said, "and we insist on the fact."

"I had a student by that name," Holliwell said, as Tom Zecca took the Honda around the circle of the fountain and onto the empty boulevard that connected the city center with the university grounds. He wondered if this were not the very student. He often ran into former students and failed to recognize them.

"Yes, you did," Tom said. "That was my kid brother Rich. You really did a job on him."

"I did?" Holliwell asked.

"Well, he still talks about your class. You really impressed him a lot."

Of the student Zecca, Holliwell could only remember that he wore a McGovern button and was very polite.

"That's why we came tonight," Marie Zecca said. "We saw your talk in the embassy bulletin, so we thought—that's the guy Rich is always talking about—we've got to go and see him."

"Well," Holliwell said, "I'm sorry it turned out the way it did."

"Whataya talking about?" Tom said. "It was fine. You pissed people off, so what?"

"How drunk did I look?"

The Zeccas deliberated.

"A little high," Marie said.

"I was shit-faced. It was purely accidental."

"So," Tom said, "a little shit-faced. You have to watch it with the altitude here. The booze can hit you hard."

"I should have remembered that," Holliwell said. He thought of the Tecanecan plates on the car. "You're not with the embassy here, are you?"

"No, we're stationed down in Tecan. It gets slow down there, so we drive up here every few weekends for a little R and R."

They were pulling into the night's downtown traffic. Holliwell considered the concept of Tecan as "slow."

"San Ysidro doesn't offer much," Marie said of Tecan's capital.

"Not unless you like midget wrestling or cockfights," Tom said. "Or other pleasures we won't get into. You can get all of those you like."

"But Tecan has nice beaches," Marie said. "Really the nicest beaches in the world."

The floral clock sped by them on the left. Signs flashed. Sony. Sears Roebuck. Eveready. He could see the neon signatures of the downtown hotels.

"I know people down there," Holliwell heard himself saying. "I may go down there before I go home."

The Zeccas were silent for a moment.

"If you were going down tomorrow," Tom Zecca told him,

"you could drive down with us. We're starting out around the middle of the day."

Holliwell was troubled by the feeling that he had expected the Zeccas to say something of the sort.

"I couldn't ask you to do that."

"Why the hell not? You'd have to share the back seat, though, because we already promised this reporter a ride."

"No. It would crowd you."

Marie Zecca turned in her seat.

"Listen," she said, "if you really want to go down tomorrow we don't want you going any other way. We would really genuinely like to have your company."

"It's very nice of you to say that."

"It's the truth," Tom said. "You know, the lady beside me is an old social worker type from way back. We'd enjoy rapping on the way down and we'd enjoy showing you our part of the country."

"The dusty part," Marie said.

"I couldn't get a visa in time for tomorrow."

Tom shrugged. "The Tecanecans have a consulate at Zalteca on the way. They'll write you a visa. No problem."

"Hey, that's me on the right," Holliwell said as they came up to the Panamerican block.

"Tom Zecca pulled over. "Nice place," he said.

A question occurred to Holliwell as he was about to get out of the Honda.

"Marie," he asked, "where were you a social worker type?"

"Well," Marie said slowly. "I worked for AID in Vietnam for a while. But it's family therapy that interests me."

"I understand," Holliwell said. "How about you, Tom? Were you over there?"

"Sure was," Tom said. "You?"

"Yes," Holliwell said. "Me too."

The three of them sat in a charged silence that filled the car. In the instant they were bound, in excuses and evasions, in lost dreams and death. If any of them were to speak it would come forth, the place names of that alien language, the mutual friends and betrayals and crazy laughter. It would end, as it always did, in that dreadful nostalgia.

Holliwell climbed out of the car.

"I don't think I can make it," he told them. "But if I change my mind maybe I can call you in the morning."

"That'll be fine," Tom said. He had taken out a card and was writing on it. He handed Holliwell the card through the open door. "Just call as early as you can."

Holliwell put the card in his pocket and stood in the Pan-american's driveway waving goodbye to them. Marie Zecca called something he could not make out.

What a curious evening, he thought. Shivering in the cold wind, he took the card Zecca had given him and read it.

> THOMAS ZECCA
> UNITED STATES EMBASSY
> SAN YSIDRO, TECAN

That was all it said. There was a local address written across the back.

Holliwell went inside and walked across the lobby toward the elevators. The restaurant beyond the bar was crowded now; it was Rotary Club night. Compostelan Rotarian couples were dancing and it would not be too much to say that they swayed to the music of the marimbas. They were better dancers than one might expect Rotarians to be. Closer to their folk roots than the pale Rotarians of the North, Holliwell thought.

The adjoining bar was almost empty; there were deep plush banquettes and idle waiters. He straightened up, sauntered into the bar and sat down where he could watch the dancers. He was into his second scotch and considering the practical wisdom of ordering something to eat when his waiter inquired whether or not he were Mr. Holliwell.

He was. The waiter brought him a telephone, its signal button flashing silently. Holliwell assumed it must be Oscar—but a wild hope soared in him that it might, by some magic, some mercy of travel, be the Señora Obregón.

"You fuck," the voice on the line said. "Communist son of a whore. You fuck your mother and you're going to die in Compostela."

Holliwell's eye had been following the undulations of a Compostelan Rotarian rump, encased in beige silk.

"Who is this?" he asked.

The man on the phone did not hang up. Holliwell sat

holding the receiver to his ear, frozen before his drink and his little dish of peanuts. The marimbas rose and fell.

"You Communist pig bastard. We shall kill you slowly. You shall die here. Die and long live the nation!"

He put the receiver down and rapidly finished his drink. Another was on the way when Oscar came in smiling and patted him on the shoulder.

"I wish I could have been there," Oscar said earnestly. "It would have been a great pleasure."

"Apparently I got through to somebody," Holliwell said. "My life's just been threatened. Just now. Over this telephone."

Oscar looked at him. "You're very white." He walked down the bar to where the phone had been set and dialed the operator. He was asking if the call for Mr. Holliwell had been directed to the bar and whether it had come from outside the hotel.

"I don't think you have to worry, Frank. It came from outside and they called your room. It's only because of the lecture."

"It was a really innocuous drunken lecture," Holliwell said.

"They won't do anything to you. They can't harm an American. Everyone knows who they are."

"It's extremely unpleasant," Holliwell said, "to get a call like that."

"But of course," Oscar said, "that's why they do it. It's more unpleasant to get a bullet in reality. Be grateful you are protected. Be grateful you're not me."

Oscar ordered them more to drink.

"Frank, I have to beg a favor of you. I ask you to go to Tecan for me."

Holliwell leaned his chin on his hand.

"Do a favor for me, Oscar. Don't get me involved in your games."

"My games? Whose games, Frank? You know they want you to go. You can do anything you like down there. You can warn these Catholics about their situation, you can conspire with them, make them a donation—who cares? Only go and be seen and this resounds to my credit. You see," Oscar explained, "it's someone's idea. That's what makes it important."

"You're talking nonsense."

"Yes," Ocampo said. "Nonsense. Ridiculous. They are ridiculous and I am ridiculous. But that's how it goes. Some-one has an idea, Frank, and that someone has to have his way all down the line." He moved closer to Holliwell with one of his opaque Indian smiles. "There are just a few steps, under-stand? You go. You are seen to go. You get home and some-one asks you what you saw and you can tell them Russian submarines or you can tell them the heavenly chorus—it doesn't matter. Yes, it's ridiculous but these people control my life. I get the credit if you go."

"I'm afraid," Holliwell said, "that you're deluded."

"I assure you," Ocampo told him, holding the strange smile, "that I'm not."

"I mean that literally," Holliwell said.

He had clutched for a moment on the notion that Oscar Ocampo was now insane. But there was Marty Nolan. And Tom. And Marie, the social worker type.

"There are delusions, Frank, but not mine. Beleve me when I tell you my life is in danger. You risk nothing but I have to get out of here. And I have Patrick. And they can get me a job in the States."

"No, they can't." He was trying almost desperately to sober. Very deliberately he pushed the drink in front of him toward the bar and closed his eyes for a moment. "They can't do that anymore."

Oscar spoke to him in a low voice, the smile closing.

"I see more clearly than you. I beg you."

Holliwell took Tom Zecca's card from his pocket and held it flat against the bar where Oscar could see it. With all the concentration he could summon he tried to read Oscar's ex-pression as Ocampo looked down at the card.

"Who is this? Do you know the man? Have you heard of him?"

Oscar read the card, looked away and shrugged.

"Never. I don't go down there. I have no idea who he is."

"What if I tell you that he came to my lecture and that he offered me a ride to Tecan tomorrow?"

Ocampo was confused, plainly; he looked unhappy.

"I don't know what to say. Maybe they do everything by multiplicity. You know? Maybe everything is multiple." He was silent for a moment. "Clearly, if you go—I want it known it was for me. But maybe it's coincidence, no? There is still coincidence, is there not?"

"Maybe there isn't," Holliwell said. "Maybe we've located ourselves beyond coincidence. You see more clearly, Oscar— you tell me."

Ocampo did not answer him but ordered them both another drink. Holliwell declined. As Oscar's drink came, the bar telephone began to flash again and they both watched it.

"Señor Holliwell?" the waiter called out over the music. They shook their heads; Oscar held up his hand in a gesture of refusal. The waiter, who had brought the phone, looked at them both and then walked off with it, saying something into the receiver.

"It's not bad they think you're a leftist. In reality it's safe."

"You don't know what you're doing, do you, Oscar?"

"Yes, Frank. What I'm told. To escape."

"Some lecture you got me," Holliwell said after a moment. "Who in hell were those turkeys?"

"Turkeys?" Oscar asked. "*Pavos?* Well, usually it's the same faces. People with little to do."

"But these days," Holliwell said, "it would seem that everyone has something to do."

Ocampo drank.

"There was a woman there who was very beautiful indeed and her name was Mariaclara Obregón. Back there in the happy realm of coincidence. I imagined that you might introduce us further."

Oscar smiled and nodded.

"Mariaclara. The most beautiful and intelligent. Our Minister of Social Services. This is progressive no? A woman, beautiful?"

"Well," Holliwell said, "that was then."

"In my present circumstances," Oscar told him, "there is nothing I wouldn't do for you, Frank. In any circumstances, truly. But Mariaclara—you have to take my word because I know—unavailable. Committed. Without hope."

"It doesn't matter now."

"All the same," Oscar said dreamily, "we're all whores here. Because of you. I mean, of course," he explained, "because of the U.S."

"That's your story." It was an old taunt of Holliwell's. Meaningless now.

"It's too bad, eh, Frank?" Ocampo took his thought. "We no longer can argue."

The drink was closing in on Holliwell again. He took the bar with both hands to fight it off.

"All right. What about Nicolay? Who's Nicolay?"

"Ah, Nicolay," Oscar cried. He laughed with such contempt that it was almost affectionate. "Nicolay is just a . . ." He shook his head to find the word. "Just a turkey."

When Pablo returned to the Paris Bar, the Callahans were nowhere in sight. Cecil, still working the bar, paid him no attention. He sat down on a stool, his eyes fixed on Cecil's round bland face, working himself into a tight-lipped exaltation of rage.

"What the fuck, man?" he demanded of Cecil at length.

"Keep you voice down and you damn head on straight," Cecil said without looking at him. "You been hired."

"Yeah?" Pablo asked. "No kidding?"

Cecil shook his head at Pablo's fecklessness.

"No kiddin'. Anythin' wrong wif dat?"

"Not a thing," Pablo said.

"Den you and me got no problem, eh? So if I tell you what you gone to do you gone to sit and listen and not sell me no tickets, ain't dat right?"

Pablo laughed. "Sure, bro."

"In de mornin' I gone to have your passport and your gear for you. You take it, you go to de bus terminal and you get de bus to Palmas. Palmas, you understandin' me?"

"I understand you."

"Dat bus under way at ten in de mornin' and you got to be on it because de commander say so and you best do it. Dese people don' wait on you desires."

"The thing is—what about tonight?"

"You can sleep up topside here tonight," Cecil told him. "And you don't say nothin' to a soul about your billet or how you come to get it. When I give you you gear you pay me twenny dola."

"I thought I paid you, Cecil."

"Eh, I don' wan' you tickets, mon," Cecil said. "I 'splain dat one time. Dis here is trouble. I be goin' to trouble on you behalf. Natural ting is you pay me for it."

"You're the only game in town, ain't you, Cecil?"

"*Precisamente*, mon."

Pablo went out and found another bar and watched darkness fall over the piers. With the quick failing of light, the place filled with banana loaders. Feeling crowded out, Pablo went to sit in the park beside the navy building where he had spent part of his afternoon. The stations of the afternoon birds in the ceiba trees were taken up by the birds of night.

Gypsy, Pablo thought. Gypsy mongrel like my mother. He could remember very clearly his morning walk with the dogs in the brake outside of town and the cold inside him when he shot them down. Then the sun on the scaled skin of the trailer going home.

His line was playing out; there was poison in his blood. For the sake of the little boy it was better that he not be there. Better that the woman abuse him with her damned unconsciousness, leave him without clothes, leave him to ratburgers and television all night, than that Pablo be there to bring the curse down, bring the knowledge of bad blood, bring murder.

From the naval barracks there sounded a bugle call, and the sentries at the gate were relieved with a halfhearted precision that would have given the loosest Coast Guard admiral a case of the chokes. Pablo thought the bugle call was the saddest sound he had ever heard.

Son of a whore. The words made him tremble and he repeated them to himself with a fascination that chilled his blood. Pablo, son of a whore. *Hijo de puta.* Pablo. Sometimes it seemed that was the world's whole message to him—that was all it ever told him. He could catch it in every roll of laughter and see its meaning framed in the mildest eyes.

Let one of these half-nigger *gibrones* try it on me, he thought in a sudden rage. Let one.

Let one and the strange metal figure would form under his hide and death be.

He looked around the darkened park in alarm; he had not checked it out when he sat down. There were a few rummies settled with their bottles on the guano-dappled benches. Two of them were watching him. He smiled at them. The smile seemed serene. Try it, scumbag, was what the smile said. Whatever you got, try it and see.

Son of a whore. Even my fucking dogs knew it, he thought, and suddenly, absurdly, he was mourning his dogs, numb with grief, and in a moment he was crying for his son, smiling at the two rummies, waiting for a move. Try it and see. The two rummies stood up and wandered toward the pierside.

Pablo, son of a whore himself, now father to another one.

Well, Pablo thought, maybe he won't know it or maybe he won't care, he won't think that way. Maybe the world will be different then. But it won't, he thought, it won't ever be except the way it is with people fucking you over and putting their handles on you to turn you around by. Mex mestizo mulatto nigger spic. Malinche. "Tell me, brudduh, you a black or a white mon?" Gypsy mongrel. Son of a whore.

Now, why, Jesus, Pablo asked from his bench in the Parco de los Heroes de la Marina, Puerta Vizcaya, Compostela— why in the fucking fire do you run it this way? In need of quietude now—the hard-bought speed rattling in his skull—he walked the half block to a *tienda*, bought a bottle of Flor de Cana and returned to the darkness of his bench. Brown-bagging it, only in this fucking country they didn't give you no bag.

He drank his rum and watched the running lights on the little draggers that ran beyond the breakwater, and the freighters, lit like pinball machines along the wharves. The naval sentries before the gate of the naval barracks paid no attention to him.

What if the world got different? If it was different it wouldn't have me in it, I'm nothing anybody wants and that's for sure. I damn sure ain't anything I want, he thought, so what the hell is the use of me? No use at all.

Unless maybe. He reached into his pocket and bit a piece off the little yellow pill; he was drunk enough, it seemed to him, for it not to send him spinning through the impending night in a state of whacked-out hyperanimation. Unless maybe something comes along. And he began to dream of a sunup when something had come along and the world was different and he was in it after all. There would be a great summoning of powers and dominations; Pablo himself would be a power and a domination, a principality, a mellow dude.

Big easy Pablo, the man of power. It was a warm happy vision but it went funny on him as such things often did. For the first time in a while, however, he was not angry.

He stood up, waved to the sentries and marched with his bottle straight into the Paris Bar. Cecil looked unhappy with him. But the wariness, the genuine caution with which Cecil watched him sit down was pleasing. At the far end of the bar, a drunken man was playing a tape recorder he had somehow acquired.

"*Chinga*," the drunken man said into his recorder and pressed the replay button. "*Chinga*," the machine replied.

"*Maravillosa!*" cried the drunken man.

Pablo laughed and the man laughed back, unthreatening, unafraid. A happy thief.

"Hey, that's good," Pablo said. "You teach him how to work that, Cecil?"

Cecil only looked vexedly at him.

"Hey, Cecil," Pablo said, "I want to ask you something, man. Promise you won't get pissed?"

Cecil took the cigarette he was smoking out of his mouth and set it in an ashtray. He raised his boxer's jaw toward Pablo.

"What do you think is the use of me?" Pablo asked.

For a long time Cecil stared at him, then slowly his shoulders sagged and a smile spread across his wide scarred face that lit it from chin to hairline.

"De *use* of you?" Cecil asked, incredulous.

"Yeah, man. What do you think the use of me is?"

Cecil, in a moment, was wary again but his smile held.

"You mean to me, brudduh?"

"No, no," Pablo said. "The use—you know. The use of me."

"Well now . . ." Cecil began. A throb of laughter trembled in his throat. "Dat be hard to say, you know."

"Cecil, I'm the first fucker in the world knows that. But right off . . . what would you say the use of me was?"

"Oh, you just drunk," Cecil declared. But he could not control himself. "De use . . . imagine askin me dat? De use . . . de use of you?" He slapped the bar and gave a quiet whoop.

Pablo shrugged and drank from his bottle. Reassured, Cecil

brought him a glass. They poured one out for Pablo, one for the bartender, one for the thief with the tape recorder.

"De use of you, mon? Same as everbody. Put one foot to front of de other. Match de dolluh wif de day."

"That's all?"

"Sure dat's all. Good times, hard times. Mos' certainly dat's all."

"Don't you think everybody got some special purpose?"

"Hey," Cecil demanded, "what I look like—a preacher, mon? Purpose of you and me to be buried in de ground and das hard enough to do. Be buried in de sweet ground and not in dat ocean." They drank their rum together.

"Dreamin' be de ruin of you, sailor. Be de ruin. Old chap, you too young to be worryin' after dose tings. Be burnin' out your mind."

"It is burning," Pablo said. "Burning out."

"Go to sleep, Pablo," Cecil said, not unkindly. He handed Pablo a key across the bar. "Go upstairs and sleep it off, mon."

Pablo took the key, surprised that Cecil did not charge him further for it. As he went up the narrow stairs, he heard Cecil in a low voice explaining to the thief in Spanish what it was that Pablo had asked him. The thief giggled.

"*Y yo?*" the thief asked after a moment. "*Para que sirvo?* What about me?"

As Pablo was prowling the rat-infested darkness over the bar, a door opened and a girl in a tight blue dress looked at him from her lighted doorway. There was a little statue of the Niño de Praha on a dresser beside her. Pablo stumbled toward her, then, mindful of his wallet, turned away.

"It's a Walt fucking Disney true life adventure, sweetheart," he told her. "That's all it is."

The mission's mail that morning was wedged to the rail at the bottom of the steps leading up to the veranda. From the top step, Justin could see that among it was a letter with a Canadian stamp—for Egan from his nonagenarian mother, and the monthly newsletter of the Fellowship of Reconciliation. This door delivery service was something new; until a month or so before it had been necessary to drive to Puerto

Alvarado for mail. Justin suspected that the extension of postal convenience did not indicate any advance in the state services of the Republic, but rather that the Guardia, probably in the person of Lieutenant Campos, was opening and reading, however imperfectly, their mail.

Out beyond the road and the narrow beach, the ocean had assumed its winter's morning contour—it was pale and flat, mild-seeming, without affect. Within two months, the spring winds would be up and there would be storms and rain. The days might be easier to get through.

It had been weeks since she had heard from Godoy. On the rare occasions when they met, they exchanged polite, ecclesiastical greetings. This might be sound strategy—but Justin, who was as prudent and sensible as anyone, found it wounding and frustrating. And there was no work at the mission. No one came. No one. They were not needed.

She went listlessly down the steps and gathered up the mail. In addition to the letter from Egan's mother and Fellowship she found a second one for him, from the Devotionist provincial in New Orleans. There was also one for her, in a yellow flower print envelope, from her sister. The tab seal on the magazine was broken; all the letters had been opened and resealed with wads or soiled Scotch tape.

Back upstairs, she sat down in a wicker chair with the mail in her lap and leafed through it again. The clumsiness of the resealing, the absurdity of the dirty tape made her shake her head in contempt.

You bastard, she thought, enlarge your lousy life. Egan's ancient mother, my worn-down sister—they have no secrets from you. But the provincial's letter might be another matter.

The letter columns of Fellowship were filled with a controversy over whether or not the antiwar movement in the States should use its supposed influence with the Provisional Government in Saigon to implore a degree of clemency for the new regime's enemies. The An Quang pagoda had been closed. Justin put the magazine aside. Her long tanned fingers, clipped and scrubbed, tore the wads of tape from Veronica's daisy-patterned envelope and she lifted out the letter inside, handwritten on personalized stationery in the same design. The letters from Veronica arrived, or at least went forth, about once every two months. Often when pictures had been enclosed, the letters arrived with the pictures removed. During her best years there, Veronica's letters had sometimes made her feel like crying for the two of them; on this particular morning she was certain that she would never get through the three daisy-dappled sheets without coming apart. But she read.

Veronica had at last joined the Purple Sage Cowbelles. She was not the only Catholic woman in the Cowbelles—there were two Basque ladies who went to the same church, Our Lady of Mercy in Tatum, eighty miles away. Veronica drove the children there and back each Sunday morning. The stock were, for the most part, healthy and thriving in their winter pasture. But the coyote problem was bad, their population had increased and with calving time coming up the darn things would be a menace. Morton had shot eight of them one day, contrary to federal law, but they were prowling the edges of the spread as though they knew that calves were soon due. She herself had shot a few.

The winter was fairly mild, with the temperature above zero most of the day and fairly little snow. Down south, the ski resorts were hurting and the summer pasture might be drier than it should be. But the sunny days made you gay instead of gloomy; she and the younger children had done some Nordic skiing and Morton and the boys were enjoying their snowmobiles.

The library in Arrow had spent the last of its budget getting its collection of *Star Trek* books up to date—it was enough to make you scream the way that library wasted its funds on trash books and detective stories and the blandest best sellers. Their collection of Dickens was falling to pieces, they had no Stendhal, not a single Thomas Hardy, no Thomas Wolfe, no F. Scott Fitzgerald and Joyce, forget it. There was nothing worthwhile for the kids to read, to cut their teeth on in a literary way. The kids watched crap on television, and it was really crap too.

The trouble with the library, Veronica said, was partly old Mrs. Rand's ignorance and partly the blessed Mormons and their vigilant censorship. As if the television wasn't bad enough, they used their influence in Boise to force the really interesting network shows off the local stations. Justin could be sure they weren't waning in power in that part of the country; still they weren't as bad and as bigoted as they'd been in the old days, in their parents' days. And even if everything that people said about Catholics were really true about the Mormons, it shouldn't be forgotten that they had their good points, that there were plenty of fine decent people among them, no one should ever call them hypocrites, though some did.

Like most of the Gentiles in Idaho, Veronica was forever damning the Mormons with one breath and commending their rectitude with the next. Justin herself had not been so even-handed. It had been her habit at home to refer to the tablets presented to Joseph Smith by the angel Moroni as the Moronic tablets; in her junior year of high school a girl named Ada Bengstrom had had the wit to punch her in the mouth for saying it once too often. Ada Bengstrom, Justin reflected, was Veronica's nearest neighbor now. Her name was Ada Parsons and she belonged to the Purple Sage Cowbelles.

When the stock were in summer pasture, if they took on help, Veronica hoped she might get Morton to take two weeks off and they might go to New York, which she loved—if not there then to Palm Springs, where they had spent their honeymoon, or even to Maui, where she had always dreamed of going.

It had been two years since Justin had seen her sister—during the last trip home. And Veronica had looked lovely with her tanned country face and her horsewoman's slow grace and an expression of such despair in her light eyes that Justin could hardly speak to her without stammering. It was self-pity really, Justin thought, that made Veronica's letters so oppress her. The forlornness she read into her sister's life was as much her own.

Of the two of them perhaps Veronica was the plainer, the less ambitious, certainly the less arrogant. But it was she who had more knowledge of the world, at least in its North American manifestation. She had worked in New York, as a publisher's reader after college; she had spent three years working for a community newspaper in Los Angeles. But she was back home now—a rancher's wife with too many kids, married to a good-natured incipiently alcoholic Finn whom she pestered toward Catholicism. Arrow's own culture vulture who would drive most of the night to see a dance company, drive as far as Salt Lake for the national company of an O'Neill or a Chekhov play or a touring opera.

She could, Justin thought, indulging her own fantasies,

have got herself a newspaperman. Or even a doctor, some kind of professional capable of conversation beyond cursing out the posy pickers in the Sierra Club or the price of feed.

Little enough she herself knew about that kind of thing. On one of the visits home, when Justin had been lecturing—handing out threadbare pastoral advice and textbook family counseling—Veronica had turned on her. "Christ, I wish I knew as little about it as you do," Veronica had said.

Justin put the letter aside.

And what did either of them know and where had it gotten them? The promising, brainy Feeney sisters—May now called Justin playing Sister of Mercy in the crocodile isles and Veronica playing Carol Kennicott in Arrow, pop. 380.

Before her, the ocean rolled lightly against white sand, the plantain leaves hung still. The inaction after such elation, the delay, most of all Godoy's intrusion into and subsequent disappearance from her life weighed her down. How stupid it was, she thought, how adolescent and egotistical to invest such promise in a single man when the suffering of Tecan had been before her so long and she had done nothing but simmer in indignation and go by the book. But she was lonely too, on one level it was as simple as that, she needed a friend, a guide. The blank soulless world she had confronted at twenty lay again before her like the limitless unmoving sea; she would have to reconcile herself to it again, as she had then, to find in it meaning and self-transcendence, to make the leap of faith. Again.

There had been child murders along the coast, cruel and gruesome. Local children called the undetected killer The Bad Monkey and that was what the cries of *"mono malo"* were about. Someone was killing children. She was alone, the sun rose and set over the ocean. She picked up Egan's mail and went inside to his quarters.

You can go along for years, she thought, walking dreamily across the kitchen toward Father Egan's door, and you think you're there—then sooner or later you realize you've got to make the jump. And this one—toward man or history, the future—call it whatever—was harder for her. She accepted the revolution, she had for years—but she was critical, arrogant, better at the forms of humility than the substance, not so good a lover of her neighbor as herself. So there it was at her feet, another death-defying leap.

For a moment, at Egan's door, she thought about death and the defying of it. What was death, she wondered, and what did it mean to her? A proper essay for the novitiate, a nunnish reflection.

She rapped lightly on Father Egan's door several times, then slowly pushed it open. Egan was sprawled across his cot, still dressed in his khaki work shirt and tan trousers, his Detroit Tigers cap on his head, the laced work boots on his feet.

Justin went toward his unconscious figure, slowed by dread. He'd dead, she thought. He's really died. "Father?"

She stood over him looking for signs of life and after a moment she understood that he was breathing; she could see the slow heaving of his shoulders and hear the irregular wheeze of his exhalations against the mattress. His hands as well as his boots were soiled with black earth.

"Father Egan? Charles?"

She put her hand against his damp shoulder and shook him. Very slowly he raised his head from the mattress, even more slowly turned, and looked at her with utter incomprehension.

"Are you all right?" she asked him.

"Might I," he asked, "have a paper?"

"A paper?" Justin asked in astonishment.

Egan had begun a cetaceous wallowing to right himself. Justin noticed that his pills were at his bedside and that the Flor de Cana bottle stood on his desk.

"You can't mix those," Justin pointed out to him. "You'll kill yourself."

Father Egan managed to place his feet on the floor and sat with his arms folded, head down.

"I can't do anything about a paper," Justin told him. "But I can point out that we have a shower. And that there's a change of clothes available."

"Shut up," Egan said sourly. "Just . . . shut up, Justin. There's a good girl."

She walked to the far end of the room and considered him.

"Did you mix those pills and rum?"

"No," Egan said. "Don't worry about it."

"You were out last night. Where on earth were you?"

The puzzled look on his face frightened her.

"Oh, yes," he said presently. "Yes."

"Well," Justin said, "may one ask where?"

"You wouldn't understand," Egan said.

Grim suspicions assailed her. Just how crazy is he? she wondered to herself.

"I might," she said. "Try me."

"I was out at the ruins."

Justin watched him, holding her position at the farthest extremity of his cluttered room. "But why?"

"I can't tell you that. Under the seal."

Justin went out and put some coffee on for him. He preferred the Irish tea that sometimes came from home but that morning there was none available. When the coffee was ready she carried the pot and one cup on a tray to his quarters. Egan was still sitting on the cot, staring at the scrubbed wooden floor. She poured him out a cup of the thick native coffee.

"There's fruit in the kitchen," she said. "And there's mail." In her fright at his condition she had set the letters down on his desk. She handed them over. "We've got Fellowship if you want to look at it. There's a letter for you. And we've got a flash from the provincial."

Egan took his mother's letter and set it beside him.

"It's all been opened," Justin told him. "Whether by Campos or by someone higher I've no idea."

The priest shrugged and began to remove his stained shirt. "What does the letter from the provincial say?"

As she was opening it, he stood up and began undoing his belt buckle. "Oh, hell, tell me later. I've got to clean up and get to work. Answer it in whatever manner you feel's appropriate and I'll sign it."

While Father Egan carried on with his undressing, Justin went outside and read their letter from the Very Reverend Matthew J. Greene, to whose directives she and Charlie Egan were bound by sacred vow.

Monsignor Greene's letter finally and unequivocally closed the mission. It contained airline ticket vouchers and orders for them to report, prior to the twentieth of February, to the Devotionist House of St. Peter Martyr in Metairie, Louisiana. They would have been informed by the mission country's ecclesiastical authorities, the letter went on to say, that an intervenor had been appointed by the bishop of the diocese to take charge of the mission house grounds and supplies, and to supervise the property's transfer to the Millimar Corporation of Boston, the parent company of International Fruit and Vegetable, to whose control it now reverted. They were reminded that funds to cover the last quarter of the mission's expenses had been disbursed and that no further funds would be forthcoming.

"There is no reply to this one, Charles," Justin said in the empty slatted hallway. Egan was in the shower. "This is the one."

In fact, no one among the church authorities in Tecan had informed them of anything, nor had International Fruit, which had a large district office in Puerto Alvarado. It meant, Justin thought, either that the local diocese was simply proceeding in the Tecanecan style or that someone in the hierarchy was delaying the operation for unfathomable reasons.

As for IF&V, they must be simply waiting; in spite of rumors that Millimar was planning Tecan's first Florida-style resort at French Harbor, they seemed content to let the church sort out its minor schisms before taking over. Eventually, of course, they could go to the government—the President was by way of being a junior partner in the firm—if they saw the need for any dispatch. Things worked better in Tecan if you were IF&V.

When she went back into Egan's quarters the priest had changed and, red-eyed, was gathering up his books.

"You can read it, Charles. It's a final notice. We're not replying."

"Fine," Egan said. He picked up the provincial's letter, wadded it and threw it in his wastepaper basket.

"Our ticket vouchers have arrived."

"Really?" Father Egan asked. "They've sent us tickets before. They must have forgotten. That's the profligacy that goes with being tax-free. So now we've each got two tickets. If we hold out down here long enough maybe they'll send more and we'll take our entire flock to New Orleans with us."

"We don't have a flock anymore, Charles. Haven't you noticed?"

"*I* have a flock," Father Egan said.

"And the order's dissolving. Tax-free or not, they're really broke."

Egan looked at her blankly. "I can hit Hughie up for a thousand dollars U.S. God knows whether it'll get here and how long it will take." Hughie was his younger brother, a former Devotionist seminarian, now a liquor wholesaler in Seattle. "But it'll be the last grand I get from him."

"Do it then," Justin said.

"Personally I'm prepared to move to a hotel in town. Or I might try to trade those vouchers in and buy myself a little house inland. Don't stay on my account, dear."

"It's not on your account, Father Egan."

So it could go on awhile she thought. And they might yet be needed.

"What's your citizenship?" she asked Egan, possessed of a sudden thought. "It's U.S., isn't it?"

"It's U.S. For over thirty years. Since just before Pearl Harbor."

"Right," Justin said.

Just at the door, she stopped.

"You know what's funny?" she said. "The rest of the team —I hardly remember any of them. I mean Mary Margaret Donahue was here for five years and I can't remember what she looked like. Don't you think that's strange?"

"Yes," Egan said. "But it's like you. Myself—I remember them all. I don't forget people."

He began to type as she went out; she walked to the veranda and commenced pacing its length. The idleness was destroying her, she thought. Egan at least had his imaginary endless book; she had nothing. As she paced, she kept watch for the fish seller and for Epifanía to come with her basket to do the laundry. The laundry, especially Egan's, was a rotten job, yet she half hoped that Epifanía would stay away like the rest, so that she herself would have labor for the afternoon. But if Epifanía too failed to come, their situation would be even more grotesque. Pathetic as it was to have in the visits of a washing woman a last hold on duty and reason, if Epifanía and the fisherman stopped coming the place would be utterly shut off from the community of French Harbor, completely without intercourse, pastoral, social and even commercial. As though, she thought bitterly, they were there to buy fish and have their laundry done.

Then she thought she saw Epifanía walking along the beach

road and even while she wondered why Epifanía was without her basket, she saw that it was not Epifanía at all, not a black offshore-island woman at all—but Father Schleicher's friend, the community-planning trainee from Loyola, barefoot, her hair in braids and wearing a bright print dress. Almost, Justin thought, in disguise. She went down the steps and stood in the road until the woman came up to her.

"You look lovely," Justin said. She did not try to smile. "Out for a walk?"

"To see you," the girl said. She looked at Justin gravely, though she seemed to be mastering excitement. "I bring you a message from Xavier Godoy."

Justin's heart turned over.

"He says you must be ready for an action."

And will I see him? she wanted to ask. But she asked simply: "What do we have to do?"

"You must have a place ready for men to go if they are hurt. Where they can hide until we get them out."

"We have," Justin said. "But there'll be a risk if the place is really searched thoroughly."

"We think it won't be. Not everywhere."

"Then," Justin told her, "we have such a place."

"We have to know if you have antibiotics and dressings. Also whether you yourself can treat the wounds of bullets."

Justin pursed her lips to keep from trembling.

"We have all the medical equipment we need. I can treat a bullet wound—I can extract a bullet if the wound's fairly superficial. I've done it. But I'm not a surgeon. With really deep bad wounds all I can do is try and stop the bleeding and the pain."

The Tecanecan girl listened with her eyes closed. They were both visibly trembling now.

"At what time can I expect business?" Justin asked.

The girl shook her head quickly. "We here don't know. We'll be told."

"O.K.," Justin said.

"What about the old Father Egan? Will there be trouble because of him?"

"He's ill," Justin said. "And he's not a bad man. He won't be trouble, you can depend on that."

"Well," the girl said, "that's it then."

That's it then, Justin thought. At last.

"Will I see Xavier?"

The young Tecanecan drew herself up at Justin's naked breathless question. But suddenly she was smiling, a soft and kind smile.

"Maybe you will see him. I don't know. Who can know in these things?"

"Of course," Justin said, smiling back. And they were holding each other's hands.

"But you musn't say anything to anyone. I know you understand that."

"Good glory, yes."

"Then good luck."

"Good luck to you. And to those who fight."

"To all of us," the girl said. "To our Tecan."

They embraced quickly, and the girl with a little curtsy that might have been nervousness or upbringing or a show for onlookers hurried along the sandy road toward town.

Justin ran up the steps and leaned panting in the doorway. She looked at her watch—it was nearly eleven. There was plenty of time—there was too much. If the fisherman failed to come she could drive into Puerto Alvarado and buy groceries from the Syrian, enough for extra mouths if necessary but not so much as to arouse suspicion.

When the prospect of the long afternoon's waiting began to oppress her she remembered the laundry. Thank God for it! If Epifanía came she would give her some money and send her away.

Without a word, she gathered up the scattered dirty clothes from Egan's room, then fetched her own laundry bag and set the load down by the kitchen sink. There was no need to tell Egan now; it was best that, if there were people to treat, he should know at the last minute. There was always the chance, she reminded herself, that Godoy would not come, that she would not see him, that she would have to handle it all herself. It would be all right.

As she watched her scrub bucket fill with well water from the tap old prayers came to her mind. Justin drove them out, sorting the wash, lighting the stove.

You don't pray to that God, she thought, that God of meaningless battles, of unconsoled poverty and petty injunctions. Perhaps Egan was right when he said that they had it wrong—wrongly written down. It was superior and uncharitable of her to be such bad company, to ignore him so. Perhaps his thinking was closer to hers than she imagined.

When the bucket was full, she went off to look for soap.

So, she thought, let God be in those children on their carousel, in Godoy, in these people proud and starving. Because if not there, then where would He be and to what purpose and what would it matter?

She put the steel bucket on the stove and opened a fresh white bar of soap.

A violent red sunrise assaulted Holliwell's eyes as he awakened. He had not drawn the curtains and his room was bathed in its light—the tiles of the floor, the dressing-table mirror, the sheets of his bed stained a color like blood and water. Outside, the sun was rising into smoky rain cloud over Misericordia, the eastward peak. He eased his feet onto the tiles. It was the dry season, he thought. The rain clouds had no business in that sky.

During the night, there had been three calls, each promising him a painful death forthwith. Each time it had been a different voice, once it had been a woman's. He had not neglected to call the switchboard before collapsing into bed; he had asked them not to put calls through. But the calls had come.

He stood up and in the next moment he was sick, on his knees over the toilet fixture, gripping the sleek rounded edges of it—his body running sweat, his hair plastered to his skull in the faint breeze of the bathroom ventilator. For a few moments he thought he would die there.

Presently, however, he was upright; he showered and brushed his teeth. As he cleaned up, the events of the previous night came back to him in small paroxysms, each jab of memory occasioning him a minor convulsion.

The red glow had not softened when, wrapped in a towel, he went back into his bedroom. He walked to the window and saw the sun higher but still fixed in its prism of rain cloud and smoke from Santiago. Its broken light dyed the still surface of the pool below, was reflected on the waxy surface of the leaves of the trees along the hotel's wall and on the white-washed walls of the city beyond them. Blood red were the tin roofs of the shacks on the lower slopes, the chrome and windshields of the cars on the highway that led to the airport. He drew the curtains, dressed, and pouring himself a drink, drank the straight scotch in cautious sips until it was down and easing him.

His watch read seven-thirty, local time; the daily plane for Miami left at eleven. He spent the next hour and a half in chill combat with the switchboard until he had determined that there was no one at Aerochac to take a reservation. Between calls he drank and paced the floor, smoking his duty-free Kents one after another. The flights were almost always filled the day before departure, and as for standbys—there were always enough people crowding the Aerochac desk at the earliest possible hour, ready to slip some clerk a five for such cancellations as might occur. If he had troubled to make the reservation the day before there would have been no diffi-culty, he could even have done it through the hotel. But he had not planned to leave so soon.

More and more frequently as he paced his curtained room, the thought of calling Tom Zecca came to him. With the thought came the recollection of a poem he had once heard read, about a mouse so frightened it went to the cat for love. But he was not a mouse—he had always been good at taking care of himself. He was neither a coward nor a small animal. The fact was that in spite of what he might tell himself or others, he simply did not have enough direct knowledge of present conditions in Compostela to be able to interpret the degree of danger his threatening calls represented. There had been killings, there was no question of that. And he no longer trusted Oscar Ocampo enough to accept his reassurances.

His confidence rose and fell irrationally. He became drunker. Shortly before ten he made contact with Aerochac—there was nothing. Standbys? Standbys were being turned away.

If at sunrise, he thought, he had summoned the presence of mind to go straight to the airport he could probably have bought someone's seat from under them .It was too late for that now. Grimly, he made a reservation for the following day.

It was not going to be a pleasant twenty-four hours. There would be more calls. He would be confined to the hotel, messengers of death would pursue him through its grounds. Oscar would importune him.

Soothed by the whiskey, he thought further of the ride to Tecan. He put the card with Tom Zecca's number on it beside the phone. It was almost ten-thirty; if he did anything, it must be soon.

He knew shortly that he would go to Tecan. There was every reason for it now. He could not face flying home as he was, to the safety of white winter, terrorized, more crippled than when he had come. He had business down there. On the coast near Puerto Alvarado were things to be seen that it was his business to see, his secret business, the business of his dry spirit. He refused to be frightened away.

Of course, there were the islands just offshore, and the ocean. And he had never driven the stretch of Pan-American Highway between Santiago de Compostela and San Ysidro.

Holliwell finished the drink in his glass and went to the telephone. It's what you want, he told himself. Don't obsess over it. Do it.

Marie answered. She sounded pleased enough. It would be fine. Finer still since he had only one bag. Plenty of room.

Holliwell hung up, a little stunned at what he had set about. They would call for him at the hotel at twelve-thirty. There was only time to pack, check out—and go.

When the Zeccas' car pulled up, he was on the street side of the hotel wall having his shoes shined by a feral twelve-year-old. He leaned against the oily stone, regardless of his best dark shirt, his suitcase behind the heel of his disengaged foot, a Saigon reflex, a half measure against snatchers. The boy was whispering to himself, working over Holliwell's second shoe with elaborate snaps and flourishes of his cloth.

The Zeccas waved and smiled and left their engine running. There was a balding young man in the back seat. His expression was amiable.

After an unconscionable amount of time the boy proffered up to Holliwell his shined shoes with a deferential smile.

There were sores on the boy's gums.

Holliwell felt around in his pocket and came up with what proved to his embarrassment to be a U.S. dollar. He handed it over. The shoeshine boy took the dollar and looked quickly up and down the street. His sunken little chest expanded in triumph; he gave Holliwell a smirk of contempt, picked up his box and fled. Two older city Indian boys were advancing on him along the tree-lined avenue, racing barefoot under the palms of the traffic island to cut off his retreat. One of them held a screwdriver handle up in his fist. The blade would be sharpened to a cutting point.

"What did you give him?" the amiable-looking young man in the back seat asked Holliwell, as he climbed in the car with his suitcase. "What'd you give him—a buck?"

"It was all I had," Holliwell said. "Forgot to get change."

"Good for him," Marie Zecca said. "He had a good spot there."

Tom was watching the pursuit in his rearview mirror. Clutching his box, the smaller boy had turned the corner but the other two were gaining fast.

"Good for him if he gets to keep it."

They drove toward the Old City, where the Avenida Central broke up its act, rounding the seventeenth-century cathedral and dissipating, delta-like, into the back streets of the market. Indians in straw sombreros with marital knots in the band carried loads of cured hide, squat women in white carried fresh-killed turkeys or stacks of cheap hammocks to sell in front of hotels like the Panamerican. With the hand of experience, Tom Zecca guided his gold-colored Honda through the crowds, past the Salvadorean *chorizo* stands and the shops selling tail pipes and stolen hubcaps and dried beans.

"Kind of reminds you of market day in Danang," he said.

The blond young man in the back seat beside Holliwell was named Bob Cole; he sat rigid, staring out at the market streets. He was pale and overweight in an unwholesome way; his teeth were crooked and yellow from smoking. Holliwell sensed a peculiar tension in his frame; Cole held his hands clutched against his knees and the khaki cloth around his grip was moist. He seemed somehow atremble. At first, Holliwell thought he had been drinking.

"It's all the way," Cole said.

"What do you mean?" Tom Zecca asked him. "You mean it's all like Danang? You mean after you've seen one market-place you've seen them all?"

Cole never looked at him.

"He means the Third World," Marie said. "The pre-industrial world, right, Bob?"

"Yes," Cole said.

"When you get too far from Madison, Wisconsin, it gets unsanitary," Tom Zecca said. "The people get funny-looking and it's hot."

"Tom," Marie said, "stop teasing."

They passed the reeking meat markets, the third-class bus station with its cluster of dormitory hotels, and followed the rutted streets to an intersection where the road to the banana lands commenced—the back way out of town, through the side which Santiago de Compostela presented to most of its countrymen and subjects. Within a mile or so of the last cluster of hovels the plantations began.

"My grandfather," Tom Zecca told them, "always said to me—kid, you don't know how lucky you are you live in America. Back there it's all shit. You take your hat off and you eat dirt. Here you got it made."

"He must have been successful," Cole said.

"He burned his bridges and he was tough. He lived to see his son be Man of the Year. That was in Toledo, see. They have a Man of the Year every year and my old man was Man of the Year twice. He had a real camel's-hair coat and my grandfather would come up to him when he put it on and rub his fingers on the cuff and shake his head."

"America," Marie said, "success—the whole bit. My family was a little like that. Only we didn't have any Men of the Year in mine."

"Have you ever gone to Italy?" Holliwell asked.

"Oh sure," Tom said. "The Bridge of Sighs. Florence. Verona. Marie and I once spent two weeks in Taormina. Well, the old man flipped. Sicily? What the hell you want to go to Sicily for? It's all strunz there."

"That means it's all shit," Marie explained.

"I suppose I understand how he felt," Bob Cole said.

"Eh," Zecca said, in a tone of mock menace. "Watch it."

After about an hour of the banana trees, they came to a town called La Entrada. There were railroad yards there and the stacks of an industrial complex. The town had a great many shops and a bank with bright wide windows through which one could see decorative plants and fluorescent lights.

There were neat stucco houses with chain link fences in front of them; the square had a new church of triangular concrete slats in the North American suburban style and a playing field with basketball courts.

"They got themselves a steel-rolling mill in this town," Zecca said. "Old Compostela—little by little—it's coming up in the world."

"And Tecan," Marie said, "little by little it's going down. Or under. This year there's a banana disease and a coffee disease. They get the worst of the quakes."

"When new diseases are invented, Tecan gets them first," Tom said. "And of course they hold fast to the old ones."

"And of course," Bob Cole said, "they have our continual attention and assistance."

No one answered him.

"Are you from Madison?" Holliwell asked Cole after a while.

"No," the young man said. "Never been there."

After a few more miles of bananas, Holliwell helped himself to the water jug in the car and went to sleep again.

When he drifted out of his whiskey doze, they were driving a curving road in uplands that might have been Colorado. The hillsides were pine-clad. There were meadows of rich green grass and wildflowers intersected by fast-rushing streams that ran clear over smooth rock, trout streams they might have been, looking pure enough to drink. The roadside window carried a fragrance of sun-warmed evergreen.

"They must have looked for gold here," he said dreamily.

The Zeccas turned and looked back at him.

"Welcome back," Marie said.

Bob Cole was leaning forward in the seat, his face nearly pressed against the window.

"They did," he told Holliwell. "It was a man called Martínez Trujillo, one of Alvarado's captains. He used Alvarado's techniques. He would gather the Indian leaders and give them until dawn on a certain day to produce the weight of his horse and armor in gold. If they didn't he burned them alive. He never got any, of course, because there isn't any up here. Never got a nugget but he kept on burning Indians. He burned thousands of them in these mountains."

"The gold was all down in the swamps where it didn't

belong," Zecca said. "Under the mud. No one's ever found gold up here."

"What became of Martínez Trujillo?" Holliwell asked.

"He burned a few too many Indians," Cole said, "and he never had them baptized. The friars complained. Martínez Trujillo was a New Christian and the Inquisition got him in the end."

"And burned him, we hope," Marie said.

"The histories are vague. He appears and disappears. He was a minor unsuccessful conquistador. Impatient and cruel. Probably just stupid."

"History is tough on guys like that," Tom said.

Cole told them that was as it should be.

Cole, Holliwell thought, was a man who respected history. History was always affecting to be moral and to be just.

"Another loser, another prick," Tom Zecca said. "You ever see the murals at Bonampak? These characters all deserved each other."

"Well, you can't really say that," Cole said.

"What can you really say?" Zecca asked.

"It's still going on," Cole said. "The same thing. It's unresolved."

"Do you think," Marie asked, "that the Indians knew where the gold was all the time?"

"Who knows?" Zecca said. "Who knows what they knew?"

A few kilometers further along the highway, they pulled off onto a freshly paved track that curved through the pine forests. A short distance in, a sign beside the track read: "Lago Azul Lodge, Global Fishfinders, Houston, Texas."

"The bass lake," Holliwell said. "I've heard about it but I've never been up here."

"Well, I've done got some beauties out of here," Tom Zecca said. "Biggest was over twenty pounds. God only knows what the record is."

"Twice that," Bob Cole said. "Maybe bigger."

The paved road began a descent and, rounding a turn, they saw the lake itself, immense and truly blue, girded on the near shore by flame trees and then by sharply rising palisades. There were no boats in sight. Its uncanny blue surface shivered under the faintest of breezes; a flight of black ducks was crossing it at midpoint, flying in a V wedge inches above the shimmering water.

"Good God," Holliwell said.

After twenty minutes' descent they pulled into the grounds of the lodge itself; a cluster of neat huts with bamboo lattice windows. Near the lakeside, above a series of piers where aluminum boats were moored with their outboards up, was a large building, open on all sides, with wicker shades curled under its wide winged roof. Its decorative style was tropical-Bavarian and fixed to its walls were the mounted carcasses of outsized largemouths, some of them bigger than sand sharks. On the muddy strand beside the piers a few reed pole boats had been drawn up.

They parked beside the building and climbed out stiffly. The lakeside air was warm, the vegetation about them more tropical. There were palms near the shore and parakeets in the flame trees.

The open-sided building was a restaurant; it had a fireplace with German beer mugs on the mantelpiece above it and more, dozens, of the outlandish stuffed bass.

"Where are the Global Fishfinders?" Holliwell asked.

"Just be grateful they're not here," Tom told him.

They took a table near the lakeside and after a few minutes a black waiter came out to serve them. His English and his air of deference and bonhomie under pressure might have come from Houston with the fishermen.

Bob Cole and the Zeccas had bass. Holliwell called for beer and then for an omelet, which was huge and fishy.

"Everybody know the story of Lago Azul Lodge?" Cole asked them.

Holliwell had not heard it.

"Let's hear your version," Zecca said.

"This lake," Cole said, "used to be called the Lago de los Camaidos. But back in the thirties an American airline bought it and the land around it with the lodge in mind. The airline figured that los Camaidos had too much bad history in it and they wanted their customers to feel more at home. So they named it Lago Azul and they stocked it with largemouths from breeding tanks in Louisiana. As you can see, the largemouths thrived, they grew to enormous proportions. Also they killed every native species in the lake. The Indians who lived by netting the native fish starved, their nets couldn't hold big bass. A lot of the lake birds—some of them didn't exist any other place on earth—died out completely because the monster bass ate their young.

"The only problem was that these big bass wouldn't take a hook. They simply could not be caught on a line. So the tourism angle went by the board. After a while, the airline sold out to Global Fishfinders, who were a bunch of rich Texas doctors, and the Fishfinders developed some kind of Arkansas shiner that the bass would take on a hook. Now they'll take plugs if they look enough like shiners. Eventually, the Indians learned to spear the bass. Some of the birds survived."

Cole fell silent. Tom Zecca took up the tale. "So now—every few weeks, a planeload of gringos turns up in Santiago and they bus them out here. They make a few jokes about the country and the people, they go around yelling '*Sí, senór*,' and 'Hey, Pedro,' and they fish. Every night they sit in here and get drunk and talk about the niggers back in Texas compared to the niggers down here in Compostela. I tell you, this is the Forest Lawn of fishing, a bigger bunch of drunken bigoted assholes than these Fishfinders you couldn't come across."

"When we come," Marie said, "we try very hard to avoid the times they're around. It's not much fun then."

Zecca was watching the birds on the lake. Cole smoked one local cigarette after another.

"Marie had her fanny pinched by a Sun Belt executive type once when we were down here."

"You should have let it pass," she said.

"I sent him home in a neck brace to straighten his head out," Tom told them. "That's what diplomatic immunity is for."

After lunch, they trudged back to the Honda and took up positions.

"There are jaguar in these mountains," Tom said as they drove back to the highway. "Wouldn't you like to see one of those babies?"

Westward, the land sloped downward, the pine forests thinned and they drove over high desert cut by steep barrancas. Within an hour, the Sierra was behind them, the land sandy and cactus-ridden, picked over by lean cattle and skeletal burros. They passed an occasional burro cart laden with cords of pine wood but there were very few people to be seen.

It was an empty desert of a place. In the western distance the slopes of another range rose; these were the mountains along the Pacific coast, fleecy marine cloud hung over them.

They turned south well short of the coastal mountains and came in sight of a town centered on the copper dome of a basilica and surrounded by green irrigated fields.

"That's Zalteca," Bob Cole said to Holliwell. "Where you and I get our visas for Tecan."

"Zalteca de las Palomas," Tom Zecca said.

Before long they were passing the gates to fincas and little wood and adobe villages.

"This is another place known to sportsmen the world over," Zecca said. "Here it's the annual dove shoot."

"Yes, it's very big," Cole said.

"Every year," Zecca explained, "the doves migrating south pass through this valley. The Global Fishfinder types and similar sportsmen come down to shoot them. And all the villagers outside of town burn down their houses."

"Why's that?" Holliwell asked.

"Well," Zecca said, "it goes like this. We're out in the brush with our fowling pieces popping away at doves when suddenly this distraught granny appears. We don't understand a word she says but she's really upset. She shows us this column of smoke and leads us to a heap of burnt-up shit that she claims was the home of her ancestors. If we try and ignore her she gets whinier and nastier and louder and presently a crowd of locals appears. They're wearing machetes, they smell of cane juice and they're looking at us in a most unfriendly manner. So we say—what the hell? We're all mogul Fishfinders out for a good time, we all own condominiums somewhere, we kick in twenty or thirty bills apiece to buy granny a new spread. Let's say there's six or seven of us. The old woman gets a hundred fifty, maybe two hundred. If she's lucky she can find another bunch of blasting-away gringos and do the same number on them. When the season's over everybody throws together a new bunch of sticks to live in and has a party."

"They've been doing it so long," Marie said, "that it's taken on a religious significance."

Zecca laughed. "As an anthropologist you should be interested in the cultural layers. A little crude insurance arson. Gringo baiting. Renewal."

"And the auto-da-fé," Holliwell said. "Perhaps a subconscious reference to Martínez Trujillo."

"You could do a paper," Bob Cole said.

"I could indeed," Holliwell said. "I'm working on a multi-volume study of mankind called *The Aesthetics of Horseshit*. I want to beat the sociologists at their own game. I'd happily include a chapter on Zalteca."

Tom Zecca had begun to sing *"Cu cu ru cu cu, paloma."* His wife joined in briefly.

"You don't sound as though you take much satisfaction in your work," Bob Cole said.

Ah, Holliwell thought. The representative of history.

"That's not true at all," he told Cole. "I've been temporarily sidetracked. But I go to bed every night with a profound sense of satisfaction."

"Really?" Cole asked.

"Oh, yes," Holliwell said. "I live for my work. Every day is different."

Cole nodded thoughtfully.

"How about *your* work," Holliwell asked. "Are you getting off on it, as we say?"

"Well," Cole said, "I suppose I've been sidetracked too."

"It's very hard to fix one's eye on the Big Picture," Holliwell said. "Don't you find that?"

"Yes," Cole said.

They were driving through the cobbled streets of town. Small boys ran beside their car offering threats and guidance.

The central square was nearly empty under the afternoon sun. A man lay asleep at the foot of a eucalyptus tree with a tray of chewing gum beside him. There were a few wrought-iron park benches that looked as though they might have been imported from Paris a hundred years before by some local philanthropist of means; they were covered with parakeet shit, and mongrel dogs lay asleep beneath them.

Zecca parked his car in a space beside the basilica; the church's dome was held together with wooden scaffolding. The boys who had been following the car approached across the deserted square in an attitude of movie-hoodlum confidence. Zalteca was used to gringo tourists. Tom Zecca engaged the largest boy to watch over the car.

Walking wearily, they made their way down the street of

public notaries and public letter writers to the Tecanecan consulate. After several rings of the outsized doorbell, a teen-aged girl admitted them to a parlor filled with tropical plants and girded by whirring electric fans. In the adjoining room, prosperous-looking children were watching dubbed Yogi Bear cartoons on a color television set.

The consul's wife appeared after a while; in her tight sheath skirt she had the appearance of an attractive woman turning gradually into a caricature from a Rivera painting. The consul's wife led them into an office where there were still more fans and a monumental ebony desk with an Olympia type-writer in the middle of it. On the wall behind the desk were a crucifix, a portrait of Tecan's celebrated President and a tin-type of William Walker's last defeat.

There was some difficulty about the visas for Holliwell and Cole; between the lady's drawling Tecanecan and the whirring of the fans its nature was obscured to Holliwell's ear. The difficulty had to do with its being Sunday, with its being siesta, the consul's absence, the proximity of Lent, the config-uration of the planets and the phase of the moon—whatever it was, it got away from him. He stood obstinate and uncom-prehending while Cole nodded sympathetically. When the woman, with a melancholy smile, had finished her elimination of possibilities, Holliwell simply began over again—citing the necessity of his immediate departure for Tecan, the misfor-tunes that would befall both him and the country if he failed to arrive in time, hinting at the displeasure in high places that would be the result of his delay in Zalteca. Zecca, responding, came to his aid, producing a U.S. passport with a red cover. A diplomatic passport, Holliwell supposed.

It turned out to be a matter of money. Travelers who insisted on crossing the border in the face of the many diffi-culties at hand paid twice the rate for their visas. Twelve dollars instead of six.

He and Cole set their twenty-four U.S. dollars on the con-sulate desk. The lady, without glancing at the money, seated herself, typed out the visas and stamped them in the two passports. The children in the meantime had torn themselves away from Yogi Bear and were gathered in the office door-way, watching their mother work. As the Americans left, the consul's wife shooed them away and back to the screen. The twenty-four dollars stayed where it was, on the desk.

When they returned to the central square and their car, Holliwell and his company found the boys gone but their hubcaps in place. Zecca opened the hood to see that the battery had not been stolen. All was well.

On their way back to the Pan-American Highway, a little boy of hardly more than six ran toward the car, demanding to guide them. Zecca avoided running over him with some difficulty.

"Well, that's Zalteca, folks," Zecca said.

"Not such a bad town really," Marie said.

"No," Holliwell said. "Not really."

"When you're in Tecan," Zecca said, "you'll think about it fondly."

They stopped at a filling station on the edge of town, filled the tank with the highest-grade gasoline and drank Coca-Colas.

South of Zalteca the land flattened out altogether; the line of the coast range disappeared and only fulsome clouds marked the proximity of the ocean. It was desert, the barest of cattle land, brown grass, dust. East of them the Sierra petered out into a low regular slope that seemed to be covered with a jungle of thorns.

Within half an hour they were in sight of what appeared to be the border, a cluster of kiosks of different colors, a line of trucks, and most incongruously in this empty landscape, lines of people blocking the road.

The border between Compostela and Tecan proved to be an affair of some social complexity. The Compostelan dimension consisted of three adjoining green buildings atop one of which the national banner hung lifeless from a peeling flagpole. The highway was blocked by a series of speed-trap bumps, the bumps were green-striped on the Compostelan side; on the Tecan side the stripes were yellow. Four Compostelan border policemen in green tropicals and Wehrmacht-style caps lounged together in the shade of the customs shed, a fifth was making what appeared to be a halfhearted inspection of a truck loaded with kerosene stoves. From the perfunctory nature of his poking and prodding about the truck, he appeared not to have had his turn at AID customs school.

The real action was all on the Tecanecan side. There, six or so trucks were lined up at the side of the road while Tecanecan customs men in coveralls went over them with screwdrivers and flashlights. The difference in ambiance on the far side of the border was reinforced by the presence there of the Tecanecan Guardia Nacional, whose uniforms, resembling those of American paratroopers complete with the laced boots and colored scarves, were freshly pressed and spotless and quite different from those of the ordinary customs inspectors. The Guardia were occupying themselves with a long line of young foreigners who had been lined up in the middle of the road beside their shoulder bags and backpacks and who stood, facing Compostela, squinting into the sun and looking frightened and unhappy.

Zecca had parked his car so that its front tires surmounted the first Tecanecan speed bump; those foremost in the line of colorful young travelers could exchange glances with the passengers in the Honda at a distance of a few feet.

"It's hard to get into Tecan if they think you look funny," Zecca said. "It's even harder to get out."

There was a sergeant in charge of the line of funny-looking foreigners. The sergeant was black, although it was not a part of Tecan where many black people lived—the Guardia Nacional pursued the tradition of stationing the members of the gendarmerie as far as possible from their native region. This made assignments fairly predictable in Tecan; it was not a large country and its only regions were the mountains and the land on either side of them.

The sergeant was repeatedly inspecting and commenting upon the hippie gringos. From time to time, he would seize hold of a boy's long hair and pull him out of line, caress the hair while making kissing noises with his mouth, shout something at the youth and shove him back in line. He had a repertory of spits and sneers and snarls and his smiles were not good-humored. When he came to a girl who struck his fancy, he would pause contemplatively and feel her up. No one seemed to be protesting his behavior.

"Shit," Zecca said, "they must have caught someone with grass."

"I think someone should have a word with that guy," Marie said.

On the opposite side of the road, another event was in progress. A cow had fallen into the ditch that marked the frontier and entangled itself in the wire the Tecanecans strung on their side of the line. A crowd of local boys, whose proper business was assisting tourists through customs, selling cold drinks or begging, were amusing themselves by stoning it to death. The cow had so totally engaged their attention that they ignored the Zeccas' car.

The animal had lost its footing and was lying with its back legs tucked under it, its hooves tearing ineffectually at the dirt and wire while the rocks crashed down on it from every side. The boys would exhaust their handful and then run off into the sandy fields to gather more. Each stone was received by the cow with a soft bellow. Its eyes and nostrils were beginning to show blood.

"Look at that, for Christ's sake," Marie said. "Are we going to do something about this bullshit?" she asked her husband.

"Hang on," he told her. "Everybody give me their passport." The Honda's passengers gave him their passports; he climbed out from behind the wheel and held a brief dialogue with the officials on the Compostelan side.

Holliwell and Bob Cole sat watching the boys stone the cow. As they watched, one of the smaller boys looked over at the car, wiped his hands and approached them with a glass jar. He thrust the jar through the open window into Holliwell's face—inside was the largest scorpion Holliwell had ever seen.

"Two dollar," the boy said.

"No," Holliwell said. "No, *gracias.*" For a moment he thought he might be being threatened. If he failed to produce two dollars the boy would drop it on his chest.

"One dollar," the boy said.

Marie Zecca let out a fetching little scream.

"No," Holliwell said. *"Otra vez."*

But the boy only made a farting noise at them and ran back to throw more rocks at the cow.

"That thing must have been nine inches long," Marie Zecca said.

"Smaller than that, surely," Bob Cole told her.

Tom Zecca came back clutching the brace of passports.

"What happened?"

"A kid just tried to sell me a scorpion," Holliwell said.

"Hell, you can't give them away around here. This is *alachán city.*"

"I suppose," Bob Cole said, "it's considered a souvenir."

Marie Zecca grasped the back seat and turned to Tom.

"Look, man—those nasty little kids are murdering a defenseless animal and over there that goddamn Guardia is abusing women and children. Can we do something about this action?"

"Sure," Zecca said. He handed the passports back round and started up the car, easing it over the Tecanecan speed trap. This forcing of his nation's border attracted the Guardia sergeant's attention; he came toward them with languid belligerence, walking with his hands on his hips.

"*Buenas tardes, sargente,*" Tom Zecca hastened to say, when the Guardia stood beside his window. He thrust the red passport into the sergeant's hand. The Guardia looked at it through the reflecting sunglasses that were as much a part of the Guardia uniform as the paratroop boots. Within a moment of inspecting the passport, the sergeant drew himself to attention and saluted energetically.

"*Señor Capitano, bienvenidos a su casa.*"

Zecca thanked him for his kind greeting and returned his snappy salute.

"What about the cow?" Marie whispered.

From where they were now parked, Holliwell was looking out nearly eye level with the young Europeans and North Americans who were trying to cross the border. A number of them, boys and girls both, had begun to cry.

"Sergeant," Tom Zecca said, "I'm sure you know how women are. My wife here is disturbed by the misfortune of that cow. Can something be done?" His Spanish was effortless, unashamedly American in accent.

"*Capitano,*" said the Guardia, smiling with Zecca, "*claro que sí.*"

He walked over toward the ditch, drawing the automatic pistol from the web belt at his waist as he went. Bracing his legs, he fired the weapon three times, a few inches above the hairline of the tallest boy. The gringo youths in line recoiled at the firing. The boys dropped their stones and scattered crouching, diving for cover. Some cringed along the shoulder of the highway, sad-eyed waifs awaiting the sensitive photographer, their hands clasped over their heads.

The cow was so startled at the burst of fire that it freed itself from the wire in an awkward lunge, gained its feet and succeeded in hauling itself out of the ditch. Liberated, it trotted up to the Pan-American Highway, eluded a charge by the cursing Compostelan customs cops with a bovine end run and took off down the center line, headed for the capital.

Zecca waved his thanks.

"*Que le vaya bien, capitano*," the sergeant called, and returned to the line of quaking travelers. The Honda and its passengers drove past their wistful glances.

"It's lousy about these kids," Zecca said. "But I can't interfere in that."

"They can't all be carrying dope," Holliwell said.

"No, he just got one or two. He'll let the rest out when he's had his fun."

"They really are pigs, the Guardia," Marie said. "Actual pigs."

"What happens to the ones with the dope?" Bob Cole asked.

"Best not to think about it," Zecca said. "It was very dumb of them to buy it here. They were probably turned by the guy who sold it."

"I didn't know you were a captain," Holliwell said after a while.

"That's because I didn't tell you. But I am. U.S. Army. I'm with the military mission in San Ysidro."

Bob Cole stared at him.

"Don't you feel a little . . ." Cole let the question die.

"A little what, Mr. Cole? I feel just fine."

"O.K.," Cole said. He turned to Holliwell. "Can you imagine what that feels like—especially for a college kid? Standing there, taking that abuse, waiting for those bastards to go through your stuff?"

"I know what it feels like," Holliwell said. "I dream about it."

"That was no dream back there."

"No," Zecca said, "that was an average day at the gates of Tecan."

As they drove south, the wind carried dust clouds that sometimes forced them to close the car windows. With every kilometer the land seemed more brown and infertile, the cattle fewer, the corn scantier and more stunted. A squat brown volcano came into view in the southwest; the wind whipped its faint smoke trails into the lowering sky.

"I'll tell you a Guardia story," Tom Zecca said. "Our

Caudillo in the capital lives in a house with a hundred and fifty rooms. The grounds take up about twenty-five city blocks square and there's a wall of cactus against the fence. The whole complex is patrolled by German shepherds, real ones—from Germany. When the old man bought them he was told that they had to have steak every night to be happy and alert—so the palace is serving up steak dinners for over a hundred of these huge mutts. The dogs probably eat more meat than the population of Tecan.

"One morning, El Caudillo arrives at his desk to find eight guys from the Palace Guardia detachment on their knees in front of it. The palace commandant is his little brother Arturo and Arturo is wailing on these guys, yelling and carrying on and beating on them with the butt of his sidearm. It turns out they've been stealing the dogs' steak, sneaking it home to their families. Arturo's beside himself, making points with big brother. A breach of the President's trust. Treason to the nation. A disgrace to the most honored branch of the service. And so on. One of the Guardia is already half dead from Arturo's beating on him.

"Now this is a thorny problem. These characters know all the security arrangements for the presidential palace. They know where all the bodies are buried—we're in Tecan now, so I'm speaking literally. You can't fire these men, you've got to shoot them or forget about it.

"Amid the weeping and the dull thuds, El Hombre considers the scene and ponders deeply. Finally he tells Arturo to knock off and let them go. From now on he says, all the Guardia and their families get steak every night just like the dogs. AID will pay for it somehow. The Guardia crawl over to El Hombre, they cry on his cuffs, they lick his boots. He's got their loyalty for life. They'll all walk over their grandmothers for him.

"All except the dude little brother's been beating on too much. He's too punchy to be properly grateful, so they shoot him."

Marie uttered a soft vibrating wail, indicating fear and loathing.

"Life in Tecan," she said.

"But observe the craft," Tom said. "Observe the crude but sound statesmanship. The bastard hasn't been in power all this time for nothing."

"Have you been inside that palace?" Holliwell asked Tom.

"*Claro*. Many times. Even partied there."

"The parties," Marie said, "are ghastly. It's like a Dracula movie but without the class."

"The last party I went to," Tom said, "was after I'd been out to the islands, so I'd been peeling. I mean my skin was peeling from sunburn. Up to me comes Arturo—drunk out of his gourd, as is customary. He grabs a fistful of skin off my nose and calls me a gringo."

"You didn't tell me about that," Marie said. "What did you do?"

"What did I do? I smiled and saluted. Is Arturo a sadistic little creep? Should I have cold-cocked him and rubbed him into the carpet? *Claro*. But I represent the flag, *comprende*? In my small way, I represent Policy. I had my dress whites on and two years in grade."

"He'll get his," Marie said.

"Not if we can help it, my dear. If we can help it, he'll be the next President."

"There must be someone better than that," Holliwell said. "Someone acceptable."

"Well, Arturo's a stopgap. While Policy decides what to do next. Mind you, Fat Frank really likes the guy. He likes the whole family. He thinks they're American-type people."

"That's a quote," Marie said. " 'American-type people.' Because they speak English to him."

"Fat Frank?" Holliwell asked.

"Ambassador Bridges. Some people call him that."

"But not us," Tom said.

Bob Cole was staring out at the hills to their left. The desert ended where they rose toward the Sierra and the further hills showed dark green.

"That's coffee up there," he said after a while. Holliwell thought that Zecca was glad to hear him speak. Cole's silence had been making him uneasy.

"That's right," Tom told him. "Good grade and low price, they tell me. But what do I know?"

"Then there's probably an insurgency in progress up there," Cole said. "Given the situation."

"Yeah?" Tom Zecca asked him coolly. "Why do you say that?"

"The way I understand it," Cole said, "wherever you've got

coffee in this country, you've got an insurgency. They go together."

"There's a degree of truth in that," Tom said.

"Is there one going on up there?"

"What do you hear?" Zecca asked him.

"I hear there is. That it's centered around Extremadura. Among the Indians there."

"Who says that?"

Cole looked on Captain Zecca with a sagging smile, his mossy yellow teeth briefly displayed.

"There was a piece in the international edition of the Miami *Herald* last week. It was off the AP wire—I think the dateline was San José. You must have seen it."

"I saw it," Zecca said. "Might be something to it."

"Well," Cole said, turning his gaze back toward the hills, "I'm thinking of going up there."

"I wouldn't," Zecca said.

"You oughtn't to," Marie told Cole. "I've been around there. If I were you I wouldn't go up there right now."

"I'm just doing my job. Like you folks are. Like Mr. Holliwell."

What job? Holliwell thought. What does he mean?

"If I know you're up there," Zecca said, "I'm going to worry about you. The Atapas don't like strangers around in the best of times and they're not nearly as tranquil as they look. Especially these days."

"Do you suggest I register my presence with the embassy in San Ysidro?"

"Honest to God, Mr. Cole," Zecca said, "I don't know what to suggest. Except that you not go."

"I understand," Cole said.

They drove on in silence over the dusty plateau. The coastward volcano was abreast of them, a second, larger rose ahead. To Holliwell, they seemed freakish mountains; only malignant gods could inhabit or inform them. They rose solitary out of featureless tableland, bare, without harmony, unbeautiful enough to appear exactly what they were— burst excrescences on Tecan's pocked dusty hide. A geology lesson, he thought. They communicated a troubling sense of the earth as nothing more than itself, of blind force and mortality. As mindlessly refuting of hope as a skull and bones. The landscape was a memento mori, the view ahead like a dead ocean floor.

"Scary," Holliwell said.

Tom and Marie laughed.

"We thought it was only us," Marie said.

"The Tecanecans are very big on their volcanoes," Tom told Holliwell. "They're on the flag and the national seal. They run up and down the country along a fault. First thing a local will ask you when you come in-country is whether you've seen the volcanoes or not."

"Key-to-the-country kind of thing?"

"I never had it put that elaborately," Tom said. "I don't think anyone here thinks they're the key to the country. They're just big things for *turistas* to gawp at. I mean they're there and they're huge and uniquely Tecanecan, so the Tecs are proud of them. It's their duty to be."

"What does the national poet say? Is he on about them?"

"They don't have a national poet to speak of. They never had a Rubén Darío in Tecan. Never saw the need for one."

"There's a verse about the volcanoes in the national anthem though," Marie said. "I can't remember how it goes. It's pretty trite."

"The first movement of Brahms' First," Tom told them. "That's the national anthem. Moving as hell. In the old days before the Marines came the Tecanecan Army could goose-step to it. The Marines made them knock it off."

They began to pass more buses on the road. The number of dirt roads with signs indicating villages off the road increased.

Tom slowed down, wary of children and cattle on the highway, sounding his horn at turns to warn the burro carts that appeared more and more often now as they approached the capital. From time to time, they passed a lone Indian bent under a load of firewood. People looked down at the dirt as the car sped by them.

"What I wonder," Bob Cole said in his strange tremulous voice, "is whether the people down here have to live this way so that we can live the way we do."

"I'm just a soldier," Zecca said. "But I think the answer to that is no. It sounds too simple to me."

"But it's not a simple question," Marie said brightly. "It's a really complicated one."

Cole turned to Holliwell.

"How about you, sir? You're something of an expert. What do you think the answer is?"

"I have to confess," Holliwell said, "that I haven't figured that out. There are lots of gaps in my expertise. I don't know what the answer is."

"We have to believe it's no, don't we?" Cole asked. "We couldn't face up to it otherwise. Because if most of the world lives in this kind of poverty so that we can have our goodies and our extra protein ration—what does that make us?"

"It makes us vampires," Holliwell said. "It makes us all the cartoon figures in the Communist press."

"What if you found out it were true?"

"Me? What I do doesn't matter. I'd go on doing what I'm doing."

"How about you, Captain?"

Zecca took one hand from the wheel and turned partway around toward Cole. Marie kept her eyes on the road.

"What are you, Mr. Cole?" Captain Zecca asked. "Some kind of an agitator?" He asked the question humorously, with more of Toledo in his voice than he usually permitted.

"Not at all," Cole said.

At the approaches to the Tecanecan capital of San Ysidro, the Pan-American Highway wound down in switchbacks from the high desert into a lush tropical plain beside a great lake. As they started the descent, the sun hung over the low hills of the coffee country and the contours of the two visible volcanoes softened to show Holliwell a more insidious menace. They were running late. After sundown, the inter-capital truck traffic would be on the road—a mortal risk.

"When you were in Vietnam," Holliwell asked Cole, "what did you do there?"

In the expectant silence that filled the car, Cole seemed to force an answer.

"I was in the Army," he told them. "In the Army there for three years because I extended."

"Is that right?" Zecca said.

"I started with an infantry platoon, a second lieutenant. Then I was on staff, with intelligence. Then later . . . I went back. With AID. And then I went back again as press, free-lancing."

"You must have liked it there," Zecca said.

"In a way," Cole said, "I liked it very much."

The captain smiled thinly.

"It held a fascination for you. A kind of moral fascination, am I right?"

"Well . . ." Cole began. "Yes," he said.

"I can understand that very well. Right, Marie?"

"Sure," Marie said. "A lot of our friends were like that. We were a little like that too, weren't we?"

"We sure were," Tom said. "And we were courting, so that lent color to our moral fascination."

"I never found time to go courting," Cole told him.

"Too bad," Zecca said. "You find time to get laid? Or weren't you interested?"

"Sexist talk," Marie hissed softly. "Jeez."

Holliwell asked Cole if he had been much in the delta. He had been. He had been out to the island and met the coconut monk.

"He's in jail now, that guy," Tom said. "They locked him up."

"That's a mistake if it's true," Cole said.

"It's true," Holliwell found himself saying. "And they didn't lock him up by mistake. They know what they're doing."

"Fucking-A," Zecca said.

Cole only shrugged and looked more unhappy.

Fields of bananas grew on the slopes above San Ysidro, introduced there from the east coast. The town below was a white seaport city with the lake doing duty as ocean. It was a lake twice the size of the Lago Azul but lifeless from four hundred years of ill use. Its surface was still and dark. The declining sun had passed over it.

They drove past a summerhouse among the young banana trees, a pocket villa hung with Japanese lanterns. Below them, a mile or so from the foamy edge of the lake, was a reservoir, surrounded by a cement wall.

"The Marines put that in during the nineteen thirties," Zecca told them. "You can drink the water here. Only drinkable water between El Paso and God knows where."

"That at least," Marie said. "So our presence here hasn't been all bad news."

Cole stirred in his seat, his thoughts apparently fixed on the coffee country. Holliwell lit a cigarette.

Entering the capital, the Pan-American Highway made a brief promenade into town, running along the lakefront past several blocks of crumbling, incongruously Victorian mansions and lit by cast-iron streetlamps of antique Parisian design. After less than half a mile of this, it broke up into unpaved narrow streets.

San Ysidro, in its tuck of the lake valley, was losing the light. The cramped streets near the lake were suddenly dark, scantily lighted, but alive with the din of a half-seen crowd. Driving slowly, Zecca put his head out of the car window to see past the screen of dust and crushed insects that fouled his windshield.

On corners, vendors sold roasted maize from pushcarts, barefoot families made their way along the damp walls, ready to press back against them as cars passed. At the intersection where there was a little light, groups of young men in bright plastic shirts stood together drinking rum, listening or singing to someone's guitar. There was much music to be heard—but these streets were not festive or lyrical. The mood was restless —febrile, Holliwell thought—furtive. The songs were short on melody, driven and mocking, calling forth from those who listened a hard humorless laughter. Holliwell could not understand a word of the shouted, perversely inflected Tecanecan Spanish that went back and forth in the darkening streets as they passed. He and Cole were tense and silent.

"Late at night," Marie said, "these are bad streets."

Holliwell caught a whiff of marijuana on the air, something he had never experienced before in a public place in a Spanish-American city. From a nearby street, he heard what seemed to be screaming.

"Pretty lively for this time of evening," he said.

Zecca pulled his head back in and steered carefully round a turn.

"It's always lively on this side of town. It's one big bad party."

Someone fired a water gun at Cole's closed window. Cole looked at the dirty water streaking down the glass beside him.

"Hey, Cole," Zecca said, "a lot of the people here are from

Extremadura. You could find out a lot by checking it out over here, discreetly. In the daytime."

"I think I'd do better out there, don't you? I mean, I'd feel kind of heavy-footed around here. I'd be drawing crowds."

"You're gonna draw crowds anywhere," Zecca said. It was uncertain whether he was speaking generally in reference to the country or of Cole.

Holliwell began to notice that there were a surprising number of cars in the narrow streets, most of them American cars only a few years old. They drove along a block of open arcaded shops and came on a cathedral square centered on a monumental obelisk. The rotary around it ran its course like a mechanized feeding frenzy, a riot of oversized cars in every condition, bad driving and ostrich optimism.

"Well, shit," Zecca said, and drove the Honda into it. Marie clung to the back of her seat, her face on her arm. Cole and Holliwell held to the top of the car interior.

They went halfway around the rotary and up a wide, park-sided avenue that ran between the cathedral square and another plaza, visible in the distance, where there were neon signs and taller buildings—office buildings lit on every story.

To one side of the avenue along which they drove was a forest of low trees, divided from the broad clean sidewalk by a high barred fence. On the other side there was more greenery. There, only the tops of trees were visible because the thick wire fence along the street was backed with a wall of cactus.

"On your right here," Tom Zecca said, "behind the wire and the cactus and the German shepherds is the palace of the President. Over there is the Central Park and the Zoo, famous for its three-legged cow.

"There are about ten thousand people bedding down in that park now. They're a lot worse off than the people back there in Mamalago. But the nearest shack is more than a mortar's distance away from the Palace. That's a trick we taught the President. Anything closer is patrolled by the Guardia. The cracks in that obelisk back there came from the earthquake ten years ago. The people in Mamalago moved into the park and some of them never moved back. Then more folks came down from the hills and took over the houses in Mamalago. If you're in Mamalago it's rough, but it's better than the park. Mamalago and the park are better than the shanty towns on the west slope. If it were still light, you'd have got a good look at the cathedral and you'd have seen the Palace of Culture beside it."

"Where they have the midget wrestling," Marie said.

"What's the obelisk for?" Cole asked.

"Usual shit," Zecca said. "Victory and independence and successful struggle. Tecan always wins. It won the Second World War."

It was a dead-hot city, sea level and without hope or promise of an ocean breeze. As they drove along the ceremonial avenue, the day's heat welled up from the earth; the mixed smell of the jungle plants and of cheap gasoline threatened to close off breath.

As they passed the palace gatehouse the smells, the sight of the sentry box in its well of light under the jacaranda, the brown sawed-off soldiers in MP's helmets brought Holliwell such a Vietnam flash that he was certain that they must all be feeling it together. It awakened in him so potent a mixture of nostalgia and dread that in spite of the morning booze-up which was still fouling his blood, he began to feel like a drink.

No one said a thing.

When they made the turn into traffic at the end of the drive he half expected to see noodle restaurants beside the cinema with its cheap imported karate thriller—but there were record shops and *farmacias* instead and the street vendor sold roasted nuts and *empanadas* and the city smell was of cigars and pomade and dust instead of fish sauce and incense and bougainvillea.

Some things were the same though. The empty stares, the demented traffic—even the newly built bus station had about it something of the curving hand-me-down art deco of downtown Saigon. There were beggars clustered about its doors with little paper cartons full of cigarettes or chewing gum and fruit or sometimes only brown outstretched open palms. And the markets would be behind the bus station, where they always were, in Tecan as in Danang or Hue.

"As close to the bus station as you can get," Bob Cole said, "will suit me fine."

"You're not trying for Extremadura tonight?" Marie protested. "You'll get there in the wee hours. You'll have no place to sleep."

"My little red book says there's a through bus in two hours," Cole told her. "I'll wander around town a little and get it."

When they pulled up at the bus station both Tom and Marie turned around to check that their car was out of traffic.

"Stay the night with us," Marie said. Tom, beside her, was nodding.

"No, thanks," Cole told them. "Look," he said to Tom Zecca, "maybe someone from the consular office should know I'm up there. If that's the case, you tell them. O.K.?"

"You're making a mistake," Zecca said. "That's the advice of the consular office. As conveyed by me."

"Well, it doesn't matter," Cole said. He climbed out of the car and started into the crowds in front of the bus station. The beggars were on him at once.

"How do you like that?" Marie said. "He's out of his mind."

Carefully Zecca pulled the car into traffic again, and rounded the bus station block.

"He broke up with his wife," Tom said. "I think I remember him telling me that."

In the market behind the station the stalls were beginning to close. The streets at this end of the city were very like the streets at the lakeside with their mud roadways and high broken curbs. The same morose groups were gathered at corners.

"Shit, the guy's crazy," Zecca said. "He'll get macheted up there. And he better not wander off from the bus station or he won't even get that far. This is no town for midnight strolls."

The Zeccas lived in a house high on the slope above the town, a street of middle-class houses with little stucco walls in front of them. At the end of their comfortable street, the shacks began, cut off from the bourgeois fortress by a barricade of barbed wire, rusted road signs and sheet metal: as they drove the Honda into their garage and began unloading their gear, a chorus of unseen dogs set up a cry from one end of the street to the other.

A smiling young maidservant met them at the door. She took as many of their cases as she could manage and led them into the living room.

The house was new but tasteful and pleasant in a severe colonial style. The tiles looked as though they might have come from Spain, the oak beams were weathered and supported at their moldings by metal studs. Oak beams were not just for fun in Tecan—the number and mortality of her earthquakes was appalling.

It was a small house, by no means sumptuous, with a homely American smell.

Marie argued the maid out of making them dinner and sent her back to her quarters to watch television. The television was in the maid's room and her opportunity to watch the dubbed soap operas had made her the foremost storyteller in her barrio.

"Well, we can go out or I can make us up something simple. Like ham and eggs."

"There's a big production of a place, La Finca, a few blocks from here," Tom Zecca said. "Steak in the local style. *Muy Auténtico*. Lots of music and red bandanas flapping."

"Speaking just for me," Holliwell said, "I'm not very hungry. But I'll go along with anything."

"Well, I'm not too hungry myself," Zecca said. "Don't know why."

"Maybe no one's hungry," Marie said.

"Looks like no one is," Tom said. "But I think everyone would like a drink." Holliwell nodded gratefully.

They took margaritas in a small garden, closely bound by vine-covered walls and banana trees. There was barely room in it for the green metal table and the chairs that had been set around it. Marie put out glasses and two large blenders full of margaritas.

"Someday," she told Holliwell, pouring the drinks into the frosted glasses, "I'll tell you about the day I was sitting out here and an iguana fell in my lap."

Tom took his drink. "And me—goddamn it—I missed it. I was at the office. I have to reconstruct the whole scene in my imagination."

"As I remember it," Marie said, "the cops came. People poured into the street, crossing themselves."

They drank and after a moment Tom said: "What about that Cole guy? Now there's a questionable character." It struck Holliwell as odd that Captain Zecca would raise the matter of Cole's questionability with him. He looked across the table and saw that Marie was shaking her head sadly. Perhaps they were just relaxing.

"I suppose the question about Cole," Holliwell said, "is who he thinks he is and what he thinks he's doing."

"Do you mean does he think he's Régis Debray?"

"No," Holliwell said, "I mean beyond that."

"Beyond that?" Zecca asked. "Beyond that isn't necessarily my business. Beyond that he's a Vietnam burn-out. A pilgrim."

"There's a lot of us," Holliwell said.

"You see yourself as a burn-out?" Marie asked. She turned to her husband. "I wouldn't have described him that way."

"Maybe just badly seared," Holliwell said.

"Everyone that ever saw that place is a little fucked up," Tom said, leaning his stocking feet on the delicate table. It was easy to picture him at the Diplomat Hotel or some BOQ bar, a younger man, harder case, second-generation tough, hungry. "It was the dumbest damn thing we ever did as a country, no question about it."

"Well, we told them so at the time," Marie said. "Nobody listened until it was too late."

"No," Holliwell said, "we told them and they didn't listen."

"AID?" Zecca asked. "That was your cover?"

Holliwell became afraid. It was a misunderstanding.

"It wasn't a cover," he insisted. "I wasn't an intelligence specialist or even a contract employee. I mean, you know how it is." He was staring at his drink. The Zeccas watched him. "They come to you. Someone has a girlfriend in Saigon, he wants to stay there, so he has to make work for himself, he has to make up a report to file. So what an anthropologist knows—family relationships, the relationship of an uncle to a nephew, a younger cousin to an older cousin—it all goes into the hopper. Nobody gives a shit about it—maybe nobody ever looks at it. But it ends up—pardon the expression—intelligence."

"We know exactly what you mean," Marie Zecca said.

"Did you learn the language?" Tom asked him.

"I picked up a certain residue. No," he said. "I never really did. I depended on a few local people and we spoke mainly in French."

The thought came to Holliwell that he had spent much of his life depending on a few local people, speaking some lingua franca, hovering insect-like about the edge of some complex ancient society which he could never hope to really penetrate. That was his relationship with the world. And he himself— more and more losing touch with the family he had made, a bastard of no family origin, no blood or folk. A man from another planet forever inquiring of helpful strangers the nature of their bonds with one another.

"I don't know how I got into family structures," he heard himself tell the Zeccas. Tequilla. Insidious. "It was archaeology I liked. The ruins, the traces, you know. I would have liked, I think, to dive. To dive for galleons."

"Maybe you will yet," Marie said.

"The family," Holliwell said. "It's so strange, you know. I never had a family of my own to speak of. And the one I've raised I don't believe I understand at all. As far as other people's families go—I'm absolutely ignorant."

"Christ," Tom Zecca said. He was relaxed now, merry with the end of the drive. "With guys like you in the shop no wonder we lost the goddamn war in Nam."

They all laughed.

"No," Zecca said, touching his arm to reassure him. "I'm kidding you, bro. You're O.K. You're a straight shooter."

"I hope our friend Cole comes down O.K. He worries me a little."

"How about it, Holliwell?" Captain Zecca asked. "You think he's a spook?"

"You'd probably know more about that than I would," Holliwell said warily.

"I'll tell you something, Doc Holliwell . . . I don't know much until I read my mail—that's the situation we've got working here. Maybe there's a line on him in the pouch tomorrow."

And maybe, Holliwell thought, a line on me.

"Well," Marie said, "he'll be up there tomorrow wandering about among all those disgruntled *macheteros*. Feel for him, guys."

"We do," Holliwell said.

"Poor useless bastard," Zecca said, pouring out his creamy margarita. "He doesn't know who he works for and he doesn't know what side he's on. Even if he's ours, he's not a hundred percent sure. You take a dude like that and the next thing you know you've got a double agent, the most dangerous goddamn creature walking."

"They have short life spans," Marie said, "that's one thing about them."

"That's the only good thing," Zecca said.

Marie moved the second blender into position.

"But damnit, those people up there are screwed. They're getting dumped on in the most incredible fashion."

"You better believe it," the captain said. "For untold fucking generations they've been living on beans and lizards to grow coffee for the bastards that run this country. Now we've found copper up there and the idiot greedhead generals who own it are throwing them off the land—sending them down here to beg or starve. Nah," Zecca said, "who am I to knock Cole? It's no wonder they're fighting back."

"Are they?" Holliwell asked him.

"Are they seriously fighting back? I wish I knew. I'm supposed to. I can't depend on dip-shits like Cole. One of these days I'm going to have to exercise my ass and go find out. I go up there in a chopper and they've got the weaponry, I'll know in a big hurry."

"It's not worth worrying about," Marie said. "If this place goes, they know where to find us. We're fatalists. That's what you've got to be, see. You've got to be a fatalist."

They drank from the second blender.

"How much do you know for sure?" Holliwell asked. "If you don't mind telling me."

"O.K.," Zecca said. "There's a basic, quite justified piss-off all over the country. It's particularly strong up in the Sierra where the Atapas live and the Atapas have a history of banditry and trouble-making. They can handle modern weapons but we don't really know if they have any or if they have, what sort. If they've got, say, ground-to-air missiles—El General is in big trouble. Likewise if they've got a cache of AKA's. Here in town, anyone with a brain or an honest buck to turn hates the government but probably won't move. Here the trouble is students, rich kids most of them—they're divided into factions, Fidelistas, Trots, Maoists—the usual spectrum. Over on the east coast people tell you time stands still, nobody expects trouble over there. In my opinion that's complacent because if anybody lands armament it'll be over there, not on the Pacific coast. And it's hard to fly stuff in here because we gave them an outrageous air force and we trained them in radar detection."

"Sounds sort of standard," Holliwell said.

"It's not, though. Because now the morons who run this joint have given every anti-government faction a common cause with that copper grab. The unemployment rate is like sixty percent here. The streets are full of teen-age kids with nothing to do but rip off whatever's handy and go to the karate movies. You could make a tough little army out of those kids. Inept, disorganized, sure. But you'd have to kill whole bunches of them—they'd be the cannon fodder. El General would stink worse than usual in the nostrils of the world. Bad scene," Zecca said. "The question is—does the Guardia stay loyal? Answer—probably."

"And when the Guardia goes in—we advise them?"

"Mr. Holliwell," Zecca said. "Doctor! We put this government in for our own interests. We trained the Guardia. Our ambassador thinks the Pres and his family are American-type people."

"There's a grain of truth in that," Marie Zecca said.

"You're a Communist," Captain Zecca told his wife. "She sings 'Guantanamera' at embassy lawn parties."

"Under my breath," Marie said. "Fat Frank wouldn't recognize it if he heard it anyway."

"O.K.," Zecca said. "The Guardia will have American weapons and support. The support will be mealy-mouthed and covert but it will be there."

"And what do honest folk like ourselves do then, Captain Zecca?" Holliwell inquired.

Zecca put away another margarita.

"It's too late. It's too late, understand. The usual shit will go down. You and I, Doc, maybe we know something about the country. But it's too late. If we don't back them now, we'll have a Russian submarine base in Puerto Alvarado—maybe a missile base this time. See how that goes over in Dubuque, in Congress, in the White House, for Christ's sake."

"Fucked again," Holliwell said.

"I'll be gone," Zecca said. "My tour is almost up. Then they can send in the types who like the Guardia's style. The headhunters, the Cubans, the counterinsurgency LURPSs. And the guys who enjoy saluting animals in tailor-made pink uniforms."

"And where will you be then?"

"I don't know," Zecca said. "Not some place like this. They owe me."

"It's not all one thing or another, you know," Marie said. "It's not us being bad guys all the time. Only assholes think that. Pious assholes."

"Don't call him a pious asshole," Captain Zecca commanded his wife.

"I don't mean him," Marie said, and Holliwell thought she was beginning to cry. "I don't mean you," she assured him. "I agree with you. I don't even mean Cole and Cole really *is* a pious asshole."

"You have to go on hoping for the best," Zecca said.

Marie nodded. "You have to have faith."

"Only pious assholes have faith, Marie," the captain said.

"Up yours," Marie told him. Holliwell drank another margarita. It was all in fun.

"Let me tell you something," the captain said suddenly to Holliwell. "In Nam I spent two years in combat intelligence. In that time I interrogated maybe hundreds of prisoners and *chieu hois* and I never once let the Arvins get away with torturing any. I'm speaking of torture in the strict sense. I never did, in any of the time I was in that place, anything I thought was cruel or dishonorable. You believe me?"

"Of course," Holliwell said.

"I never sat still for shooting up civilians, not even up north. I never clipped an ear or set fire to a hootch and I never countenanced it. I conducted that fucking war honorably and so did my people. I did that to the greatest possible extent, sir, and it wasn't easy in my position. Moreover, I thought it was a crock, a stupid hopeless crock. It was dumb and it was inhuman by its nature. But me," Zecca said, turning his fingertips inward and tapping his heart, "I'm not. I make that claim."

"It's true," Marie said.

"I don't claim virtue," Zecca declared. "I don't claim to be a kindly man. I claim to be capable of honor."

"I also claim that," Holliwell said.

"I took an oath," Zecca said. "I fulfilled it and I fucking fulfilled it without compromising myself. Takes a little working at."

"Surely," Holliwell said.

"The Army didn't send me down here to be a chaplain to the peasantry or to feed the birds or conduct an agrarian reform. It sent me down because I'm supposed to know about the lay of the country from a military point of view. In terms of intercontinental defense."

"Of course," Holliwell said, "intercontinental defense. And you're beginning to feel compromised?"

"No," Zecca said quickly. "Not at this point."

"Excuse me," Holliwell said. "Do you expect to conduct your career in one American-sponsored shithole after another, partying with their ruling class, advising their conscripts in counterinsurgency and overseeing their armaments, and not compromise your oath or your honor? Because that sounds very tricky to me."

"You don't know the facts, mister," Marie said.

"I know a few," Holliwell said. "Beyond that I know what you tell me."

"I know what you know," Zecca said. Holliwell folded his hands on the metal table. In the circumstances, he had gone too far. "And this is what I tell you—that when they evict those people over the mineral rights, I hope to Christ we'll be on our way to another posting. O.K.—that's a cop-out, it's a quease. But you've got to think in terms of the large scale, the . . ."

"The Big Picture."

"The Big Picture," Zecca said with a grim smile. "Thank you, sir. But you don't know what's really going on here. Neither does Cole. He thinks he does but he doesn't. He knows more than me but I know more than him, do you follow me?"

"I think we went to the same sort of schools," Holliwell said.

"Tom and I both went to St. Bonaventure," Marie told him. "In Olean, New York."

Captain Zecca was drunk. So was Marie. So, to his own reckless satisfaction, was Holliwell.

"I'm sorry," Holliwell declared. "I don't approve of the American presence here."

"Someday," Captain Zecca said, "I'm going to work with the Chinese. Someday somewhere the conditions are gonna be right and me and the Chinese will get something going—I don't care if it's Africa—maybe even China."

"Wouldn't that be great," Marie said.

"I'm a fucking master of destiny," Zecca said. "My family is related to Napoleon's. I'm gonna get down with those Chinese."

"Listen to him," Marie said. "I hope you realize we're all drunk here."

"I realize it," Holliwell said. "I wouldn't have it any other way."

"But, Jesus," Marie went on a little sadly. "I wish we could trust you. I mean, we don't even know who you are and here we're talking about the Chinese."

"You know who I am and you can trust me," Holliwell said. "Personally, I enjoy talking about the Chinese."

"Well, one day," Zecca said, "this army will get me and the Chinese together and together we are gonna be the fucking Yellow Peril."

"Include me in," Holliwell told him. "As far as possible."

"There have been Chinese for five million years, man," the captain said. "I don't know how long there's been Zeccas but I know there's one thing that Zeccas and Chinese have in common. We know how the world goes." He took a little salt from the edge of his margarita glass and rubbed the grains between his fingers. "We know the price of salt. The Americans forget, if they ever knew. But Zeccas and Chinese will always know."

Holliwell toasted the ancient wisdom of the Zeccas and the Chinese.

"Cole doesn't know shit. Fat Frank doesn't know shit. El General—well, he's an ape. You, sir," he said, addressing Holliwell, "I don't know what you know. I won't presume to speculate. But things don't work the way people think."

Holliwell shrugged. "I know that my redeemer liveth," he said. The Zeccas stared at him. It was too Protestant a text.

After a moment, Tom laughed.

"We have a proverb, sir, in my grandfather's country. In his island. I'm positive they have the same proverb in China. It goes 'To trust is good. Not to trust is better.' "

"A *salute*," Marie said, and they drank the last of the margaritas.

"To Sicily," Holliwell said.

Captain Zecca's face seemed suddenly drained of good feeling. In the light from the living room, the shadow of his thick brows masked his eyes, high cheekbones and the arch of his nose covered the play of his thin lips.

"To the price of salt," he said, "and the ten pains of death. Which is all we really know."

Marie sighed. Holliwell held his seat until Captain Zecca rose from the table. He had seen such drinking parties in Vietnam and sometimes they ended badly. Zecca had begun to "sir" him rather a lot, a bad signal.

"Next month," Captain Zecca said, as they all staggered off to show Holliwell to his quarters, "we have to have twenty barrels of green beer. The way things get done in this country we better get on it now."

The room to which Holliwell was shown was small and comfortable, typical of the house; a touch of suburbia, a touch of Spanish formality. It had its own bath.

"Green beer!" Marie said. They shook hands all around.

"Good night, Doc," the captain said. "Great ride."

"Really," Marie said.

Holliwell thanked them profusely, excessively.

Washing up in the small neat bathroom, he could hear them plainly when he turned off the tap. They were in the kitchen.

"St. Patrick's Day," Captain Zecca was telling his wife. "It's in March."

"Oh, you're kidding," Marie said.

"Like hell I'm kidding. I've got to locate this individual who can dye beer green without poisoning the whole station."

"That's too goddamn ridiculous," she said.

Sitting on his bed, Holliwell could still hear them.

"Some Kraut, maybe. They've gotta have some Kraut over at the Germania brewery. Maybe he can do it."

"He'll think you're crazy."

"Fuck him."

"Tom—in this town—they'll dye it with old socks and deadly nightshade."

"We'll find a Kraut," Captain Zecca said. "We'll make him drink the first barrel."

Marie was giggling as they went to bed.

"Green Tecanecan beer for St. Patrick's Day. That's the living end. Will anybody mind if I stick with *agua mineral*?"

Holliwell heard them laughing together until he went to sleep.

Pablo woke to the goony birds. He had propped a chair against the doorknob; he was lying in a soiled mesh hammock in a bare evil-smelling room. Roaches in the size and quantity of delirium were scurrying across the slat floor, stripes of hard sunlight came in through the closed battered shutters. He struggled out of the hammock and took a Benzedrine at once. On the floor, he found an empty pack of the local cigarettes; he poured his remaining tablets into the packet and folded it away in his shirt pocket.

His clothes and his body were sweaty and rank and it had been days since he had been able to brush his teeth properly. This was a particular discomfort to a young man of Pablo's fastidiousness.

Downstairs, Cecil was cooking *refritos* in a kitchen off the bar.

"Don't you never sleep, Cecil?"

Without a word, Cecil came out of the kitchen and threw a plastic bag on the bar that contained Pablo's passport and his *turista* card. Beside it he placed the blue duffel bag that Pablo had come south with.

"Twenty," Cecil said. "Damn cheap at de price."

Pablo paid him.

"De bus station—you know where it is. Take de bus to Palmas—make sure. In Palmas go on down to de quays and you see de *Cloud*. Das de name of her—de *Cloud*. Goin' to be your new home."

"See you, Cecil."

"Hope so, mon. Hope you be doin' all right. Find out de use of you, all like dat."

"Shit," Pablo said.

Cecil watched him walk out with his gear and went back to the beans.

The bus to Palmas ran past mile upon mile of banana plantation. One of them was enclosed by a chain link fence surmounted with barbed wire; at its gate was a Coca-Cola sign with its center board replaceable for the inclusion of the name of the establishment on whose behalf Coca-Cola was prepared to extend its welcoming logo. The sign read: "Coca-Cola—Bienvenidos a—LA COLONIA PENAL."

The bus stopped often and it was crowded. There were a few women with children but most of the passengers were young plantation workers wearing machetes hung in leather sheaths from their belts. Listening to them speak together in a soft-edged Spanish of which he could pick up scarcely a word, Pablo fell victim to his wonted suspicions. That they were mocking him, taking counsel in avian trills and hisses to plot his undoing, seemed as obvious to him as the cloudless sky and the green mountains. Pablo was scornful of their ill intentions; he was armed, as was his custom, with a Dacor diver's knife strapped to his calf and the automatic pistol holstered against his armpit.

But the passengers in the bus aroused within Pablo another sensation and it was one on which he scarcely dared reflect. As his guarded glance swept the people pressed close around him, he felt that he could anticipate every smile and gesture that he saw. There was a secret self inside him that knew their rhythms and their stirrings, even knew their thoughts. In the hot cramped space he realized suddenly that he had some kinship of the blood with these dark stunted people whom he so despised—that they were, however distantly, his mother's people and in that way, his own. It did not make him feel in the least warm toward them.

Palmas was a gas station at the end of a dirt street that led past mean wooden shacks to the ocean. Pablo climbed off the bus with his gear and walked the length of it. He paused at the dockside—there were a few shops and bodegas and the office of the captain of the port. Tied up at the two piers were two dozen local shrimp boats of seventy or eighty feet, their wheelhouses painted in bright tropical colors like the local buses. There was no craft in sight that looked as though it would be the Callahans' powerboat. He put on his Macklin Chain Saw hat, took his sunglasses from the pocket of his shirt and looked from one quarter of the harbor to the other. Nothing but shrimpers. He walked out on the pier, set his bag down and leaned against a piling, cursing under his breath.

From behind the tinted-glass windscreen of the *Cloud*, Mr. Callahan and Freddy Negus watched Pablo on the pier.

"That's our boy," Callahan said.

"Gawd," Freddy Negus said.

"What's wrong with him?" Callahan demanded. Callahan was drinking a rum and soda and the sight of it in his hand at so early an hour made Negus uneasy. "He showed up, didn't he? He's just a deserter, that's all." He saw Negus glancing at the drink in his hand and put it down beside the Fathometer. "I mean, what do you want, for Christ's sake? Billy Budd?"

"You hire these monkeys and then I got to keep them in line. I'll tell you, Jack, I'm getting plumb wore out with it. We could have taken on a local crew for this."

Callahan picked up his drink angrily.

"I told you, Freddy, didn't I, Freddy, that I did *not* want a native crew for this? I need people I can control and who need me. I need a guy with a little technical savvy who's a long way from home and who can't take to the hills if the deal goes queer. A deserter is perfect. That boy you're looking at is gonna work out fine."

"Gimme a dope run any old time," Negus said. "At least you know what you're up against."

"Hell, Freddy," Callahan said, "you been out in all the weather. An old pirate like you." He stepped unsteadily over the hatchway and into the galley for another drink.

"Maybe that's the problem," Negus said. "We're all getting a little old for privacy." He kept on watching Pablo, fretting down on the pier. "And when's Deedee coming back? We want to clear tonight."

"She drove over to Pico to find a dentist," Callahan said, measuring out his rum. "She'll be back in plenty of time."

"Fuckin' 'ell," Freddy Negus said. He put his baseball cap on and went out on the little bridge beside the wheelhouse, squinting into the sun.

"Hey, you!" he called down to Pablo. "Pablo! Come on up here."

Hearing himself hailed from one of the ratty shrimpers, Pablo picked up his bag and started along the pier. There was a white man in a baseball cap on the bridge of the largest of the boats; the man was waving Pablo aboard. It occurred to him that the Callahans' yacht must be lying to offshore somewhere. He had suspected contrabanding but nothing so complex.

"Tabor?" the man asked him when he stood abeam of the

shrimper. A black man who had been painting bright yellow numerals on the vessel's prow turned to look at him. Pablo nodded.

"Come aboard, Tabor."

Pablo stepped over the rail. The man who had called him was tall and lean, tanned, with lazy faded blue eyes. He indicated a hatchway behind the wheelhouse and followed Pablo through it.

"I'm looking for the *Cloud*," Pablo explained.

"You're standing in her," the tall man said.

Mr. Callahan came forward from the galley, a glass in his hand.

"Well done," Mr. Callahan said. "Right on time."

Pablo turned from the tall man's steady gaze.

"Christ, Mr. Callahan. You told me you had a powerboat. You didn't say nothing about shrimping." He felt disappointed and betrayed. It was not at all what he had looked forward to.

"You don't see any sails, do you?" the tall man asked him. "This is a powerboat."

Pablo turned to face him. "No question about that."

"What's happening right now," Mr. Callahan said, "is that you're being engaged as a crewman on the shrimp boat *Cloud*. We're registered out of Marathon, Florida. We're licensed to fish in the territorial waters of the United States, of Mexico, Belize, Compostela and Tecan. Any other questions will have to wait. O.K.?"

"What am I working for?" Pablo asked bitterly. "A percentage of the catch?"

"That sounds like a question to me," the tall man said.

Pablo looked at the man again. From his accent, Pablo made him out to be a white Bahamian. Hope Town, Spanish Wells, some sorry-ass town like that. A mean redneck.

"Let me introduce Mr. Negus," Callahan said. "My number one."

Pablo nodded. Mr. Negus shifted the plug of tobacco in his cheek.

"And let me hasten to assure you that you're not being taken advantage of. If we were looking for cheap labor there's plenty to come by down here. You'll do fine but you've got to go by our rules."

Negus was looking out at a pier through the hatchway.

"Where you from, son?" he asked Pablo.

"Texas."

"Lay out your gear for us." He indicated Pablo's bag and the deck of the passageway in which they stood. For the first time, Pablo noticed that the interior bulkheads were paneled in dark wood, the rubber-matted deck was spotless. He opened his bag and spread his store of worn work clothes, toiletry bags and slickers across it. Negus crouched to rifle through it and immediately picked up the plastic bag that held Pablo's passport and tourist card. He handed it over to Callahan.

"We ask everyone to do that for us," Mr. Callahan explained. "These days you can't be too careful." He looked the passport and tourist card over and returned them. Negus took Pablo's wallet from him. There was nothing in the wallet except what was left of his money. Negus gave him back his wallet and motioned him up against the bulkhead. Pablo leaned forward on his palms.

"Sorry," Mr. Callahan said.

In a few moments Negus had the automatic and the diver's knife out on deck. Grimly, he turned out Pablo's trouser pockets one by one.

"What's all that for?" Mr. Callahan asked mildly.

"Just for protection."

"Now how in hell," Mr. Negus wanted to know, "did he get down here trussed up with all that weaponry? Don't you think it's a bit odd," he asked Callahan, "that they didn't get it off him?"

"Nobody ever searched me," Pablo told them. "I come down to Vizcaya on the bus."

"The bus? All the way from the States?"

"Yes, sir. All the way from Matamoros, Mexico."

Negus sighed in exasperation.

"I mentioned that it would be our rules," Callahan said to Pablo. "If any of that troubles you"—he motioned back toward the shacks of Palmas—"we'll pay your way back to Vizc and wish you luck. Otherwise—our rules and no questions. That way you'll make out very well indeed."

"O.K.," Pablo said. "I guess I'm with you."

"You can't keep that pistol while you're aboard," Callahan told him. "You might have an accident. The knife, O.K."

Negus gave him his Dacor knife. "Wear it on your belt where a man can see it, sailor."

"Welcome aboard," Mr. Callahan said, and took his drink aft.

He walked through the galley and into a dark compartment where the forward ice hold should have been, closing a door behind him. Pablo looked from the well-stocked bar in the galley to the tinted glass fronting the pilothouse. At the forward end of the passageway in which he stood was a Modar UH transmitter and a CB. There were A and C Lorans and what appeared to be a seventy-eight-mile-range radar scanner. The wheelhouse cockpit had a brand-new recording Fathometer. From the dock the *Cloud* had appeared to be a moderately clean eighty-five foot shrimper. Inside she had the appointments and equipment of a cutter.

"I take it," Mr. Negus said, as he watched Pablo look over the electronic gear, "that you're familiar with this stuff?"

"More or less," Pablo said.

"Everything the latest boats carry, we carry," Negus told him. "Your big Texas boats have all this stuff."

Pablo did not contradict him. They went out on deck and Mr. Negus led him aft. Between the mainmast and the upright outriggers, some kind of extra compartment had been constructed. Its uppermost section rose above the level of the main deck and was boarded over with three-by-five hatch covers. This, Pablo thought, would be the compartment into which Mr. Callahan had taken his drink.

Pablo decided that he would venture an observation.

"Never seen that space on a Texas boat," he said to Mr. Negus.

"You'll see it on plenty of boats down here," Negus told him casually. "When a man takes his family out, he needs more space. The *Cloud's* a home, you understand. It's a lifestyle."

"Oh," Pablo said.

There were two ice holds, empty and with their hatch covers off. Aft of them a hatchway led down to an airless lazaret where there was a single bunk and some bales of chafing gear.

"You can sack out for a while if you like," Negus told Pablo. "But we're going out before sunset and I want everybody standing to."

"Roger," Pablo said.

"Tino can fix you up with boots and whatnot when he's finished painting. He'll show you around. Once we're under way you come on up to the pilothouse and we'll tell you what you need to know."

"Yes sir," Pablo said out of instinct.

Down in the lazaret, he took off his cowboy boots and lay down on the bunk. The sheet smelled freshly laundered, the pervasive odor of diesel fuel made Pablo feel somewhat at home. A powerboat.

He lay low for a while, listening to the slap of water against the boards, the sounds of the quiet harbor. At some time during his rest, the woman came aboard; he heard them call out to her from the pilothouse and then her voice with theirs in a muffled echo through the holds that lay between his quarters and the dark compartment.

Late in the afternoon he looked up to see the black man who had been painting the bow framed in the hatchway above him. The man dropped a pair of white rubber boots down the hatch: each boot had a rubber glove stuffed inside it.

"*Vámonos, muchacho.*"

"*Sí,*" Pablo said. "*Momento.*"

He rolled out of his rack and put on a pair of clean woolen socks, pulled the boots over them and jammed the gloves in his pockets. The black man stepped back to let Pablo climb topside and extended his hand.

"*Soy Tino.*"

Tino's hand was like a shard of coral. Pablo wondered what Tino made of his own soft hand.

"Pablo."

"*Buenas. Usted es norteamericano, no?*"

"Texas."

"Dat's what I figger," Tino said.

"Sure is a fine boat."

"Surely is. Dushi, we say on my island."

"Which is that?"

"Sint Joost," Tino told him. "You see it couple days."

"Be my pleasure to be the fuck off this coast, I'll tell you."

Mr. Callahan, looking fresh and sober, was standing on the dockside in conversation with a Compostelan in a smart naval uniform. They were laughing together. Pablo saw them exchange sealed manila envelopes and shake hands heartily. Negus, who had been leaning on the rail beside the pilothouse, sauntered back to Pablo and Tino.

"Reckon we're just about set," he told them.

"You don't want the net rigged?" Tino asked. "Don't want the outriggers over?"

"Fuck it. We're not fishing tonight and we don't have to put on a show. Weather's nice, so we won't need the stabilizers. Just get up steam and we'll ease along out."

Tino took off for the engine room.

"Like the boat?" Negus asked Pablo.

"Dushi," Pablo said.

Negus did not smile.

Holliwell traveled down the Río de la Fe from a town called Tapa. The Zeccas together drove him there from San Ysidro. If Captain Zecca had received a line on Holliwell in his workday morning's mail, he gave no indication of it. At the same time, it seemed to Holliwell that they talked less on the drive than they had before and that their talk was more bland. On the dockside, they shook hands with him gaily and assured him that it had all been fun. Holliwell, quite sober now, felt inexplicably forlorn watching their Honda disappear down Tapa's single muddy street, headed for the potholed, switchbacking mountain road back to the capital.

In the guidebook Holliwell carried, the local boat was recommended because it afforded a leisurely journey in the course of which one might inspect the magnificent gorges of the river valley, see the Indian towns on the bank and the landings where the *hacienderos* waited for their mail and their mailorder luxuries from the capital. Unlike Compostela, Tecan had no highway between her coasts; east-west surface transportation was by boat along the river. It was a route much used by Forty-niners during the California gold rush to avoid the journey around Cape Horn; an arduous and malarial journey in those days that killed a quarter of the men who undertook it. Now the traffic moved by diesel-powered launches manufactured in Bremen, and the one moored at Tapa's dock looked new and fairly well maintained. Holliwell, for the Zeccas' convenience and his own impulse to flight, had booked passage on the night *rápido* and engaged a cabin.

An Indian boy carried his bag aboard for a quarter; he found his cabin small but very clean, with a brass-knobbed wooden door opening on an interior passageway and a second, louvered door opening to the deck. The sheets on the bunk were starched and spotless; there was a ceiling fan, mosquito netting, even a glass and a jug of *agua purificada*. Holliwell took a bottle of the local rum from his suitcase and mixed himself a rum and water. When he finished it, he drew back the mosquito netting, lay down on his bunk and went to sleep.

Rápido or not, the boat stopped many times during the night; so often that Holliwell within the first two hours of darkness was moved to rise and take his bottle out on deck. The night was clear. The mountain ranges rising close over the river on both sides cut off the moon from view but its deflected light lit the rocky peaks and cliffs, the treetops and the slow-seeming tawny river. Night birds and howler monkeys sounded from the banks, their calls echoing in the gorges. Holliwell sat down on a gear locker and looked up at the stars. According to his guidebook, there were jaguar in the valley.

The finca landings were lit by the headlights of parked jeeps. The forks of white light would flash of a sudden from the bank ahead, lighting the dun river in their glow, and the boat would slow and ease toward the bank until the searching spotlight over the wheelhouse picked up the vehicle and the waiting men together with a thousand spinning moths, their bright wings flashing a thousand colors in the glare. Into this well of light, the Indian deckhands would toss the starboard hawsers and the men on the bank secure them to rusty weighted barrels while the vessel's fantail swung completely around in the invisible current and her engines labored full astern. When the boat was steady against the bank, the engines still rattling astern, the deckhands would push a wooden gangway from cargo deck to bank and, running as though under fire, would commence to carry ashore a few dozen sacks and crates. These the finca's peons would carefully load in the waiting jeeps. Within a few minutes it would be over, the hawsers cast back aboard and the boat under way again. Astern of them, the landing would quickly dissolve into jungle darkness, like a theatrical tableau suggesting dreams or fairy spectacle.

In the Indian villages along the Rió de la Fe there were no jeeps nor were there electric lights of any kind. The people on the bank would signal the boat with torches and the offloading would be lit by the pilothouse searchlight and a fire burning in an open pit beside the bank, with the hawsers secured around stumps. Handshakes and greetings would be exchanged on the run; the language of discourse was not Spanish. Boys would leap aboard from the outer darkness, prowling the decks like scavengers, accosting the few cabin passengers in sight with things to sell—feathered rattles, stuffed lizards, a live snake in a jar. Holliwell, ever conscious of thieves, would watch his unlocked cabin door, although there was little behind it worth stealing. At the last possible moment, the boys would leap ashore in the firelight and the boat continue its slow passage down the river.

Although it was difficult to see in the darkness, the smoke and the confusion of lights, the Indian villages seemed to Holliwell as poor and mean as the slums of the capital. There was a distinct sour smell to them, not quite fecal, but like rust and congealed blood. And in spite of their size and remoteness, they seemed to him like some North American cities he knew in that what they brought to the landscape that surrounded them was not a sense of settlement and advance but of concentrated misery, despair.

Between stops, he walked the upper deck—the few other cabin passengers were not in sight. For a while he leaned with his elbows against the rail and watched the men in the pilothouse. The helmsman was an Indian like the rest of the crew, wearing a wide Panama bent out of shape with the brim turned up and down to resemble an Australian bush hat, staring out into the darkness with a faint smile. Behind him the captain bent over a chart in the light of a desk lamp, shielded from reflection by a tar-paper shade. The captain was a heavy red-faced man of some African blood with fair wavy hair, wearing a starched white shirt and narrow black necktie. Neither man appeared to speak to the other.

In time the mosquitoes drove Holliwell back to his cabin, and he lay down on his bunk buried behind the netting, smoking. He was thinking about his wife and his daughters, and how, though he had stayed—would never leave now—he had lost them. He had thought to do everything right—he believed in love. There had been something, perhaps, that it was not possible for someone like himself to know and his not knowing it had lost them. The hard way, little by little, without an outcry of any sort.

Thoughts of loss could be cauterized with drink. The alcohol he had been consuming since the start of his journey was a regular part of his metabolism now; he was half drunk, almost at peace. He nearly slept.

When he went out on deck again it was getting light, the sun rising over flat jungle and grassland where lean cattle grazed. The mountains were behind them to westward, rising abruptly in a massive escarpment that burst into bright green with dawn. Within minutes they were coming into a town of sorts—a city. Unpainted wooden houses with slant roofs stood on stilts above a black beach where gulls picked at piles of refuse and open clay gutters emptied a viscous stream into the brown river. Puerto Alvarado.

As the launch pulled for the right bank, Holliwell could see ahead a line of tin-roofed warehouses where two freighters stood at moor, and beyond that the river widening into a delta bordered with mangrove swamp, and beyond all, almost motionless in the morning light, the expanse of pale green ocean. While they tied up, Holliwell worked on his expense records, then gathered up his luggage.

The hustlers on the deck, offering to carry his bag or shine his shoes, spoke Caribbean English and required eye contact of him. Holliwell's shoes were already polished to a high gleam. He attempted to oblige with the eye contact but his eye was uneasy; he was scanning the dock for menace. The most menacing presence he could detect was that of the Guardia Nacional—four troopers and an officer, who exuded a floral aroma and regarded him in an unfriendly fashion. A few yards behind the Guardia pack—at the edge of the dockside street—a tall black man in a white shirt stood beside a Willys jeep of World War II provenance.

"Paradise?" the man asked Holliwell.

"Lovely," Holliwell told him.

The man took Holliwell's bag from him with a sure hand and placed it in the back of the jeep.

"Wait," Holliwell said to him, "there must be some misunderstanding here."

The black man frowned at him.

"Mon, I just as' you if you goin' to Paradise. You tol' me O.K."

"No," Holliwell said. "I'm not going to Paradise."

The man turned toward the boat in no particular hurry. Holliwell retrieved his bag lest he incur some manner of fee. At the dock, the last Tecanecan passengers were disembarking under the Guardia's glare. There appeared to be no other gringos aboard.

"Where you want to go then?" the tall man asked Holliwell.

Holliwell looked at him and at his jeep.

"Well—to the Islas Airlines office. And the airport."

"Jolly good," the man said, taking the bag back. "I take you to the office."

He climbed in beside the driver and they started up. The river-front streets had little Spanish about them. The peeling wooden houses, the tin roofs, might have been in Kingston or Belize.

"How about the airport?" Holliwell asked.

"You not goin' there today, mistuh. Nor tomorrow neither."

"How come?" Holliwell asked, feeling a bit alarmed.

"Because Islas got only one plane and she's over in Respina and she not about to fly. They got to get some parts from up San Ysidro. Carry dem over on de boat when they feel like."

"Christ," Holliwell said. The streets and the people in them were more Latin American as they approached the center of the city. Indians with marriage bands around their sombreros carried slaughtered turkeys and heaps of faggots over the cobblestones.

"If it was my airline," the driver said, "I run it differently. But it's not."

"I guess I'll check in at the office anyway."

"Humm," the driver said. "Want me to wait?"

Holliwell thought about it.

"No, don't wait. I might be a while and maybe I'll get lucky."

"Thas a good way to think," the Paradise driver said. "Thas the way I think."

In front of the Islas office, he paid the price demanded and took his bag.

The office was in a part of the city off the central plaza, across from the government technical school. It was decidedly Spanish America here. The high curbs were set with ancient paving stones; the cathedral he saw through the jacaranda trees of the plaza was at least as old as the late eighteenth century. There was an old stone building beside it of about the same date, with Guardia sentries at its doorway. The *judicia*.

Behind a desk in the airline office, an Oriental woman sat listlessly on a high stool, projecting inexpressible melancholy —Masha Kuligina with another life to mourn, upon whom karma had bestowed exotic rebirth and strange displacement. Holliwell realized at once that there would be no good news from her. In the most decorous and formal Spanish at his command, he inquired the state of transportation to the islands. She answered him, as he knew she would, in English.

Things were more or less as the driver from Paradise had described them. The plane was in Respina. Another plane had been dispatched to the capital to obtain needed parts but had not yet returned. There was no question of alternative arrangements because the government regulations about the franchise were very rigorous. The islands and the coast were a military district and could not be overflown by any aircraft other than those authorized. There was indeed a boat that ran to the islands but it ran only on Wednesdays and Saturdays, the same days for which the plane was scheduled. A boat had left that morning. The journey was over ten hours because it stopped at several places along the coast as well as at each of the five offshore islands. One waited on the quay in the morning for a place, it was always very crowded.

"You speak English very well," Holliwell told the woman. "Do you speak French also?"

The woman looked at him sadly. In his irritation, the observation and question had been a bit patronizing, an impertinence to a Vietnamese woman of culture such as this lady unquestionably was. She allowed him to realize this and smiled without a trace of good humor.

"Of course," she said.

Of course, Holliwell thought. *Bien sûr*. Our worlds have touched before and we both know it, don't we?

In any case the small opportunity he had offered himself for second thoughts on the spot seemed just about removed. Now he would be obliging Ocampo. He was there; he was *being seen*, as Oscar had put it, to be there. He glanced about the broken streets and wondered by whom.

Taking his bag once around the square, he paused on a guano-spotted bench to have his shoes shined yet again by a gaunt nine-year-old. It was a grim little plaza; the people lounging in it were as poor as any that Holliwell had ever seen. The interior of the cathedral, though it contained some good carved *santos*, was mainly a Babylonian horror with mindless rococo gilding and a curious encoffined Christ. When he had finished inspecting it, he carried his bag down a street of notaries and public letter writers to the clapboard riverfront.

The jeep was parked in the declining shade of the customs shed, its driver stretched out in the front seat with the brim of a Ralston Purina cap pulled down over his face. The ships at the adjoining wharf were loading sacks of coffee beans and the longshoremen working them wore sweatbands across their foreheads and machetes at their belts which gave them a piratical look.

The sleeping Paradise driver awoke to the whistle of a diesel launched from the interior which was pulling for its berth. He raised his hat and looked at Holliwell sympathetically.

"We goin' to Paradise, you and me?"

"I guess we are. How much to go there?"

"Ten dollars," the man said. "And I didn't say pesos, did I? I said ten dollars U.S."

Holliwell shrugged.

"The tourists always sayin' I told 'em ten pesos," the driver said as they turned to watch the arriving boat. "Never told anyone dat. Ten dollars. One with Mr. Hamilton on it."

"I got you," Holliwell said.

There were three gringos on the steamer, all going to the Paradise. A short rounded man with a deep tan, a gray goatee lengthening his thick jowls. His wife or girlfriend, gray-blond with a leathery brown face like a boot about to crack. A thin, florid man wearing a Yucatecan Panama.

The driver took their bags and everyone exchanged small nods. Holliwell sat in the back, beside the slight man with the Panama.

"Ralph Heath," the man beside Holliwell said, as they drove over a straight dirt road through the mangrove swamp. The man held his Panama in his lap.

"Frank Holliwell."

"Been here before?" He was an Englishman of about fifty, with a mean-featured hard little face. A drinker—the pouches under his eyes were the only slack part of him and distended veins ran down the sides of his nose.

"Never."

"Alvarado's a hole. But it's a nice coast if that's what you're after. Coming place."

"Are you down here often?" Holliwell asked him.

"Once or twice a year. Sometimes on business, sometimes just for the beer."

"From England?"

"I live in Miami now," Heath told him. "I have ever since our fruit company merged with yours. You're American?"

"Yes," Holliwell said. And after a moment, he shouted to Heath over the engine noise. "How do you like Miami?"

"Never looked back," Heath said.

They drove under the mangrove wilderness, which opened to sandy beaches and palm groves; the road was only a packed sand track near the water's edge. The cheerlessness of Puerto Alvarado fell away in the sunlight.

The drive took hours. They sped past clapboard fishing villages in the palm groves where nets were drying on poles along the beach and brightly painted boats with cabined wheelhouses were hauled up, buccaneer fashion, on raked plank dry docks beyond the tide line. Almost every house had in front of it a small garden of plantains and an overturned double-ended skiff. Farther from the ocean were the miles of fruit company houses, numbered and painted yellow. A good half of them appeared to be unoccupied.

On the beach road they were constantly passing women carrying baskets or pots on their heads. From time to time, Holliwell would see a basket that looked to have the ghost of an African design or a pot inlaid with a highland Indian pattern. But for the most part they were factory-made, bought in Alvarado or from a passing Syrian. Between the villages or

on the edge of them were some compounds of vaguely ecclesiastical design that looked as though they might be mis-
sions. Holliwell said something to Heath about its being a fine
place to be a missionary in.

"Too damn many of them," Heath shouted to him. "That
was your company's policy in the old days—the more of the
bastards, the merrier. They're regretting it now."

"Why's that?"

"Why? Because they're a pack of reds. Why shouldn't they
be? They don't work for a living like you and me. I'm assum-
ing you work for a living."

"I teach," Holliwell said.

"Ah," said Mr. Heath, and he fell silent for a while.

"It isn't religion they need down here," Heath declared
after five minutes. "They've had plenty of that. It's the Pill. If
this coast had half the population it has it would be in damn
fine shape."

Heath was speaking at the top of his voice, conceding their
driver only the virtue of some necessity. The couple in the
front seat stirred and half turned round in embarrassment.

"Then who would pick the fruit?"

"Hardly any fruit to pick these days. Less than half the
crop there was ten years ago. We package coffee and bananas
now—we've lost most of the bananas to blight. The next thing
we need to package is tourism and we don't need all these
imported Jamaicans for that. The other way round—we need
less of them."

The couple in the front seat cringed visibly. The driver, one
arm resting on the back of his seat, looked with an amiable
countenance at the track before him.

"In the old days," Heath said, "when the bananas had a few
bad years the pickers moved on. No more. The sensible thing
for us to do is to airlift the lot to the Pacific coast where we're
bloody crying out for pickers. It's the sensible thing, so naturally these psalm singers are determined to stop us doing it.
They turn the people against us and against the government.
They're masters of propaganda."

"Really?" Holliwell asked.

"God, yes. Down here they're meek and mild. Lambs. Then
they go abroad and thunder for blood and revolution. They've
got powerful friends, you know, and they use them to the hilt.

Dignity of man," Heath said sourly. "Where I stand a man's got dignity or he hasn't, rich or poor the same. You can't bestow it on him. You can't send it to him in a CARE package."

"I don't really know the situation," Holliwell shouted back. "So I can't say."

"Fair enough," Heath told him. "You're one among many."

The hotel called Paradise was neither as transcendent nor as banal as its name. It consisted of a number of simple wooden bungalows around a well-tended garden. At some distance from the bungalows was what appeared to be a disused airplane hangar but which revealed itself on closer inspection to be a terraced dining room, open to the beach. Where the tool shops might have been there was a kitchen and a crescent-shaped bar; an old nineteen-forties jukebox stood at the edge of the large cement floor between the bar and the decks of tables, blasting Freddy Fender's rendition of "El Rancho Grande" into every square foot of covered space. At the water's edge was a dock with a couple of numbered boats tied up to it and a shack with a diver's flag painted on the roof.

Not paradise but nice enough. In the office bungalow a hefty Spanish woman registered the guests and dispensed keys to the bungalows.

Holliwell stowed his bag in the plain bungalow and took a cold shower, the only kind available. When he had changed clothes, he poured himself a drink and went outside to sit in the shade of an arbor of bougainvillea.

After he had been sitting for a while, a dark-skinned young man came up from the bar, where he had been drinking a beer with the driver, and asked Holliwell if he wanted to go diving.

Holliwell looked at the young man and then at the placid ocean. The question aroused in him a thrill of fear and also a longing for the depths, for the concealment and oblivion of blue-gray light at sea level minus seventy.

"It's been a while," he said.

"If you want," the young man said, "we run you through a checkout in the morning. Bring it back. You been certified?"

"Yeah," Holliwell said. A reliable-looking kid, he thought. Undersea images flashed in his mind, fans and parrot fish, silvery barracuda. Things being what they were, why not?

The young man gave him a card with the diving package rates. Holliwell put it in his pocket. As the young man walked back toward the dive shop, Ralph Heath came by carrying a glass of white rum and soda.

"Going diving, are you?"

"I'm thinking of it. I haven't in a long time."

"Nor have I. I got thumped on the head in Bogotá eight years ago and I haven't been able to dive since. Only wish I could."

"Did you ever dive around here?"

"Oh, yes. Here and in Jamaica. Malta. Yap in Micronesia. I was very fond of it."

"How did you come to get thumped?" Holliwell asked.

"Accident," Heath said. "I'll tell you—Playa Tate's a good place for a dive. That's about six miles south of here. There's a reef close inshore—then she drops off about three quarters of a mile out. It's a wall—a real chiller-diller, that one. Grand Canyon."

"Many sharks?" Holliwell asked sheepishly. It was a question one was not supposed to ask.

"Well," Heath said, "this is the eastern Carib, chum. You're likely to see the odd shark out there."

"I suppose," Holliwell said.

"Another good place is near there. By the American Catholic mission. There's one reef that starts in about eight feet of water, then slopes down to forty, then flattens out and drops a mile out. Good snorkeling there as well."

"How's the shop here?"

"Quite good actually. Sandy's a good boy. I used to dive with his father ten years or so ago. Nice family they are. Head and shoulders above the rest of them around here."

"I think I will go out," Holliwell said. "I'll go look up Sandy in the morning."

"You'll have a jolly good time, Holliwell," Heath said.

Pablo leaned idly on the rail as they cleared the harbor, the rubber work gloves still in his back pocket. His want of a bath was bothering him acutely now and he wished that he had asked them about it while the boat was still hooked up to a dockside water line. If there was a woman aboard, he reasoned, the *Cloud* must have a head and shower somewhere.

No harm in asking, he thought after a while; there might be enough water from the evaporators or a fresh-water supply somewhere aboard. They seemed to have everything else. He went forward to the wheelhouse and leaned his head through the hatch. Negus and Callahan were in the cockpit chairs.

"If we got some time now and there's water enough, could I clean up? I ain't shaved nor showered for a while."

Negus looked from Pablo to Callahan.

"There's enough," Callahan said. "Right behind the galley. Knock first."

He went back to the lazaret to get some fresh clothes and his toilet kit and then up to the galley. Behind it was the door to the dim compartment into which Mr. Callahan had earlier disappeared with his drink. He knocked twice on it.

"Hello," called the voice of Mrs. Callahan.

"Sorry," he said.

"Come on in."

He opened the door just as Tino, out on deck, was hauling away the hatch covers that closed off the windows of the compartment from the outside. As the space filled with light he saw that the compartment had the same dark paneling as the forward passageway, that there was a striped chaise longue, some captain's chairs with brightly colored cushions, even a bookcase. In the center of the stateroom was a round table with metal studs, an electric fan resting on it. Mrs. Callahan was sitting in one of the captain's chairs under a lighted wall lamp, a book on her lap.

"On your right, Pablo," she told him. She pulled the terry-cloth robe she was wearing a little farther down over her tanned thighs. It was all she had on, Pablo thought.

"I'll go easy on the water."

In the pocket of Mrs. Callahan's robe, Pablo espied a bottle of pills. There was a small swelling distorting the patrician contour of her high cheekbone and long jaw.

"Yes, do," she said.

Pablo had him a shit, shower and shave; his thoughts were carnal. Soaping down, he sang to himself.

> "I ride an old paint
> I ride an old dan
> I'm going to Montana for to have a hooly-an."

The water was warm, hand-pumped out of an overhead pipe through a rubber nozzle. He shaved slowly and deliberately, his shoulder propped against the bulkhead beside the mirror, riding with the slow roll of the boat, still singing.

When he came out, Mrs. Callahan was watching him, leaning her head on an elbow, her hand covering her mouth. When she took her hand away, he saw that she was smiling.

"Do you play the guitar?" she asked him.

"No," Pablo said, feeling surly and put down.

"What a shame," Mrs. Callahan said.

He climbed out of the fancy compartment, the kit and soiled clothes under his arm, and went out on deck. Low even seas slid westward under the light wind, over the horizon was a thin line of cloud, nearly pink in the fading light. Big bitch thinks I'm comical, he said to himself. She thinks I'm the fucking entertainment.

Tino was checking out the net's chain line as Pablo tossed his things down into the lazaret.

"Callahan bring his old lady every trip?"

"Mostly does."

It was not his custom to speak of white women with dark people but resentment and desire made him uneasy and perverse.

"She spread it around any?"

"Lister engine," Tino said, nodding toward the casing of the outrigger's auxiliary motor. Pablo watched him drop the chain line on the deck and walk over to slap the top of the casing. "You can work it from right here or from the cockpit. Can haul it up by hand on the windlass if you needs to."

Pablo fixed his eyes on the tall St. Joostian and leaned against the upright outrigger. He was being turned around again. He watched the other man's eyes and thought of the denticled palm.

"We ain't fishin' tonight," Tino said, "but I tell you in case like. Over dere—" He pointed to a rolled-up smaller net against the port rail. "Dat's de tri-net. We haul her up every half hour maybe on a lay line. You ever been shrimping before?"

Pablo only stared at him.

"Well," Tino said, meeting his stare, "you best be told so you know what you doin'. Got to know what you doin' out here."

"Is that right?" Pablo asked him.

"Believe it," Tino said, and picked up the chain line again.

"That's real good of you, Tino."

"*Para servile*," Tino said softly.

During the next two days, the *Cloud* ran the coast of the Isthmus. Most of the time they were out of sight of land, in the seas between the Swan Islands and Serrana Bank. Pablo watched and listened, made himself useful and kept his nature to himself. It was like a breakdown cruise; they were testing the electronics gear and the auxiliary diesels; making plans to which he was not party. Mainly, he realized, it was he himself that they were observing. Tino, Negus, both of the Callahans would engage him from time to time in strained quiet conversations that varied in nature according to their several styles. He made it his business to be pleasant, incurious and resourceful in small matters. He had a turn at the wheel, he replaced a Raytheon tube and sunned himself on the hatches. Once, when they were anchored off Gracias a Dios, he had a skinny dip and was confirmed in the conviction that Mrs. Callahan had eyes for him. The swim also gave him a chance to study the boat's dynamics from the business end, and although he was no engineer he could see that even in basic construction the *Cloud* was not what she appeared. She had what the Coast Guard would call a false hull; a squat duck of a shrimper at first and even second glance above the waterline, her lines were modified to make her capable of formidable speed with the diesels engaged. A contrabander, as he had assumed.

On the morning of the third day out, they dropped the hook off Palmas and every one of them but Tino set about getting drunk. Their intemperance worried Pablo, who thought it unbusinesslike. They smoked a great deal of grass as well and tried to press it on him. Pablo had settled himself into three Benzedrines a day and he did not care for marijuana; it made him feel turned around. An indistinct notion presented itself to him: that the company's undisciplined self-indulgence might eventually be turned somehow to his advantage. But for the moment he was content.

After siesta, on the same day, the lot of them held a conference in their improbable saloon space. Pablo was not invited. He had found that standing in the forward ice hold he was able to hear quite clearly everything that was said on the far side of the bulkhead, but he knew better than to employ this convenience prematurely.

When the afternoon passed and he was not summoned, he felt confident that they were satisfied with him. In the evening, he and Tino took the anchor in and lowered the stabilizers. Mrs. Callahan cleaned the kitchen. It seemed he was in.

In the years since the city's history had caused the decline of the lakeside district, the most desirable section of Tecan's capital was in the hills west of the center, on the only slope not occupied by squatters. Most of the embassies remained on the Malecón beside the lake but a few had moved to the hillside neighborhood; it was in this section of Tecan's capital that the Zeccas maintained their pleasant house.

The slope section had always been known as Buenos Aires. Its central area of four blocks or so was the remains of a colonial suburb destroyed by a series of earthquakes and contained the remnants of a baroque church and a colonnaded building which had been a theater, a market, or the palace of the Inquisition depending on the books one referred to. A market was what it had become, and it had probably always been one.

The outer streets of Buenos Aires, between the colonial core and the new residential sections, had been set out in the nineties by a class of people who had been to Paris once or twice and remembered it imperfectly but fondly. Any foreigner taking a turn round the Buenos Aires district and attempting to pursue the promise of an isthmian Montparnasse would be disabused as quickly as a stroller among the flats and terraces of a production of *La Bohème*—but here and there, among the beggars and the Indian vendors, a streetlight, a gray stone high Renaissance structure, a mansard roof might bring a fleeting taste of some dead comprador's lost city of light. The gentry responsible for this modest hall of mirrors were melancholy internal exiles. But they were also great dreamers, so it was impossible to be certain just how far, during the brief period of agrarian prosperity and large foreign loans, they had intended to pursue this fancy. Their greatest achievements in its realization were marked by the blighted lakeside barrio; Buenos Aires, like the Paris of Thiers, had been early aborted. But for reasons of recent history, that section had held its thin illusion more successfully. Squatters who tried moving into some of the empty buildings were summarily dealt with and sometimes murdered outright by the Guardia, an indication that there must be a continuing affection for the district on the part of a faction in the present regime, men of sensibility less taken with Houston and Atlanta than their colleagues and relations.

There were many religious houses in the area now, minor government offices and the chambers of professional men. The National University used a few buildings there, and there seemed to be a great many private language schools doubling as pensions whose brochures were available through foreign travel magazines. High on the slope, the President's family was constructing a new, glass hotel.

Early on a winter morning, just after first light in the hour before the day's heat descended on the inland sea, a young woman in jeans and a neat white blouse was walking downhill past one of the grander of the gray stone buildings, humming to herself and carrying a stack of books and a thin plastic briefcase. Obviously a student, her very presence, her books and high spirits, contributed to the decorous European veneer of the neighborhood.

She was at the point of entering another stone building a little further down the hill when she slipped on a worn marble step at the street entrance. She kept her footing but her books and the briefcase scattered over the pavement. Bending to recover them, she looked up to see a slight elderly man in a lightweight Italian suit advancing to help her. The man had just stepped out of a Fiat in the narrow street; as soon as he was out the door the car sped away.

The man was elegant and professorial, as he briskly gathered up the young student's fallen books; he smiled in a dignified way and spoke to her softly to ease her embarrassment.

It was a charming incident in its contrast to the petty cruelties and palpable brutality that characterized so much of the street life of San Ysidro. The two, student and professor, looked like the kind of people for whom the Malecón and the Buenos Aires district had been constructed.

"What an opportunity," the elderly man was saying. "In my

youth one could always make the acquaintance of a pretty fellow student in this way."

"One still may," the girl said gaily. She was naturally pale, though blushing under the compliment. Her face was angular and handsome; in body she was a bit squat and not altogether suited to jeans. The old man carried her books as the two of them went into the building before which she had had her small accident. A worn brass plaque on the door identified it as a residence of the Christian Brothers.

Once inside they walked up a dusty flight of stairs and to the head of an immaculate corridor which had windows with lace curtains at each end. A European brother met them there, politely asked their names and told them that room five had been engaged for their seminar. The corridor had plastered walls and a wooden floor on which their steps reverberated.

In the room numbered five, five men sat at a polished round table. All five stood at the elderly man's entrance; they seemed to strain toward him, wanting to touch him. He was the object of their happiness.

"Compañeros," the elderly man said, *"salud."*

The terseness and dignity of his greeting held them in place. They took their seats again.

With a courtly smile, the old man placed the stack of books he had been carrying on the polished table, and extended his hand to the young woman.

"I am Aguirre," he told her.

The girl took his hand and held it. Her accident had in fact been the signal for his safe entry.

"We met once, Don Sebastián, but you wouldn't remember me. When you left we were all afraid . . . never to see you again."

"But here I am," Aguirre said. "And I'm not Don Sebastián to you, *compañera.*"

All in the room were smiling now. Aguirre himself was not well and was extremely tired. Within the past week he had visited foreign friends in several countries, had even made the transatlantic journey from Prague, a process which never failed to exhaust him utterly.

In Prague, in addition to business, there had been late nights with his old friends from the Spanish war—much spinning out of the past and hardly any talk of the future. Their relentless nostalgia discouraged and exasperated him and to his own grief he had found many of his old fellow soldiers—brothers and more than brothers from the terrible days of the defense of the University City—tiresome and redundant. Even more depressing to him than the burned-out nature of so many old comrades had been the occasions of his lack of communication with the young. These, fortunately, had been few—but they frightened him. His courtesy had served to conceal much impatience with empty nostalgia, rhetoric à la disco, self-indulgence and mindless bohemianism. He was relying on the same courtesy now, for few in the room had anything to tell him, in spite of his three years' absence from Tecan. He was eager for action, for hard information that would complete his strategic assessment, that would move things forward. There was only one person in the room who could provide for his requirements in this regard and he had now to wait, benign and courtly, until the real conversation could take place.

As he pretended to listen to young Comrade Rodo present her report on the student situation in the capital, he used his time as valuably as he could trying to read in the faces of the men around him, in their manner and demeanor, some record of the three years he had lost of Tecan. Of course, they in their turn were seeking out the reverse side of the record in watching him. The concentration that seemed focused on Rodo's assessment, as she shuffled her coded aides-mémoire, was profound.

Across the table from Aguirre sat an Atapa Indian called a la Torre. Taller and more broad-shouldered than most Atapas, he was otherwise physically typical of them. The Atapas were a Malay-like people, and even their artifacts resembled those of Southeast Asia. During the conquest, the Spaniards had thought of the Atapas as docile, although in the period before independence they had come to learn otherwise.

A la Torre himself was a small landowner and while it would be unfair to speak of him as vicious, he was, drunk or sober, feared by Indians and whites alike. A kulak, the Russians might call him. But their social designations did not apply well in Tecan.

Several attempts had been made on a la Torre's life both by

gentry concerned with mineral rights and ultra-right fanatics. Each had failed and some had occasional mortal consequences. He was the unquestioned leader of the southern group of Atapas, in spite or because of the ways in which his life differed from most of theirs. In his youth, he had been converted to Adventism by North American missionaries, but his enthusiasm for the gospel and its evangelists had evaporated during his two years at the National Technical College, obviated, it seemed, by his discovery of the Republic and the machine.

His experiences had left him with a curious and volatile variant of the Protestant ethic. He was an unstinting and indefatigable worker of strong ambition and great physical strength. His small holding, given over to scarce and hence relatively valuable vegetables and a small dairy herd, had been cleared from scrub jungle by his own muscle and sweat. When he had occasion to hire the labor of his fellow Atapas he paid them as generously as possible and supervised their work through terror. Yet his society had forced him to see his own and his people's work as a humiliation, surrounded and dominated as he was by those who did none or lived off that of others.

All work to a la Torre was physical work. Doctors and teachers he recognized as necessary, but they were not workers. Making reluctant exceptions for these professions, he was consumed by a serious and quite personal hatred for large groups of people whom he saw as living without working. The rich and the priests did none and he hated these most of all. The bourgeoisie did none. Nor did the gringos, the *gachupines*, the soldiery. Their existences consisted in living by trickery off the work of others and he was prepared to kill them in good conscience as he would those he caught stealing or cheating him at cards. He was thoroughly honest and a leader, not cruel but unyieldingly just in accordance with his perception of justice, which owed something to that of the Adventist God.

Looking covertly into his black Tonkinese eyes, Aguirre shuddered. The man was so thoroughly the emotional product of social forces as to pose a dilemma, one that Aguirre might find the energy to discuss over good Pilsener with his old comrades in the Charles Square. In terms of socialist human-

ism, a la Torre was almost too good to be true. That history
has provided us in our poor country with such treasures,
Aguirre thought gratefully! And *que huevon*, the old man
thought. Invincible!

Seated beside the formidable Atapa—owlish, effervescent
with wise humor and contained intelligence—was another
personified dilemma, Héctor Morelos de Medina, one of the
few surviving members of the old Communist Party of Tecan
and one of Aguirre's oldest friends. Ironical, learned, the best
of company and, most rare in San Ysidro, a true wit—
Morelos ran a bookshop in the Buenos Aires neighborhood.
For many years as a Communist in Tecan he had led a
terribly dangerous life, endured exile, acted with the greatest
bravery in the face of torture and excruciating sacrifice. Now,
like Aguirre's other old friend in Compostela, Oscar Ocampo,
Morelos had become a North American spy. Intelligence
abroad had not identified the motive for his defection but it
did not seem to be ideological. Presumably it was banal like
Ocampo's. Aguirre had always been close to Morelos; certainly he preferred his company to that of Stakhanovites like a
la Torre. On the other hand it could not be said that he was
profoundly shaken. He had known many defectors in his lifetime and plenty of them had construed for themselves the best
of motives. Sometimes the nature of their treason was objective only. It was disagreeable and regrettable for Sebastián
Aguirre to now consider his friend Morelos an enemy in war,
but it was certainly not impossible.

Señorita Rodo finished her report and everyone nodded. She
was Urban Youth, Studentdom, Woman; an essential. A good-
hearted rich kid who might or might not have a mean streak
for good or ill when the time came. No question of guts; she
was risking interrogation by the Guardia. Aguirre gave her his
choicest approving smile.

Beside Rodo—the moderates. Agustín Baz, a manufacturer
of soap, a mestizo of poor origin who had worked his way to
enlightened wealth and been rewarded with sharp dealing and
extortion at the hands of the ruling clique. He was also in
competition with foreigners. Most of the local capitalists endured and took what they could for themselves; Baz had the
gift of resentment and more balls. He preferred facing revolution to being openly cheated. Baz was as honest as a la Torre

and ran the clandestine organization in San Ysidro effectively.
He had moments of tactical brilliance. Yet, he would not go
the distance, Aguirre thought. The man was no traitor and no
weakling but they were simply not fighting for the same things
and Baz would finish in Miami, embittered, a *gusano*, as the
Cubans said. He himself had not the remotest idea that this
would come to pass, but Aguirre, listening to his report on the
state of the nation's finances, felt fairly certain of it. Naturally, he was always ready to be proven wrong.

Next, inevitably, the priest—at the moment another essential. Monsignor Golz was of partly Swiss origin, another honest man conversant with and not unsympathetic to Marx.
Inspired by the example of Calles, a disciple of Gustavo
Gutiérrez, he thought of himself as an intellectual. Aguirre, as
much a connoisseur of *engagé* priests as he was anticlerical,
thought him fatuous. But there was no question in his mind of
the necessity of having Golz, and in his portly, priestly way,
Golz was a fanatic. Aguirre was much more certain of Baz's
ultimate desertion than of Golz's. His fanaticism might take
him either way—one could never be sure with priests.

The moderates, Baz and Golz, were ill at ease. They were
aware of the patronizing and faint scorn of nearly all the
other participants, and the monsignor, as he described conditions on the Caribbean coast, was particularly aware of the
distaste and distrust with which the terrible a la Torre
watched him. Even young Rodo curled her lip as she listened.
And of course Morelos, the CIA stool pigeon, was least able
to dissemble his amusement at this ecclesiastical presence.

Listening carefully to Golz's report, and giving no evidence
of any suppressed contumely, was the man whom Aguirre had
come to see. He was a man in his middle thirties, dark-
skinned and massive, with a face not easily forgotten. His hair
was thick and straight, he was bull-necked and broad-faced
and down the length of his broken nose from brows to nostrils
was a jagged crooked scar, showing the red imperfectly healed
flesh of a deep wound. The coarseness of his features and
the disfiguring mark of violence seemed to sum up the fortunes of a Tecanecan *campesino*; in fact the young man's
origins and career were in no sense proletarian. His father had
been a botanist at the Institute of Sciences and he himself had
degrees in art and in art history from the University of Cali-

fornia. For years he had been a moderately successful painter, spending most of his time in New York and in Mexico City; presently he was chairman of the Art Department at the National University. He was on social terms with the families of several presidential henchmen and with quite a few Americans in the diplomatic community.

He was the man, Aguirre thought, reassured, watching him nod encouragement to the rambling monsignor. They thought well of him abroad. The Americans thought they knew him, liked him, had no reason to fear him. He looked as vital, as capable as ever. He was the man who would lead—during the revolution and afterwards. Among those in the room, only Aguirre and the young man himself realized this. The realization had taken Aguirre a long time to arrive at; the young man himself seemed always to have known it.

From his suit pocket, Aguirre drew a forbidden cigarette— Benson & Hedges—and waited, smoking, for the mock council to draw to its conclusion. The scarred young man was his only true collaborator among the lot of them and there were things now that required urgent consultation.

The pro forma strategy session was not ended easily. All participants required a stroke for their self-esteem, the spy required reassurance. Roles had to be assigned and *abrazos* exchanged with the venerable and distinguished visitor. It seemed a long time before they had all gone and Aguirre was left alone with the scarred man, whose name was Emilio Ortega Curtis.

When they were across the table from each other in the abandoned conference room, Aguirre lit another cigarette and offered Ortega the pack. Ortega smiled and shook his head.

"How was Prague?"

"Beautiful as ever. A bit subdued, as you may imagine."

"Well," Emilio Ortega said, "too bad. But that's their problem, of course. How did you find our friends abroad?"

"How?" Aguirre weighed his words. "Cautious. Patronizing. *Faux naïve.*"

"Then nothing's changed."

"Nothing essential. Tell me about Tecan."

"As they say in the Koran, Don Sebastián, no one has promised us tomorrow. But I think, my friend, you've lived to see the revolution."

Aguirre's frail heart began to beat in his throat.

"And have I just seen the provisional government—more or less?"

"Some of it. The same sort of people. Except, of course, for Morelos. Whom we know is a Yanqui spy."

Aguirre nodded. "Sad, no? I can't know how you feel, Emil, but—myself—I'll miss him."

"I miss him," Ortega said. "I've already mourned for him."

They sat without speaking, observing something like a moment of silence for the man's treachery.

"If one must have a moral," Ortega said, "I propose: Look too long into yourself and you won't know whom you're seeing."

"He was always," Aguirre said, "an exquisite ironist."

"Well," Ortega said. "Small suffering countries don't require ironists. When we require ironists we'll produce our own. Without help from the United States."

"But not too many, one hopes."

"The representatives of our provisional government—what did you think of them? The 'usual suspects'?"

"Yes, I suppose. I have hopes for Golz, as priests go."

"I do too," Ortega said. "His organization within the church was built very discreetly and subtly. He's lined up some solid ones for this stage."

"Godoy, I think, is his man, no?"

"Godoy is among his chiefs. Like him, but not a man to my taste."

"You're not Spanish enough to appreciate Godoy."

Ortega shrugged. He was indifferent to the legend of Spain and the self-obsession of Spaniards. Even Tecanecan *criollos* like Aguirre, with their peninsular pieties, offended his *indigenismo*.

"I'm a man of UCLA," he said. "In spite of what they say, we weren't all mystics in Los Angeles."

"Clearly not," Aguirre agreed, then changed the subject. "You're aware, I hope, that the gringos have filled up the country with spies. Their activity is more than routine. We have this from primary sources abroad."

"We're aware. They're here for the show, so we're making it hot for them. In fact, a la Torre shot one in the mountains last week."

"You're joking! A U.S. citizen?"

Ortega was unable to repress a smile; in a moment his expression sobered.

"Not merely a U.S. citizen but an imported gringo."

Dr. Aguirre whistled between his teeth.

"A man named Cole showed himself in Extremadura. He claimed to be a journalist and full of sympathy and he expressed great interest in visiting our military formations. He had just come from Oscar Ocampo. A la Torre took him up to First Brigade. He talked a great deal and he demonstrated familiarity with every sort of weapon. He had been in Vietnam—he told us this himself. We held back awhile—we wanted to be fair and avoid a provocation. The third day there he was court-martialed and executed."

"I approve," Aguirre said. "Let them stop taking us for fools. Let them find out that Yanquis die as easily as peasants. And perhaps," Aguirre said, "the regrettable time has come to do something about Oscar. He seems to enjoy making difficulties."

"The time has come. But we have to clear it abroad—or so we're told."

"I grant you dispensation," Aguirre said. "Let the Compostelan comrades have him." He stood up from his hard-backed chair and began pacing the room. Then tiring, he took a different chair. "Thank God for the Atapas," he said, his eyes closed. "The Fascists truly screwed themselves when they went mad over those mineral rights. They tore the last spines out of the social structure."

Ortega smiled in agreement.

"For forty years," Sebastián Aguirre said, "we worked to bring the Atapas to our side and like pious donkeys they ignored us. It would have taken us forty more without the mineral grab."

"We have them now," Ortega said. "Moreover, the government has taken to drafting more and more Atapas into the Guardia to find reliable troops—and also of course to demoralize them. When these Indians get out they're changed men. And right now half of the Guardia is Atapa."

"My God," Aguirre said, "it's going to happen! I don't know if I ever believed it."

"There were times, my friend, when you were the only man in the country who did."

"Morelos and I," Aguirre said.

There was a tray in the center of the table that held a pitcher of cold coffee and some cups. Ortega poured them both a quarter cup and they drank.

"I want to talk strategy now," Aguirre said. "Is there a chance that Señor Morelos or these good brothers have placed some electronic instruments here? A bug?"

"We have had help from abroad to determine that. Not here."

"You must realize," Aguirre told him, "that I have instructions for you. More help from abroad. Most of it is so much shit. So now I'll ask you what you propose to do."

"With pleasure. Sunday—a demonstration here in the capital. A dangerous one, a bad one—but as you'll see a necessary one for our purposes. They'll bring in more Guardia from the mountains. A day passes and we hit the Libertad Guardia barracks on the edge of town in small force with automatic weapons. The Guardia troops there are slightly less than half of them Atapas—we don't expect to take it but anything can happen and we'll see. Should we take it, we won't try to hold it but we may gain some arms and recruits. While this is happening the main force will move. The five Atapa brigades will take command of the cordillera and liberate the fincas. In a single offensive they can close the Pan-American Highway north of the capital, close the Pacific highway and the river. The Guardia will never dislodge them, even with aircraft. This is the important thing, and you may depend on its not being in the newspapers. We've had tons of automatic weapons and surface-to-air missiles flown in and we haven't lost a single shipment. Guardia troops going into the mountains will meet Atapas more numerous and better armed than themselves. They will have no support whatever from the population. The Guardia air arm has no experience against surface-to-air missiles and the bastards don't know how to fly anyway—at least not in a combat situation. The gringos trained them in close air support and if they try doing what they've been taught they'll cease to exist in those mountains within an hour. The ground-to-air missiles are miraculous; they're easy to hide and two half-trained men can use them. They'll be the only ordnance from the socialist bloc we're using and they're untraceable."

"Instructions specify Israeli weapons wherever possible."

"Well," Ortega said, "in that respect instructions are wise. Everyone knows the Israelis handle supply for the gringos here to see to the Guardia's needs and Israeli weapons for the most part are what we'll use. If they're captured we can say we got them from the Guardia."

"Bravo," said Sebastián Aguirre.

"Now prior to the main thrusts we have a diversion on the Caribbean coast."

"Interesting," Aguirre said, "but it's proverbial they don't care to fight down there."

"Forget proverbs. It's going to be a good test. We'll hit the foreign property there and we'll kill some notable sons of bitches. The Yanquis are convinced things are safe there, they think it's a little apolitical paradise and they want to use their property to build resorts now. We shall disillusion them and upset the digestion of their guests. Maybe we can capture a Club Med, eh, Sebastián?"

"Very bad for our fighters' morale," Aguirre said drily. "And what would the French say? Did Golz's man Godoy organize this?"

"To his credit, he did. He arranged for excellent weapons from the old-time smugglers there, so the enemy will be badly outgunned, at least in the beginning. It will frighten the gringos, move troops from the real theater of war and politicize the population. Godoy also cultivated the active support of some progressive missionaries."

"An effective man, for sure."

"No doubt of it. Now we can't depend on success here—the methods are primitive, the Guardia may intercept our weaponry, we may not prevail. But nothing is lost if we fail here and it's a traditional region of exploitation. We owe our people a front there."

"One word of advice," Aguirre said. "Don't leave Godoy running a diversion. He's too good, especially with the Indians."

"I agree. While the southern Atapas are fighting under a la Torre, we'll have Godoy with the Atapas in the north. A former Guardia officer, an Atapa, will be in military control."

"It's going to work," Aguirre said finally.

"Clearly. The mountains are the key, the Atapas. The roads and the rivers closed, the coast unsafe, insurrection everywhere! Every night rockets in the capital. Within ten days we'll have Tecan. San Ysidro falls as an epilogue."

"Abroad," Aguirre said, "they're afraid of the North Americans."

"This is shortsighted of them, with all due respect. They, of all people, should be aware of how it's going in the world. For one thing we have a most moderate non-Marxist manifesto prepared and the North American embassy will be among the first to get copies. More importantly, a lot of gringo asses got kicked forever in Vietnam and Congress will never authorize any intervention on behalf of this present government."

"Very good," Aguirre said. "We can give the Yanquis the stick and the carrot—their own favorite method. We'll be killing off their lousy spies while we're reassuring them. They've got that coming for their own murders."

"Precisely," Ortega said. "And what can they do—destabilize us? Destabilize Tecan?"

The two men laughed together.

"I want a drink," Aguirre said. "I want to drink to this now in case I die tomorrow."

"Only one, compadre," Ortega said. "You're a living treasure of the nation at the moment and I want to keep you that way."

"A piss-poor treasure."

"Nonetheless," Ortega said, walking toward the door, "you are hereby nationalized. Later I can lay flowers on your monument—now I require you alive."

During the time that Ortega was out of the room, the beating of Sebastián Aguirre's heart made him clutch his breast. He felt nearly pulverized with excitement at the prospect of victory yet terrified as he had never before been of loss. Someone had said that the second-saddest thing in the world was not to achieve one's life's ambition and that the saddest was to achieve it. Who had said it? A Frenchman? Clemenceau? No, no. Oscar Wilde. He sat looking through the curtained window at the pseudo-Parisian façade on the building across the street.

After a few moments, Ortega returned carrying two glasses and a bottle with a few inches of Spanish brandy. He poured out the liquor and handed a glass to Aguirre.

"Salud," Aguirre declaimed, and drained his glass. Ortega

was amused and touched at the antique chivalry of his style. He returned the toast.

"Where in the world," Aguirre asked presently, "did you find a la Torre? The man makes me tremble."

Ortega laughed.

"Yes, a la Torre was a find. A fierce one, no?"

"It isn't his ferocity," Aguirre said, "it's his essence, his life. The man is history. The personification of every Marxian insight. Everything I've ever believed about socialist humanism—it's true in this man."

"So true," Ortega said, "as to be a vulgarization."

Aguirre laughed in spite of himself.

"*Compadre*, we are all vulgarizations of history. We have to live it out by the day—life, unlike sound philosophy, is vulgar."

"Indeed. And you approve of Golz? And Godoy?"

"Golz, yes. For this stage certainly. And even more of Godoy, although I know you dislike him personally."

"You've rarely met the man, Don Sebastián."

Under Ortega's disapproving eye, Sebastián Aguirre poured himself another small brandy.

"I've never met a la Torre until this morning, still I approve of him because of what I know. Now let me tell you something about the Godoys of our world."

We'll be off to Spain, damn the place, Ortega thought. Always Spain. Why not Algeria? Why not Angola, Vietnam, China?

"In Irún we faced the Carlists. I can tell you, my friend, they were superb fighters and they had great conviction. In a way, they were the most reactionary of all the Fascist troops. We called them Fascists too but they were not really such. They were fighting a jihad."

Ortega nodded politely.

"I don't think you've ever heard me speak against the Spanish Republic," Aguirre went on, "but between ourselves there were some rather sordid bourgeois elements active within it. Some of these thought to act progressively and enrich themselves at the same time through the seizure of church lands in the north. Madre de Dios, what a storm this produced. In the name of Juan Carlos, this fugitive from a Velázquez, led by their priests and by mounted aristocrats—the real thing,

Emilio, not like these *ratones* here but men who spoke their language and their dialect—they turned out to destroy us in the name of Jesus Christ."

"Like the Cristeros in Mexico," Ortega suggested.

Aguirre made a sour face. "The Cristeros were the stage of farce. An imitation, a primitive caricature."

Ortega felt the first surge of sympathy he had ever felt for Cristeros. Farce to the *gachupín* Aguirre because they were brown Americans and not men of Holy Spain.

"These Carlists were in the grip of a metaphysical politics from which grew baroque mutant fruit. There arose such arabesque absurdities as anarcho-Carlism—all men would be equal and all political organization rooted in the sky. The preposterous Carlos would be king-surrogate for Jesus Christ himself, who would be the true, directly responsible King of Spain. Under His reign there could be only virtue and honesty, liberty, equality, fraternity based on the Sermon on the Mount. Imagine it, Emilio, we found ourselves fighting creatures out of Engels' history, men who in their hearts believed much of what we believed, who should by rights have been shoulder to shoulder with us, but were fighting us to the death. Well, we could never say so in those days and circumstances but many of us admired them."

"Courage and conviction are always to some degree admirable," Ortega said with a shrug.

"And you, Emilio, say 'so what?' And I agree. But let me tell you that I think that Godoy is a bit like those men. I think he fights for the peasants and the Indians because whether he knows it or not, he deeply desires the just rule of the Lord. Probably, he will never realize this—certainly we must hope not, for his sake. I'm sure he sees himself as a humanist and a student of Marxism. But I think unconsciously it is the kingdom of God he fights for. Emilio, the best revolutionaries, the first Communists may come from among such men!"

"This must be what I don't like about him," Ortega said, smiling. "I admit only that he's good at his job and for now that's good enough for me."

"Ah, yes," Aguirre said archly. "UCLA. He fights for Christ and you for John Dewey."

"Tell me, Sebastián," Ortega said, pouring out a brandy for himself, "what shall we do about our late comrade, Morelos?

In fact," he told the old man, "I've already decided. But I should like your opinion all the same."

Aguirre was taken aback and impressed. He felt justly chastened. Ortega had terminated the anecdotes and the levity with talk of treason and its consequences. It was calculated, brutal and to the point; it reminded Aguirre of the Old Man. The Old Man might have done it the same way. How right he himself had been, Aguirre thought, in deciding that Ortega must lead.

"Do you think me sentimental?" Aguirre asked his young leader. "Do you imagine I would plead for him?" Only once in his career had Aguirre opposed an execution for reasons of friendship and his advocacy had nearly cost him his own life at the hands of André Marty and the NKVD clique. Only Stalin's intervention had saved him. Never again had he undertaken to defend one condemned and though he had suffered in his conscience as a result, further reflection had always convinced him that the policy of unyielding severity was ultimately correct. In the case of Morelos it was not in question. There could be no mitigating circumstances to regret here.

"Perhaps I'm sentimental," Ortega said, "because my first instinct was somehow to spare him. For his long service and his gray hairs. I thought we might dispatch him abroad with his ten favorite classics in the presidential airplane. Or wrap him in ribbons for the Yanqui embassy."

"But now you think otherwise?"

"Tomorrow, when our people here are underground and you and I are in the mountains with First Brigade—Señor Morelos will be arrested by the Guardia as a proven Communist. Then you may be sure he'll howl for the gringos and he'll learn whether they retain any interest in him after he's no use to them."

Aguirre finished his brandy.

"This," he said, "is only simple justice." He would not himself have handled it with such studied harshness. But he was not made to be a leader.

"Now let me tell you something, Don Sebastián—pardon me for addressing you so—we are fighting for a new Tecan with a new leadership. The leader will not be John Dewey and he will certainly not be Jesus Christ. Not Bolívar, or Jefferson

or the ghost of Pope John. Not, as we say, the People. Nor
even the Party, because all of these entities are either dead or
not yet truly formed."

"Who then?"

"With permission," Ortega said, "and with your invaluable
assistance—me!"

"Am I to take this for cynicism, Emilio?"

Ortega looked away from him and out through the curtained window.

"Cynicism? That I—a plain man, a mediocre artist, perhaps
even a mediocre fighter—take it upon myself to bring justice
to our accursed suffering country? To bring health to her
children, dignity to her desperate poor? To replace her absurdity in the eyes of the world with pride—to make housing,
hospitals, schools for her masses of ignorant? To leave sound
philosophy and engage life which we both know to be so
vulgar? To dispense life to some and death to others in the
name of a form of humanity which for all we know may
never exist?"

The old man listening to Ortega rose from his chair. Ortega
turned his back on him.

"Hombre," Ortega said, "there is no Jesus Christ. There is
no philosophy in a shack or in the gutter. There is not yet
even such a thing as the People. There are only poor creatures
like you and me, my comrade—and we propose to bring these
things about. We propose unto death."

Ortega turned toward Aguirre again. "Cynicism? I would
have to be mad, would I not, to cherish all this cynically—in
the name of my own glory? Perhaps I am mad to propose
these things at all. Yet, as an act of faith, I do propose
them."

Aguirre fixed his eyes on Ortega and took a step toward
him. The old man spoke truly of himself when he said that he
was not sentimental. He had heard such words from the cynical and the mad. He had seen much of war and executions,
death and cruelty. He raised his palsied hand in a fist.

"I don't know," he said to Ortega, "whether one may thank
History. She's a cold bitch. But I thank her now. I thank her
with love that I've lived to see you and this day. I beg her to
allow me to see the days that are coming. You are my son,
Ortega . . ." The old man laughed with pleasure and to cover

his emotion. He could say no more and advanced no further. It was time to refrain from embracing. Perhaps, later.

Ortega returned his salute with a smile. He was embarrassed at having run on. He supposed that the suggestion of his cynicism had provoked him; moreover he was an artist, a man of temperament.

"And you, my father," he told Aguirre. "Without you— nothing. I thank you."

If the gringos could see us here, he thought, it would amuse them. "So," old Aguirre said. "Death in one eye and dishonor in the other, eh. We shall have a drama."

They raised nearly empty glasses to each other.

"Victory," Ortega said. *"Patria o muerte."*

The dark came down quickly after sunset. The lights of the coastal fishing boats grew dimmer and more distant abaft; eastward the evening star was rising, the wind steady. The *Cloud* plowed into its faint resistance making seven or eight knots. From the galley came the smell of frying steak.

Pablo sat beside the after hatch, watching the wake in starlight. Freddy Negus came out on deck and called him forward for chow.

Mrs. Callahan was leaning over the galley stove, a rum and tonic secured on a rack beside her. Strips of sirloin were warming on the pan, there was a huge pot of boiled greens.

"She's a good feeder," Pablo said. He was cheerful.

"Oh, you bet," Mrs. Callahan said. "Get yourself a drink and go sit down."

Pablo helped himself to a moderate measure of light rum and took it down to the fancy paneled compartment. The crew's lounge. Tino came down behind him, smelling of diesel fuel, and ducked into the head to wash.

At opposite quarters of the mahogany table, drinks set before them, were Negus and Mr. Callahan. Pablo picked himself a chair and sat down. After a moment Tino came out of the head, ducked up to the galley to draw a Coke from the freezer and joined them.

Pablo looked around at the men in the compartment; all of them were watching him. Callahan looked boozy and affable.

Freddy Negus, scratching his ear, looked unhappy; Tino, sleepy-eyed now, expressionless.

"What do you think, Pablo?" Mr. Callahan asked.

Pablo smiled. "What do I think about what, Mr. Callahan? You got a nice boat here. She's a good feeder. I ain't even done any work yet."

Mrs. Callahan, in the galley, was humming "Amazing Grace."

"You will, though," Callahan said. "For example, can you handle an M-16?"

"I don't see 'em every day. But I'm familiar with the weapon."

"We may be dealing with unpleasant people and we may have to defend ourselves. How's that grab you?"

"That's how it always is," Pablo said. After a moment, he said: "I hope you're not talking about the U.S. Coast Guard."

"Christ," Negus said to him, "you think we plan to shoot it out with the goddamn U.S. Coast Guard? I was hoping you had more sense than that."

"Local-type cops, maybe?"

"Not too likely either. If we have that kind of problem we tend to run. We're a lot faster than we look. Thanks to our engineer."

Pablo surmised that Mr. Callahan was referring to Tino. He nodded.

"It's thieves I'm thinking about. We have a few exchanges to make with various parties that we'd like to see secure. Just so everybody keeps their side of the bargain."

Pablo sipped his rum with satisfaction. It was everything he might have hoped.

"You got the right man, no shit, Mr. Callahan. I never backed out of a hassle in my life and I never let my people down neither."

"We your people?" Negus asked him.

"You treat me right, you're my people. Anybody that knows me knows that."

"We don't let our people down either, Pablo," Callahan told him solemnly, "and we've been in business a long time."

Pablo raised his hands, palms up.

"Good enough!"

Mr. Callahan rose to his feet. "Let's have another drink, *compañeros*. . . . Deedee," he called to the galley, "come and have one with us." He started toward the single step that led up to the galley space and in climbing, tripped and staggered. Negus and Tino exchanged looks as he did so. For a moment, the Callahans whispered together in the galley, then returned; Deedee Callahan carried a tray with the bottles of rum and of tonic and some iced glasses. When she had settled herself in a captain's chair everyone except Tino poured himself another drink. Then it seemed Mrs. Callahan was lighting a joint. She passed it to her husband, who passed it to Tino. Tino took two deep tokes and passed it on to Pablo. On this occasion he smoked some and passed the joint to Negus. Negus passed it back to Deedee Callahan without taking any. It went around again in the same fashion and then Mr. Callahan declined a third toke.

"Das all for me," Tino said.

"Me, too," said Pablo.

"Well," said Mrs. Callahan, "the more for me."

Pablo felt her eyes on him. He looked through the smoke into their blue watchfulness.

Tino stood up suddenly.

"Goin' forward," he announced. "Got to watch de bottom out here."

"What about your chow?" Negus called after him, but he was gone.

Mrs. Callahan leaned back in her chair and finished the joint. Callahan was pouring himself another drink, Negus moodily finishing the one in his hand. The woman worked her joint down to a ring of resin, balancing it on her lip with a hemostat. When it was finished, she put the hemostat away.

"Want to help me out, Pablo?"

"Sure," Pablo said.

From the galley, they could see Tino sitting in one of the cockpit chairs, his head and shoulders faintly green in the unnatural light of the Fathometer. A soft merengue was coming in over the UHF; Pablo watched Mrs. Callahan's lower body, encased in the tightest of faded denim jeans, sway mellifluously to its beat. She was gathering metal plates from an overhead dish rack. For the first time he noticed a printed sign posted over the stove that read YOU BETTER BELIZE IT. When she turned to him he was laughing at the sign.

"What's funny, pardner?" She smiled and brushed the damp hair from around her eyes. He could not tell how old she was—forty, more or less. Her face was lean, creased around the eyes, sun-cured. When she set the dishes down on the counter beside the stove, he felt her breast brush his bare arm, the nipple distinct and distended under the soft cotton of her sweat shirt.

"Just feelin' good," Pablo said.

"Feelin' good is easy," Mrs. Callahan said. She said it with such gravity that he felt compelled to reflection.

"No," he said after a moment. "Not so easy."

They watched each other, locked in the drug; she was looking at him with wary amusement, still easing to the merengue.

"Funny kind of boat this is," Pablo said.

"Yes," Deedee Callahan assured him. "This is your basic funny boat. Now do something for me, Pablo. Give the boys their vittles."

She took the steak from the pan and placed a strip on each of the five dishes. On each dish she spooned out some of the greens from the stewpot, then handed two of the plates to Tabor. She winked at him and motioned with her head toward the dining compartment.

Pablo did not chafe under his servitude. He served Negus and Mr. Callahan graciously, setting the steaming plates before them.

I goddamn well got her, he was thinking. Any old damn time.

When he went back into the galley she gave him a plate for Tino in the cockpit. He brought it forward and placed it on the chart table; Tino gave him a brief bad eye in return. Pablo smiled. The man must know, he thought, what was passing between himself and Mrs. Callahan.

There was a plate for him steaming in the galley; he brought it down to the table and seated himself across from Negus and Callahan. Mrs. Callahan joined them presently, carrying her own plate and some *salsa*, salt and pepper on a tray. The *Cloud* took the gentle seas with a slow fore-and-aft pitch.

"Beats shrimping," Pablo said, breaking the silence that had settled over the dinner table. He assaulted his tenderized steak with concentration.

"We'll do some shrimping by and by," Mr. Callahan told him. "But as you have undoubtedly surmised—shrimping is not how we make our way through life."

"Yeah," Pablo said. "I surmised that."

"What else you surmised?" Negus asked him.

"You told me not to ask questions, cap," Pablo said, "so I didn't ask you any." He looked around the table. "I'm easy to get along with."

"Fred," Mr. Callahan said to Negus, "you're the best seaman in the world but you're a balls of a politician." He turned his soft look on Pablo. "What we're wondering, fella—you being lately in the Coast Guard and all that—is what you make of us. We're interested in your educated guess."

"O.K.," Pablo said. "You're running something. I would have said dope but I don't think so now. If you were going up to the States from a Dutch place like St. Joost I'd say diamonds. But you say you're not messing with the States." He cut himself another piece of steak. "Computer parts maybe. Calculators, like that. Only this boat's not big enough for a high-scoring run with that kind of weight. And the whole deal feels sort of heavy-duty. Between one thing and another— guns. That's a good old-time trade."

"Yes, it is," Callahan said.

"If we're going to Cuba," Pablo said, "we got our work cut out for us."

"We're not going to Cuba."

"Well, good. If it's not there it could be any one of ten or a dozen places. There's lots of petty-ass politics down here, right? I don't even follow it."

"All right," Callahan said. "Let me give you the word on a need-to-know basis as it were. You don't need to know where we're going. In a day or two we'll be in Nieuw Utrecht on St. Joost taking on ice and groceries. After dark we're loading cargo on the other side of the island. What we want from you is a little help with the groceries and what we especially want is you standing by while we take on the cargo. Also when we deliver it, because that's the moment of truth, *hombre*. You'll get to do some shrimping tomorrow night too, in case you're interested."

"I wish someone would tell me what I stood to get paid," Pablo said.

"When we figure our costs," Negus said, "we'll tell you."

"It's a reasonable question," Callahan said equitably. "You can figure on at least five hundred a day for the next few days. It'll beat your Coast Guard pay."

"I guess so," Pablo said.

"Think that'll keep you happy?" Negus said. "Because we have to keep you happy. We insist on it."

"I think everybody's gonna do all right," Pablo said.

Everyone in the cabin laughed; Pablo found it disconcerting.

When dinner was over, Negus and Mr. Callahan took their coffee to a small compartment aft of the central cabin and closed the teak door behind them. Pablo found himself on mess duty with the lady once again. The radio in the cockpit was tuned to one of the missionary stations that broadcast Jesus messages—the Baptist missionaries had the most powerful transmitter in the islands.

"Whereunto shall I liken the Kingdom of God?" a youthful Nebraskan voice inquired over the UHF, "it is like leaven . . ." Tino was making notations on his Loran chart.

She had gone back to smoking grass. It was the strongest grass Pablo had ever drawn of and she seemed to take joint after joint of it. After two or three tokes, the enveloping papers grew moist and tarry with deep green resin. Pablo declined. When the washing up was finished they went back to the cleared table.

"What brought you down here, Pablo?"

"Just wandering around," Pablo said. He was thinking that they were all the same.

"You're kind of a throwback, aren't you? In the jet age?"

"I been on plenty of jets," Pablo told her.

"Didn't you like the Coast Guard?"

"I liked it all right until they started turning me around."

"I thought that was what they were all about."

"Some guys will sit still for anything," Pablo explained. "They got no self-respect. Any kind of militaristic trash, they don't object to it."

Pablo had picked up the anti-militaristic angle working at the Coast Guard district headquarters in Boston and incorporated it into his line. It had worked fairly well with the girls around there, and Mrs. Callahan, although not so young and tenderhearted, seemed to be a little like them.

"So you got radicalized, is that it?"

Pablo felt as though he had been softly counterpunched. He rolled with it.

"I had this CPO on my case who was like a Fascist-type guy. He kept at it, so I cold-cocked him. Broke his jaw. I was looking at time, see what I mean? So I skipped."

"Is that a literal story, Pablo," Mrs. Callahan asked sympathetically, "or is it kind of symbolic?"

"What?" Pablo asked. He did not necessarily insist that women believe everything that they were told, but he was not used to their calling him a liar.

She put her joint down and looked sincerely thoughtful.

"The thing is," she said, "when you hear the same kind of story from a lot of different people you wonder about the little details. Because no two things ever happen the same way, do they, Pablo?"

"I guess not," he said.

"Of course, they don't. So you tell me that story and right away I want to know—because I'm a curious sort—what's special about Pablo Tabor. As opposed to all the other guys who broke the CPO's jaw and so forth."

Smart, he thought. But smart or not they were all the same.

"A jaw got broke," Pablo told her, "and it wasn't mine. Somebody tried to fuck with me. So I'm over the hill and on this boat and that's my story."

"And they call you Pablo. Is that a nickname or what?"

"It's my name," he told her.

"But it's Spanish."

"My mother was Indian," Pablo said. It was true to an extent, but to what extent was a question lost in centuries.

"I knew it," Mrs. Callahan said quietly.

That's what she goes for, Pablo thought. He had run across it before. He was aware that she had eased her chair against his and he felt her body again, her long leg in smooth clean denim.

"This funny boat where you live?" he asked her.

"So it would seem," she said. "It just goes on and on."

"Maybe you don't like it too much."

"It has its moments."

When he put his hand against her soft sheathed thigh, she was suddenly somber.

"Goodness," she said.

He slid his hand down to her knee and back up, fingering

an inner seam and the flesh it lined. Then he closed his fist and rested the back of his hand on the film of denim. It was a physical stalemate. With Tino in the cockpit, Callahan and Negus on the other side of a door, there was nothing more he dared do.

"You take your pleasures where you find them, do you, Pablo?"

"My kind of life you do."

"Mine too," she said.

She turned her head to look at him and he saw that under the weathered skin, the various set wrinkles and the small boozy sacs below her eyes—there was something like a kid about her.

"Hey," he said after a moment, "we're gonna get in trouble." He was embarrassed at the standoff and his palms were beginning to sweat.

The woman laughed silently. "Trouble?"

"Ain't we?"

"What's a little more trouble," she asked, "on this funny boat?"

The small teak door to the inner compartment opened and Freddy Negus put his head out. In the moment, Pablo decided, Negus had seen all there was to see.

"Jack would like you with us for a while, Deedee. If you don't mind."

She rose slowly from under Pablo's hand, her own hand touched his shoulder. "Right you are."

Negus was watching Pablo as he held the compartment door for Mrs. Callahan.

"Why don't you get some sleep, son?"

"Thought you might want me to take the wheel from Tino."

"Tino's all right. If he wants a few zees we can go on automatic for three or four hours."

"Well, O.K. then." He stood up and stretched. "Guess I'll go back aft then."

Negus nodded and they exchanged good-nights.

Ambling back to the lazaret, Orion ablaze over the starboard quarter and the sea rolling easy under the boards, Pablo paused to lean over the rail. He was flushed and horny with his conquest of the soft rich lady. As he lounged, scheming in the starry darkness, he became aware of voices sounding from somewhere in the innards of the boat. He was standing over the forward ice hold. The voices were those of Negus and Mr. Callahan.

Pablo took a look around and lowered himself into the half-covered hold; its interior still smelled of shrimp and of another substance, vaguely familiar but beyond his recall. There was a half inch of water on the flooring.

Moving to the bulkhead closest to the compartment in which he had taken dinner, he pressed his ear against the damp boards. It was almost completely dark where he stood, except for the scattering of stars visible beyond the edge of the hatch cover overhead.

"The old Jew's losing his grip," Callahan was saying in his whiskey-confident voice. "He's hitting the sauce. There's a certain vacancy there."

"I wouldn't attempt to exploit that," Negus replied. "I think it would be unwise."

"It would be plumb fatal," Callahan said. "Even half out of it old Naftali's worth ten of the punks you see around now."

"Speaking of punks . . ." Negus began—but Callahan cut him off.

"Speaking of punks—stay off the kid's back. I don't want him getting all disgruntled and paranoid. We don't have to live with him long and he's going to come in handy."

"Handy for what?" Negus asked. "For playing kneesies with Dee is all."

"You playing kneesies with him, Dee?"

"I confess," Pablo heard her say; he was startled. "I was playing hot kneesies with him. I dig him."

"If you fuck him," Callahan said, "that rather makes him one of the family. I think that's going too far."

Negus uttered a series of low cautioning obscenities. "I wish the governance around here would pull its socks up. We're doing serious business and the whole vessel's stoned, drunk or sopored."

There was a brief silence and then laughter.

"Pablo's all right," Callahan said. "For our purposes."

"I gotta admit he ain't as bad as some of 'em," Negus said. "He's a hard-ass and that's good if he knows his place in things."

"I think he does," said Mrs. Callahan. "Pablo Tabor is one

of life's little yo-yos. He wants to please and he'll do just fine."

His ear pressed against the cold sweating woodwork, Pablo's mind beheld the picture of a red yo-yo on a red, white and blue string with a store sticker on it that said "Made in Japan." He had forgotten that he was high; he was more puzzled than angry. I'm gonna fuck her brains out, he thought.

Negus was swearing again. "You see the fucking weaponry he had on him? He was armed to the goddamn teeth. Shit!"

Another silence and Negus said: "Tino don't like him."

"Tino's not too big on the whole number," Callahan said.

"Well," Deedee Callahan said, "Tino's a fucking mystic. How can you go by Tino?"

"I'm inclined to go by him," Negus said. "I been with him fifteen years in all weather."

Crouched in the hold, Pablo heard a step on the deck above him. He heaved himself against the boards and saw a shadow pass between his hiding place and the night sky. It would be Tino, he thought. Coming up from the lazaret. From going through his gear. He bent lower and listened.

"Naftali still take his money up front?" It was Negus.

"First thing that happens is Naftali gets his dough. He'll be on the pier with his hand out."

"Chrissakes," Negus said, "that old boy rakes it in. I seen him peel off hundred-dollar bills like they was lempiras. I think he keeps it all in his hotel room, I swear."

Pablo was thinking of an old boy in a hotel room full of hundred-dollar bills when he was startled once more by a sound on deck. He looked up and saw the outline of a man directly above him. It could only be Tino again. After a few moments, the man moved off aft. Pablo waited, too anxious to eavesdrop further, and then climbed silently out of the ice hold. He saw no one. For a while he leaned on the rail expecting to be challenged—but there was no further sign of Tino and he was reassured. He went down into the lazaret, found his gear in good order and climbed into his rack.

Negus and the Callahans sat late in their paneled cabin while the *Cloud* ran on automatic. Tino was brewing coffee in the galley.

"We getting ice and fuel from the Perreiras this time?"

Negus asked. He was hunched in a captain's chair, his bony arms folded on the table. Callahan sat across from him nursing a glass of soda water. His lady reclined on a short sofa, her feet up, reading *High Times*.

"I don't think so," Callahan said. "I think we'll get grub and parts from the Perreiras, then after dark we'll go over to Naftali's outfit in Serrano. We can get fuel from him along with the goods."

"What'll we tell Perreira?"

"We'll tell him Naftali made us a better offer. He won't press it. He's not aggressive."

"Always wondered how Naftali got away with running that operation," Negus said. "You'd think the Dutch would know it. Or the Americans."

"Maybe they do. Anyway it's Naftali's property, he owns it and he's pretty fucking careful. Or else Mossad owns it and they're super-careful."

Tino came down from the galley carrying a cup of coffee and took a chair. He spoke briefly to Negus in Papamiento.

"You're unhappy," Callahan said to him.

"I don't like dat mon," Tino said. "Pablo."

"Hell, I don't like him neither," Negus said. "But he ain't supposed to be a nice fella. He's our sonuvabitch."

"You approved him, Tino. You said you'd ship with him."

"So I gon to," Tino said.

Callahan kept his eyes on the engineer.

"You're sort of off the whole enterprise, in my opinion."

Tino smiled sadly.

"De ting can be done, capt'n. De money's good."

"I think," Negus said slowly, "that Tino's concerned about the way things are being done lately."

"Meaning what?" Callahan asked.

"I ain' sayin' dat, Fred. You sayin' dat, not me."

"Look Jack," Negus said, "you have to admit that we been getting lax. You been drinking a lot, there's that. You been drinking on the job, so to speak. The both of you been acting like there's no tomorrow. I mean, the days are past when you can operate down here in a spirit of fun like."

"You can ask anybody around, Freddy, and they'll tell you we're the most professional, the most reliable vessel in the commerce. That's always been true."

"It's been true in the past, Jack."

"If we weren't good, Naftali wouldn't work with us."

Negus looked down at the tabletop.

"I'll tell you—sometimes I'm surprised he still does."

"Well," Callahan said, "you give me pause, Freddy."

"I'm sorry, skipper, but there it is. Sometimes it feels like we're just floating a party."

"We do like we've always done, Fred. The only difference is we seem to be losing our confidence."

Negus was silent.

Callahan reached across the table for the bottle and poured some rum into his soda.

"Maybe you're right about getting old for it. Could be it's the beach for you, old stick. Maybe you should get back to that saloon in Hope Town."

"I just hope to see it again," Negus said.

"Nowadays," Tino told them, "so many *droguistas*. A mon get killed quick."

"Young Pablo reminds me of a *droguista*," Negus said after a while. "That's what bothers me about him."

"He's a Coast Guard deserter," Callahan said. "Hasn't been around long enough."

"Know who he reminds me of," Negus said. "That dude we had the trouble with . . . you know. Can't even remember his damn name."

Deedee put her magazine aside.

"Oh, dear," she said. "What an unpleasant thought."

"Dat was bad," Tino said.

Negus nodded in somber agreement.

"Well," Callahan said, "we dealt with it. I trust we won't have to do that to anybody again. However," he said, "should the occasion arise . . . we won't be found lacking in resolve."

Freddy Negus stood up and walked to the hatch that led up to the galley.

"It ain't a matter of Pablo, Jack. It's the whole thing. I mean, Tecan's no milk run. Those Tecs lay hands on us, we've had the fucking drill." He leaned in the hatchway for a moment and went back to his chair. "El Jefe's got a lot of new technology. He's got more boats and they're faster. He's got helicopters. The Yanks give him whatever he wants. They tell him what he wants."

"We've always run the same risks, Fred."

"Damnit," Negus said, "we were younger. We were tougher and more squared away. And you were . . . more responsible."

"Obviously," Callahan said, "if you don't have faith in me we can't operate."

"Fred's been brooding," Deedee said. "He's been thinking about that albino dwarf El Jefe keeps."

Callahan sipped his drink.

"Oh," he said with a smile, "the one who chews people's privates off."

Negus flushed.

"There is such a creature, Jack, I hate to tell you."

"Snowflake," Tino told them. "Copo. Das his name."

"Tecan is a mixture of the old and the new," Deedee said.

"Look," Negus said, "there are times when the two of you act stark crazy. Now we gonna keep this damn boat right end up and do our business or what?"

"I'll come through for you, Fred. You do the same for me. Are you guys with us or not?"

Tino nodded silently.

"Of course I'm with you," Negus said. "Always have been. Just I get the feeling sometimes you're flirting with disaster."

Callahan grinned with adolescent mischief and winked at his wife.

"If it be now, 'tis not to come," he declared. "If it be not to come, it will be now. If it be not now, yet it will come. The readiness is all."

"Ripeness," Deedee Callahan said.

"It's readiness, Dee."

"I mean taking a risk is one thing," Negus told them. "Fucking around for kicks is another."

"I like ripeness better," Deedee said.

"You like it," Callahan said, "because it's sexier."

With the air tank tucked into the gunwales under the bench on which he sat, Holliwell smoked and watched the green coastline—palm groves, banana plants strayed from the plantations, beach heliotrope of outsized luxuriance. Sandy, the dive master, ran his thirty-six-footer at full throttle, slapping the hull over the placid water; the bow took spray over the windward side that soaked the STP jacket Holliwell had worn against the sun.

Sandy was a long, spare man with a freckled English countryman's face darkened by the suns of Tecan and West Africa. He lounged in the stern, one loose hand over the stick, one elbow on the rail, leaning out to see the water ahead. His long black hair was bleached at the crown, parted at the middle of his skull like a nineteenth-century Russian peasant's, and this with his sharp black eyes deep-set under thick low brows brought a kind of dervish flair, a Rasputin intensity, to his appearance.

In the boat with Holliwell was a family of five Cuban-Americans from Miami. The father was stocky and muscular, his hair worn in a brush cut, his jaw jowled and pitted from relentless shaving. His wife was buxom and fleshy-faced yet with a long-legged trim frame, a Floridian body honed by dieting and Gloria Stevens. There were three boys between twelve and seventeen—the oldest vulpine with a nearly complete moustache and muscular like his father, the two younger quite like their mother; over the waist of each of their bathing suits sagged a tube of buttery fat. The parents spoke to each other in Spanish, the boys in American Adolescent. All of them ignored Holliwell.

"Could be seein' turtle over this reef," Sandy told the boys. "Good place to see dem."

"Aw-*right*," said the middle boy with enthusiasm.

"Would they bite you?" asked the smallest boy.

Sandy laughed. "Turtle bite you? Turtle don't bite you. Maybe take you for a ride."

"Hey," the seventeen-year-old said, "I could go for that."

When the children's parents spoke to Sandy it was in a formal and imperious way, as though they were used to service. Sandy answered them with deference.

Three hundred yards offshore, Sandy killed his engine and hopped forward to put the anchor line down. Everyone looked over the side. The sky's light sparkled back at them, reflected and refracted from the reef tops below—a long line of peaks curving out toward open ocean.

Sandy gave them the dive plan. The current was southerly. They would dive straight out from the stern, up-current. Then they could follow a semicircle of reef tops, cross a sandy bottom and follow the edge of a drop back to the boat with the current behind them. There was black coral there, Sandy told them. The site was called Twixt by the people of the coast.

Holliwell stared down at the liquid light of the white reefs. They were, after all, what he had come to see. He took a deep breath and put on his buoyancy compensator, his backpack tank, and bent to wrestle on his weight belt. Sandy put his own tank on with the ease of a man donning a sweater. The Cuban-American bustled about, trying stays and buckles—the head of the house overseeing procedure. The woman and the youngest boy were not going down. While Holliwell put his boots and fins on, Sandy checked out the gear of the younger of the two boys who were diving.

"Ever see any sharks around here?" the younger boy asked, as casually as he could. Holliwell admired his sangfroid. Testing his own regulator, he turned to watch Sandy answer.

"No sharks here," Sandy said simply.

It turned out that the younger boy was diving with Sandy, the oldest with his father. It had been so ordered.

"Want to come with us?" the dive master asked Holliwell.

"I'll just follow along," Holliwell said. "I'll be all right." He was not in fact a very experienced diver but the dive seemed easy enough.

Holliwell went over last, carrying two five-pound weights, wearing trunks and a tee shirt to ease the shoulder straps on his sunburned back. On the jump-off, his mask filled almost to eye level; he let the water rise in it, pinching his nostrils to equalize pressure. When he saw the reef tips rising around him, he cleared his mask and checked the depth gauge on his wrist. He was forty-five feet below the surface. He settled over a punch-bowl depression on the bottom; his fin tips stirred the milk-white sand there. The visibility at this depth was marvelous—over a hundred feet, perhaps two hundred. Black and golden angelfish swarmed around him as though they expected to be fed. There were parrot fish and convict tangs in uncountable numbers. The reef descended in terraces from its highest peaks, from each terrace elkhorn coral stretched in tortured fantastical shapes between the domes of brain coral. Below him wrasse and groupers glided by, a boxfish watched him shyly from behind two prongs of elkhorn. When he paddled out from the plateau on which he had rested, two trumpet fish came along with him like scouts. He swam clear of the next terrace and let the weights take him deeper; on the edge of vision he saw a barracuda—fairly small, certainly under three feet—prowling the edge of the swarm to pick off stragglers. When he leveled off, he was at sixty feet and the ocean floor still sloped downward under his fins. Far off and about forty feet above him he saw Sandy and the Cuban boy outlined against the shimmering curtain of the surface, swimming away from him.

On the next terrace he saw the black coral. There seemed to be acres of it, dappled with encrusting yellow infant sponges, and circling down he felt as though he were flying over a lava field grown with daisies. When he was closer, he could see the coral's root and branch patterns. It was sublime, he thought. He could feel his heart beating faster; his blood coursed through him like a drug. The icy, fragile beauty was beyond the competency of any man's hand, even beyond man's imagining. Yet it seemed to him its perfection provoked a recognition. The recognition of what? he wondered. A thing lost or forgotten. He followed the slope of the coral field. Down.

It had been years since he had taken so much pleasure in the living world.

At about ninety feet, he confronted the drop. The last coral terrace fell away and beyond it there was nothing, an immensity of shadowy blue, an abyss. He was losing color now. The coral on the canyon wall read blue-gray as he descended; the wrasse, the butterflies, the parrot fish looked as dun as mackerel. A gray lobster scurried along the cliff. Enormous gray groupers approached to have a look at him. In a coral crevice, a spotted moray drew back at his approach, then put its head out to watch his bubble trail with flat venomous eyes. The surface became a mirage, a distant notion.

He was at a hundred and ten and his pressure gauge, which had pointed twenty-five hundred p.s.i. at the jump-off, now read slightly under eight hundred. It was all right, he thought, the tank had no reserve and no J valve; he would have enough to climb back as the pressure evened out. At a hundred and twenty, his exhilaration was still with him and he was unable to suppress the impulse to turn a somersault. He was at the borders of narcosis. It was time to start up.

As soon as he began to climb, he saw shimmers of reflected

light flashing below his feet. In a moment, the flashes were everywhere—above and below. Blue glitters, lightning quick. The bodies of fish in flight. He began pumping a bit, climbing faster, but by the book, not outstripping his own bubble trail.

Some fifty feet away, he caught clear sight of a school of bonito racing toward the shallows over the reef. Wherever he looked, he saw what appeared to be a shower of blue-gray arrows. And then it was as if the ocean itself had begun to tremble. The angels and wrasse, the parrots and tangs which had been passing lazily around him suddenly hung in place, without forward motion, quivering like mobile sculpture. Turning full circle, he saw the same shudder pass over all the living things around him—a terror had struck the sea, an invisible shadow, a silence within a silence. On the edge of vision, he saw a school of redfish whirl left, then right, sound, then reverse, a red and white catherine wheel against the deep blue. It was a sight as mesmerizing as the wheeling of starlings over a spring pasture. Around him the fish held their places, fluttering, coiled for flight.

He started up too fast, struggling to check his own panic. Follow the bubbles. Follow the bouncing ball.

As he pedaled up the wall, he was acutely aware of being the only creature on the reef that moved with purpose. The thing out there must be feeling him, he thought, sensing the lateral vibrations of his climb, its dim primal brain registering disorder in his motion and making the calculation. Fear. Prey.

He was running out of air—overbreathing and overtaxing the expanding contents of his tank. The sound of his own desperate respirations furthered panic.

When he had worked out a breathing pattern and reached the first terrace, he found that he had enough to curve his ascent with the slope of the coral. At forty feet, he saw a sandy punch bowl like the one in which he had stopped but the forests of elkhorn were everywhere the same and the anchor line was nowhere in sight. Looking up, he saw Sandy outlined against the surface, coming down at him.

Sandy grabbed Holliwell's pressure gauge, read it and shook his head in reproach. He pointed to the right and upward along the slope. Holliwell followed the coral ridges as long as he could. The fish in the shallows swam placidly, unperturbed. When he found himself sucking hard on the regulator mouthpiece, he eased up the next thirty feet, taking three breaths on the way. And there, in another dimension altogether, the boat rocked gently, the youngest of the Cuban boys leaned over the side to watch the shifting surface, lost in reverie; his mother thumbed through *Cosmopolitan*. The shoreline glowed green beyond the hot blur of the beach, the line of banana jungle broken only by a white wooden building on a solitary hill, surmounted with a cross. Holliwell turned over on his back and swam to the boat's ladder.

The boy and his mother watched as he took off his gear. Before disconnecting the regulator from the tank he checked the gauge once more; it read just a hair over empty at sea level.

"That's as empty as it gets," he told the people in the boat. The charge of primary process he had experienced at a hundred and ten feet put him in danger of becoming garrulous.

The boy looked at the gauge. "None left at all?"

"Empty," Holliwell said. "Just like it says." He was ill at ease with the boy and he sensed a certain artificiality in his own manner. His own children had not been this age for five years or more; he had forgotten what it was like. Out of touch again, he thought.

"How come is that?" the woman asked.

"Just ran it out," Holliwell told her cheerfully.

"What did you see?" the boy asked him.

"Lots of great fish," he said. "And beautiful black coral."

"And we can't take any," the woman said. "Such a shame because it's so beautiful."

"I'm sure it looks prettier where it is," Holliwell heard himself say pompously.

The woman inflated her cheeks and shrugged. She was not a bad sort, Holliwell decided. They chatted for a few minutes. The family's name was Paz; they lived in Miami, had lived there since 1961. All of their sons were born there. The man was a dentist, she herself was in real estate. They were visiting her brother, who had five hardware stores in Tecan. Holliwell told her that he was a professor; she had lived in the States long enough to remain unimpressed.

Sandy and the middle son were next up; the boy climbed aboard and fixed a smirk on Holliwell. The dive master got out of harness in a single easy motion.

"Now what you want down theah, mistuh?" he asked Holliwell. He was smiling. "I nevah tol' you go down theah."

"Just wanted a look, I guess."

"Sandy made him get out of the water," the middle son announced. Señora Paz and the youngest boy gave Holliwell dutifully accusatory looks. Then Señora Paz asked sharply after her husband and eldest son. They were under the boat, Sandy assured her, playing among the elkhorn coral.

After a few minutes, the dentist surfaced and climbed aboard. He was elated after his dive and his amiability extended even to Holliwell.

"Where the hell were you?" Dr. Paz asked Holliwell. "I never even saw you." His English was almost completely unaccented.

"Sandy made him get out of the water," the middle son said.

"Just down too deep," Sandy said soothingly. "A bit too deep and de air run out faster."

"What's the attraction down there?" the dentist asked.

"Just the drop," Holliwell said.

"How far you think she drop off dere?" Sandy asked him, laughing.

"A long way," Holliwell said.

"Nine hundred meters," Sandy said.

"Is that possible?" Holliwell said.

Sandy let his smile fade. His nod was solemn, his eyes humorous with certainty.

"I'm tellin' you, mon. Nine hundred meters."

When the youngest boy wanted to know how far that was in feet, Sandy was uncertain.

"It's about two thirds of a mile," the dentist said. "I thought they taught you that in school."

"Yeah, dummy," the middle son said to his brother.

"How about that," Holliwell said.

Then the oldest boy surfaced with an empty tank.

"Orca, orca," the two younger boys shouted. "Orca surfaces at last."

The youth's eyes were shining as he climbed up the ladder. It was hard to dislike anyone, Holliwell thought, when you watched them come up from a dive.

"Gosh," the boy said to Holliwell, "we didn't see you anywhere."

"Sandy made him get . . ."

Señora Paz hushed her middle son with a frown and a raising of her chin.

They motored back to the hotel dock making small talk. At the dive shack, Sandy, who knew a big tipper when he saw one, helped the Pazes wash and stow their gear and was jolly with the boys. Holliwell put his own gear away and sat down on the dock. After a while Sandy wandered down and joined him.

"How long you been divin'?" Sandy asked him.

"I've been certified for two years. I don't do it much anymore."

Sandy looked out to sea. "Lost a mon on dat drop other year. I follow him dom near two hundred meters but when I turn off de mon still goin' down."

"Suicide," Holliwell said.

"Das right. Mon take de sleepin' pills and go down."

"It must have happened more than once."

Sandy nodded. "I don' lose nobody," he said. "Got to be dere own chosen will."

Holliwell felt himself shudder. "Did you think that's what I was doing?"

"Oh, no," the dive master said quickly. He touched Holliwell on the shoulder in the Caribbean way but avoided his eye.

"I won't make the dive this afternoon," Holliwell told him. "Maybe you could leave me off around French Harbor. I'd like to snorkel down there."

Sandy guessed that it would be all right. French Harbor was on the way. He told Holliwell that if he requested it, the Paradise kitchen might pack a lunch for him. They walked together toward the hotel buildings.

"There was something down that drop this morning," Holliwell said. "A big shark, maybe."

Sandy stopped walking and looked at Holliwell, holding his hand on his brow to shield his eyes from the sun.

"You see any shark?"

"No."

"Then don't be sayin' shark if you don' see one."

"Something was happening down there."

"I tell you don' go down that far, Mistuh Holliwell. I give you de dive plan. When you down so far, das not a good place."

"Why's that?"

Sandy walked on; Holliwell followed him.

"Dat drop, people see tings, den dey don' know what dey seen. Dey be frightened after."

"Was it always like that?"

"Jus' dangerous divin', das all. Surface current and de drop is cunnin'. You get deeper den you know."

"So pretty, though."

"Jus, as pretty on de top," Sandy said. "Always prettier in de light."

"Yes," Holliwell said. "Yes, of course."

Justin was trying to reread *To the Finland Station* in the afternoon shadows of the veranda. She had almost dozed off when she saw the man snorkeling along the southern end of Playa Tate. For days now, her dispensary had been ready to receive wounded insurrectionists; each night she had spent awake and prowling in the light of her hurricane lamp among the stacks of stretchers, the basins and the small array of surgical instruments—listening to the government radio until it went off the air and then to U.S. Armed Forces radio or the BBC foreign service. Sometimes she would turn the volume down and tune in Radio Havana. Nights were long.

It was high tide and the swimming man crossed over the inner reef and headed for the roadside beach in front of the mission steps. Only a few hundred yards past the steps, a sizable stream ran down from the foothills of the Sierra, carrying with it all the refuse and infections of the hillside barrios. Its small estuary was a dirty place to swim. The shrimp that lived there grew to great size and Justin had often seen boats from the hotels up and down the coast come at night to gather them. Moreover, she knew that in the water offshore there was a deep channel where hammerhead sharks came in to feed upon the shrimp.

The man would be a tourist from one of the hotels. There would be many more before long as the fruit companies liquidated their unprofitable plantations and converted to the resort business.

The swimmer's absurd sportive presence irritated Justin considerably. If he persisted in staying near the channel, she would have to go down and wave him out of danger and she was not in the mood for personal engagement. To her further annoyance, the man came out of the water by the mission pier, took his fins off and sat down on it. Two women carrying laundry on their heads passed the pier and Justin felt as though she could see the false smile he gave them, hear his fatuous *"Buenos diás."*

While Justin was watching the tourist on the dock, Father Egan came out on the veranda.

"There's someone on the dock," he said to her.

"A tourist. Snorkeling through."

"What do you think he wants?"

"He wants to sun himself on the glistening sands of Tecan. That's what he paid for."

"But why on our dock?"

"Because he owns the place. Chrissakes, Charlie, go ask him."

She watched Egan make his way down the steps, slack-jawed, shuffle-gaited. His deterioration was proceeding at an alarming rate; he had aged dreadfully in the past months, sometimes he seemed to her almost senile.

Egan was talking to the tourist now; the tourist had accepted a cigarette and a light from him. An odd pair they made—the tourist tanned and muscular, towering over the priest's gray, lumpish figure. The two of them turned toward the mission building; Egan was pointing into the forest behind it. She stood up impatiently and went inside to make herself some coffee.

It had all been smoke before, Godoy had said. Perhaps it was still.

One time, she thought, they will require something from me other than my well-exercised reverent attention and prayerful expectation. People—men, when you came down to it—were always dreaming up glorious phantasmas for her to wait joyously upon. Justice. The life to come. The Revolution. There are limits, she thought. Justin Martyr.

When she went out with the coffee, Egan and the snorkeler were sitting on the pier in conversation.

Well, she thought, why not, we're all tourists now. For weeks no one had come. Campos had some method of keeping them away.

After a few minutes, Father Egan came huffing up the steps.

"Know who he is, that fellow? He's an anthropologist. He had business in the city and now he's come to see our ruins."

"Yours and mine?"

"Haw," Egan said. "Clever kid."

But Justin was growing anxious about the swimmer.

"And did you volunteer to take him back and show him?"

"Yes, I did. And I asked him to dinner on Friday."

Justin looked at him in dismay.

"Go down and un-ask him," she said in a steely voice. "We can't have him here."

"We certainly can."

"We can not!" Justin almost shouted.

"May one ask why?"

She looked away, out to sea.

"Good heavens, I suppose we can go to town and have dinner. I don't understand what the objection is. Do you think I'm so unpresentable?"

"It's not that," Justin said. Better to let it go, she thought. The chances were that the man would not come back. Or that Egan would forget. She watched the strange swimmer now, saw him sit waist deep in the water putting on his fins. He began to crawl toward deeper water. He was not far from the river channel now. If he continued as he went, the bottom would slope sharply and without warning he would be over it. It was no place for a tourist to be—the sharks, and the bottom covered with sea urchins. A few feet short of the surge channel, she saw him crumple up and stop swimming. He was splashing, clutching his knee. Justin stood up. The tourist had crawled into the shallows and was in the slight surf, both hands folded over his wound.

Damn you, she thought, you asshole tourist.

"He's hurt himself," Father Egan said helplessly.

"He stepped on a goddamn sea urchin is what he did. Either that or something took a piece of him." She went into the dispensary wing, snatching up a bucket on her way through the kitchen. In the bucket she poured a pint of ammonia and then diluted it with well water from the tap. She hauled the solution down the veranda steps and across the road to the water's edge. The swimmer was sitting upright now, with his back to the ocean. When he saw her, he was squinting in pain, his teeth clenched, pale under his tan.

"Watch where you're sitting, sir. There are sea urchins all around you."

The man turned on his side and eased toward her, feeling the way before him with his swim fin. She put out a hand and he took it in his, leaning his weight on her, dragging the injured leg. His mask was up on his forehead.

Justin guided him out of the water and had a look at his leg. Sure enough, his left knee was swollen and purple with small spine ends visible through the skin. Justin poured some of the ammonia solution over his knee and rubbed it in with a cotton swab.

"You can also piss on it," Justin explained.

"It's not so easy to piss on your knee sitting down," the man said.

He was looking grateful and embarrassed. He was a tall well-built man; his face, in Justin's eyes, bespoke softness and self-indulgence. But perhaps it was only the pain and his being a tourist.

"I'm really sorry to be trouble. Are you from the mission here?"

"Yep." She took a hemostat from a kit and lifted a spine end off the mottled flesh of his knee. "Hey," she said, "I got the end out."

"I'm sure you have more important things to do."

"Oh, stop it," Justin said. She went after the second spine and pulled it out. "That's gonna be sore for a while but the real bad pain will stop very soon. It's nothing serious."

"I guess I was lucky."

"I guess you were. When you doubled up I thought a shark had hit you."

"A shark? Right here?"

"There are sharks in the channel here. And a carpet of sea urchins. And the water's polluted. It's like a harbor."

"I'd better restrict my snorkeling to Playa Tate then."

"You should," she said. "This is a lousy place for it."

And what now? He should be given an aspirin, put in the shade. He did not appear to be in shock. Nursey business for the tourists.

She helped him across the dirt road, sat him under a ceiba tree and went back up to her dispensary for aspirin.

"Poor fellow," Egan said as she passed through the kitchen to replace her bucket. "A nice chap."

"Yep," she said.

As she went down to him, two young loafers from town walked by along the road and paused briefly to mock him. He was indeed mockable, she thought, with his swim fins in his lap and the mask and snorkel still fitting on the front of his skull and his Day-Glo kneecaps. An absurd and unnecessary person.

"Have an aspirin," she said. "Have two. Forgot the water."

He took the pills and swallowed them. Some color was coming back to his face. In the scattered afternoon sunlight that shone through the great ceiba's branches, she noticed that there were two identical and very nearly invisible scars on his right earlobe and that a small piece of the lobe itself was missing.

"My name is Frank Holliwell," the man said. "I was just talking with your Father Egan."

"Is that right?" When the man's ear was out of the sunlight the small scar disappeared. "How will you get back now?"

"The boat will pick me up." He looked at the angle of the sun through the ceiba leaves. "They should be by anytime."

"You O.K. now?"

"I feel a lot better."

"Good. Take care now."

"I understand I'm coming to dinner on Friday."

"No, I don't think so," Justin said, blushing. "I think Father Egan means to go into town with you. If he's well enough."

"I see."

"We're in a state of disarray. We're closing down soon." There was something in the man's affectless stare that made her uneasy. She glanced quickly at the scar, visible again in the sunlight. "They'll have to get along without us."

"You're a nun?"

"That's right," she said.

He asked her what order she was and she told him. He went on nodding as though the Devotionists were familiar to him. Catholic.

"They used to rap you on the knuckles, right?" she asked lightly.

"Not on my knuckles. I had Jesuits for that."

"Oh, I see. Well, that's . . . classy."

"Are you coming to dinner with us too?" he asked. She was startled by the manner in which he put it. It was as though he was flirting with her. What's the world coming to? she thought. And how would I know?

It sometimes happened to Justin that she would relax a bit and speak earnestly and directly to a man and the man would think she was becoming flirtatious. It was annoying. It had something to do with the way she looked.

"No, I can't," she said. "I've got a whole dispensary to pack."

"What's it like being a nun these days?"

"Oh," she said, "well, there are all kinds of nuns."

He *is*, she thought, he's coming on. He probably can't help himself. That's what that softness in his face is all about.

"What's it like for you?"

"It's medieval," she said. "And otherworldly."

She was pleased when he laughed, in spite of herself. "What's that business on your ear, Mr. Holliwell?" Put him on the defensive.

The question seemed to surprise and embarrass him.

"It's a tribal scar. I got it in Southeast Asia."

"Really? Where?"

"Indonesia," he said quickly. "Celebes. I'm an anthropologist."

"And you were being one of the gang."

"Yes," he said, "one of the bunch. I asked for their smallest size."

The buzz-saw whine of a large outboard sounded on the ocean; they both turned to see the Paradise dive boat on its way to Playa Tate.

"Well," she said, "take care of your foot. Be thankful you knelt down on a baby one or we might have had to open up your leg to get the spines."

"Thanks," he said.

"And try to keep it clean."

"What?"

She laughed at him. "Your knee."

"Oh . . . yes. Look, maybe I'll see you again. At the ruins or somewhere. I'd like very much to talk."

"I'll be pretty busy."

"Packing and telling your beads."

She smiled at him and turned away. He was impertinent and patronizing and for all she knew, depraved. He was the kind of man she thought of as "cheesy." But he was sort of nice. And not just a tourist, she thought; Justin was innocently snobbish in the extreme.

Back on the veranda, she felt a little high. The very recognition of her exhilaration was enough to depress her; she was shortly guilty and ashamed. Air-headedness. Petty foolishness. The thought of waiting through another night was dreadful. But she would have to. She would have to go on believing in them.

She leaned on the rail, gripping it until her knuckles were white.

"Christ, it's impossible," she said.

Egan was in the kitchen. Drunk.

"Now, now," he said. "There's a good girl."

Pablo opened the hatch to dazzling sunlight and stepped out on the hot boards of the afterdeck, barefoot and shirtless. The *Cloud* was tied up by a cement pier in a town of red-tiled roofs. The streets, unlike those of Palmas, were paved, the walls of the harborside buildings were whitewashed. Over the port captain's shed was a double-masted flagstaff displaying a banner with a white cross on a star-dappled blue field and the horizontal tricolor of Holland. Beyond the town was desert, grown with cactus and thorny acacia. Across a sparkling bay lined with limestone palisades, a low white peak rose like a cone of salt.

The water lines were over; Pablo picked up a hose and laved his head and face with a jet of fresh water. The water was good and cold. Spring water. Wiping it from his eyes, he saw Tino approaching.

"Like to start d' day wid some beer?" Tino asked pleasantly.

"You kidding me?"

Tino motioned him toward the rail. Stacked up on the dock

were a dozen cases of Amstel beer. A yellow-haired Creole driving a forklift was lowering more beside it.

"You go get 'em, sailor," Tino said, slapping him on the shoulder.

Pablo took his morning Benzedrine; a barbed wave of resentment ran through him. Fucking pull and tote. He climbed over the rail and took a closer look at the town.

At the end of the pier was a market square dominated by a gabled stone building with "Perreira Brothers" lettered over its central doorway. To the right of it, behind a garden wall enclosing royal palms and banana trees, was a government building marked by the same two flags.

Two seagoing tugs were berthed at the adjoining pier, one flying U.S. colors, the other Dutch. Beside the tugs were two small Venezuelan freighters. As far as Pablo could see, there were no other craft in port.

He lifted a crate of Amstel, carried it aboard and set it down beside the forward hold. After a while, he fell into the rhythm of hauling; the speed, the sweating, the sun on his body made him feel powerful. When the beer was aboard, there were cartons of frozen meat for the reefer, then greens and fruit.

Each time Pablo shouldered a box past the shuttered main cabin, he heard the voices of the people conferring inside and although he could not make out what was being said there was something about the very tone in which they spoke that made him think of high fortune and the big-time score. He began to take less pleasure in his donkey work and to feel turned around.

After a little more than a half hour, he decided that he would take a break, let the cartons pile up on the pier for a while and get out of the sun. Tino was down in the engine space, working on the diesel.

In the shade of a hatch cover, Pablo contemplated the scheme of things. He kept thinking of the old man called Naftali who was with them in the cabin now, and who lived in a hotel room amid piles of hundred-dollar bills.

He had made his move, he thought. He had put a thousand miles between himself and the life of petty day-by-day. McPhail and his like, the crummy trailer, the chickenshit, that bitch and her ratburgers. He was out where it mattered; out here, he thought, you made it big or you went under. He would go under or go back and let them put the irons on him and do the time. But if he made it big, he might go back and no one could touch him. Or he might settle down, on some island, a better island than this one—and be like the men you read about in *Soldier of Fortune*, men who had lived the life of adventure in hot countries and by their strength and cunning made it big, gotten rich, and who lived exquisitely in plantation houses high above the harbor with beautiful native wives.

People liked to get you thinking you were small-time. That way, they made out and you got fucked. It was that way now, he thought, they were in the cabin talking big-time scores and he was hauling groceries for them. They might pay him or they might not; he was a yo-yo to them. One of life's little yo-yos.

But the fact was, they were old and soft. They were making it big, they had made their move, but they were soft. Callahan was a rummy. What were Negus and Callahan together compared to him? Surely, he thought, their day was over. It was someone else's turn now, someone smarter and tougher. And it was all in your mind; if you let weak people buffalo you, they would keep you down. He had been letting them do it all his life and it was time to call them on it. He was young, he was strong, a soldier of fortune. He had seen them up close, they were nothing much.

Naftali with the room full of money, he had not seen. But Naftali was an old man, was losing his grip. Was he as bad as all that? He, Pablo, might see about that; you had to take risks, there was nothing for free. It was a new ball game on this ocean. He began to suspect that things were going his way.

Then Tino came up and yelled at him—the black son of a bitch actually cursed him out in front of the other niggers on the dock; he was put back to his loading. As he labored under the bales of netting and the boxes full of spare parts, a chain of recall ground against his memory and every insult and humiliation he had ever been forced to bear flashed before him, as bright and hurtful as though he were enduring each again.

When the last of the stores were aboard, he took another

Benzedrine and shortly thereafter made up his mind. They would never pay him, he realized. They took him for a fool. It was time for another move. A man doesn't live forever, he thought. You don't make out playing it safe. He had tried being Joe Citizen and he had ended up sharing a trailer with an ignorant whore and a kid he couldn't support. No more. If you let yourself be anybody's man you ended up like everybody.

In the afternoon, Tino sent him to the port captain's office to get the *Cloud*'s papers stamped and the fishing permit renewed. By the time he got back aboard, the conference was over. The cabin shutters were lifted and Naftali had departed unseen. The Callahans were in bathing suits.

Pablo asked if he could take a shower.

"Go ahead," Callahan told him. "We're finished here."

Callahan looked pretty good, Pablo thought, harder and trimmer than he ought considering his age and the amount he seemed to drink. The sight of Mrs. Callahan in her bikini stirred Pablo's resentment and strengthened his resolve. He noticed that Negus had started in drinking beer.

"We're going to the beach," Deedee said. "Up at the new hotel. Anybody else want to come?"

Pablo shook his head.

"Tino," she said, "you come. I want to see if you'll show your legs."

"Oh no," Tino said. "Not me."

"I don't think he can swim," she said to her husband.

"I de bes' swimmer," Tino told her with a sad smile.

"You'll find Naftali at the Hollandia if you need him," Callahan told Negus. "He'll probably sack out, I don't think he's feeling well." He looked over his men with an air of good-natured proprietorship. "Think you boys can stay out of trouble until we get back?" As he asked the question, Pablo noticed that a gear locker beside the gallery was swinging open. Its upper drawer was piled with tubes and radio parts—various things that mght be worth keeping under lock and key in port. His automatic pistol was in the lower drawer still in its leather holster. On the locker handle hung an open padlock.

"Guess I'll wash up now," Pablo said. He went back to the lazaret to get his towel and clogs and some clean underwear. The space was close and airless without a seaborne wind to cool it; the boards enclosed each hour of the day's heat.

When he had finished showering, the locker still hung open. He changed clothes on deck, leaving his boots beside the hatch with his wallet and passport under his socks, and put on his sunglasses and his Macklin Chain Saw hat. With the cap down over his eyes, he sat down in one of the cockpit chairs, turning it round on its swivel so that he could face the main cabin and see the open locker.

In the cabin, Negus reclined on a wooden bench, his feet up on the table and his back against the bulkhead. He had been up all night and had started drinking in the morning. There was a glass of neat rum on the table, a few inches from where his legs rested.

Tino was in the engine space with another St. Joostian, working on the Lister. Through the planking, Pablo could hear the rattle of their tools and their soft curses.

In his swivel chair, Pablo felt clean, cool and ready. He was waiting for Negus to fall asleep. As he willed Freddy Negus into slumber, he had a look at the publications stacked beside the Modar. He found two U.S. Coast Guard code books, laminated and stamped "Secret," and the Coast Guard frequency chart, all current. Along with these were code books of the Tecanecan and Compostelan navies, so similar in typeface and binding to the U.S. books that it was apparent they had been printed by the same outfit. The Spanish in these was obscure to Pablo, but the military frequencies and codes were listed.

When he heard Negus begin to snore, he put the books down quietly and stood up and walked barefoot into the galley. Negus was asleep down in the main cabin, not ten feet away from him, his head resting on a lintel in the paneling, his mouth open. Pablo waited a moment with his eyes on Negus' drawn face and listened to Tino and his mate work in the engine space. The quiet rhythm of their labor went on unbroken. Still watching Negus, he reached into the lower drawer of the open locker and drew out his holstered pistol. Pistol and holster in hand, he backed off silently to the cockpit and furiously set about getting himself in harness. Negus was still snoring when he finished, Tino still tapping away on the Lister with his assistant. With shirttails over his trouser tops, Pablo walked out on deck, picked up his boots and sat down on the edge of the after hatch. He put his passport and wallet in his pocket and casually put on his socks and cowboy boots. He made himself wait for a moment, then climbed over the rail and walked slowly along the cement dock toward town. There was still no one in sight aboard the *Cloud*. On his way to the market square, he could not resist touching the pistol under his arm.

When the slant of the sun lit the cockpit windows to a green-tinted blaze and the sunlight crept across the galley and the cabin below it, Negus woke up and held his head in his hands. After a while he stood up, shuddered and went out on deck shielding his eyes. He found the water hose beside the after hatch, turned the pressure on and held it over his head and drank from it. Tino, in a grease-spattered purple tank-top shirt, came up and took the hose from him.

"Where's the kid?" Negus asked him as he drank.

Tino rolled the water in his mouth and spat it out on the deck.

"He not with you?"

They looked at each other and stalked around the boat in search of Pablo. Negus called his name. They checked the lazaret and looked through his gear.

"The fucker flew," Negus said.

"Lef' his gear."

"I didn't see his passport there."

They went into the galley and leaned against the stove. Negus rubbed his eyes.

"Maybe he won' come back," Tino said.

"Took his piece out of here," Negus said, slamming the gear locker shut. He did not bother to lock it.

"I fin' him," Tino said. "No place he can go I won' fin' him. Not on dis eye-land."

"O.K.," Freddy Negus said.

"Wan' me to bring him back?"

"Find out what the hell he's up to and let me know. We'll figure it from there."

"Ya," Tino said.

Negus watched him walk briskly down the cement pier. As he went, two young islanders who had been sitting on a piling stood up and fell into step with him.

Holliwell finished his rum, thought about having another and decided on it. He poured it quickly and guiltily; he was drinking as he had not done for years and still smoking. Propped in a wicker chair on the porch of his Paradise bungalow, his feet on the pastel rail, he looked out over the layered ocean.

Raw rum drained the disease of his mind. His thoughts were focused by an act of will on the pale-eyed woman at the mission beach. He remembered quite clearly the cool sure-handed motion with which she had guided him from the surf. The lightest of touches, a gesture almost, but she had put all her strength behind it. For a few seconds she had supported him. Curious. Indicative of what? Trust. Confidence. An insolent assurance, an unthinking self-superiority that was wonderful to see. A nun.

Thinking of her made him laugh. In his solitary laughter there was admiration, contempt and jealousy.

It was very beguiling, that female arrogance. There were women who could not refrain in their dealings with men from intimating that it was they who were more at home in the world. Who could not forbear, all unprovoked, to run up their mythic pennants. Instrument of Birth. Shroud Weaver. Bent never Broken. It became very primitive very quickly. Talking some commonplace like genocide or the weather they performed a hula, a series of mudras. Your eyes are hot and deluded, they signaled, ours are clear. We have suffered your rantings, your violence, your febrile illusions and endured. We can look on all things the same, we can imagine serenity. Grow up, they said.

The responses were various and complex but all involved equally primitive rage. Snatch! Stuff, cooze, undoing, unclean. Go bathe yourselves and be suitable for our fantasies. And you can't hear the sound of our Bull Roarer!

He took more rum and filled his glass with warm Popi-Limón. The ice in the bar bucket had melted.

He liked her, it was that simple. He could say anything he liked or nothing at all and the spooks and hirelings could report anything that he said and it would make no difference. He felt sure enough of that.

Was she then at home in the world—the *modern world*, like the Jew in Nolan's strange arrested hypothesis? She seemed to think she was. The question would not have occurred to her. He would put it to her; that was in his line, after all. Who do you think you are and what do you think you're doing?

One way or another it must seem possible to her that the world could be ordered to suit her scruples and inhabited with satisfaction. In the name of God or Humanity or some Larger Notion—a new order of ages with a top and a bottom and sides. Right consequences following right actions. A marvelous view of the world, he thought. If it prevailed it would produce its own art forms, its own architecture, its own diet.

In Saigon, he had once smoked opium with a young officer of airborne troops who had described himself as a winner. "If you oppose me," the young officer had explained, "I will win. You will lose."

"Always?" Holliwell had asked.

Every time, the officer had explained. Because the compulsion to lose was universal and only a handful of people could overcome it.

Holliwell had ventured the opinion that it must be very strange to approach every contest with the certainty of success.

The officer was an unimposing man. He wore eyeglasses so thick that one wondered how he had come to be in the Army at all.

"What I think is strange," he had said, "is approaching them knowing you're going to lose."

Saying it, he had fixed Holliwell with a look of unsound satisfaction. The eyes behind the lenses were knowing and tolerant and demented, but the point was well taken and he had scored a success ad hominem in that very moment.

Positive thinkers.

How could they? he wondered. How could they convince themselves that in this whirling tidal pool of existence, providence was sending them a message? Seeing visions, hearing voices, their eyes awash in their own juice—living on their own and borrowed hallucinations, banners, songs, kiddie art posters, phantom worship. The lines of bayonets, the marching rhythms, incense or torches, chanting, flights of doves—it was hypnosis. And *they* were the vampires. The world paid in blood for their articulate delusions, but it was all right because for a while they felt better. And presently they could put their consciences on automatic. They were beyond good and evil in five easy steps—it had to be O.K. because it was them after all. It was good old us, Those Who Are, Those Who See, the gang. Inevitably they grew bored with being contradicted. Inevitably they discovered the fundamental act of communication, they discovered murder. Murder was salutary, it provided reinforcement when they felt impotent or unworthy. It was something real, it made them folks and the reference to death reminded everyone that time was short and there could be no crapping around. For the less forceful, the acceptance of murder was enough. Unhappy professors, hyperthyroid clerics and flower children could learn the Gauleiter's smirk. The acceptance showed that they were realists which showed that they were real.

Rum was making his poisoned leg throb.

There was no reason to get angry. At his age one took things as they were. Despair was also a foolish indulgence, less lethal than vain faith but demeaning. One could not oppose the armies of delusion with petulance.

It was necessary to believe in oneself. Very, very difficult. One was a series of spasms, flashes. Without consistency, protean, infantile—but one would have to do. The loneliness was hard.

In the greening twilight, he thought of the great silence that had settled on the reef. The fear and the muted coral colors hung in his recollection like fragments of collective memory, a primordial dream. Closing his eyes, he could hear again the rhythm of his breathing and feel the panic drugs surging in his blood.

He had no business down there.

Three men carrying firewood came down the road, their bent figures outlined against the aqua and scarlet horizon. Approaching the Paradise grounds they turned off to follow the shore where their passage and their burdens would not worry the nerves of sensitive guests. It was a diorama of toil and poverty, and Holliwell, in his easy chair, felt suitably guilty. B. Traven—but they were all south of cliché, so it was simple reality. Familiar moral frissons qualified as insights. Carrying wood always felt different depending on your health, your state of mind and the time of day; sitting in a resort watching the peons was always the same for people whose education prepared them to do it properly; the final emotion was self-pity.

He had no business under the reef. Nor had he any business where he was, under that perfumed sky.

He reminded himself that he had his business like everyone else. It was as real as anyone else's and so was he. His business was done in University Park, a perfectly real place though recently constructed. It was to husband and father, to teach, even to inspire, and to endure. These things were not trivial. A monstrous pride might despise them, but honor could not. Because who does one think one is?

At times one has only a slender notion. One is only out here in this, whatever it is.

Whirl. People disappeared and were said to have died, as in war. Or their contexts changed like stage flats leaving them inappropriately costumed, speaking the wrong lines. Some disappeared in place, their skulls hollowed out by corrosive spirits or devoured by parasites.

The world and the stations of men changed ruthlessly; the funhouse barrel turned without slowing. The fall of last week's airplane sends amazed salesmen down the ledge. The coral polyps and sawfish receive a dry rain. In suburban shopping centers the first chordates walk the pavement, marvels of mimesis. Their exoskeletons exactly duplicate the dominant species. Behind their soft octopus eyes—rudimentary swim bladders and stiletto teeth.

Just out here. Each one alone. The rest is fantasy.

It had been to consider too curiously to consider so. As the stars came out, fear broke over his heart like a dawn of unwholesome colors. Rags in the wind, the taste of a tannery. It was a childhood image.

He drank more but the rum didn't do it. That's what you get, he thought.

In the last hours of afternoon, Pablo sat pacing himself in the E Wowo Bar, drinking light rum and doing speed. Well after dark, he hit the street; he felt himself an instrument of stealth and strength. He followed the palm-topped wall of the Governor's Palace, grim, almost angry.

Naftali's Hollandia Hotel was two blocks beyond the palace on the far side of the street. Pablo sauntered across, strung tight and trying to loosen it down. Trying to ease it, cool it.

The Hollandia was no more than a two-story stone house with a little garden behind its pastel gate. Four tiled steps led up to its veranda. Pablo mounted them quickly and went inside. The foyer was deserted, the cubicle-sized desk unattended. In a curtained room behind it, someone was watching television, a comedy with music, in Spanish from the Caracas station. No one came out when Pablo went upstairs.

The second-floor corridor smelled of varnish and insecticide. At the far end of it a loosely fitted shutter creaked in the gentle wind and lightly battered the window casing. The sound covered Pablo's soft steps as he went along the hall.

There was only one transom showing light and it was at the windowed end of the passage, above the room numbered eight. Across the hall was a water cooler with a plastic glass resting on it. As he passed the cooler, Pablo glanced back over his shoulder toward the stairs, then placed himself beside the door to room eight. He was disturbed to hear voices sounding from inside, speaking some foreign language he had never heard before. Dutch maybe. But after he had listened for a while, he determined that there was only one voice, a single speaker. The voice sounded vacant and slurred, like that of a drunk man talking to himself.

Well, well, thought Pablo. You put yourself away a little early, my friend.

He went to the cooler and silently filled the plastic glass. Then he crouched down outside the door and began to pour the contents of the glass underneath it. The door opened at the first spout.

Standing above Pablo was a hawk-faced man in a blue bathrobe and carpet slippers who was pointing what appeared to be an automatic pistol down Pablo's throat. The hand holding the gun was unsteady but purposeful. Pablo set his plastic glass down and rested on one knee, a genuflection.

"What's this, sailor," the hawk-faced man inquired, "the wine of astonishment?"

When the old man leaned down to take Pablo's weapon from beneath his open shirt, Pablo realized how unsteady the man's hand actually was. Had he not been thrown so off balance himself, he might have tried a move. But he had lost for the moment. The sclerotic nature of the old man's movements both frightened and encouraged him.

"Come visit," the man said to Pablo. "I been expecting you all night."

"Not me," Pablo said, blinking under the shaded light of

the room. "We both got the wrong people. See, I was playing a joke on a friend of mine."

"Aha," the man with the gun said. "Funny."

"Honest to Christ," Pablo pleaded. "Now just take it easy!"

"Tell me something. How easy you want me to take it?" He motioned Pablo deeper into the room. It was a room that was clean and without character, unclaimed by its occupant, everything the management's. "In my former organization when funny people poured water under our doors we would blow the door apart."

"Hey, man . . . honest to Christ!"

"If I would have done that it would have been your blood I'd see coming under my door. But I'd wait before I put my head out, believe me."

"It's a mistake is all, see."

The man carefully seated himself on the side of his bed; he was half turned away from Pablo.

"I saw you on the boat today. You stank all over the dock of petty thief." Naftali was inspecting the serial number on the stock of Pablo's service forty-five. "But a petty thief with problems. Right away I knew we'd meet again."

He had put his own gun down on the bed to look at Pablo's.

"This is U.S. government property, no?" Naftali asked. He removed the clip from Pablo's gun, set it down and picked up his own automatic. Leaning back on the bolsters, he held the gun on his lap.

"That's right," Pablo said.

"And you . . . whose property are you?"

Pablo made him no answer.

"Well, you're too late, thief." Naftali took a piece of paper from his bathrobe pocket, wadded and threw it toward Pablo. What Pablo picked up and read was a bank receipt for the transfer of gulden three hundred eighty thousand to the Amsterdam branch of the Nederlandse Algemeen Bank. The account to which the money was consigned was held in the name of a M. Blanc, a resident of Brussels, Belgium.

"Know what it means, boychick?"

"I believe I know what it means," Pablo said.

"It means you would die for nothing, thief. It means the money's gone."

"What are you gonna do?"

"You know what's customary?" Naftali asked.

Pablo took a deep breath and glanced at the door. It looked very far away. When he turned back to face Naftali he noticed for the first time the night table beside the old man's bed. The table was covered with bottles—one of Mexican brandy, another of liquid Nembutal, clearly labeled in English, yet another small one of insulin with a syringe beside it.

"I won't ask you for a break," Pablo said.

"It never hurts to ask."

Pablo turned away from the sight of the barrel.

"Fuck you," he said.

"Nothing to say for yourself? A name?"

"Pablo," Pablo said.

"Whose life is worth more, Pablo? Yours or mine?"

Tabor looked with hatred into the man's cold gray eyes. He could not stand to be the object of games.

"I'm gonna walk outa here," he told the man on the bed. "You can do what you like."

"That's right," Naftali told him. "I'm entitled."

Pablo stayed where he was.

"Tonight I indulge my every whim, why not?"

Confused and frightened, Pablo bared his teeth and tried to shrug. The man seemed extremely drunk. Or drugged. Yet his movements were deliberate. He was crazy, Pablo decided, and sick. His eyes were red-rimmed, he was pale and sweating. Sick to death, Pablo thought.

"Please," Tabor said. He knew it was a terrible thing to say.

"I think I waited for you," Naftali said. "The thief always comes."

Pablo panicked, coiled himself to spring and almost lost his balance. He was too frightened.

"You embarrass me," the old man said. Yet he was not so old, Pablo saw. Sickness and fatigue had drained him. "I'm dying."

Tabor could only stand and stare, taking each breath as it came. "Do you understand, Pablo?"

Pablo slowly shook his head.

Naftali smiled coldly.

"You are interrupting my suicide."

Tabor's mouth fell open.

"It's terrible," Naftali said. "A coarse intrusion at a solemn moment. What a rude fellow you are."

"I . . . I . . . don't know what to tell you," Pablo stammered. "I made a mistake."

"Definitely."

"I made a big mistake," Pablo Tabor admitted. "But I ain't gonna crawl, mister. Whatever happens gonna happen."

Naftali laughed and his eyes closed for a moment and Pablo considered a bolt for the door. The predatory eyes were on him before he could compose a move.

"You're young, Pablo."

Tabor swallowed.

"Have a drink," Naftali said. He reached over, took the brandy bottle from his night table and tossed it to Pablo. Catching it, Pablo held it by his chest for a moment, then took it in his right hand. He licked his lips. He was preparing to throw it in the man's face.

"Don't even think about it," Naftali warned him. "I want to see you drink."

Pablo stared at the bottle.

"No," he told Naftali. "No way."

"Think it's poisoned?" Naftali laughed again. "That would be funny, eh? I could go to eternity with a little thief at my feet. A Viking funeral. Don't worry," the old man said. "It's not the best brandy but it won't kill you."

Pablo took a sip and gently put the bottle on the foot of the bed.

"Sit," Naftali ordered him. He went across the room to a straight-backed chair and sat down with his head in his hands.

"We'll tell the story of our lives," Naftali said.

"I'm sorry," Pablo said. "I'm awful sorry. Lemme go, will ya?"

Naftali shook his head solemnly.

"An extrovert to the last, that's me, Pablo. But I'm a good listener too. Since you're here, we'll chat. But it must be about important things. Time is short."

Pablo started to speak, to plead. The barrel of the pistol was still trained on him. He put his hand over his eyes.

"I'm a thief like you," Naftali said. "An older and much

better thief. Smarter. If I were not a thief—who knows what
I'd be. A geologist. An opera singer maybe. A baritone. Scar-
pia." Still pointing the gun at Pablo, he leaned forward and
took the brandy from beside his slippered feet. "Truthfully,"
he told Tabor, "I think I would be a pianist, strange as it
seems. Now tell me—given your intelligence—if you were not
a thief what would you be?"

"The thing is," Pablo said, "I'm not a thief at all."

"Answer seriously."

"Shit, man, I don't know. Look, if you're gonna be easy
about this, would you mind if I just left?"

"I would mind," Naftali said. "Now answer."

"I got no idea in hell."

"Try harder."

"I suppose I'd be a lifer in the Coast Guard."

"Harder."

"I'd do things different." Then to his own surprise he said:
"Maybe I'd be a better father."

"Ah," Naftali said. "Now you're talking. Father to whom?"

"You want to know my story do you, mister?"

"I do. In your own words."

"I got a little boy. Nine. I was just wishin' he had a better
father. It just come to me here."

"Then why do you have to be a thief?"

"Because I got turned around. Just turned around and
around."

"Yes. Me also. What turned you around?"

"What did? Things did, is what. Things."

Naftali took the bottle of liquid Nembutal in his hand and
drank from it. He followed the drink with brandy, which he
swallowed without blinking, his eyes still on Pablo's.

"Things," he said. "Life? History?"

"Sure," Pablo said. "If you like."

A small wind chime tinkled against the closed shutter on
the window. Naftali turned toward it. Pablo saw that his hand
was still around the pistol.

"The last time I saw *my* father," the old man said, "he was
standing on a piano stool. He was showing our visitors that
there was no jewelry concealed in the light fixture. It was in a
faraway country of which you know nothing. My father was
wearing only pajamas and I had never—although I was al-

ready a graduate—I had never seen him in pajamas before. And my mother stood beside the stool and her hand was raised because she was afraid he would fall. I was there. I was also afraid. I wasn't Naftali then."

Pablo frowned. He could make no sense of it.

"Did they find any jewelry?" he asked after a moment.

"No jewelry. But in the stool there were some nocturnes of Chopin. Manuscripts in his hand. Right in the stool. So typical of my father."

"Huh," Pablo said. "Did they find them?"

"Oh yes, they found them. They came back for them. And for my parents and my sisters also. But I was gone." He picked up the brandy bottle and tossed it to Pablo. Pablo took a long drink. Naftali was listening to the wind chime.

"Hey, that's tough," Pablo said.

"Tough," Naftali repeated. "Happened a million times. Always has. Continues. History. History will turn you around every time, sailor."

"Well," Pablo said. "I hope you got your own back off the bastards."

Propped on one elbow against the bolster, Naftali shrugged.

"I had revenge. It wasn't enough." He turned toward the shuttered window again and the breeze drifting through stirred his sparse hair. "You can't get your own back."

Naftali's eyes were dulled. Pablo began to think he might come out all right.

"I keep remembering trains, Pablo. The last trains. Little gymnasia sweethearts waiting on platforms. Their parents waiting for them. And I alone am escaped to tell thee."

"What I don't understand," Pablo said, "is how come when you got all that money you're gonna throw it away."

"If you lived long enough, you might understand," Naftali said. "But you won't." He settled back beside the bolster; his hand, holding the pistol, rested at his side. "Know what Nietzsche tells us? He tells us that the thought of suicide helps bring a man through many a long hard night. Well, I'm grateful to Nietzsche for that observation—but, *danke schön*, no more nights."

Another breeze licked at the wind chime.

"All that bread, man—that could buy you a couple of good ones."

"You can buy lots of fancy nights. But you can't buy morning. Try sometime and buy yourself a short night for money, you'll see what I mean."

Talking was the thing, Pablo thought. "I couldn't be that negative," he said. "The way I see it, if money don't mean nothing then nothing does."

"I know the value of everything," Naftali said. "I've stolen it all and I've sold it all."

"Life is life. You just don't blow it off. Not me."

"A little cinder in the wind, Pablo—that's what you are. You're telling me—who set such store on my survival—that life is life?"

"It's me gonna be alive in the morning," Pablo said. He hoped it had not been rash of him.

"What for?"

"What for? Well . . . to keep it rolling, I guess."

"To keep it rolling," Naftali repeated. "To make the world go round. Maybe it goes better without you—what about that?"

Pablo watched him warily. The man seemed balanced on the edge of consciousness but his falcon's gaze was still sharp enough.

"I never thought of it that way," Pablo said.

"Try it."

"Are you gonna let me go?" Pablo asked.

"I had three wives," Naftali said. "Each one was an idealist. All went to prison. And I, a thief, a murderer, have never seen the inside of a prison."

"You been lucky."

"Why should I let you go?" Naftali demanded. He pulled himself upright in a sudden spasm of passion. "What are you worth? Explain yourself."

"Everybody's worth something," Pablo said. "I mean— everybody's life got some meaning to it. You know—there's a reason for people."

"No kidding? A reason for you? What is it?"

"I don't know," Pablo confessed. "I ain't found out yet. But I know there is one."

"But you're vicious and stupid, are you not?"

"No!" Pablo said hotly. He was shocked and enraged. "Of course not!"

Naftali's eyes went out of focus for a moment. His gaze wandered. Pablo tensed.

"I could have put an end to everything with this," the old man said, lifting his pistol. "But I thought—no. I want to go slow. I want to remember. Can you believe it? I wanted to remember everything."

"I believe it," Pablo said. He felt himself under Naftali's cold scrutiny again.

"You're a very stupid young man," Naftali told him. "I tell you this for your own good because you need to know it."

"Can I have a drink?" Pablo asked. Naftali let him come forward and take the bottle off the bed.

"When you're dead in some gutter for a dime, what happens to your son? It was you with the son, yes?"

"Yeah," Pablo said. "It was me."

"What happens to him? He becomes a thief like his father? Or what?"

Pablo put the brandy back on Naftali's bed.

"You really give a shit?"

"Tell me."

"He won't be nothing like me," Pablo said. "He'll be the total opposite of me."

Naftali turned toward the breeze again. The wind chime sounded.

"You won't get to sniff that wind where you're going," Pablo told him.

"I leave you the wind," Naftali said.

"Aren't you scared?"

"Of what should I be scared? Of devils?"

Pablo was impressed.

"You got a real heavy rep around this ocean, Naftali. I guess you know that."

"I got a heavy rep all over," Naftali agreed. "For my avarice and my readiness to kill."

"Listen," Pablo hastened to say, "I appreciate your bein' easy about this. I wouldn't blame you if . . ." Naftali's smile stopped him. A hard, bad smile, he thought. A dead smile. He froze in his chair.

"Revenge is not enough," Naftali said. "I know." The smile faded and the hardness left his eyes. "Not revenge. Not money. Liquor. Opium. Women. All the things we like, Pablo, you and me. They're not enough."

"Easy for you to say, pal. You've had all those things."

"Not enough."

"Well, hell. What's enough then?"

"I am not the man to ask, young sir. I can only tell you what is not."

Pablo began to rise from the chair but Naftali raised the gun and waved him back down. He took more Nembutal, then brandy, and rolled the bottle to Pablo.

"Drink."

Pablo had another pull and eased back in the chair.

"Trains," Naftali said softly. Pablo saw with embarrassment that he was crying.

"I sure did come to rip you off, Naftali. Sorry I picked tonight."

"Thank your lucky stars you picked tonight," Naftali said. He kept the gun pointed at Pablo; his left hand was groping under the bolster. It came up a clenched fist.

"If you're asked—tell them I'm dead. Tell them you saw me. That there's no mistake."

Pablo nodded. Naftali extended his closed left hand and opened it under Pablo's eyes. In the colorless palm was a small bright stone; it took Pablo a few seconds to realize that the stone was a diamond.

"Take it," Naftali said. His voice was empty of intonation, running down. Pablo looked at the stone, then at Naftali.

"You're giving me this?"

"I'm giving. Take it."

It was the biggest diamond Pablo had ever seen, although he had not seen many. It appeared to be five times the size of the one in his wife's wedding ring and he had still been paying for that one when he went over the hill.

"Goddamn," he said.

"I don't want them to get it here," Naftali said.

"Goddamn," Pablo said. "You're all right, boss, no shit."

"And," Naftali said softly, "I don't want you searching my room afterwards. It has . . . bad associations for me."

Smiling like a child, Pablo feasted his eyes on the diamond.

"Since I was young," Naftali told him, "I haven't given anything to anyone. Now there's no one but you and it costs me nothing. So take it, thief. Give it to the son you talk about and tell him . . ." He broke off in a massive yawn that seemed to exhaust him. "Or keep it and lie. Do what your nature compels."

"What do you want me to tell him, boss?"

"There is a creature in another dimension whose jewelry is dead worlds. When this creature requires more of them it plants the seed of life on a tiny planet. After a while there are people and then nothing—a patina."

"You want me to tell him that?"

The pistol fell from Naftali's hand. At the sound Pablo jumped up in alarm.

"The thief always comes," Naftali said. "Weren't you told by your mother?"

"Not by my mother, no."

"Yes," Naftali said. "Always."

The old man's eyes began to roll backward in their sockets. He said something too faintly for Pablo to hear.

"Es ist eine schöne . . ." Naftali whispered. "Ach. Trains."

Pablo leaned against the brass frame of the bed and bent down to hear.

"Brain coral," Naftali whispered to him. "It's only the outer coral of the brain . . ."

Tabor took the brandy bottle and sat down on the edge of the bed. He dropped Naftali's diamond into the breast pocket of his shirt.

"Pablo!"

"Yo," Pablo answered.

"There are reefs outside, Pablo. And reefs inside—within the brain of the diver."

"I don't understand you, boss," Pablo said. He realized then that he feared to lose the old man's presence.

But he had scored in spite of everything. Had made an idiotic overplay and scored all the same. He felt forgiven, favored by God.

"In the brain coral you see the skull of the earth, the heaping of the dead. You pass it going out . . . you see it in your mind . . . it's your own brain. Sometimes among the brain coral . . . the casing of a skull. It rolls under the reefs."

Pablo stood up, lifted the shutter slats and looked out into the quiet street. He saw no one save an elderly Chinese in a

Hawaiian shirt, walking his bicycle along the sidewalk. He turned and put the brandy bottle on the dresser, catching sight of his own lean brown face in the mirror as he did so.

"Pablo!"

"Still with you, boss."

"Your name rolls, Pablo. It's your skull down there—white and round. It shines in the clear light . . . eight fathoms under the fan coral. Your skull is the counter . . . it's the only ball in this game, Pablo."

He cursed me, Pablo thought, he turned around and cursed me. The chill of eight fathoms touched his heart. A dying man's curse.

Might it be, he wondered, that a man saw the future as he went out?

"Hey, man!" He shook Naftali's shoulder, lightly at first, then harder, trying to bring him back in over the reef. But Naftali's breathing was like the slow droning of some remote insensible machine, beyond call.

He stepped back and looked around the room, fingering the bottom of his shirt pocket where the diamond was. It was still possible, he thought, that there was more jewelry somewhere in the room. If there were even one more stone like the one in his pocket, he might buy time and freedom. If there were two or three more . . . the excitement made him clench his teeth and roll his upper lip in a hungry grin.

As he reached down to take his clip and gun from beside Naftali's unconscious body another thought came to him: that it might still be possible to bring the old man back, to get help, a doctor, an ambulance. But it was too late for that. There was too much to explain, too many forces at work. It would be a foolish gesture.

Naftali's pistol was a good one—Japanese, a new Nambu, eight shots, seven sixty-five.

Pablo set about searching the drawers and paper wardrobes. In one drawer, he found a wall crucifix. The other drawers held invoices, onionskin copies of contracts, letters typed in several languages, some in a strange alphabet he had never seen before. Only one was locked and when Pablo pried it open he found a stack of nearly a dozen passports from as many countries. The wardrobes held a few pairs of slacks and a great many short-sleeved white shirts.

He searched no further; he felt very tired now and it was

dangerous to stay. He sat back down in the chair for a few minutes and drank the rest of the brandy, listening to the wind chime and Naftali's last labored breathing. What, Pablo wondered, might he be seeing now?

The speculation threw him into a sudden panic.

He's too strong, Pablo thought desperately, he'll take me with him.

Tabor got to his feet, hesitated for a moment and then went quickly to the bed and slid the bolster from under Naftali's head. Staring hard at the colorless stucco wall before him, he pressed the bolster with all his strength into Naftali's face. There was a brief spasm of faint struggle, so faint that he might almost have imagined it. When he had finished, he dropped the bolster and wiped the sweat from his eyes. He could not bring himself to feel for the old man's heart.

Before turning out the light, he glanced quickly at the figure on the bed. Naftali's gray eyes were dull, there was spittle at his lips. No question now on which side of the reefs he lay.

Alone in the darkened room, he felt bereaved. He would interpret Naftali's words not as a curse, nor as a prophecy, but as a warning from the dead worlds. He besought Naftali's forgiveness. When he passed the open drawer where the crucifix lay, he crossed himself as he had seen Mexicans do.

What now, old man? he thought, touching the diamond.

There was nothing to do but go back to the *Cloud*.

The lower floor of the Hollandia was silent and dark now; its street door had been bolted. Pablo laid back the latch carefully. Outside, the island town seemed to have withdrawn into itself. He could hear only a distant car engine, a few dogs, the calls of the night birds that had tormented him in Compostela. He went down the front steps and out through the little garden fence and it was not until he had crossed the street and started down the neat little alley leading to the marketplace that he noticed the old Peugeot with an unlit taxi sign that was parked some distance down the road from the Hollandia, and that there was a man seated behind the wheel. The Hollandia's night light reflected on what might be the man's sunglasses or the visor of a driver's cap.

Aboard the *Cloud*, the Callahans were making merry in their saloon deck; Negus was on the bridge moodily tapering off on beer.

"Where the hell you been?" he demanded of Pablo. "Who in fuck said you could just take off?"

"I got finished loading," Pablo told him. "You were crapped out, so I thought I'd go over and lift a few."

Negus staggered out of the pilothouse. He looked slack with his day's drinking, his anger weak and without menace.

"Nobody told you you could have that pistol. Give it here."

"I need protection," Pablo said, "if I'm gonna walk around these foreign places." He handed Negus his forty-five. The Nambu was tucked in his belt, concealed by shirt-front.

"This ain't the goddamn Waterman Line," Negus said, as though he had thought of saying something else instead.

"Hell, I was over with Tino before. I thought it must be all right."

"Where is Tino?" Negus asked. "Was he with you?"

"Haven't seen him since this afternoon," Pablo said. He walked back to the lazaret with Negus' frail curses behind him.

Down in the compartment, he propped the hatch cover open with a marlinspike and lay down on his rack. When he closed his eyes, luminescent ranges of coral began to form behind them.

Godoy's church was in the hills above Puerto Alvarado, a square structure of whitewashed clay with the shapeless parody of a Norman steeple over its doorway. As soon as Justin opened the unpainted wooden door she heard the babies crying. Some Indian couples had come down from the Montana to have their infant children christened. The Indians knelt gravely in the candlelight around the font, the women in their dreary cotton shawls that were never sold in shops or exported, the men in khaki shirts and trousers, clutching straw sombreros with red and black marriage bands like coral snakes around the crown. The older children knelt behind the adults, equally grave and silent.

In turns the women rose to offer up their weeks-old infants and as Godoy, unassisted, poured the sacramental drops, the church would fill with the babies' thin cries and the liturgical hum of the godparents reciting their oaths. Justin sat waiting in a rear pew, out of the light. When she had been seated a minute or two, she looked across the church and saw two men, one white and the other Negro, sitting in a pew opposite. The two men had turned to watch her; they did so unselfconsciously. One of them had thrown a lazy arm around the back of the bench on which he sat. The men were wearing cheap silky sport shirts of a bright print.

Justin ignored them and sat facing the baptismal font. When the christenings were duly solemnized and Godoy, wielding his censer, blessed the Indians and his church, the two men crossed themselves. Justin, out of reflex, did the same.

Father Godoy, with a smile, walked the Indians to the door. Each of them turned their eyes toward Justin as they passed her; not one, not even the children, glanced at the men in the print sport shirts. Godoy opened the church door and stood in the doorway, a rhombus of fiery light, shaking hands and bestowing felicitations. The Indians gone, he remained there, shielding his eyes from the glare. The surplice over his black cassock was real lace, Justin saw; it was a strangely rich thing in so poor a place. A gift from his mother, she thought. Vestments were what their mothers gave them.

The two men in the church stood up, and passing Justin, affected to examine her with an insolence enriched by four hard centuries of tradition. At the doorway, they did as well for Godoy. When the two were outside, Godoy closed the door against the fiery light and locked it.

"Thank you for coming up," the priest said to Justin. He approached her and offered his hand with the same manner and with the same smile that he had employed for the Indian parents. The recognition of this troubled Justin slightly: she decided that it was his sincerity she saw.

"I've been waiting to hear from you," Justin told him, as indeed she had been.

Together they walked toward the front of the church and Godoy went to the baptistry to blow out the candles around the font. Justin sat in a forward pew to the left of the altar. With the candles out, the church was almost in darkness, lit only by two small windows of imitation stained glass over the ceiling beams and the red sanctuary lamp.

He sat down beside her and she could barely see his face. They were close together, nowhere touching; two creatures of sacerdotal dark.

"I sent for you to tell you I was leaving," the priest said.

She was surprised at the pain his words caused her. In the silence of the church, she thought he must have heard her shocked intake of breath. She fixed her eyes on the lamp beside the tabernacle.

"The work is in the mountains. It's very important for us to be there now."

"Of course," Justin said. "Whatever the necessity . . . wherever it's going on . . . you should be." She could not get it to come out right but her voice never broke.

"In the mountains we have started collectives—*ejidos*. There are nuns working there and the Indians are organized. They've done wonderful things there, these nuns. Our *compadresitas*."

Unlike the nuns here, Justin thought, who tend to be twittish, sentimental and useless. And who are not above a rush of raw hatred for the wonderful *compadresitas* in the mountains.

"We have the land there," Godoy told her. "We have it by right of occupation and by right of law. Very soon the landowners and the copper companies will send in the Guardia to take it back if we let them. But we're not going to let them. This time we resist, you see. And all over the country we will resist."

"What about the *foco* here?" Justin asked. "Is it going to happen?"

"Absolutely it will happen. When the signal is given. Arms are on the way. And it will be soon. Absolutely."

"And how will I know what to do?"

"You'll be directed by people who know you. You must prepare."

"We might have done things here as they did in the mountains," Justin said sadly. "We might have organized collectives on the land."

"The situation is different here. Here the foreign companies have what they want and the structure is not so visible. Also one is cut off on this coast. It can be liberated only together with the rest of the country."

"I thought the nursing was enough," Justin said, bowing her head. "I wasn't looking around me. I wasn't seeing. In all this time . . ." She could hear Godoy tapping his fingertips on the pew bench, impatiently.

"Don't reproach yourself. You have your job and I have mine."

After a moment she said: "I'm sorry you're leaving."

Godoy himself was silent for a while. She waited in the darkness for his answer.

"Interrupted friendships are disappointing" was what he said.

"Yes," Justin said calmly, "But I suppose they're very much part of the work."

"Sadly so."

Sadly so. He had done her the courtesy of informing her personally of his leaving and he wanted her to be off.

"How much notice do you think I'll have," she asked him, "before the dispensary is needed?"

"You were told to be ready at the shortest possible notice. At most you will have only a day or so. It depends on circumstances."

"O.K.," Justin said.

"I must go very soon. I have many things to do before I leave for the mountains."

"Yes," Justin said. "I have to go myself." In fact she had nowhere to go. Nothing of any value to attend to except the nursing of a dying drunk.

They sat beside each other, neither moving.

Will you just touch me, Justin thought, will you do only that much? I will do whatever you ask, I will face the Guardia, I will die, I will try to kill for you, will you just touch me? Will you do something for me, to me? Will you give me your hand? Will you give me anything?

Godoy stood up and waited in the aisle for her to do the same. She rose and walked the length of the aisle with him. A key was in his hand.

"Father Godoy," she said to him. He had not looked at her, had marched her straight back to the door which he was now unlocking. "Father Godoy!" She nearly shouted it at him. "What I care about . . . maybe all I care about . . . is me! Not about this country. Only about the way I myself feel."

He looked at her in silence for a moment and then he smiled. He had a sad smile for all the wind and weather, she thought.

"I think we are all that way deep inside. But there can be a coincidence of interest, can there not? Between justice and one's feelings."

In despair, she played the schoolgirl and then the penitent.

"Of course. But before I go there is something I want to say. I want to say it because we may never meet again. My feeling for you is particular. I have come to feel about you in a particular way."

Godoy had opened the door a crack. She stepped back from the light so that he might not see the shame in her face. It would have been so easy not to say anything. And then to say it in the absurd language of the cloister. Now it was too late.

In time suspended, she watched him search for an answer, saw his brows knit, his eyes shift. Then, without looking at her, he said: "I feel the same about you." Immediately she knew that he was lying. Whatever his feelings might be, his declaration to her was a simple lie, a pacifier.

She watched the Adam's apple bob in his white throat above the top button of his cassock and the thought came to her that he must be quite good at lying. But for her he was not trying very hard.

"There you see the extent of my selfishness and foolishness."

Godoy was genuinely embarrassed and perhaps concerned for his *foco*.

"Please," he said. He opened the door and they were standing together in the white hot light. "I am your friend, you can believe that. I need you to help me. These poor also need you."

"There was never any question of that," she said. "I'll be there when you need me."

Another melancholy smile. "Until later then, dear friend."

"Yes, until later," Justin said, and went down the three whitewashed steps. The two men in print shirts were on the corner and she needed all her strength to walk past them, calm and heedless with a friendly, superior nod.

On the drive back she let herself cry. She cried from shame and from revulsion at his deceit and unctuousness. But he was right, she thought. Her feelings were a child's feelings, and they were a matter of no importance. It was she, by all the rules of all the games, who was wrong.

By the time she was most of the way along the beach road, the sun was out of sight behind the mountains. Justin parked her jeep beside the ocean, climbed out and walked to the water's edge. For a long time she looked out over the ocean before her, still in sunlight and deep blue.

In all the working systems, she thought, the weakness was always yourself—that spot of gristle in the gears. It applied on every level—even the act of getting through a day could be performed with gusto and dispatch if you kept out of your own way. Justin believed that she knew as much as anyone about self-struggle. But if I win, if I crush myself, she wondered, what will be left of me? She was not so much afraid as curious. Would what was left be useful? And if so, in what way? Would what was left be happy? And there I am again, she thought. Me.

The self was only a girl, a young thing, brought in arsy-varsy. A One True Church was a One True Church, a scientific system was a scientific system, a Revolution, no less, was a Revolution, but a broad was only a broad. It was all so obvious.

I am unworthy, she thought. You are. We are. They are. We are all fucked flat unworthy, unworthy beyond belief, unworthy as a pile of shit. Help us there, you—help us crush ourselves out of recognition, help us to be without eyes without pudenda without any of those things. Most of all make us without childish feelings. Because it's that kid inside that makes us so damnably unworthy. We'll scourge ourselves, we'll walk in the fiery furnace, we'll turn ourselves around.

To do penance and to amend my life, amen. To struggle unceasingly in the name of history. Gimme a flag, gimme a drum roll, I'm gonna be there on that morning, yes I am. And it won't be the me you think you see. It'll be the worthy revolutionary twice-born me. The objective historical unceasingly struggling me. The good me.

And if I'm not there on that morning, she thought, I won't be anywhere at all.

She walked a few steps into the mild surf, wetting her chino trousers to the knee, and cupped two handfuls of salt water to pour over her face. When she started back to her jeep it was a few minutes before twilight and the hillside across the road had started to settle into evening. The first howler monkeys were awake and signaling their alarms, the diurnal birds settling down to cover among the thickest boughs, trilling the last calls of the day.

Something was in the road ahead; Justin stopped in her tracks. It was an animal running along the inshore shoulder, but it did not run so much as prance. And it was not an animal, it was a kind of man. The light was still strong enough for her to make out some of its colors—a topping of flaxen hair, white garments that were stained.

Back behind the wheel, she could not be certain that the stains were red. They were bright, of that she was sure. No fruit she knew would stain that brightly. She could not make the stains be anything but blood.

And she understood then that the creature she had seen was the young Mennonite who had passed the mission weeks before. The hillside now was darkening and apparently deserted, the road empty of traffic. Justin shivered, turned her headlights on and started the jeep for home.

Holliwell hobbled along a rutted pathway lined with frangipani toward the dining hall. The stars were out, the wind easy.

The half dozen working tables in the Paradise's utilitarian refectory were lined up along the seaward edge of the hall. Japanese lanterns hung from the rafters above them and from wire stays in the palm grove between the tables and the beach. On the other side of the huge floor space, some officers of the Guardia were lined up at the bar, drinking rum and listening to old Lucho Gatica records on the jukebox. Looking over the line of tables, Holliwell saw Mr. Heath sitting by himself over a gin and a dish of peanuts. Heath looked up and called him over.

"Hurt your foot, did you?" he asked. His face was florid in the lantern light, his nose and the skin under his eyes marked with swollen veins.

"I kneeled on a sea urchin over by the Catholic mission. There was a nun standing by to pull the spines out for me."

"Good luck. Was that sister Justin?"

"I never asked her name. I think she's the only one there."

"Yes," Heath said. "What brought you over that way?"

Holliwell shrugged. "Nothing special."

"What do you make of them over there?"

"I don't know what to make of them," Holliwell said. "What do you make of them?"

"They're quite pleasant, didn't you think?"

"Yes," Holliwell said. "Yes, they are."

Heath and Holliwell dined on fresh dorado. As they took dinner Mr. Heath said that he had been offered a position in the fruit company's new resort enterprise.

"Old hands like me are redundant since the blight," he told Holliwell. "The profits are in tourism. So it's take that up or retire."

"And which will you do?"

Heath smiled vaguely. At that moment, Holliwell realized how drunk the man was.

"When I first came out here," Mr. Heath said, "ten bandits and myself were the only force of law in two hundred miles of mountains. Great days they were."

Holliwell nodded.

"We could put a company blanket on a tree stump—leave it for weeks and no one would dare touch it. We were respected. We respected ourselves as well. Every morning I could get up and say—*Yo sé quien soy*. Understand?"

"Sure," Holliwell said.

"My men were able to say that because I made them able. And I didn't do it by avoiding their eyes and tipping them ten shillings for smiling at me. D'ye see?" He did not wait to be encouraged. "It reflected my training."

Holliwell was about to ask him where his training had been acquired.

"Nineteen years of age I was in the legion—the Légion Etrangère. Sidi Barras. Christ, great days!"

"And you came here after that?"

For his question, Holliwell received a momentary glance of dark and profound suspicion. It was a look to stay the timid and was obviously meant to be.

"After that I was in the Ceylon police. Had a bit of trouble there . . . a damn religious procession in Kandi. I was shown the instruments, you might say. Drove off in superintendent's car after a party and that was that. Then I came out here."

"Do you ever go back to England?"

"Can't," Heath said. "She's not there, bless her. Not my England. Of course, I was home for the war. I was with the Second Army."

"Montgomery . . . wasn't it?"

Heath laughed. "Yes. Monty. Teetotaler."

When the server took their plates, he called for more gin. Holliwell, who was fighting a wave of fatigue, would try to counter it with another small rum.

"We're going to have tourists coming down here at the rate of a few thousand a month. We're going to have me spying through keyholes so the hotel staff doesn't pinch their Minoxes. We're going to teach the people to steal and we're going to teach them contempt for us."

Holliwell began to say something about jobs for the populace. About giving them a share.

"These people don't like being poor, Holliwell. No one does. We're going to teach them to be ashamed of being poor and that's something new, you see."

"That's the American way," Holliwell said.

Heath sniffed. "Don't like to see a man run his country down. Not abroad."

"I'm not doing that. I think what's best about my country is not exportable."

Mr. Heath did not hear him. "We're all wringing our bloody hands, that's it. We've been doing it since the war. Apologizing and giving in and giving over and not one black, brown or yellow life have we saved doing it. We want to be destroyed, you see. So we will be."

At the bar, the celebrating Guardia officers had grown progressively more hilarious. But a few of them, drunker than the others, were subsiding into a sinister quietude. They were not coastal people but Indians and mestizos from over the mountains and their style of being drunk was different. They leaned on the bar as though holding themselves up, communicating to each other in single shouted words, in whistles, sudden gestures, bursts of unpleasant laughter. Some telepathy of alcohol.

The Miami dentist came in, accompanied by a tall youthful man in an elegant *guayabera*. Behind them came Mrs. Paz and her sons, all combed and scented. Their entrance was cordially saluted by everyone present, not least by the officers at the bar. Holliwell gave them good evening and Heath, who apparently knew the tall man, did the same. The tall man, Holliwell assumed, was Mrs. Paz's brother.

When the Cuban party were seated and served, an American couple came in from the darkness outside, and seated themselves at a table behind Holliwell's chair. Holliwell had time to observe them as they passed.

The woman was of a certain age—perhaps in her forties, though she might also have been sixty or even older. She wore a muumuu with a coral necklace at her fleshy throat, and her hair, dyed deep black, was pasted against her temples like Pola Negri's. The man was lean, pale and thick-lipped. He had very close-shaven hair and small dark eyes; his face preserved a kind of desiccated youthfulness. He was in white, even to his loafers.

The couple's entrance induced an attitude of watchful menace in the drunken Guardia officers at the bar. But it appeared that no one knew them.

Mr. Heath watched them sit down, drawing thoughtfully on the lemon slice that had come with his fish.

"Stew Nabbs was in Key West," Holliwell heard the man say. He himself was at the point of exhaustion. Of course the rum did not revive him.

"Ugh," the woman muttered in a deep coarse voice, "the pits. *The* pits."

The man giggled. A tiny-eyed giggle.

"Well," Holliwell told his dining companion, "I'm going to bed. I'm out of it."

Mr. Heath leaned forward and addressed him softly with a bland half smile.

"You're not to go. Stay where you are."

"I'm afraid I don't understand," Holliwell said.

Heath glanced over Holliwell's shoulder at the couple and fixed his eyes on Holliwell's.

"I want you to listen to these people. They're extremely interesting."

"What a guy," the man behind Holliwell was saying to his friend. "Indictments on him from here to Seattle and he's living it up in Key West. A house, you know? A bankroll. Fuckin' guy. But it won't last."

Holliwell shrugged and frowned a question at Mr. Heath.

But Heath had settled back like a man about to listen to some beloved music.

"Stay," Heath whispered. "Listen."

"You lived with him," the woman said.

"I went by his pad up there. Off Duval. He's got a kid passed out in the garage—the kid's fourteen? Fifteen? On a tank of gas. I split. I said, 'See you, Stewart.'"

"You were his pal," the woman said.

"New York, Clyde Hotel. Aagh. That fuckin' place. Needle Park over there."

"Hey," the woman crooned. "Hey, I remember, Buddy. Do I remember?"

"You remember Phelan, the loan shark?"

"I was into Phelan," the woman said. Holliwell tried to bring her face to mind again. "You were also, Buddy. And Stew."

"Everybody was. Me and Stew were supposed to be whattayacallit. His men."

"His leg breakers," the woman said. In a sweet singsong, like one reminding a child of a lesson forgotten. "And legs were broken, in my recollection."

The man began to curse immoderately.

"How was your dive today?" Heath asked.

"I was just thinking of the dive," Holliwell said. "It was a lot of things."

The young man was speaking again.

"That little harelip from Riker's. The fuck was doing six bits a day and going to Phelan. Simpleminded. Phelan says put the arm on the little stiff. So we go to the big hotel there, the Ansonia. They got offices there, everything. Pay phone and we order shit from Riker's. An hour later comes the harelip and we jump him. He runs, he screams like a cooze. Runs up a dozen flights of stairs. Finally me and Stew get him on the top floor. We hold him over the stairwell by his feet and it rains coin. His change, his wallet, his works, everything goes—and he's upside down there making little bird noises. The whole goddamn time he never let go of that burger."

"Down the purple corridor," the woman declared, "the scarlet ibis screaming ran."

"You know what Phelan says? He says how come you didn't drop him?"

Holliwell's eyes met those of Mr. Heath.

"Twixt, wasn't it?" Heath asked. "I remember that wall very well. See anything marvelous?"

"There was something down there. I don't know what."

"Stew had holes in his shoes," Buddy told his dining companion. "He wore rubbers every day. Fucking Clyde Hotel."

"And Phelan passed away?"

"Did he ever," Buddy said.

"Did you find it frightening?" Heath asked Holliwell.

"Oh," Holliwell said, "I suppose. I gather it's a sinister place."

"It's never been my idea of a sinister place," Heath said.

"Right after Phelan got it," the man behind Holliwell said, "Stew's wig snapped. He went funny."

"Ha," the woman said, "I heard. I know what it was."

"No, Olga," the man said. He lowered his voice. "No, you don't."

The officers at the bar were much quieter now, drunk almost to silence. They neglected to play the jukebox. At one end of the dining hall, a waiter was counting out white candles from a stack on a table before him.

"We were still in the Clyde. Stew was chicken-hawking. All these kids, in and out. He dealt. He had a string."

"Those kids are lousy," Olga said. "Detestable."

"He left town. He did one."

"He did?"

"He did one. He took this chicken out."

"Curtains?"

"I'm telling you," Buddy said. "He went to L.A. I saw him there. Hollywood he went to."

"The Boulevard of Broken Dreams," Olga said.

"He had chickens on skateboards. Dolls, a couple. Hustling."

"Tray bizarre," Olga said.

"Bizarre. He was on Percodans. He was into snuffing. Him and a friend."

"Some friend."

"They had clients took pix. They ran the roads, Stew and this friend. Chicken snatching. Kids up the bazoom, they grabbed them. The freeways, like. Off the street."

"Gollywilkins," Olga said.

The Japanese lanterns in the palm grove flickered, went out, then came on again. The officers at the bar were leaving. One of them staggered past the tables into the grove, belched loudly and began to piss in the frangipani. Over the palm crowns hung an infinity of stars.

"It's the simple life down the wall at Twixt," Mr. Heath told Holliwell. "Clean down there. One sees so far."

"I was thinking it was the same up here."

"Humanist fallacy," Heath said. "Appearances deceive. There's a philosophical difference."

Holliwell was unable to answer. Mr. Heath had proved himself a philosopher and once again Holliwell caught the saffron taste of Vietnam. The green places of the world were swarming with strongarm philosophers and armed prophets. It was nothing new.

Heath was looking over Holliwell's shoulder, holding his expression of affable uninterest. Buddy had lowered his voice further, it trembled with rodential wariness.

"Chickens were disappearing. Stew had these pix. He sold them. Famous names, he says."

"Intense."

"Me, I'm shit scared. I know this is happening. Stew knows I know. His friend is a big pinhead."

"Poor baby."

"The cops are finding these *children*, Olga. Blipped. Bitty kids almost. Sans parts. It's big in the paper."

"The parents don't care," Olga said. "They sell them."

"Snuff pix, chickens, that was Stew. He was obnoxious about it. He said it was big."

"Did he say he liked it?"

"He never said. I figure he liked it, right? I was scared, Olga. I left town."

"The kids ask for it sometimes," Olga said. "They're lousy at that age."

"That's what Stew says. I says: See you, Stew. I was scared."

"This," Olga said, "is why I won't live in Los Angeles today."

When they stood up, Heath gave them a friendly nod. Holliwell forced himself not to turn around.

"Do you know how I came to notice them?" Heath asked.

His florid face held the polite amiable smile. "It was a way of laughing that bastard had. When I heard him laugh I knew what I had before me."

"Not your ordinary run of tourist," Holliwell offered.

"Yes . . . well, what's ordinary today? There's a very rubbishy sort of American loose on the world these days. If you don't mind my saying so."

"All kinds of people have money and leisure in the States. Surely you know that."

"I thought the American of thirty years ago was a better type," Mr. Heath said. "Not much savoir-faire but a sounder sort of chap."

"I know who these people are," Holliwell said. "I know what they come out of. I know more than I want to about them."

"So their dinner conversation doesn't shock you?"

"Does it shock you?"

"Not me, mate. I was there when we went into Belsen and quite honestly that didn't shock me either."

"What did it do for you?"

"It aroused my workmanlike instincts," Mr. Heath said. "I have the same reaction to . . . them."

"Olga and Buddy."

"Yes. Olga. And Buddy. They make me think—ha, boyo. Time to go to work."

"It is the same," Holliwell insisted. "Up here and down the wall. It's the same process."

"That's very tender-minded of you. Are you going to tell me all that lives is holy?"

"Not me," Holliwell said. "But even Olga and Buddy have a kind of innocence, don't they? And their friend in the story?"

"Holliwell," Heath said. "Holliwell—God may forgive Olga and Buddy and company—he doesn't have to share the world with them. You have children, I suppose?"

Holliwell confessed that he did.

"There's someone murdering children in the villages here, did you know that? He's killed five kids already."

"I didn't know. But that has nothing to do with these people."

"Don't you know your own side, man? I can assure you that I do. And when I hear that laugh—when I catch that

pong in the air I feel like our good missionary friends, ready
to go into my cure of souls. I believe that God gave the likes
of Olga and Buddy and the late Rudolf Hoess into my espe-
cial keeping. But because this civilization is corrupt and cow-
ardly, because it insists on being tyrannized by weak, bent
neurotics who don't know the fucking meaning of self-respect
or mercy—I can't do my job."

His knuckles were white on the glass of gin. He blinked and
sipped of the drink and smiled again. "So I feel frustrated,
you see."

The officers of the Guardia were leaving the bar. The last to
go whistled unpleasantly for the shy black barmaid who had
been nervously serving them; when she came up to him, he
stuffed a wad of bills under the bodice of her bright tight
dress. Then he turned and watched the two men at the table
across the hall.

"I'm a copper, really," Heath said.

"Why did you ask me if I was frightened down the wall?"

"Ah," Heath said, "Rude of me. Sorry."

"I didn't think it was rude. Just a little peculiar."

"My manners are dreadful," Mr. Heath said. "I expect I'll
have trouble in the resort business."

At Serrano on the windward shore, the frayed ends of a
norther whipped the winch chains against the stabilizers and
set the mooring lines to groaning. The dock lights showed
soiled whitecaps speckling the milky harbor. Pablo worked the
fuel line with one of Naftali's pier hands. Freddy Negus
leaned against the bridge housing, smoking, staring into the
darkness beyond the lights. He was waiting for Tino.

Naftali's men worked quickly. The crates of weapons,
greased in creosote, were loaded in the holds on a waterproof
tarp; the tarpaulin's ends were tucked down and the holds half
filled with sixteen-pound blocks of ice. Within an hour of
tying up, the *Cloud* was nearly ready to get under way again.

In other circumstances, Negus would have kept a close eye
on the loading, but on this night he let the dockers go about
their work unsupervised. His attention was fixed on the un-
lighted road that led to the pier. Across the bay, the lights of
an oil refinery glowed like the towers of a phantom city.

Slightly above them, on a cactus-covered hillside deep in darkness, were the dim, scattered lights of Serrano Town. A wall of barbed fencing and thorny acacia divided Naftali's marina from the desert wilderness outside.

The dirt road that led to the pier was blocked by two Dodge trucks parked head to head across it; fifty yards beyond them was a steel hut lit by a single naked bulb over its doorway. A man with a holstered pistol stood under the light watching the loading operation. Negus cursed and went into the cockpit.

"I reckon he's not coming," Negus said.

Mrs. Callahan was stocking the galley shelves; Callahan himself was bent over his charts.

"And what does that mean?" Deedee Callahan asked.

"He never done this before," Negus said.

Callahan said nothing.

"Listen," Negus said, leaning on Callahan's chart table. "Put it together, man. We've got this punk off the coast on our hands. Then Tino goes over and he doesn't come back."

"What are you suggesting?" Callahan asked. "That the kid did away with him?"

"By Christ, I wish I knew. But all of a sudden Tino's gone and he doesn't come back. Either he's in something he can't get out of—or else he thinks the deal's queer and he's pulling out."

"Wouldn't he have let you know?" Deedee asked.

"Hell, I'd have thought so. Maybe he wasn't able." Negus turned from the chart table and looked out through the windshield at the dark water. "It's always number one first in this business. That's the rule."

Callahan kept his eyes on the chart, not answering.

When the fueling was done, Pablo took a brief turn at loading crates. He, too, was watching the dark road that led to the pier, thinking of the room in the Hollandia Hotel where the wind chime would be sounding faintly on the light breeze. From the pilothouse he heard Negus' rasping petulant drawl. As he stepped onto the dock, he noticed that the armed man beside the shed had turned to look down the road, and that far in the distance along it was a flickering, wavering light. Pablo glanced over his shoulder at the pilothouse and jogged toward the shed.

"What's up?" he asked the guard.

The guard looked at him, shrugged and looked down the road again.

As the light drew closer, Pablo saw that it was the night light of a bicycle; a tall islander wearing a mack's violet platform shoes was pumping it along the sand-and-shell track. He pulled up beside the iron shed and wiped the sweat from his eyes. He and the man who stood by the shed spoke together in Papamiento. The rider held a manila envelope in his hand.

"Boy come up from town," the guard told Pablo. "Got a letter for Mr. Negus."

Pablo turned around and saw that the bulk of the iron shed stood between him and the *Cloud*'s bridge.

"I'll take it," he said.

"You Mistuh Negus?"

"That's right," Pablo said. "Just give it here."

The man with the bicycle spoke again. He, too, wore a pistol on a web belt around his waist.

"This man say the boy come from the city. Twenny mile. Got to give him sometink."

Pablo reached into his pocket for a handful of island bills. Gulden. He put a wad of them into the rider's hand. He had no idea of how much they might amount to; they turned out to be enough.

While the guard and the armed rider stood by, Pablo walked to the light from the shed's doorway and stood where he was still out of eye line from the shrimper's deck. He took a note out of the manila bank envelope and read by the naked bulb.

"Deer Fredd," said the note, "I muste tell you in haaste. Thees jung pog Pablo ben by Naftalie and that man by him morded. Sure bad you knowe it yeerself. You know brudeer I ben skipping wit you everie ways but thees onie gone be deadt ver us. I doont daar mov vom this place I een. Policia ben versoor. I tinkie say mouten to olde mann. Beterie saaf yoorselv. Die Shell tug standen byheer we get outen byher. Olde mann got to see hees oun way outen. We get to Curacao and that's de ende to it. Thees Pablo a ritt bastad.

"Ritten in Jesus Christ, Valentine."

Pablo put the note in his pocket. The bicycle rider spoke again.

"Dey tell de boy wait for an answer."

"No answer," Pablo said. "It's all right." Pablo pursed his lips in outrage. "Damn lucky you got up here," he told the blank-faced rider. "Really appreciate it."

In the wheelhouse, Mr. Callahan was setting his Rolex to the time signals from Corn Island. Negus ran his hands through his thinning hair as though the steady double beats from the receiver were flaying his nerves.

"If Tino doesn't show," he told Callahan after a moment, "I'm not going."

"We've just concluded that he isn't going to show," Callahan said. "Have we not?" Deedee Callahan looked in turns at Negus and at her husband, the shell of a pistachio nut clenched in her white teeth. "Stop it, Freddy," Callahan said. "Don't be an old woman."

"You're a damn fool," Negus said. "That's what you are."

"Where is our sloe-eyed boy?" Callahan asked his wife. "Where's he got to?"

Deedee put her head out to see.

"He's up on the hatches," she said. "Looks like they're about done."

"Go and stroke him," Callahan said. "Keep him out of harm's way. Freddy and I have to talk."

He watched his wife smooth her hair as she went forward.

"If you don't go, Freddy, I can't go. And God knows I've set my heart on it."

"You have to know when not to go, Callahan. I do if you don't."

"Freddy," Callahan said, "you owe me one."

"Not my bloody life, Jack. I don't owe you that."

Callahan rolled up the chart he had been studying and put it in a drawer beside the map table.

"I can't go just me and Deedee and that kid from nowhere. Those bastards on the coast—they'll take the weapons and then they'll board and sink us. I need at least one man I can trust."

"Don't go."

"My dear man, I have to go. I must. I bet the ranch on this run."

Negus looked away from him.

"Remember what happened to Otis in Grenada, Freddy? Him shorthanded and his boat full of M-1s?"

"He made it to St. Eustatius," Negus said absently. "They're good people there."

"Now here we are," Callahan said. "We've paid and we've loaded cargo. We can't quit now. I can't."

"I can," Negus said. "Tino did."

Callahan closed his eyes, rested an elbow on the chart table and put his hand over his eyes.

"Listen to me, Freddy. We won't have money on board until we deliver. Pablo wants to do us, it's the money he's after. We can keep him in line until then."

"Maybe. What about then?"

"Then," Callahan said, "kill him. In fact he's yours for the whole run. If you seriously feel he's more trouble than he's worth, deep-six him. I'll leave it to your discretion."

Negus was silent for a while. Callahan turned in his seat to read the tide tables.

"No chance of paying him off now and turning him loose?"

"No chance," Callahan said without looking up.

Negus leaned in the hatchway, his teeth set in a rictus of unease.

"Shit, if it's up to me I'll put him over as soon as we clear the reef."

"No, you won't, chum. You'll be patient. When the balloon goes up you may learn to love him."

When Deedee Callahan came back, Negus turned on her in surprise.

"Where's the kid?"

"He's right where he was," she said. "What's happening, gentlemen? Are we setting forth or not? Because this vessel's all loaded and the dock boys are wondering what we think we're doing."

"Take her out, Freddy," Callahan said.

Negus put his fishing cap on, went out on deck and shouted at Pablo to let go the mooring lines.

Callahan took the whiskey down from a pantry shelf and poured himself a shot. "And how's our young man?" he asked.

"He's in some kind of sulk. You ever see a speed freak trying really hard not to talk? That's how he is."

"In the words of a great Irish wit," Callahan said, "it's not enough to opt for silence. You have to consider the kind of silence."

"Ah," Deedee said, "that's very good. But you know something, Jack baby, I don't like this too well."

"You could have fooled me."

"He *is* bad news. He is, he is."

"Then we'll kill him," Callahan said. "Stay close to him. We'll want to know what's on his mind."

"He's not dumb. Remember that."

"Isn't he?"

"Not at all. He's pretty fucking clever."

"Too bad," Callahan said.

"So this time it's me who gets to drink if I'm supposed to stay close to him. And it's you that stays sober. Because he's not dumb and you better be on top of things."

"You're right, of course."

"Damn straight," Deedee said. "Some fun, hey, boss?"

"That's what we're here for," Callahan said.

All night they steamed with the stabilizers down, rolling almost dangerously before a dying northeast swell. At dawn a roseate raft of clouds was massed over a solitary mountain to southward. Clouds there seemed to slip away reluctantly on the wind and were replaced by others that, singly or in packs, came over the flat far horizon and made straight for the veined slopes that were brightening to green. It was San Ignacio, once English, then Colombian and Panamanian by turns, now its own, or anyone's, island.

Pablo had settled in the lee of the after hatch; sleeping in short fits, sliding into undersea dreams, awakening to the stars. Spray had started him once and he had lifted his head to see white water racing under the rails and felt the vessel's boards tremble from the power of the engines and a steady slap of the bow against the sea ahead. They had been making a speed which he could not calculate but a speed of which no shrimper on earth was capable. When she settled down to her accustomed fifteen knots he had gone to sleep again.

The rumble of the Lister engine raising the stabilizers woke him to morning. He backed off to the rail and turning, saw in the distance a white reef line and green hills fading into cloud. The deep black valleys among the hills were inlaid with rainbows.

"That's Tecan," Deedee told him.

And he recalled that she had been around all through the night, smart-talking and boozing, coming on. He had paid her no mind. She was lying across the hatch cover now, in jeans and no shirt at all, leaning her chin on her hands. Pablo felt for the diamond in his shirt pocket and found it over his heart.

He saw Freddy Negus come out of the wheelhouse and engage the windlass engine. They were settling down for the day. Negus never looked in his direction; he felt that the man was trying not to see him.

"So," Deedee Callahan asked him, "you believe in the invisible world?"

It was just smart talk, but the words troubled him. He turned over the leeward rail to piss.

"I don't know what you mean," he said.

"You don't sleep much, do you?"

"I don't feel the need of it much."

"In the Navy they say, 'All time not spent in sleep is wasted.' Don't they say that in the Coast Guard?"

"Yeah," he said. "They do."

He saw that in the smooth flesh of her shoulder there was a miniature tattoo, the links of a chain. It was tiny and elegant, a beauty. She saw him looking at it.

"Chain of Cashel," she told him. "It stands for eternity. On and on and on and on and you don't know where she starts from and you don't know whither she goes. So you string along."

She was smoking a reefer. It seemed to him that she had been smoking through the night; he had been smelling it in his dreams.

She rolled over and he looked quickly at her breasts; they were small and round, young, a paler tan than her shoulders.

"This is Praisegod Reef," she said.

Looking over the side, he saw no reef; the water under the boards looked as deep and blue as the expanse around them. He turned to look at the coast again, wondering if it could be the same coast they left three days before.

"I spent so many mornings here," she said, offering him the joint. He shook his head. "So many mornings I wonder how many. Mornings."

"On this thing?" Pablo asked.

It seemed to take her a moment to realize that he meant the boat.

"Hell, no." She was looking toward the coast with a melancholy vacant smile. "On the real *Cloud*. The real article."

"What was that?"

Deedee raised the joint to her lips and drew from it. "That was," she said slowly, "that was a schooner, boy. Seventy-footer, two masts. She was built in Halifax, she was a Lipton Cup racer and you could smell her teak before you saw her coming. That was the real *Cloud*."

"Where's she at now?"

Deedee shrugged, pouted her lips and opened them with a little groan.

"She's in times past. Sailing along in past perfect."

Pablo snickered at her. He told her she was stoned.

"I been staying awake on this dope," she said. "It's good for that."

"How come you been staying awake?"

"How come you have?" she asked. She got no answer from him. "The We Never Sleep Shrimp and Shit Corp., right? Eternal vigilance is the price of parsley."

Pablo was watching the anchor chain grow taut as they drifted to windward. The hook was fast on bottom.

"How come he put the hook over?" Pablo asked.

Deedee flipped the end of the jay overboard and rolled onto her stomach.

"Better ask *him* that, Pablo."

In the cockpit, Negus maneuvered the dial on the *Cloud*'s VHF receiver; the cabin hummed with submarine static and faint Spanish voices. He and Callahan looked at each other and sat back to wait. Callahan glanced at his watch.

Quite shortly, what might well have been an American voice came in loud and clear.

"Waterbrothers, this is Marie Truman, you copy? Over."

"Well, well," Callahan said. "There he is now." He picked up the mike.

"Marie Truman, Waterbrothers. Copy real well. What kind of night you have up there?"

"Waterbrothers, Marie Truman. Slow night. Scraping the rocks. We got us a sawfish bill. Over."

Callahan grinned at Negus.

"Marie Truman, Waterbrothers. Don't throw that away, hear? It's worth forty bucks on the beach. Over."

"Waterbrothers, Marie Truman. We'll see you-all up to Gracias a Dios tomorrow. Have a nice day. Over."

"Marie Truman," Callahan said, "this is Waterbrothers. You have a good one too. Out."

"Isn't he a darling?" he asked Negus. "He's playing he's a Texas boat. And he's got what we want and we have what he wants."

"We still got all day," Negus said.

"If we have him on VHF he's within seventy miles of here." Callahan went to the chart table and brushed a worn copy of Bowditch from on top of his coastal charts. "By his co-ordinates he's coming out from a place called French Harbor. Coming out over a reef." He took a pair of reading glasses from the breast pocket of his tennis shirt and bent to the chart. "There's supposed to be a church tower there. Anyhow it's just a hair down from Puerto Alvarado and they have all kinds of lights. So we'll run past him around dusk. See what we got to work with and take a sight bearing."

"You get the weather?"

"Beautiful weather, Freddy. Fair. Light northerly. And no moon until after midnight."

"That guy speaks gringo awful good," Negus said. "God help us if that's the Guardia we're talking to. You know," he said, "they got a lot of Yankee know-how behind them."

"Ah, Fred," Callahan sighed, "if they had him they'd want me. And here I am right on their front porch."

"Maybe they got you and they want him."

"Then how would they have his codes? Use your head for Christ's sake."

Negus went on deck and swept the coastward horizon with his binoculars.

"Nothing happening," he told Callahan when he came in. He set the glasses down in their box beside the windshield.

"The thing is, Fred," Callahan told him, "you do a thing or you don't. Now we are *doing* this thing, so let's carry on and do it without bitching all the time."

"I was thinking," Negus said. "Our people could be just a nice bunch of good patriotic Spanish boys. Probably just pay up and take their hardware. Probably wouldn't give us trouble at all."

"Then we could get rid of Pablo right now, couldn't we?"

"That's right," Negus said.

"But it's more likely they're a bunch of fucked-up *ratones*. You don't get a good class of Spanish boy on this coast anymore. Not since the cocaine boom."

Negus put his head out of the cabin hatch and looked aft at Pablo, who was propped against the lazaret with his hat over his eyes.

"Goddamn that guy," he said.

She was driving in from Alvarado with two ten-pound sacks of beans and a few kilos of fruit when she saw Campos in the road before her. His jeep was parked so that it blocked passage to any other vehicle and he stood in front of it, languidly waving her down, his Foster-Grants ablaze in the afternoon sun. Although she had firmly made up her mind not to be afraid of Campos, the positioning of his jeep troubled her. Someone would have to back off—a minor matter on the face of it but a confrontation, charged with suggestions of authority, confidence and guilt. She stopped her own jeep in the middle of the road and stayed behind the wheel.

Lieutenant Campos came forward and looked her body up and down. His attitude was not in the least jocular or flirtatious.

"Sister Justin" was all he said. She tried to find his eyes behind the reflecting glass.

"Good afternoon, Lieutenant."

He passed by her and examined the provisions in the rear seat.

"We understand you're leaving our poor country."

"Yes," she said. "Before long."

"You've been ordered to go."

"By our provincial," she said. "As soon as is convenient."

The lieutenant leaned against her jeep and looked out to sea.

"Twenty pounds of beans. Going to take them back to Yanquilandia with you?"

"We still have people to feed."

"Hippies," Campos said.

Justin was at a loss for words. It was true that some of the long-haired foreign travelers had been turning up around the mission grounds and some of them looked like settling in. She was aware that Egan had taken to spending his evenings out back and that this visitation somehow involved him. As far as she knew—and she kept close accounts—the kids in the ruins never stole. They brought in their own provisions. But the business could not have come at a worse time; somehow she would have to put a stop to it. Since Godoy's departure she had received no further orders.

"We didn't ask for these people," she said, "and we're not feeding them. The ruins are a natural tourist attraction. We're not responsible for our location."

"Hippies aren't tourists," Campos told her. "They repel tourists."

Justin had the sense that a great deal depended on her behavior at that moment. It was necessary for her to seem confident and also necessary for her to determine what Lieutenant Campos had on his mind—never an easy enterprise. Justin had little knowledge of policemen in general but through Campos she had discovered that being crazy did not stand in the way of one's being a good cop.

"So this doesn't help the country as a mission should. But the contrary."

What now, she thought, rational discourse? She had no idea how much he knew or suspected, except that she was somehow subversive. Was he simply upset further about hippies in his jurisdiction? Was this new apostolate of Egan's a weakness that he was seizing on to hurry them out of Tecan? Or was it much more, a little cat-and-mouse before he brought the whole sorry structure down—the *foco* that might or might not be, her, Godoy—with his simian Guardia fist?

By God, she thought, if he knows what I'm up to he knows more than I do.

"If you wish," she said, "we'll advise them to move along. On your recommendation."

"They're murdering children," he said. "Six children have died."

Justin let go the wheel, which she had held to like a steersman throughout the encounter, and stared at the lieutenant in horror.

"No!" was all that she could manage. Her combatant's poise deserted her.

Campos smiled. "Yes. Murdered. Six."

"These killings," Justin said, "these killings . . . they began months ago. If we had the slightest evidence or suspicion . . . the slightest . . . we'd report it."

"How do I know that?" Campos asked.

Justin fought to keep her temper in bounds.

"We have all been horrified by these murders, Lieutenant." Her fury grew, but as it did she came to realize that something more frightening and more fatal than simple harassment was going on. "We have all been puzzled by the Guardia's lack of success in solving them. You can be sure we'll help in any way we can."

"You're puzzled by the Guardia's lack of success?"

"Disappointed."

"Ah," said Campos as though soothed. "You know," he said, "it's funny. We both have uniforms to wear. I wear mine. But you—never. Are you still a nun?"

"You can consult the church authorities and the Interior Ministry in regard to that. I'm a nun. This is not the capital and we're permitted to dress for work."

"Only a confusion of traditions, then?"

"I suppose," she said.

"Then you may be sure," Campos said, "that in this jurisdiction you'll be treated as what you are."

She made herself smile. Whence came the smile and how she had mustered it she had no idea. It pleased her then to smile at him.

"We thank you, Lieutenant."

He stood about for a moment whistling tunelessly through his teeth.

"Now, Sister, have the goodness to back up your vehicle and let me pass."

She put the jeep in reverse and backed into soft sand hard by the water's edge. For a moment, the wheels spun; she cursed softly. The rear wheels spun free of the slough.

"Excuse me, Sister," Campos asked, "did you speak?" He had backed his own jeep onto higher ground and was straightening out to pass.

"No, I didn't," she said.

He threw his jeep into gear and gunned the engine briefly. "Nuns don't curse," he shouted at her. "Not at me."

And then he was off at his customary speed.

"Que le vaya bien," she said to herself as she eased back onto the track. Driving the rest of the way, she kept her attention and her mind on the road. She was very frightened and she wanted nothing more than to go back to her quarters, close the shutters and stretch out in the cool darkness. Things would come clearer to her there.

Back at the mission, she showered and lay down; for a short time, under the weight of her fear and exhaustion, she actually slept. Awaking from a confusion of dreams, she found herself confronted with a simple certainty. The notion that the Devotionist mission at French Harbor could be used as a tactical location in the coming struggle represented a coincidence of fond fantasies. It had been compounded of her own egoism and the Tecanecans' naïve confidence in the protection afforded by the American flag.

If the Movement was dismissive of Campos as a venal thug, then they had not understood his obsessiveness. To them, presumably, he was simply a sly and brutal timeserver—the ideal enemy. She herself was convinced that there was more to him than that; he had a spider's-web aura of schizoid insights around him, an odor of unclean appetites that seemed to concentrate on her. He was always asking Charlie Egan about her, asking the merchants, the *campesinos*. It was beyond suspiciousness. In a peculiar way, he seemed more intelligent than a social agent of the Guardia should be; it was as if he had succeeded in becoming everything that the other swaggering sneering bastards of his organization pretended to be. Then, if he was as unsoundly intelligent as she suspected, he would be as attached to the idea of a *foco* on the coast as the rebels were. He would have planted the idea on his superiors in the capital and he would, of course, have connected it with the straggling Devotionists. It would be, in a sense, his project too. Captain Campos. General Campos.

The whole thing suggested internal betrayal as well. Tecan was full of police informers; they would have penetrated the

Movement, perhaps to its highest level. A fiasco that dissipated the Republic's revolutionary energy would buy the government ten years. Or longer.

Can it be, she wondered, that I have come to understand this country? Impossible, she decided. It was only one of her brief attacks of common sense. A periodic seizure.

She dressed and had a drink of cold well water. She would get them a message immediately. That the scrutiny was more than routine, that something was up that would mean disaster and there would have to be an alternative plan. She had to presume that the Tecanecan Movement had developed the concept of alternative plans.

Sensible or not, the thought of abandoning her part in Tecan's liberation was bitter to Justin. They needed so much, she thought, and they had asked her for so little. To keep the dock lights on—there was nothing very suspect in that—many of the fishermen went out at night with torches, sometimes they asked her or Egan to run the generator late and keep the dock lights lit to guide their passage in. To be available for the wounded—she would have done that unrequested. But the obscene attentions of Campos made everything a hazard. The Guardia would be observant of late-burning lights. Wounded men who came to the dispensary would be drawn into a trap. Egan, who was her charge now, would not survive at all.

Decision then—hard but necessary. There were other battles and she had a life before her to fight them. She went into the office beside the kitchen where the small radio set was and sat down in front of it. She would have to call Sister Mary Joseph for help in closing, get a telegraph to the provincial, notify the consulate and the Ministry of the Interior.

She began to draft the appropriate messages in longhand, but after a moment she set her pencil down.

Campos. She had once had an erotic dream about him. His presence now bestrode her thoughts and as she thought of him a notion struck her that stayed and as it stayed, ripened into certainty. It was he who was killing the children! The notion was utterly without foundation but she felt sure of it. How could they have told her not to be afraid of him? If they had planned to kill him—she had surmised so much as long ago as her dinner conversation with Godoy but had put the idea out of her head from weak scruples—why had they not done so before? Now, from a tactical standpoint, it was too late. Or was it? Could there be some element of blackmail in the thing, could the Movement be somehow aware of his killings and consider him thus neutralized? Impossible, she thought, they were not cynical, not that way. But someone would have to go for Campos; if not, he would go on killing. Everyone, every mother and child on the coast was in his hands, living and dying through his sufferances. The torture and murder of children was something more important than even the establishment of revolution, surely. But was it not all of a piece— Campos on the coast, the President in his mortar-proof palace in the capital, the American interests that kept everything in place?

She stared down at the draft paper before her and leaned her forehead on her hands.

From outside, from the small plantain grove through which the creekside trail led inland, she heard voices. She went to the window, opened the shutter and saw the first groups of young foreigners heading for the stelae. They were mainly in couples, mainly fair, sunburned and bleached, in cutaways or sailcloth pants, in halters or bare-chested. They seemed to her incredibly innocent, vacant. But the oldest of them could not be many years younger than she herself. They passed like ghosts. None of them saw her.

Out on the veranda, Father Egan was still asleep on the hammock. His gut was swollen with sickness but his face was thinning, hollows beginning to show under his eyes and cheekbones. He had been hale and portly when Justin arrived in Tecan; now she saw for the first time his long chin and fine features. His face was a gray replica of what it might have been in his youth, the death mask of a handsome delicate young priest who could quicken a pious lady's pulse with the resonance of First Corinthians.

She did not want to bury him here, she thought, under a twisted-wire cross. There was a stone vault for him under the lime trees in California, where he could sleep with all those other shadows who had worn down their steps on carpeted altars by candlelight. Broken their hearts, minds, sex and entrails in the imperfect service of their Holy One, their Hanged Man.

He woke and saw her looking down at him.

"What's wrong, dear?" He sat up on the hammock and his belly hung down over his belt, almost to the hammock's edge.

"You've got more of them coming," she said.

He looked at her blankly.

"Your parish," she said, "is assembling."

Egan yawned. "You're disapproving of me again."

"Well, they have to go, that's all. One of us has to tell them to move on. I'm trying to get the two of us out of here with a minimum of trouble and Campos is making a stink over them."

"He was here today," Egan said. "He never mentioned them. He asked about you."

Justin shivered. "Asked what?"

"Vague questions—you know how he is. He asked me man to man if I thought you were a virgin. Man to man, he said. Then he asked me if you had ever been in California or in Paris." He stood up and brushed the hair from his forehead. "It made me think."

"And what," she asked, "did it make you think?"

The priest went past her into his own quarters and began to pump up water for his shower. He spoke to her through the open door.

"About humanness. He asked me these strange questions and I began to wonder if he was human. Then I began to wonder if I was. And you, dear, whether you were. Then I thought: What do we mean by it? Humanness. Does it mean being real and in the world and not an animal? Is it running thin, so to speak? Whatever it is—is there less of it? And is that good or bad?"

The pumping stopped and she heard him move the bottle from the shower stall and turn the water on.

"Then I ran out of categories, so to speak. Meanings just faded. I thought—a word might as well be a little plant. I thought, well, silence will do. Not thinking will do. But I'm incapable of silence or not thinking."

"You're still capable of taking a shower, Charlie," she said. "There's merit in that." He would not have heard her for the running water.

She stood for a moment looking at the blank message sheet by the transmitter and wandered into the kitchen. Immediately she saw that the stores had been broken into. The last sack of beans, which had been half full, was missing. The larder's only padlock had been broken and half of the frozen fish was gone. And the biscuit tin.

"The useless sons of bitches," she said aloud. On the next thought, she hurried to the dispensary; sure enough—a jar of codeine tablets gone, half of the Percodan. Her store of morphine was still intact, they had failed to find it.

In a rage she ran out to the edge of the veranda to confront Egan's troops, shouting as she went.

"We have real pain here, you people! People suffer here, they get hurt!"

Three young men in turned-down white hats looked up at her as though she were mad, startled from their serenity. A couple behind them actually smiled at her.

"This is a medical dispensary!" she was shouting. "Our medication is not for you fucking rich kids to get high on!" At the height of her outrage, she found herself eye to eye with the peculiar young Mennonite she had been seeing around the place.

The strange young man only stared at her with his doll's face. His eyes were blue and very bright. She could have sworn in that moment that he had painted cheeks. Justin's angry words stuck in her throat. She held to the railing of the porch, turned her head away and then backed off. Out of his sight.

As she went back inside, his image stayed clear in her mind's eye. And with it came a verse which she had always loved but which now filled her with revulsion.

"Be not afeard; the isle is full of noises,
Sounds and sweet airs, that give delight, and hurt not . . ."

She felt overthrown. Why was there so much suffering? How was it she could never do anything? Tecan. It was an evil place. Accursed.

In his quarters Egan had finished with his wash and was dressing. Justin walked in on him, took a swig of Flor de Cana and sat down in his desk chair.

"I'm going crazy, Charlie. Like you. I think we'll have to send up a rocket."

Egan tucked the tails of a clean white shirt under his belt.

"You're just afraid, dear. I know all about that, I can assure you. Remember how afraid I was?"

"I don't scare easy, do I, Charles?"

"You certainly don't."

"What am I scared of?"

The priest went to the mirror and began combing his hair.

"There's a great deal to be scared of here. I suppose mainly you're scared of Campos. He's after you, you know."

Justin looked at him in the mirror. "Charles," she said, "is he killing those children?"

Egan did not answer her. He finished combing and took a net shopping bag from beneath his bed in which there was a Bible. Then he took the rum from where Justin had laid it and put it in the bag.

She followed him out into the office.

"Is Campos killing those children, Charles?"

"I thought," Egan said, "you suspected me of it."

"No," she said. "Campos."

"Well, it isn't me," he said. "You're right about that. I don't kill. I can't imagine any circumstances in which I'd kill anyone ever."

She watched him look off toward the hillside until she thought he had forgotten where he was.

"I thought it was Campos," he said after a while. "I was fairly sure it was. But it's not."

She felt weak, almost unable to breathe.

"Then I know who it is," she said. "It's that . . ."

"It's the Mennonite kid," Egan said. "He came in over the border from Nicaragua. The police are looking for him there. Grew up on one of their farmsteads down there and lost his mind. Religious. Hears voices."

"You're hiding him."

"That's about it."

She walked up to him and seized him by the arm, trying to keep calm.

"You can't do that, you fool! He's killing little children." She was crying unawares, tears spilled down her cheeks, gathering at her chin.

"Not since he came to me. I'm talking him down. When I give him the pills Mary Joe gave me he doesn't hear the voices. And I'm going to replace his voices with mine."

Justin wiped her face with a handkerchief. "I was sure it was Campos."

"I was too," Egan said. "But no."

"What fools we are," Justin said. "This place just beat the shit out of us."

"They all will," Egan said. "All of 'em. Every time."

"The thing about that boy," she said, "he doesn't look real to me. He doesn't look human."

"You're getting the idea now, aren't you? Well, he's as real as it gets, Justin. Here or anywhere else."

"All right," she said. "All right." She began to pace up and down. Egan sat down at the desk beside the transmitter and looked at the matted floor.

"We're getting out in a hurry," Justin said. "While we do, we'll get that kid locked up and sent back to Nicaragua. I mean it's tough, but it's got to be done. Maybe the Mennonites can get him proper care."

One was not a child, she thought. One was not a hysteric, one was trained to deal with the world as it came. There were three things—to see that the Movement did not ruin itself trying to use the mission, to get the insane young person out of circulation, to get herself and Egan back to the States.

I'm not going to be afraid, she told herself. I'm going to do what I have to and if I louse it up I'll carry the weight. She was, she thought, not just anybody.

"There's a message for you," Egan told her. "Your friend Laura brought it. It seems she's a Latinist."

"I see," Justin said evenly. "And where is it, please?"

She watched Egan go into his trouser pocket and bring forth a crumpled piece of paper which he carefully straightened out against his thigh. Steady, she told herself. She felt, for the moment, strangely calm.

The message was indeed in Latin, hand-printed on bonded stationery.

NOLI RESPONDERE NI NECESSE SIT. APPARA, ET LUMINES CUSTODI. NOLI TIME.

"No response unless necessary. Prepare and remember the lights. Don't be afraid."

Justin read it over several times, using every fraction of her strength to keep hold of the suspect calm she had achieved.

The lights, of course, meant an incoming boat or plane. No problem there unless they were disposed to set down right at French Harbor. If that was their plan then everyone involved in the business would be killed outright, the President could proclaim a national holiday and Campos would get a medal. That was what was bound to happen, she thought, unless she reached them in time. They had to stay away—there could be no question of them using the dispensary. At the same time it seemed as though events had overtaken her and, unfortunately, Egan with her. Campos, as the priest had observed, was after her and she saw no point in letting him get her without a fight. With things so far along and gone, being of some use to the Movement was the only way she could accomplish anything more life-affirming in Tecan than to successfully run away from it. And she wanted to fight, wanted to desperately—in spite of her terror, perhaps because of it. It was just possible that she might have it both ways—fight *and* run. More folly perhaps, but her chances were not the best now either way and that was not entirely her doing. If she could get a message through that would both warn them away and arrange a quick meeting, they might have other work for her, worthwhile work. With things as they were, she would probably be told to drop out of it—then she could get Egan away and be free herself with a good conscience. And even warning them off would be a valuable service.

Hope, sweet and green, came to her in the midst of their ruin.

She shooed him away from the chair and with one of his dictionaries sat down to compose her own Latin message.

UTI HOC LOCO NON POSSE EST IN CONSILIO. CONGREDI DEBEMUS. GRAVIS EST.

"This place should not be used in the plan. Necessary to meet. Urgent."

She wrote it out on the sheet on which she had been composing the radio message to Sister Mary Joe. She would hold the radio messages a day, until after the meeting. If there could be one. The light in which she wrote had the red cast of sunset. She would have to keep the dock lights on, all the same.

"I wish I could pray," she said to Egan. "How I wish I could."

"There's really no need," he told her. "Everything's all right. In spite of what seems."

"Hell," she said. "No wonder you've got yourself a following."

The angle of the sun came aslant the peak of his baseball cap and lit him from another shallow sleep. Since Serrano he had been drifting into this dozing, a reptile suspension of awareness that was impervious to speed. He rose, sunburned and sweating, and went down to his quarters in the lazaret to draw a change of clothes.

From his pockets, he was able to salvage three whole Benzedrine tablets and one that was nearly crushed to powder. Immediately, he swallowed two of them. Perhaps the Callahans would have more. Yes, certainly they would. Pablo believed there was always more. He left the diamond where it was, in his soiled work shirt.

When he climbed on deck, the engines were turning over and the anchor chain winding itself around the windlass. He stood by the hatchway and watched the forepeak swing round until the mountainous coast and the declining sun lay westward. Then he went to the rail and leaned on it, looking at the weakening sunlight on the blue water, letting the bennie spin. There was a diamond in his pocket.

He blew a spot of crushed cigarette ash from the white tee shirt that he held rolled and folded in his handful of clean clothes. Things turned up if you kept your eyes on the moment. For a few minutes, with his Benzedrine and his clean clothes, Pablo was a happy man. But he was certainly in danger now; no question. It would be utter dumbness to dismiss this fact and of utter dumbness he felt himself incapable. He was all right. He was better than all right. The Coast Guard turkeys at Berry's Point were so many peons, so many stooges compared to him. His was the life of adventure. As he walked into the wheelhouse he was thinking that what he would buy next was a tuxedo. A white one that you wore a black tie with. For hot countries.

Negus was at the helm in the cockpit, Mr. Callahan leaned on his chart table and looked toward the coast.

"Mind if I take a shower?" Pablo asked them.

Neither man glanced at him.

"We may be fishing tonight," Callahan said. "You'd just get yourself all gamey again."

"Fishin'?" Pablo asked.

"Anyhow," Negus said, "the lady's using the shower. She might be a while."

Pablo took himself out on deck again, the anticipated clean clothes he carried were just a useless embarrassment now. He was nearly enraged. It was a hell of a thing not to get a shower when you wanted one. It was a bring-down. It made you negative.

He threw the clothes in a heap on his bunk in the lazaret. If they were fishing tonight, he thought, it would be for show, to have shrimp to put on the ice in the holds where the guns were stored. He climbed the ladder and stood scratching at his scroungy frame, looking over the stern as the *Cloud* picked up power and headed along the coast. His elation fled.

There would be no tying up on this coast, he should have known that. In Serrano, they might have a setup, but here the guns were for people to use against their own government. The coast here would be Reef City all the way; any passage broad enough to be worth dock space would have a town and any town must have some type of cops. The draft of the *Cloud,* even with her modified hull, could not possibly be less than eight feet loaded—so they would have to lie offshore, beyond the reef, and wait for a small boat to come out to them. Then there would be no way for him to get ashore and when the job was done it would be only the four of them on a big ocean. And whoever was in the small boat would be no friend of Pablo's.

Showerless and negative, his rush fading, he thought things over several times to make them come out his way. In this, he was not successful.

Not a word had they said about Tino. Not Word One. Back in St. Joost, Naftali's body would have been discovered. He found it very difficult to believe that the Callahans would ever be prepared to pay him off and let him go. Yet, he thought, if they had wanted to do him they could have done so by now. They were waiting for the deal to go down. For the money.

Pablo began to discern the diagram of events toward which the life of adventure was propelling him. Either the Callahans and Negus would get their money and he, Pablo, die—or he must make it be the other way round. But he was not a killer; he could not conceive of killing them. Even if they forced him—out of their greediness, their paranoia, their natural two-timing way of doing—to defend himself, he was outnumbered and lost and alone. On the other hand, he found his own death even more difficult to conceive.

"Holy shit," he said.

He tried again to make it come out all right in his mind—another coast somewhere, the diamond in place, cash in hand, a grudging admiration all around. Then a few months on the beach. Daiquiris, elegant flunkies, his tuxedo.

No help. He was boxed. In over his head—and the image of that dreadful game came to him on Naftali's dying whispers, the game with his skull. He looked at the deep green coast and was frightened.

"I can't cut it," he told Naftali. "I'm up the well-known creek."

Thinking about Naftali made him feel a little bit better because that had been a time when things had looked bad and he had made out. He had put his mind to it and scored.

So, he thought, there was something more than just human to it. There was the Power. He might be Aided—his mother had said that to him. Aided.

He prayed to Jesus and to his mother and to Naftali. They gave him to understand that in the coming days he would know.

Late in the day, Holliwell took the boat ride to Playa Tate and limped along the beach to a small dock that ran thirty feet or so from the sand to the first ridge of coral. He wore long cotton trousers, a windbreaker and a shapeless straw hat to defend himself from the force of the sun. Down a curve of the coast, he could see the beach where he had been spined and the mission building with its pier, its high veranda and wooden cross. In a way, he was spying.

At the other extremity of the Playa, the Cuban hardware dealer, brother to Mrs. Paz, lounged under a desiccated palm cabana with some men who had driven out from town. The men appeared to be local merchants like himself; the dusty late-model Ford in which they all had come was parked at the edge of the dirt road. The Cuban and his friends were drinking piña coladas, mixed in a blender that plugged into the car's dashboard.

For over an hour, he sat and watched the sun play on the coral shallows, the darting silver shapes of shore-feeding barracuda. Again and again he turned in the direction of the mission beach. It was where he wanted to be. Even with the use of his injured leg, there was no way for him to simply present himself there with discretion. But he wanted to see her.

It was hard, in the sunshine of Playa Tate, to consider repression and retribution, sacrifice and justice. It was hard anywhere for Holliwell to consider such things except as abstract functions of behavior. They were things other people believed themselves to be motivated by, his objects of study, the people who also believed themselves to be at home in the world. Wars he understood, what people did in them and believed they did and how they explained it to themselves and to others. All at once he found himself wondering again about what he would say back home when they came around to ask him. He realized now that they would surely come around to ask him—he had *been seen to go*. He might tell them nothing, he thought. Or something that explained things or obscured explanation. Of one thing he was certain—he would find out what it was she believed herself to be about over there under the wooden cross. He would find out what it was like for her; that was all he cared about.

It was a little dangerous. The thought made him smile and quickened in him a subtle fine excitement. Like the feeling that had come to him over the black coral—but not so coarse as that. It had to do with the girl. There was something of seduction in it.

He lay back on the splintering boards, his hat beside him, arms across his face, until something, a bird's shadow, the passing of a cloud roused him. He sat up then and put on his hat and saw a solitary figure coming toward him along the water's edge. When he saw that it was she, a rush struck him like cocaine in the blood and he was surprised. He had been hoping against hope that she would come that way.

Upright, his hands clutching the edges of the dock, he watched her draw closer. She was in white and he thought, at her expense, it was appropriate. Loose-fitting white work pants and a short-sleeved shirt. There was a red scarf over her hair.

When she was near the dock, he could see that her face was drawn and pale, her eyes harried and haunted and clouded with fatigue. She walked looking down at the sand.

As soon as he called to her, something like a voice inside him said: You are foolish. A middle-aged drunk, meddling. Foolish. By then he had already spoken. When she turned toward him her look was blank. He took his hat off.

"Oh, it's you," she said, and he nodded, lamely agreeing that it was.

"You shouldn't be out in the sun. How's your leg?"

"It's healing," he said. "I don't much like sitting around the Paradise."

"Don't you like it there?"

"Not much. Do you know it?"

"Not up close," she said.

"One thing I can't do is get a fin on. I'm thrown on the cultural resources of the area."

"That's a shame," she said, "because there aren't any."

He asked her if she could stop to talk; he was afraid of sounding breathless. He wanted her to sit beside him on the dock but she stood off, tensed for flight.

"How are things going?"

"Oh," she said, "not too bad."

"Packing?"

"Yes," she said. "Right."

"How long have you been here now?"

"About six years." She seemed to have to think about it. "Six it would be."

"You'll be sorry to leave then. Or will you?"

She pursed her lips as if she were trying unsuccessfully to smile.

"Yes, I'll be sorry. I'll be sorry to leave this way. To leave things as they are, when I might have helped more."

"When you talk about things and how they are do you mean the country? The conditions?" He watched her then for a hint of suspiciousness; he was reminding himself of the secret policemen who started conversations with suspicious foreigners about the state of their countries. One found them all over.

"It's a poor country."

"With tourism coming down," Holliwell said, "Things might improve."

"For some people they'll improve."

"Not for the *campesinos?*"

"For a few of them. If they mind their manners and smile a lot."

"You don't read much in the papers about the politics here," Holliwell said. "Not in the States."

"I'm sure you don't," she said.

"You do read a few things though. Guerrilla stuff in the mountains. Makes you wonder who you ought to be for."

"Good," she said.

He laughed. "People like to tell you it's the politics of bananas."

"Sure," she said, and her smile changed until it had a bitter turn to it. "It's a banana republic. I'm sure that's in the papers."

"Strategic considerations aside," Holliwell said, "bananas are worth fighting for. Any nutritionist can tell you that."

"Really?"

Holliwell stood up, his eyes on hers. There was clear light there, when the film dissolved. The film of weariness or fear.

"If you don't eat your bananas, you don't get enough potassium. If you don't get your potassium, you experience a sense of existential dread."

"Now I'm a nurse," she said, "and I never heard that."

"You can look it up. One of the symptoms of potassium insufficiency is a sense of existential dread."

"You're the scientist. I'm supposed to believe what you tell me."

"Certainly. And now you know why Tecan is vital to the United States."

"The United States," she told him, "may be in for a spell of existential dread."

"What do you think will happen after you go?"

"There'll be changes. I'm absolutely sure there will."

"They say the more it changes here, the more it stays . . ."

She was shaking her head. "Changes," she said.

"You mean . . . something like a socialist government?" It was a crude question and he was ashamed of it.

"The country is going to be overrun by its inhabitants. We may have to pay a little more for our potassium and our sense of cosmic certainty."

"So," Holliwell said, "We're the bad guys again."

"Look," she told him, "they're good people here. They suffer. Their kids die and they get pushed around and murdered. That's all there is to the politics here—no more than that. Just people who need a break."

"Will they get it?"

"If there's any justice they will."

"Is there any?"

"Yes," she said. "Even here. Even Tecan isn't beyond justice."

"But it's only a word. It's just something in people's heads."

"That's good enough," she told him.

He had not been paying close attention to the things she said. There was no need for him to draw her out and sound her politics. Instead, he had been concentrating on the way she was, and in the time it took him to spin out his net of marginal civilities he had seen, or was persuaded he had seen, what fires were banked in her. Fires of the heart, of sensibility. There were plenty of *engagés,* he thought, plenty of them were honest and virtuous. She was different; she was heart, she was there, in there every minute feeling it. This kind of thing was not for him but he knew it when he saw it; he was not an anthropologist for nothing.

It'll kill her, he thought, drive her crazy. Her eyes were already clouding with sorrow and loss. It was herself she was grieving and hoping for; for that reason she was the real thing. So he began to fall in love with her.

"Maybe it is good enough," he said.

"Even here we have history. Things change. People want their rights."

"Does history take care of people?"

"I wish I knew," she said. "Maybe in the end. In the meantime people take care of themselves."

"Yes," Holliwell said.

Lady of sorrows, he thought, creature of marvel. It was

enough for her that people took care of themselves. In the meantime.

I will show you, he thought, the war for us to die in, lady. Sully your kind suffering child's eyes with it. Live burials beside slow rivers. A pile of ears for a pile of arms. The crisps of North Vietnamese drivers chained to their burned trucks.

He thought she was a unicorn to be speared, penned and adored. He was a drunk, middle-aged, sentimental. Foolish.

He wanted her white goodness, wanted a skin of it. He wanted to wash in it, to drink and drink and drink of it, salving the hangover thirst of his life, his war.

Why, he wondered, is she smiling at me? Then in a moment he thought he knew why, although he was sure that she did not. You did not have to be an anthropologist to know.

"I'll see you tomorrow," he said.

He would never bring it to that. He was more honorable than that, an honest man. But he was sure now and he did not feel ashamed for thinking it. Exalted rather and moved at her innocence in that regard, who was so wise.

The smile had left her face; she looked at him in slight confusion, raising a weary hand to her face.

"I'm supposed to have dinner," Holliwell said, smiling. "I'm supposed to see the ruins."

"Oh, my gosh," she said. "I forgot."

"Is it all right?"

She stammered, the hand touching her scarf.

"Not, not . . . for me. I mean I don't think I can. But Father Egan will take you."

"Good," Holliwell said. "Well, I'll see you anyway."

"Yes," she said. She had turned back in the direction from which she had come, she did not look at him again. "Take care. Take care of your leg."

When she walked off he felt like crying. He stood up and walked the beach, hardly thinking of his leg. When he had been wandering around for a half hour, he found himself even with the ragged cabana where the Cuban and his friends were resting. It was their blender that attracted his eye. It was amazing how many people owned blenders in places like Tecan. Where there was electricity, even people with barely enough to eat seemed to have them. The Cuban was waving to him, motioning him over.

The man's name, it turned out, was Miguel Soyer. He was tall and youthful with a square good-natured face, warm eyes under thick Celtic eyebrows. He did not much resemble his sister.

"You were diving with my brother-in-law, no?" Soyer asked as the three men with him watched politely from behind their dark glasses.

"Yes, indeed," Holliwell said. He had been introduced to the others but had immediately lost their names. All of them had the sinister air that respectable businessmen so often projected in the South. Holliwell was not disturbed by it; it was an incongruity of appearance only, the result of a difference between Anglo and Latin expectations and masculine style.

"Twixt," Soyer said. "Beautiful."

"It was a fine day's diving."

Soyer turned and looked in the direction of the mission.

"You're a friend of Sister Justin?"

"Not really. I had a minor accident in front of the mission the other day and she took a sea urchin spine out of my knee. So we're acquainted."

"She's a nurse," Soyer said vaguely. "Now you're her patient, eh?"

"Yes."

Holliwell accepted a piña colada.

"A very dedicated woman," Soyer said. "We admire her here."

"She's very nice, isn't she?"

"Yes, very nice. Very American. *Una tipica.*"

"I suppose," Holliwell said.

"I know North America well. Once I spoke English but I'm out of practice."

Holliwell was reassuring. It was not his impression that Mr. Soyer had difficulty with the language. The three men with him held their silence.

"I was in school at Washington," Soyer said. "At Georgetown University. I was preparing for the foreign service of Cuba when the Communists took power."

"Ah," Holliwell said.

"America is so free," Mr. Soyer said. "That's what I liked. So many opportunities."

"But you chose to settle here."

"The style is better for me. I like the quiet life, I think."

"How's business?" Holliwell asked.

"It's not bad," Soyer said. He was still looking toward the mission. "We hear that Sister Justin is leaving."

"That's what she says."

"Then it must be true, eh?"

"Gosh," Holliwell said. "I guess so."

"Do you think she is a true idealist?"

"I assume so," Holliwell said. There was a silence. "Do you mean," he asked, "as opposed to a false idealist?"

Soyer slapped his knee and laughed loudly and vacantly.

"I'm misusing the language," he said. "Forgive me."

"I'm intrigued," Holliwell said. "I wonder about the relations between the missionaries and the community here. Are they good? Are they cordial?"

"Why not?" Soyer asked. Then he said: "Why ask me?"

"I wondered," Holliwell said, "what you thought about it."

"I think they're more than agreeable," Mr. Soyer said. "But I'm a sucker for Americans."

Holliwell supposed his smile appropriate and kept it in place.

"This mission," Soyer said, "Sister Justin's—I don't know what they do now there."

"She was telling me they feel kind of redundant. That's why they're going, I guess."

"Ourselves and you," Mr. Soyer said, "I speak as though I'm of Tecan because it's my home now—ourselves and you, we have a great deal in common. We have common enemies."

"Very true," Holliwell said.

"The greatest enemy," Soyer said, "is the enemy inside America. Do you think so?"

"We're all our own worst enemies, aren't we?"

"I don't mean that," Soyer said. "Not exactly."

"American politics is rather frenetic." Holliwell hesitated. "Fucked up."

"From maybe too much comfort. Everyone is comfortable."

"Not everyone."

"I see," Mr. Soyer told him. "I understand your point of view."

"I'm not very political."

"Sister Justin?" Soyer asked. "Do you think she is political?"

"No, I don't," Holliwell said. "Not at all."

He watched Soyer frown. The Cuban grunted and shook his head as though he had been given information of significance. Holliwell turned toward the ocean and saw with some relief that Sandy was bringing the Paradise boat around the outer reef.

"I don't see Mr. and Mrs. Paz," Holliwell said.

"Gone home," Soyer told him. "Only this morning."

"Thank you for the cold drink, Mr. Soyer." He got to his feet and nodded to Soyer's three friends. They nodded back.

"Staying long?" Soyer asked him.

"No, I don't think so. I only wanted a little rest after my labors."

"Listen, Holliwell—don't take the boat back. Come have a drink with us and we'll take you."

Holliwell explained that his foot was hurting and that he had writing to do.

"Ah," said one of Mr. Soyer's hitherto silent friends. "Writing."

In fact, Holliwell was in some pain. He felt dizzy and he was thinking for the first time in a while about the telephone calls in Santiago de Compostela.

On the run back, Sandy spoke to him above the engine.

"How you leg now, mon?"

"Better," he shouted. "I still can't put a fin on."

Sandy grinned. "Keep you outena trouble."

"I think it's too late for that," Holliwell said.

With the sun below the green saw-toothed ridges of the coast, darkness gathered quickly. Venus was the evening star. She hung low over the eastern horizon and the unbroken sea beneath her transit was dulled to the color of lead. The wind rose in that quarter, setting a roll beneath the *Cloud*'s counterfeit boards but nowhere breaking the skin of the sea's expanse. Across the sky, Deneb and Vega twinkled beyond a calligrapher's stroke of purple nimbus.

Freddy Negus, holding to the wheel, had pulled the night shade down behind the cockpit. Callahan, a drink in one hand, stood beside the wheelhouse hatch running his infrared binoculars along the coastline.

"How's traffic?" Negus asked him. "I'm getting blips on my scope here."

"Let's light it up," Callahan said.

Negus threw a switch that lit the running lights in the stabilizer mast and the work areas around the hatches. Callahan went forward to light a spot on the forepeak.

"We're gonna be out in front of Port Alvarado presently, boss," Negus said.

Callahan refilled his glass and bent to inspect the digits on the Raytheon and leaned over his chart table. He turned the Loran signal up so that it was audible and timed the tones on his watch.

"We're getting there, Freddy. What's your bottom like?"

"Bottom is marbles," Negus said. "A couple of yards to starboard and we'd be sitting on them."

Callahan hung in the hatchway, looking coastward.

"I got Puerto Alvarado light," he told Negus. "I see the bastard. If you could get me a mite more speed, Freddy, I would love it. So we have a tiny bit of daylight when we drop the buoy."

"I can get you twelve knots on just the main engine. That's what you got."

"Puerto Alvarado," Callahan said, pronouncing the city's name in careful Spanish. "I see the banana piers and I believe I see the national streetlight."

"Some hole that place is," Negus said. "Had to get some of my boys out of jail there once. No trouble either. Being a British subject meant something in those days."

Callahan studied the harbor.

"They planted a few light buoys in these roads since I was here last," he said. He glanced at the Raytheon scope. "Lot of boats around with lights."

"That's how it is out here," Negus said. "Nothing faster than ten knots. Nothing coming our way."

Callahan checked the Loran digits and his charts.

"Very shortly we'll get on the CB. Right around the point."

Callahan had taken the rum bottle from the galley shelf and was pouring himself another drink, easing the neck of the bottle against the glass so that Negus would not hear him, when Negus stood up in his chair and turned around.

"Look at this, Jack. I got a fucker on here bearing three-forty. He's coming at us and he's coming fast."

Callahan put his drink in the galley rack, ran into the lounge to slam his wife's door twice and ran out on deck with the glasses.

"I don't see him," Callahan said. "He's not lit."

"Bugger fucking all," Negus said.

Deedee Callahan was standing beside her husband in the next moment, straining to see into the near darkness.

"Engage the diesels, lover," he told her. "Do it faster than anything."

She ran around to the engine space and had opened the metal hatch when she heard her husband laugh.

"He just lit up," Callahan called to them. "He's a dragger."

Negus looked out the windshield at the fresh lights.

"He must have been making thirty. You sure he's a dragger?"

"He's the Rastafarian Navy," Callahan said, watching through the glasses. "He's going right into Alvarado."

Deedee came forward wiping sweat from her forehead.

"Is there an explanation for him?" she asked. "Or is he just stoned like us?"

"Probably be his lights don't work very well," Negus said. "He wants to get in before United Fruit runs him over. And he's souped up for running ganja."

"Don't want no more," Deedee Callahan sang, "midnight rambles no more. *Que vida.*"

"Where's that fucking Pablo?" Negus asked.

"Sacked out. Leave him." He bent over the Raytheon and marked his Loran chart. "O.K.," he told them, "Freddy's going to find me a hole in the wall."

As they looked on, Negus turned the *Cloud*'s head toward the reef and cut speed. Everyone watched the Fathometer.

"Gotta be it," Negus said after a minute. "Ninety and ninety and sloping up."

"Engine stop," Callahan said. "And drop the hook so we don't drift on the marbles."

Deedee was on deck peering into the darkness.

"You don't get more than a flash glow from Alvarado light," she said. "It's around that point."

Callahan was at his chart table with a piece of chart paper before him.

"Let me get a quick line of sight here," he said.

"There's an aviation beacon on that mountain," she said,

shielding her eyes from the glow of the deck lights. "It's on your Loran chart."

"I got it," he said. He marked the coordinates from the Raytheon on his line-of-sight chart and x'd in the aviation beacon. They were waiting for the boat to swing full around on its chain.

"Two dock lights at sixty degrees off the beacon. Over them there's a building with a cross on it."

"That's fine if those dock lights are on all night," Negus said. "But whoever they are must be using a generator because there's no electricity out here."

"They'll be on," Callahan said. "We were told they'd be on."

He marked the dock lights on his handmade chart and put it under the Bowditch.

"Now," he said, "Deedee, go turn that bozo to and get the marker buoy over. It's time to talk to the customer."

The CB was silent as Negus dialed in.

"José," Negus said into the night, "you get those pumps for me?"

"Absolutely, Mr. Fry." It was a different voice, but relaxed, easy with English.

"That's just fine," Negus said, and hung up the receiver. "Think he sees us?" he asked Callahan.

"No question about it," Callahan said.

Deedee and Pablo came in slightly breathless. At Deedee Callahan's call, Pablo had been huddled in the lazaret hatch close to Naftali's pistol, looking at the Puerto Alvarado lights with longing and dread.

"Hi, kids," Callahan said to his wife and to Pablo. "Now we're going to open up the arms locker."

Pablo watched Callahan unlock the gear locker in which his automatic was stowed. There were half a dozen other pistols beside it. Seeing his weapon, Pablo took a step toward it.

"Leave it where it is," Negus snapped at him.

"No, Pablo," Callahan said patiently. "We're unlocking them, we're not going to wave them at passing shipping." He stepped through the galley and down into the paneled compartment and there, with another key from his key ring, opened what looked like a teak book chest between two lounge chairs. The chest had a small automatic rifle of foreign make and a number of shotguns. When he had unlocked the chest, he closed it again.

"It's very frustrating," Mr. Callahan explained, "to look for keys when you're in a hurry. In the meantime, let's everyone remember that we're a few miles offshore with all our lights blazing like Christmas. So let's preserve our workaday respectability and demeanor and leave this stuff where it is. Until we need it. Which of course we all hope we will not."

"You're so right," Deedee said.

Callahan picked up the glass of rum he had been drinking. "Now," Callahan said to Pablo, "you and Deedee are going shrimping."

"I don't follow you there," Pablo said.

"Mrs. Callahan will explain." He put his hand beside his wife's ear; it was a caress of sorts. "And while you're out on deck, Dee, put a watch cap over your hair, O.K.? So you'll look like a gringo shrimper and a not a Rhine maiden?"

She went into her quarters and came out with a black watch cap and a green down vest. She tucked her hair under the cap and winked at Pablo.

"Let's go, Tex," she said to Pablo. "Let's go get the hatches clear."

When they were on deck, Callahan sat down in the cockpit chair and drained his drink. He picked up the rough line-of-sight chart he had made and smiled at Negus.

"We'll take her out on the Bonaire radio beacon. Right out on one-eighty. At eleven hundred we'll have her back here along zero-zero-zero."

"Aye, aye," Negus said, and swung the bow toward the open sea.

"We'll have the net over," Callahan went on, looking at the Raytheon scope, "so you better keep the speed way down. Eight or nine knots, no more."

"Hey, Jack, lay off the sauce, will you? We got a lot of time to kill and you're like to get me started."

Callahan made a placatory gesture with his slim small hand. They heard the stabilizer engine cough up and chain line being dragged across the deck.

"Damn Tino," Negus said.

Deedee Callahan appeared in the galley in work gloves and

white shrimper's boots, the watch cap tucked down to her eyebrows. She took the rum bottle and a handful of joints down from the shelf.

"Hey, man," she said, eyeing the level of the bottle, "I thought it was you staying sober tonight. I thought it was me could get snackered."

"You may get as snackered as you see the need of," Callahan told her.

Negus looked over his shoulder.

"What are you gonna do, missus, have a party back there?"

"Why not?" she said. "We gotta head all those little nasty things. You know," she told them, "I was once quite fond of shrimp."

"Don't bother heading them," her husband said. "Just get it in there and make sure it's all shrimp."

Negus reached out from his chair and took the bottle from her.

"That's my limit," he announced when he had drunk. "First we work, then we can get fucked up. That's the way you're supposed to do it."

"Are we using the tri-net?" Deedee asked.

"The hell with it." Callahan stood up and went to the hatchway and looked out at the black ocean. With the net and stabilizer down, the *Cloud* had begun to roll at an angle not at all commensurate with the mild weather.

"What's the Pablo situation?"

"He's quiet," she said. "He wants to know what he's gonna do when we get back to the marker."

"Well," Callahan said thoughtfully, "tell him a little about it and make him feel important. But don't let him get drunk and lose his splendid air of authority. Keep him otherwise occupied."

"I'll massage his cock while he heads shrimp, how's that?"

They passed the bottle around again.

"Hey," Deedee asked, "you sure you want me to tell him about the operation?"

Callahan looked aft to the stern, where Pablo was straightening out the folds in the dragnet.

"Hell, why not? I want him to feel he has a future with us."

Negus laughed hoarsely.

"But watch him, Deedee. Watch him good. If he starts acting agitated like there's too much on his mind, we want to know about it."

"He always acts that way," Deedee said. "So how will I know?"

"Intuit," Callahan told her. "Intuit darkly, and get back with him. He shouldn't be alone at all from this point."

When she went out, Negus set the wheel to one-eight-zero and they settled back in their cockpit chairs. Negus lit his pipe.

"Jack, damnit," he said after several minutes, "this here op . . . I wouldn't give . . . well, I wouldn't give you a Panamanian peso . . ."

"Do you have to?" Callahan asked, interrupting him. "Must you fucking say it again?"

Negus fell silent again. But only for a short time.

"That's a damn fine woman, Jack. I hope you're taking good care of her."

"She takes care of me," Callahan said. "She takes care of us all."

In a clearing, three stelae stood in file, an even distance apart. Their bases were sunk in morning glory vines but some of the vines had been cut back to reveal the inscriptions and hieroglyphs.

The clearing had been part of a village plantation at different times; wax beans and wildly mutant gourds grew around the slight rise where the three standing stones were. It was bordered on three sides by tall ramon trees. A small stream, originating in the mountains, ran beside it toward the sea.

The place was an obscure joint property of the fruit company and the President's family, adjoining the land donated to the mission. On certain maps it was marked as an archaeological site but—with the exception of the three stelae—it had been haphazardly denuded of its antiquities long before. A few adventurers hunted there still, at moderate risk. It was a forgotten place.

On the fourth side of the glade was what appeared to be a hill but was in fact a pyramid covered in jungle. It had been excavated forty years earlier, the apartment floors strained and sifted, the chacs removed and crated and sent to Philadelphia.

In the days before the arrival of antiquarians and smugglers, the people of the coast had buried their dead in the patch of salty, infertile soil that was closest to the plinths themselves. Some nameless ones were still interred there—the unknown and the Disappeared. Egan himself had come upon the corpse of an Indian child, somehow strayed from the Montana, and buried it beside the stream. A passer-by, following the path that led from the ocean to the falls at the head of the valley, might miss the stones and the buried pyramid entirely, in the filtered light and the many shapes and shades of green.

Now, Egan came up the path as the sunlight faded like mist from the forest, carrying a plastic briefcase and talking softly to himself. People were waiting for him at the stones. They were foreigners from the North, from South America and Europe. There were more than a dozen of them; their tents and hammocks were spread throughout the clearing. Young people of their sort, rarely seen before on that coast, had been turning up in increasing numbers, as though there were something for them there. Father Egan would come out and speak to them.

The easternmost stela, discolored from years of rubbings and centuries of weather, faintly showed the outline of a human figure, a man in a feathered headdress. The makings of a fire had been laid before it. As Egan took his place beside the stone marker, a slim young woman with a bandaged arm poured kerosene on the pile of sticks. The foreigners watched, reclining against their packs and ground cloths. Sitting apart from the rest was a hulking blond man with thick-browed elfin features and bright blue eyes.

When the fire was lit, Egan turned away from the group and leaned against the stone, eyes closed. It seemed to him he had a text. There was a cane fire in his brain. Wet-eyed, he rounded on them.

"Why seek ye," he demanded, "the living among the dead?"

Someone giggled discreetly. Marijuana smoke floated on the still air.

"What are you doing here, children, a place like this?" He steadied himself, leaning on the stone. "You know when the

Easter angel asked the woman at the tomb why she was crying she said: 'Because they have taken away my Lord and I know not where they have laid him.' "

In the highest boughs, spider monkeys were singing out last reports, their sentries calling in from evening stand-to as the bands settled down for the night.

"Taken away," Egan said. "Mislaid. No wonder she's crying. Wouldn't you? Don't you?"

A few of the young people affirmed that they did.

"Of course you do. We all do. No matter how smart you are, some things are very hard to lose."

A girl with a fever began to sing. She lay resting her head on her companion's lap.

"This is a dead place," Egan said. "It's a boneyard, that's why we're here. It's history," he told them. "It's the world."

"Not my world," said a man who was older than the others and drunk. "Not by a long shot."

Egan ignored him.

"It's another city on a hill, you see. An earthly historical city—very grand. Here we celebrate what dies. What fails. What is mislaid."

"What about the bright side?" the man said. "Is there one?"

"Certainly," Egan said. "But it has nothing to do with you. You're not on it."

Pablo and Deedee sat under the work lights aft of the ice hatches, mounted on upturned shrimp baskets, their backs against the lazaret. Over the open hatches the coiled net swung like a dun banner, anchored between the paired stabilizers and the chain drag line. The drag lay covered in a confetti of brightly colored chafing gear that was heaped over it; the pile looked like the wreckage of a carnival float. Before them, under the bright lights, was a living creeping jambalaya, a rapine of darkness and depth. In thousands, creatures of hallucination—shelled, hooded, fifty-legged and six-eyed—clawed, writhed, flapped or devoured their way through the mass of their fellow captives, the predators and the prey together, overthrown and blinded, scuttling after their lost accustomed world.

"Dig in, Pablo buddy," Deedee said. "I guess you know a shrimp when you see one, right?"

Pablo stared silently into the mass of struggling life at his feet. Deedee stood up, walked carefully to the edge of the swarm and plucked from it in her gloved hand a two-foot barracuda. Grasping the struggling fish behind its row of teeth, she tossed it over the side.

"Poor baby," she said. She worked with a joint between her lips. "Might be another one in there," she told Pablo, sitting back down on the basket. "You want to watch where you stick your hands."

Pablo leaned forward, picked up a shrimp and looked at it in his palm.

"There you go," Deedee said, "That's one right there. When you have a basket full of those little fellas you stick it down in the hold. If we were the honest folk we pretend to be we'd take their heads and legs off. But we're not, so we won't."

He did not care for the way she watched him. She was smiling and high, but there was a guilty wariness beneath her chatter and high spirits. Pablo knew little about shrimping but he believed he knew rather a lot about female anxiety. How they looked when they were turning you around. How they smiled when they were scared.

He crushed the shrimp he was holding in his right fist and with the fingers of his left hand, pulled its head off. The gesture of petty violence seemed in no way to alarm her. She went on looking him happily in the eye but he knew she had seen and interpreted his vague threat. She was very tough, he thought, she was different from other women. And they were playing a game. The thought of games was hateful to him now, it savored of Naftali's whisper.

"The rest of these beasties—the non-shrimp—just let them lie. We'll hose them off the deck later."

He kept his gaze fastened on her and she looked back at him until he felt foolish. She was better at games than he was. He was beginning to hate her. He was beginning to be afraid of her, of her more than the others.

"The first time I ever did this," she told him as they filled their baskets, "a man threw a barracuda at me." She took the joint from between her lips and let it die on the wet deck.

"Huh," Pablo said, keeping his eyes on his work.

"I was going to throw that one at you. But then I thought better of it—indeed I did."

"It might have bit me," he said.

"It might have. And then where would I be?"

What he wanted, he realized, was to fuck and to kill her. The realization made him even gloomier because he believed that such impulses were particular to him alone. It touched his self-respect. Moreover, he could not be sure whether she was only teasing him or really coming on now. It was like it kept changing. Confused and increasingly angry, he could think of only one strategy and that was to listen and wait and sound her.

"You gotta be crazy," he said. "I mean you gotta be crazy, a good-looking woman like you out here on this turkey."

"That makes two of us," she said. "At least."

"Yeah," Pablo said. "But I'm just passing through." So saying, he shuddered. He felt a nearly prayerful hope it might be true.

"Cast a cold eye," Deedee said, "on life, on death. Horseman, pass by." She was weirdness itself.

Within forty-five minutes they had enough filled baskets to cover the ice completely in one hold and to cover half of it in the second. Pablo stood on the ice bars receiving the baskets from Deedee as she passed them down. When the shrimp were stowed, she got the stabilizer engines going and he helped her spread the drag line again. They sat down on their baskets and drank some rum. It was good light Puerto Rican rum, better than the stuff they usually brought out.

"A very fine place for shrimping," Deedee Callahan said. "If we're ever in that line again we'll have to remember it."

Pablo looked out at the surrounding ocean. There were other boats in sight now, four or five of them, lit and working.

"Could be the fisheries patrol come down on us any minute," Pablo said. He said it to have something to say, bitching to bring her down and to make himself feel better.

"I wouldn't worry about that, Pab, we've never been boarded, ever. They check out the numeral and the colors. When they're close enough to see you're gringo they leave you alone. Unless of course they're looking for you."

"But that won't happen, will it?"

She took a drink of rum and passed him the bottle.

"Well, I haven't said anything. And the boss hasn't and Freddy hasn't. Have you?"

"That's a joke, ain't it?"

"Yes," she said, "ain't it?"

"They don't trust me," he said sullenly, nodding toward the wheelhouse, "I know that."

"If they don't trust you they must have a reason. What would the reason be?"

"You playin' cop or somethin', Missus Callahan?"

"We're playing Pirate," she said. "I have to trust you. So do they. Otherwise you'd be walking the plank. That's how it is in Pirate."

"What about that nigger stayed back in St. Joost?"

"You mean Tino?" He was trying to stare her down again; she was looking back at him, easy-natured. "We don't usually refer to Tino as a nigger," she told him pleasantly. "He's an old friend of ours. We're a little concerned that he's not with us but we're quite sure he won't talk to anyone."

"Everybody's a snitch sometime."

"That's a word I don't like," she said. "I dislike it and I dislike the way you say it. It makes you sound like a punk."

Pablo was genuinely surprised.

"Nobody never called me punk," he said savagely when he had mustered the force.

She smiled and sighed. "Nobody never? In your whole life?" In the next moment she was coming on. "You're a fine figure of a man," she told him. "Cultivate your higher qualities."

While he was thinking of an answer, by the time he had decided to say he guessed he was quality enough for her, Mr. Callahan came aft and looked at the catch in the holds.

"Real good, shrimp people," Mr. Callahan said. "Now let's bring the nets up again. We're running out of time."

There were not so many shrimp in the second catch and they had to pad the baskets with chipped ice and junk fish to get the second hold covered. Negus came out and worked with them until the nets were secured and the hatches tight over the holds. Pablo observed that Callahan was drunk again. Even Negus in his silent dispatch did not seem altogether sober.

"We're gonna lose these other boats," Callahan told them. "Then we're going in without lights and fast."

"And he'll be there," Deedee said.

"I like it," Callahan declared, "it's going well." He smiled at Tabor. "Is it going well for you, Pablo?"

"Sure," Pablo said.

Deedee leaned on his shoulder.

"We're happy back here. We're a team."

When Callahan and Negus went back to the cockpit, Deedee stayed where she was, cuddled against Tabor. They both watched as Callahan made his way forward, a little more unsteadily than the roll of the *Cloud* demanded. Pablo reached in his pocket and swallowed the last of his Benzedrine.

The drug's action when it came was disappointing and curious. For a fraction of a second he could not remember where he was and he was overcome with fear. But the rush passed and then he was better. He asked her for more rum and while he drank it she held to his arm. For a while he was calm and sad and grateful to have her beside him.

"You're a good man," she told him soothingly. "You're O.K. and you're going to be even better."

"I like the sound of that," Pablo told her, and then he laughed. Almost giggled. She seemed sympathetic; she laughed with him.

"How long you been with that man?" he asked her.

"Forever," she said, and they both laughed again.

She rolled a joint and they drank a little more.

"If you been with him forever," Pablo asked, "how come you're coming on to me?"

"Heavens to Betsy," she said, "I thought you'd never ask. I didn't think you noticed."

They laughed at that too. They were smoking her heavy Jamaican weed. But then he decided there was something wrong with what she had said or the way she had said it. Things got tricky for him again.

In the cockpit, Negus put the wheel on manual and they steered north, the compass needle over the Raytheon fluttered. The other boats fell away southward.

"God grant it goes easy," Negus said. "It's been such a damn . . ."

"Gonna stay ashore now, Freddy?"

"Oh, crikey," Negus said heartily, "you'd best believed it.

I'm too old and brittle for this sort of thing anymore. You said a true thing when you said that."

"I will grant you," Callahan said, "that this one was difficult. Without Tino and with Tabor. I will grant you that. But I told Deedee . . . I told her I need a bad guy I can keep in line."

"I been telling you for years, Jack, you can't just pick up any dingbat these days for something like this. You're bound to get wrong ones. Must say I think you drink too damn much for a man of business."

Callhan did not dispute him.

"What you got Deedee to aft yonder?"

"Taking care of him. She's a smart girl."

"With all due respect and up to a point that's a true thing about her," Negus said. Then he looked over his shoulder from the chair and lowered his voice. "He goes, don't he? Afterwards?"

"I'm not without principles," Callahan said. "I propose to do my duty by the world and the international shipping lanes. He goes."

"And Deedee knows that?"

"She knows."

"Just so we're clear on that," Negus said. "Because she's soft on him in a way. Taking care of him, you know, that could mean anything to her."

"I know what it means to her, Freddy, and so do you. Soft on him isn't quite the word, is it? Dee isn't sentimental in the least."

"No, hell no. She ain't sentimental. She's . . . like we know she is."

"Perverse."

"However you want to say it."

"She likes edges. She thinks he's a stud. He's got shit between his toes and he's going to be dead tomorrow. That's what she likes."

"Yep," Negus said. "That's the way I see it. That would be her way of looking at it."

"Me, I think she's splendid. One-of-a-kind kid. She suits me."

"Yep," Freddy Negus said, "she does. You and her—you're adapted to each other naturally."

"Not exactly made in heaven," Callahan said. "But we like it. Edge players as we are. You suppose he could possibly figure out why she's breathing on him?"

Negus laughed. "Well, I couldn't if I was him. And I think I seen about everything."

"But what's right and what's wrong, eh, Fred? You can't have sex without mortality. That's a biological fact."

He began to pour himself another drink. Negus lifted the glass from his hand.

"No more, boss. Not until afterwards."

Callahan watched Negus throw the full glass over the side.

"Right," he said. "It's getting time to darken ship and get on triple zero. Another couple of minutes."

"I'll be on the forepeak when we got in. We ought to check on Dee from time to time."

"She'll handle it," Callahan said. "She has a gun. Let me do the checking, Freddy. It'll work out better."

"Sure," Negus said. "That'd be more your job than mine."

"You know," Father Egan said, "I'm reminded here of another city." He uttered a reflective clerical chuckle. "When I was preparing to be whatever it is I've become I was sent to work in a hospital. Comfort the dying. I remember the mortuary there—it was very Victorian. Neo-Renaissance. In the foyer there was an inscription in Latin. 'Let smiles cease,' it said, 'let laughter flee. This is the place where the dead help the living.'"

The older man in the group got to his feet muttering.

"Bummer!" he shouted at Egan. His heavy face grew red with anger; he raised cupped hands to amplify his voice, and screamed. "Bummer!"

"I'll describe a picture to you," Egan told his congregation. "I'm sure you're familiar with it. A group of men are standing over a pile of corpses. They're smiling and they have guns. Some of them have tied handkerchiefs across their faces but not to give themselves the raffish air of banditti—because of the smell." His eyes went vacant. "What are they looking for in that pile? Has one of them dropped his watch? Never mind."

The priest wiped his mouth with his sleeve and took a

cautious step forward. "That's the big picture, children. That's how it is now. That's why you see that picture every week in all the magazines. You know—there are variations, the people, and the uniforms come in different colors, but it's always the same picture."

Around them the silences and the darkness deepened. Ramon nuts pattered to the ground through a web of leafy branches, making a sound like soft rain.

"Now why," Egan asked, "are we made to see this picture week after week until it's imprinted on the backs of our eyes and we have it before us dreaming and waking? Is it that we're meant to see it? Is it the cunning of dice play, children? Is there, in short, a message for us?"

No one answered him.

"Will those dead help the living?" he asked. "Are we to seek the living among the dead? What does it mean?"

A youth with a full dark beard who was sitting cross-legged on a waterproof poncho roused himself.

"The Holy One is among the dead," the young man declared.

The girl who had started the fire turned and stared at him.

"Oh, no," she said softly.

Egan stood with his hands clasped under his chin, his face uplifted, his eyes closed.

"And yet," he said, "and yet—where, eh?" he opened his eyes and peered at them across the firelight. "Because you can stare into faces of the dead—I've been doing it for years, I ought to know—and you won't see anything. Anything more than plain death, I mean. You can look as sharp as you like, you can pray for a sign, for something, for the slightest hint of something . . . more. Not forthcoming."

He sighed and shook his head.

"You can look into the dead face of the world, try to catch it unawares—no good. You keep looking, you tell yourself you've seen something, some little imitation, you know, of something . . . living. The Living. Or the Holy One, whatever. But it's no good. You won't. It won't reveal itself that way."

He had been standing, swaying, dangerously close to the fire. The heat warned him away.

"I mean—you look outward. To the stars, to the farthest nebulae. Not a sign. Or you look in. Do it!" he told them.

"Look in! Close your eyes and look down from the outside in and what have you got? Blisters. Skin, eh? Flesh, parasites, sour guts and a little concupiscence. Then we're down among our several intoxications and delusions and we find our minds, the little devils, the devious protean things. Anything more? A glimmer?"

Some of them sat with their eyes closed looking in. Others stared at Egan or into the fire.

"Maybe yes," Egan said. "Maybe, eh? Who knows down in that mess? But maybe there is something. A little shard of light. What is it?"

"An anchovy," the drunk said. "An undigested bit of beef." He turned and walked off toward the dark tree line, carrying a box of Kleenex.

"Marley's ghost," he said as he went. "The ghost of Christmas future."

Egan never seemed to hear.

"It's the why and wherefore," the priest said, "that little radiant thing. I've never seen it, you know, but it has to be there. It's the life. The Life. There's all this death and this dying and it's the only difference. It's the only difference things make," he told them.

"There aren't angels," Egan said. "There's none of that. Thrones. Dominions. All that business—it's rubbish. But there's life. There's the Living among the dead. I mean, you can't ever quite see it, can you? You'd hardly know it was there but it has to be, doesn't it? It's only mislaid."

He was dizzy, his chest felt hollow. He steadied himself against the stone again.

"Because it's there—everything's all right."

He tried to see each of them among the shadows and flickering light.

"That's the Holy One among the dead, son," he told the dark-bearded youth. His eye fell on the strange blond man, something made him look away.

"You have to try and find it, see?" Egan said. "If you can't find it you have to believe in it. If you can't believe in it you have to hope you will. If you can't hope then all you can do is love the idea of it. Love it at a distance if that's the best you can do, children. Love it like a secret lover."

He seemed perplexed by their silence. He walked around the fire into the semicircle they had formed.

"It's the only meaning in all of things," he said. "There aren't any others."

Pablo had lost sight of her face in the glare of the overhead work lights; she was standing by the rail stretching. He moved to the rail opposite and looked for the lights of the other boats he had seen working nearby. No other lights were in sight now.

They seemed to have shifted course. The angle of the wind was different and the low troughs came at them from a different quarter, making the sea seem rougher. He moved out of the glare of the lights, picked out the pointers at the top of the Dipper and lined up Polaris a little off the bow. The new course was northerly. A freshening wind made him feel cold.

"I'm tired," he said. "I expect I'll be earning my pay soon."

She was smoking marijuana again. He smelled it as she went across the stern to sit down on her overturned basket. She never stopped. From her knit basket she took a straight cigarette and a bottle of Puerto Rican rum; she uncapped the rum and took a deep swallow.

"Won't I be earning my pay soon?"

He could see her face well enough now. She was smiling at him in a way that made him feel as though she had never seen him before. He shivered and that seemed to make her smile the more. She stood up and brought the joint and the bottle across the deck to him.

"Soon, baby. That you will. Now have yourself a drink of this here."

The rum was good, clear and light, much better than the thick stuff they drank in the cockpit. She pressed the joint on him and absentmindedly he smoked more of it than was good for him.

"Thing is," Pablo said, "I don't understand. Things been happening and I don't understand. Like something was going on."

"Something's always going on," she said. And while he was trying to read her look, all the lights went out together. Only the instrument lights in the cockpit showed, reflected in the windshield and the faint glow of the interior lights from between the louvered shutters over the saloon housing. The *Cloud* shifted course again and someone—Negus—came out on deck and opened the engine panel. When he slammed it shut again, the boat began to pick up speed. The whole frame of the vessel shuddered, a wind picked up where there had been little more than a steady breeze—the *Cloud* was running like a crash boat.

Negus had gone below again; he came out now wearing a slicker. The bars of light from the saloon compartment had disappeared. Negus was crouching in the forepeak, a pair of binoculars around his neck.

"Away we go," Mrs. Callahan said.

The sensation of moving at such speed in what seemed an ordinary shrimp boat was dreamlike, almost comical. Pablo stared down at the white water that rushed under their bow.

Deedee sat on a basket near the lazaret hatch, hugging herself, the knit bag on her lap.

"Sit down before you fall over, Pablo," she said. "We're going faster than you think." She lit a straight cigarette in the lee of the lazaret housing. "Let's get out of this wind and Mama will tell you how it is."

Following her down into the darkness of the lazaret, his first thought was that it was not right because their clothes were foul. They had been working shrimp. And because she was smoking and there were oil cans and engine rags.

When she sat herself down on the chafing gear he sat beside her. It was the first close touch he had of her since the night in the galley that seemed so long before. He was fighting to hold Pablo now, to hold within himself the thinking, calculating Pablo—because even as he sat with her, that self was being crowded out by lust and a shadow. The lust had a rubbery bubbly taste; the shadow, he knew well. It had few emotions but it was an angry frightened shadow.

She pushed his cap off and brought his head against her shoulder and put her chin on the top of his head.

"This is how it is, Pablo," she began. Pablo closed his eyes to listen. Somehow he had the notion that his mother would tell him something.

"We have some boys to deal with on the coast here and we don't know who they are. It could occur to them to take our

goods, our boat, everything—and pitch us over the side. It's
happened. So we need a little display of sincerity. We need a
crazy old boy like you who's so mean and nasty looking they
think he might feed them a few just to hear the funny noises
they'd make. Then look at it from their side. Everything's
COD. Maybe it's a little old-fashioned but that's us, see, that's
the way we do it. They've got money for us. Now we might
just take their money and do them in—that's happened too."

She ran her fingers along the back of his neck.

"So. So, honey . . ." Cuddling him. "So they come out in
their boat and we load the stuff. You go along so everybody
feels all right. They usually have to make more than one trip
and going in they'll feel better because even if they don't have
all of their delivery they have you. And you'll be riding along
looking so bad and crazy that whatever they'd like to do—
they'll decide it makes more sense to stick to the deal. So they
bring you back with the last load. We take our money. *Buena
suerte* and *viva la causa*, that's it. It's not a desperate situation
even today. It's got rules. You're riding shotgun."

He began to laugh or by now it was the shadow. He listened to her laugh as well.

Then he went after that wet fouled denim for the sweet
flesh inside, peeled the sweat shirt off her and licked her
breasts, the nipples, above them below and around, the nipples themselves again.

"Crazy stuff," she said. "Crazy stuff."

Her watch cap had fallen off and her hair spread out
among the strands of chafing gear. She was thrusting her ass
against him—soft, round, damp under the wet film of denim
—unzipping his fly. She forced him back against the bale; she,
him!

"No need you holdin' me down," he said. It was the
shadow talking.

But by answer she bent and put her teeth against his penis.
Then she raised herself on her hands and feet like a cat
stretching and kicked off her shrimping boots, then peeled
down the jeans that encased her. Naked, she lay facing him
against the bale. Pablo took off his shirt and undid his belt
until his dungarees were down about his ankles.

She was laughing still.

"Don't you take off your boots when you have a lady,
Tex?"

"Never you fuckin' mind."

She answered him by taking his right hand and putting it between her thighs and the skin there was as smooth as the surface of a glass of buttermilk on a summer's day. She closed his hand over her, his thumb in the cleft of her buttocks, his fingers playing over the down and labia. He put his face into her neck, then sought out her shoulder where the arrogant tattoo was and then, wanting it without delays, put his face between the thighs and with his mouth and tongue took all such pleasures there as he could see or imagine. She had wriggled partway up the heaped bale until her body was above his, and with her posture strangely erect, her head thrown back, slipped down on him time after time, impaling herself, until they both had come.

Deedee was still moaning softly when he saw that the hatch at the top of the ladder was pried open. He could make out the stars.

"The hatch," he said.

She reached out for her bag and the bottle.

"Scared of trouble?"

From the way she said it, he could not tell if it was challenge or consolation, so he did not answer.

"We're not having trouble on this boat," she told him, "not about you and me. And the reasons for that I cannot tell but in another day."

So, warily, he settled down, and though he did not like the way she had spoken to him, presently he was hard again. Or it might have been the shadow's lust. He took her once more, trying now to hurt her—but she could not be hurt in that way; every thrust he made she somehow met, met yielding, as though she were ready for every moment. So he could not hurt her, could not gentle or humiliate her. And when he started to come and to pull out, she held him, letting go little by little as it pleased her until he was seeing lights on the overhead and he thought he would pass out cold.

He was very high, higher than he had ever been. His thoughts twisted off into spools, arabesques, snatches of music.

Deedee was putting her clothes on. Automatically, he buckled his trousers.

"Don't you have any gentleness in you, boy?" she asked.

He looked toward her unseen face. Fear sat on his chest, its talons in the muscles of his breast. He had seen a shadow pass the hatch. He was certain.

"You mustn't be afraid," she told him softly.

Hearing her say it was a terrible thing for him.

"Someone's up there," he said.

"That could be, Pablo. It's all right."

All right. And he was in a rank-smelling trap at a loss to understand how he had got there. Beside him in the darkness his soft-bodied enemy soothed him in a voice like gold wire.

"'Hey, hey," she said, nudging him slightly, "it's all right, my man."

All right. But they were going to kill him. He had been through the question before and that was the way it had come out.

"You set me up," he told her.

"Don't be silly," she said firmly.

As she said it, he stopped trembling. She had set him up and there was no more to it. He was among crazy people, in an empty landscape tasting of salt rubber, smelling of scale and death. They were about killing him. He sat very still waiting for her to move, listening for sounds on the deck above.

"Settle down now," she said, as though she were talking to a horse.

He was quite settled down now. There was no more reality to him than to the blossoming bougainvillea he thought to see in the darkness or to the music that he heard. Things were inside out but he was strong.

He made a loop of the chafing line and by a blind stroke caught her around the throat. One of her hands came up to struggle with the noose but the other was reaching into darkness. Pablo, twisting the line with all his strength, his mind serene, took a moment to react. Deedee brought up the butt of the pistol she had taken from her bag and cracked him hard across the upper lip, nearly getting the underside of his nose. He let go the line and went after the pistol; he could not see what had hit him but he knew it must be one.

She was shouting now, shouting for her husband in a choked nightmare voice. When he had forced the pistol from her right hand, he pressed his head down against her chest to keep it low and took Naftali's Nambu from beneath his seabag.

There was true light in the space now. On the ladder someone with a flashlight was searching out the darkness. Pablo
rolled her across his body—it was as though they were making love again—her teeth were sunk in his arm. As she passed
over him, he jammed the barrel of the Nambu under her
down vest and fired two of its eight shots upward. He felt her
teeth release him, she was flung onto her knees beside the
bale. Two shots came from the ladder, at least one of them
striking the woman. She rolled over on her side, her knees still
together. The compartment was spinning with illuminations;
Pablo thought of fireflies, wet spark plugs. His ears were
hammered shut. Against the flat lower section of the bulkhead
he was unhurt. When he fired at the man who was on the
ladder, he did so with confidence, as though he had nothing
but time. And in a second, he knew he had been on target. He
heard the shuffle, the groan, the gun strike the ladder's bottom step and slide across the deck. The man fell behind the
beam of his own flashlight, invisible and motionless. Pablo sat
panting in the darkness, waiting for the figure behind the light
to move. The moment he started to his feet, there was another
flash; Tabor's leg went out from under him and his head
struck the slanting overhead. He knelt and fired two shots into
the space behind the light's beam. There was a groan and a
man spoke—it was Callahan—but Pablo could not make out
what he said. Then Pablo discovered himself to be shot; there
was a bleeding wound in the thick part of his calf, in the
back. He ran his finger along the shin bone and found it
unbroken. The bullet might only have cut him and passed
through but it hurt. He would be all right, he thought. He had
power enough to fox them all and live. There was another
one.

From the open deck above, he heard Negus' voice calling
the Callahans by name. He began to go up the ladder backwards, sitting for a while on each step. Negus' voice sounded
far away, carried off by the wind. At last, he was sitting
framed in the hatchway. There was no sign of a light. His
head bent low, he glanced around his shoulder and saw
Negus, holding a shotgun and crouching anxiously beside the
after hatch.

"Jack?" Negus asked, and reached for a light he had set
down on the hatch cover.

As Negus reached for it, Pablo turned full around, got off a shot, then flung himself out of the hatchway and scuttled across the slimy deck like one of the creatures that had swarmed there during the evening. His shot, he knew, had missed. His leg throbbing, he crawled for darkness, his steel-hearted killer's trance deserting him. Negus was after him, rounding the hatch for a shot. Pablo, terrified now, cowered in the scuppers, he had two shots in the little Nambu and the light was bad. Then he saw Negus stumble backward, make two little capering backward steps and fall back against the hatch cover. The shotgun discharged heavenward.

Pablo, uncertain of what he was seeing, came to realize that Negus had slipped on the deck. It was a miracle of God. He hesitated for a moment, saw Negus try to bring the gun to bear and shot him. It seemed to him that he had missed again. Negus dropped the shotgun on the deck and was looking down at it, cursing softly. He turned toward Pablo.

"You stop, you hear! Just stop it!" There was a catch in his voice. He was hurt.

Pablo lowered his gun.

"Don't yell at me no more, Mr. Negus. Get back there against the rail."

When Negus stood clear, Pablo lowered himself on his good leg, and picked up the shotgun.

"Oh, you dirty monkey," Negus said. "You little son of a bitch. What'd you do?"

He seemed furious. Pablo felt as though he had done some-thing wrong.

"They're down there," Pablo said, pointing to the lazaret hatchway. "You look down there, you'll see them."

Negus walked stiffly to the flashlight on the hatch cover, took it and went to the top of the lazaret ladder. Tabor stood behind him, keeping him on the top step as he played the beam over the silent space.

"You dirty fucking monkey," Freddy Negus said.

"They were turning me around," Pablo explained. "You was too."

"Well, they ain't turnin' you around no more, bucky," Negus said. "They're dead. You killed them."

"Well, they were," Pablo said. He felt remorse and disgust.

Negus sat down on the hatch, his arms folded over his stomach.

"I don't know how the hell he took it in his head to hire you. You were just a wrong number."

From the cockpit, they could hear the RDF's steady null signal, sounding over and over, a noise from space.

"Goddamn foibles and human error," Negus said, "you got such a little margin anyways and them two always overplayed it." He coughed and spat thickly on the deck. "Figured you were fun or something."

"Well, I can't live for fun," Pablo said. "Some people can afford to but I can't. A lot of times people try and turn me around and they always find that out about me."

Negus stood up and started forward, paused and went on, holding to the rail.

"I'm not walking well," Negus told Pablo.

"Me neither. But you're gut-shot."

When they reached the wheelhouse hatch, Pablo started in; Negus stayed him with a hand.

"I don't want no blood in there."

Pablo understood. Negus sat on a gear locker and looked out to sea; Tabor leaned on the rail. There were no lights in sight, or ridges to block the great field of stars. The pointers and Polaris were over the starboard quarter.

"You got no sense, son," Negus said. "Why'd you ever come aboard?"

"I needed to. Thought you needed me."

Negus spat again. "But we didn't, did we? No need on anybody's part."

"Guess not," Pablo said. "But that's the breaks." He was beginning to think there might be a way in which he was going to make out after all. Most of all, he was wondering if there was any more speed on board.

"Now what we got, kid, is a Mexican standoff. You know what I mean?"

"No," Pablo said. But he was intrigued and encouraged to hear things put that way.

"I'm hurting. I got a slug in my gut. I don't know but that . . ." He let go. "But you're hurting too, kid. You can't get nowhere from here. Nothing on that coast for you now. You'll pile her up or the Guardia'll get you or the pirates will. You're bleeding, boy, you're drawing sharks, you see what I mean now?"

Pablo listened in silence to the beat of the null tone.

Negus stood up and leaned on the rail a few feet away from him.

"I can take this vessel anywhere. I can get us anywhere. Clear."

"How?" Pablo asked.

Negus grew enthusiastic.

"Oh, by Jesus Christ, boy, why, plenty of places. San Ignacio. Colombia. One of the islands there. I got friends in all them places. I can get us a doctor. We can sell our goods, man. Emeralds. We can get them." He was trying to see Pablo's face in the faint light that came from the cockpit. He was smiling.

"What would you tell them there? If we got to Colombia—one of them places?"

"Well, a thousand things. A thousand things, hell . . ." He was talking faster and he began to laugh. "They don't give a goddamn what you done or where you been if you got cash or goods. We'd have it made."

Pablo was straining toward hope. That it might all be true. There were moments when they both believed it all.

Negus drew his breath painfully, and encouraged, went on.

"Listen, Pablo. You're using twenty gallons an hour out here. More than that. More. You goin' to be sailing in circles."

When Pablo did not reply, he grew more heated.

"You be out here, boy, you'll see things day and night. Stuff that ain't there. I know what I'm talking about. You don't ever want to be alone out here because the stuff you'll see sometimes it ain't there and sometimes it is. When it is it's worser. I know. I'm the one that knows. And me takin' us in, old shoe, we'll be home free. Home. Free. They know me, man. They don't care." He laughed and ran out of breath, and Tabor saw that the man was lying to him, talking for his life as though to a child. Turning him around.

Years before in a town Pablo knew, the bootleggers had chained an old boy to an anchored oil barrel at low tide, chained him up for the high water to come in on him. There happened along this young child out where he had no business and the man talked to the child and begged and hollered at him to go for help. But the child fogot or his parents told him better not to say and the tide came in over the man four feet and they only found out about the child afterwards.

Pablo looked at his weary enemy and was sorry.

"Well, O.K.," he said. "Let's do it."

Negus' delight was so great that, sorry as he was, Tabor couldn't keep from laughing. The old dude was whooping and shouting like the drunkard he was, going on about emeralds and cocaine and private villas and his face was happy as Christmas morning when Pablo blew him away. It was necessary to hold the dead old man up against the rail so that he would not become a burden. Holding him up hurt Pablo's injured leg, so the two of them leaned over the rail side by side for a while. Fellow travelers. Then Tabor bent down, took hold of Negus under the knees and pitched him over. The null tone went right on sounding.

He remained at the rail, his elbows resting there, his hands clasped, and looked up the Dipper. He had been watching it edge around Polaris through the night. Perhaps because of the wound, he felt cold. Now he and the creatures in the ice hold were the only living things aboard.

His work done, Pablo became afraid. An unfamiliar emotion oppressed him which he came to recognize as loneliness; a loneliness deeper than he had ever experienced.

"Jesus help me," Pablo said aloud.

He missed them, that was it. A crazy way to feel, because they were low-down people, they were just shit as people and they had certainly been turning him around. Not the way he missed Naftali—Naftali was all right. But them being dead now, all of them, it was hard to take. It put a strain on him. Cecil, he thought, that black bastard was the root of it.

Then he thought of speed and how that would be the ticket. On his way to the sleeping quarters he stopped in the cockpit and looked over the navigational gear. The compass bearing was set for zero-zero-zero and the constant null tone signified that this was where it should be. They had gone out on one-eighty from the marker and were headed straight back in—no problem there. On the chart table he found Callahan's rough line-of-sight chart; in one corner Callahan had written the Loran digits he had noted at the spot. For the moment things were all right but later, up near the reef, he would have to do his own steering and find the market in darkness. And there would be the men on the coast, those money-crazy bird-talk-ing people. Perhaps his mother's people.

He took a light and went into the head where the shower was and found an unlocked cabinet under the small sink. Up front there were first-aid kits and soap and every kind of downer, all of them prescribed for a Dolores Callahan. In his impatience he swept them aside; he found aspirin, aloe pow-der, ginseng, exotic shampoos. Not until he was on the edge of despair did he find, on the bottom shelf under the pipe, a small bottle containing six Desoxyn. He clutched the Desoxyn bottle and bent his head against the shelf in gratitude. Less impatient now, he looked through the rest of the scattered bottles and found a jar of pain-killing tablets. He recognized the gray half-moon pills and their brand name because they were the things that Kathy took for menstrual cramps and he had used them as speed back home.

Pablo sat on the deck of the head, swallowed two Desoxyn and one of the pain-killers and made a bandage for his wounded leg. There were no exit or entry holes, only a scythe-cut wound along the side. It did not seem serious; there was not much blood. He would do.

With the light at his feet he sat in one of the lounge chairs of the saloon to let the speed and the pain-killer do their work. A ridiculous place it was, the saloon, with its teak and rattan and Spanish table. He recognized it now as a third hold, the sort they had on the big Texas boats. The Callahans had made it into a floating parlor. And it suited them, he thought, it was their idea of fun and high living. The wooden louvered shutters at deck level could keep it cool at sea but it was really just a hidey-hole, set everywhere with fans and as cramped in its fancy way as the lazaret.

When he felt better he went to Deedee's compartment and opened the teak door. There was a wide bunk bed against the bulkhead and a steel bookcase with a great many books. On top of it was a picture of both Callahans on a lawn with a lot of tables and lawn umbrellas behind them. Callahan, looking young and thinner, was standing behind a bench upon which sat his wife, who looked very much the same. Her blond hair was tied back severely and her smile was sweetness itself; her legs, in tight breeches and gleaming boots, were crossed in comfortable self-assurance. Callahan's hand was on her jacketed shoulder. Her own hand, in a string glove, rested on his.

Pablo turned the picture face down. The room smelled of saffron.

The Callahans would have to go with Negus now.

Tabor hobbled up on deck, bringing two stationary flashlights with him. Scanning the night horizon, he saw no lights in view; he would have to risk some light of his own to get the thing done. But to bring the bodies up from the lazaret by main force was more than he could manage. He switched the flashlights on—one beside the hatchway to light the compartment, the other beside an after hatch to light his work space. Then he engaged the tri-net motor and swung the bar amidships; the chain line, coils and chafing gear spread out around him like a collapsed circus tent. From among the heap, he seized an end of chain line and, grasping it under his arm, eased himself painfully down the ladder, pulling a web of coils behind him.

He came to Callahan first and linked two sections of chain line under the dead man's fleshy shoulders. When he thought the links were secured, he went topside and set the tri-net bar to hauling upright. The coils and chain with their burden rattled up the hatchway like a receding tide; Pablo stationed himself at the top of the ladder to ease the corpse through. With Callahan netted and swinging above the deck, Pablo loosened the chain from under his shoulders, swung the bar outboard and lowered away.

It went easily. Pablo had been standing by with a gaff in case the netting or the body fouled the overworked engines. But the chain settled, the net spread out without bird's-nesting and Mr. Callahan rolled off into the quiet ocean and disappeared.

Pablo rested then, nursing his throbbing leg, looking around for lights, for aircraft, for a wall of mountains against the sky northward. When he felt up to it, he went up to the cockpit to check the speed, the bearings and Fathometer. The speed was steady, the Fathometer read over eight fathoms and unchanging, the compass needle was fast on triple zero and the null as constant as Polaris.

Topside, he started up the Lister again to bring back the net to center line. A second time, like a diver, Pablo descended into the Lazaret compartment, dragging chain line behind him. He found her easily enough and pulled her into the coils. Her death's darkness smelled of suntan oil. The net hauling, he guided her up the ladder and out of the hatchway.

When the tri-net boom was lowered and the web offered her out she did not go so readily as her husband had. The colorless hair, almost phosphorescent over the water, spread itself among the coils, her down vest was caught on a cross wire, her legs, akimbo, were wrapped in the chains. In the end, he had to bring his light to the rail and cut her free from the webbing. The chains snapped loose, and then upright, her hair held on its ends by the coils that enshrouded her like a veil, she fell. Wide-eyed, as though eight fathoms held some new curiosity—like a figurehead, dolorous, an image of destiny—feet first into the water.

So Pablo had done with his dead and he switched off the lights. The null tone and the engines went on throbbing and the pointers held their places. He smoked and took another pill. He felt that his unseen presence on the ocean was ceremony enough for them.

"The answer"—Father Egan was saying—"I think they have it on the prayer wheels. Do you know what it says on the prayer wheels?"

Most of them had gone to sleep. From among the group only the girl with the bandaged arm, the feverish girl and her boyfriend, the dark-bearded young man and the blond giant remained to listen. A few others had gathered around a fire at the base of the overgrown pyramid and were smoking marijuana and passing a bottle of colorless rum. Their laughter sounded a muffled echo off the ancient stone.

"On the prayer wheels it says, 'The jewel is in the lotus.' They turn the wheels round hundreds of times a day. The little flags flutter so the wind says it. The Jewel is in the Lotus."

The feverish girl moaned and stirred in her lover's arms. Egan stopped speaking and looked at her and saw that she had the dengue. He had had it himself several times. He would have to get her some medicine, he thought, and for a moment he forgot what it was he had been preaching to them. Then it came back to him. The girl, he thought, was like a lotus and the pain in her overbright eyes a jewel.

"The lotus," he told her, "is sweet and fragrant, beautiful in life. But it's fallible and it's born for death. It's sown in corruption. But the jewel—" He felt his arm go numb and when he tried to raise it he could not. "The jewel is undying and beyond time. Beyond measure. The jewel is the meaning, you see."

A high-pitched cry sounded from somewhere in the deeper jungle, a cry that might have been human. Something surprised in the dark.

"You're the lotus. Your dear bodies that you're so fond of. You're the lotus. The jewel is in you." Egan laughed and brushed his sleeve across his mouth again. "The jewel's in hock to you. And the whole world of mortality is the lotus. And the Living is the jewel in it. That's the bright side."

He looked for the drunken man who had heckled him, but the man had gone away.

"It is sown in corruption," Egan declaimed, "it is raised in incorruption. It is sown in dishonor, it is raised in glory. It is sown in weakness, it is raised in power! On the bright side— everything's fine. You'd think they'd have no business here whose place is on the bright side. Here—it's whirl." He put out his hand and described a spiral with three fingers. "Whirl is King and it's lonely and in shadow, but over there—well, that's life over there, that's where the Living belongs. But," he said, and tapped his palm with his forefinger as though citing some father of doctrine, "the Jewel is in the Lotus! Why?"

He looked at them each in turn.

"Why, children?"

"They were all still, watching.

"Because," Egan thundered, "they're as lonely as we are! The Living is lonely for itself. For the shard of itself that's lost in us, the jewel in the lotus." He paused to draw breath.

"Isn't it wonderful after all? That we're secret lovers? Because why else would the Living be concealed within this meat, in all these fears and sweats, the Holy One among the dead? Why would he hide himself in Whirl to give meaning to a pile of corpses? Why isn't a *campesino* just an animal with a name? Why not? Why is there any meaning in a heap of dead? Or a lost kiddie. A sick little girl, a drowned . . ." A

shudder ran through him and he paused again. "Because the
Jewel is in the Lotus out of loneliness and secret love. He
doesn't have any choice."

Exhausted, he leaned on the stone. Then he thought of
something that he had once read. Or perhaps he had written it
himself.

"It's hard to see," he told the young people. "You never
know when you see the Living. The eye you see him with is
the same eye with which he sees you."

The girl with dengue put her hands on her companion's
shoulders and pulled herself upright.

"The bands broke," she said, half singing. "The bands
broke on Faithful John's heart." The boy who was with her
tried to ease her back down; she fought him. "The bands
broke on the heart of Faithful John," she screamed.

Egan had sunk to the ground and lay resting against the
stela. It seemed to him that he had made it come out all right.
His hand was on his briefcase, over the bulge of his bottle of
Flor de Cana.

"No, no," he told the girl kindly. "That's not the same at
all. That's a fairy tale."

Justin had spent the morning making inventory and talking to
a man from the shipper's office in town. They had told her
that it would be easier and more economical to load the
mission's promptuary equipment on shipboard at Puerto Alvarado than to ship it by way of the capital. He would have a
ship with available holding space quite soon.

A short time after noon she was standing in the kitchen
when she turned and saw the young Tecanecan woman to
whom she had spoken on the beach the week before. The
young woman had come up the front steps without a sound.
Justin had never learned her name.

"I don't think I can come here again," the young woman
said. "Only in emergencies."

Justin led her into the kitchen.

"You're right. You shouldn't risk coming here. I sent you a
note through the sexton."

"I have an answer for you from those in charge," the young
woman said. "They agree that you can't be involved further.

They say only continue to leave the dock lights on, this is all they ask."

"That's not much to ask."

"They say it's well you're preparing to leave. We're all in great danger now. If things don't happen soon we'll have to go for the mountains."

"Will it be soon?"

"I think so but I know very little. Only those in charge know."

"Well," Justin said, "I suppose I'm out of it now."

"You're out of it. But listen—when it starts, nobody is going to be safe. There are medical supplies here and they'll be wanted."

"When we go I'll lock up as much as I can in the building. They're at your disposal."

"If it should be that you're still here when it comes, you might be safer with us. You can make your own decision. I'll try to get word to you beforehand but there may not be time."

"Thank you," Justin said. "I'll be all right."

"They also say thanks. Those in charge."

"Yes," Justin said.

As the girl was leaving, Justin went a step after her.

"How's Father Godoy?"

"Gone," the girl said. "Gone to the Montana."

When the girl was gone, Justin felt desperate. Desperate to leave, to be gone—because their idleness and uselessness seemed more shameful than ever now that they could not actively help. Her work now would consist in persuading Charlie Egan to leave with her.

Thinking of Egan put her in mind of the man she had seen at Playa Tate and who was supposed to be taking the priest to dinner. He was a very self-confident man, very assured, rather arrogant. It seemed to her that she came very close to disliking him. For some reason, she did not altogether. It might be that he reminded her of someone, she thought.

Then the weight of things came down on her. The six years, everything that had happened since the day of the fiesta, Godoy, the child killings. A storm broke inside her, leaving her feeling for all the world as she had felt sometimes as a child—ashamed of her own triviality and insignificance, ashamed above all of her own body and its gross necessities, its rankness, its sinfulness, its carnality. She had stopped eating then, hoping to die. She found now that she couldn't stay still, couldn't put one thought in front of another, couldn't cry. She stood in the kitchen staring through the open door at the rectangle of raw mindless sky and waiting, more alone—and more lonely—than she had ever been.

Holliwell had had a hard day and he spent a large part of it trying not to get drunk. Finless, he had been going back and forth between the hotel beach and his bungalow. The hotel was suddenly full of people who described themselves to each other as contractors, and although they reminded him in some ways of the contractors he had known in Vietnam, they seemed to him at once more sinister and less colorful. Pale and foul-mouthed, they were everywhere—drinking beer at the water's edge, crowding the bar; they talked about Bogotá, Managua, Zihuatanejo and what they called Cancún City. Many of them seemed to be old acquaintances of Heath and Señor Soyer, the Cuban hardware man. Others were friends of Olga and Buddy. When they were quiet it meant they were on about coke or emeralds. It was as though there was some convocation of evil elements, a jar culture oozing out and discovering itself.

He parked his rented jeep beside the road, mounted the mission steps and walked straight into her in the kitchen. She looked ominously solemn.

"You know I don't know your name?" Holliwell said.

"Justin Feeney," she said. Perplexed, he thought, and weary.

"Is Father Egan around?"

She shook her head.

"He's back in the ruins. I'm sure he forgot about dinner with you. I should have told you he would."

"Maybe I should go back and talk to him."

"It's too far," she said. "It'll get dark and you'll lose your way. And he won't go with you. He's out of it."

Holliwell turned to look at the sky's light.

"He's in a bad way," Justin Feeney told him.

"So be it," Holliwell said. "I sure would like a look at those ruins once."

"How's your leg?"

"Fine," he said. He looked at her; it seemed she had not moved at all since his coming in.

"You must have rented that jeep and everything," she said. "I'm really sorry."

"Nothing to be done, I guess."

"Do you like brandy?" she asked.

"Sure."

She went into the dispensary wing and came out with a small bottle of medicinal brandy and a bottle of *agua mineral*.

"You have some," Holliwell said, when she had opened them. She seemed not to hear.

"I'd take you back to the ruins myself if there was time," she said. "But there isn't. It'll be too dark to see anything."

"Another time." He felt her eyes on his face as he drank.

"Listen," he said when he had finished the brandy, "how about you coming in to town with me? I'd just as soon not go back to the Paradise."

"No," she said, and laughed nervously. "No, it's not possible."

"Sure?"

"No," she said firmly. "Not possible."

"O.K.," Holliwell said. He wanted not to leave. "Do you suppose I could have another brandy?"

"You shouldn't," she told him. "Your system's been poisoned."

"My leg's fine. The rest of me could use a little bracing."

"You shouldn't," she told him.

"Well, hell," Holliwell said. "Checked at every turn."

"All right," Justin said. She went back into the dispensary and when she came out she had two bottles of brandy, together with the bottled water. When she poured his, she poured one for herself.

"Is something wrong?" Holliwell asked, seeing her.

"I'd like to go into town for dinner," Justin told him. "I will."

"You will?"

"Yes," she said. "Yes, please."

Holliwell was smiling uncertainly.

"Fine," he said after a moment.

"We could go," the nun said, "to the Chinese restaurant in town. It's not too bad."

"That's fine," he said.

There was something wrong, he decided. It was not the bad atmosphere he had brought from the hotel, or his disorientation or the pain in his knee, which burned now with the liquor. The woman was on wires, her eyes were wide open and staring, her mouth slightly open as though she had received a blow. She had the most beautiful eyes, he thought.

"Why don't I drive in," Justin said. "You can leave your jeep here if you like."

"You're afraid I'll pass out at the wheel?"

"You might well," she said. "But I just thought you'd be more comfortable."

"That's kind of you," he said. "I would be."

She was trying very hard to be cool, he thought, enjoying herself a little; she seemed to really want to come along with him. But she could not quite get it together. She was up to something. Drinking his drink, watching her, he felt a certain regret at having come. He was thinking that there was going to be trouble and that she knew it and was afraid. And although he was certainly neither a spy nor an informer, although his visit was an innocent one—he was not the company she should be keeping.

They drove in silence through the brief dusk and into the night. The ghostly sparkle of the sea was on their right; on their left the darkness compounded itself into the mass of the Sierra. It was a ride on the edge, among half-seen and unseen things, an increasingly tense and uneasy-making ride for Holliwell. He caught glimpses of wood fires through slat doorways, of fires in the cane fields. Beside him at the wheel, a frozen-faced female stranger possessed of some taut strength he felt himself to be somehow taxing. But it was beautiful there; the wind was what God had meant the wind to be, fresh from the ocean, unsullied by time. Smaller breezes stirred against the sea wind's breast, carrying an iodine smell, a smell of jacaranda, of flowers he knew by half-forgotten, six-toned names from across the world—me-iang, ving, ba—the smell of villes in Ban Me Thuot, cooking oil, excrement, incense, death. The smell of the world turning. War.

It was wrong for him to be there. He had chosen to live where the world turned wrapped in illusions of peace, where all odors startled, the soul slept and dreams were only dreams. This fate-scented night brought up his wariness, his body tensed, he watched from behind the lights with the rapid eye movement of nightmare. It was war here; his nerve ends shivered like the polyps of the reef, vibrating to guns which he could almost hear.

"It's beautiful here," he said to her, as they turned inland and the jeep labored up a grade to the low cliffs over the delta.

"I guess it is," the strange young woman said. The nun.

Over the dim lamps and the encircled glare of Alvarado's naked lights, he could make out, far out to sea, a tiny beacon. It would be Camarillo, the nearest of the Corazón Islands. It was a sweet island. He had friends there once. He knew that he would not be seeing it this time around.

Descending toward the streets of town, he looked at her from time to time, trying not to let her catch him at it. She seemed, superficially, to have thrown every grain of her energy into the driving; she sat erect and rigid and the expression of mild shock in which her face was set never changed. She was stone beautiful, he thought; to his eyes outrageously and provocatively beautiful, an impossible nun. And stone fierce now, her beauty suggested steel to him, steel that drew blood, the Queen of Swords.

"Not a bad town as they go," he called to her above the engine's whine. She nodded without looking at him, and showed her white upper teeth between the soft parted lips. He could not make himself look away from her then. She was the only person in the world. He needed to find her out and love her. Bad luck, he thought. Bad luck for both of them.

She guided him along mud streets, past square cement houses to the Gran Mura de China. It was a lime-green wooden building beside the river, the interior done up with a little halfhearted chinoiserie. There were plastic tables and fringed lanterns and a three-dollar dragon tapestry over a counter where a pale middle-aged Chinese woman leaned beside her abacus. A party of four Greek ship's officers were eating steak and eggs at one end of a long table in the back of the room.

Justin exchanged a few pleasantries with the Chinese woman and then took Holliwell up a flight of stairs to a balcony where there was a table with a window overlooking the slightly fetid harbor. The breeze was fresh enough to make it the most pleasant table in the place. Dragons notwith-standing, there was nothing to be had that night except tough steak and eggs and jalapeños. They started out with Germania beer, served them by a Chinese girl of twelve or so.

"You must have been very young when you came," Holli-well said.

"I was twenty-two," she said. "I did my last year of nursing with them—the Devotionists."

He wanted to ask if she had desired to go where springs failed not.

"Why them?"

"It must have been a newspaper ad," she said. "Isn't that silly?"

He thought it was very peculiar. He was silent.

"I was in Los Angeles at Cedars Hospital. I came from the country, you see, from Fairfield, Idaho. I didn't like Los An-geles. I was after God, all that. They wanted me."

God. All that. Yes, indeed, he thought. Life more abun-dant. More.

"I always thought of them as being in another century. I mean more than the others."

"No," she said, "no more than the others. They have lots of good women doctors."

He nodded enthusiastic agreement.

"A lot of religious used to think of them as low Irish. Still do, I guess."

"I know that to be true," Holliwell said. "Part Jesuit as I am. There is a grain of truth in it, is there not?"

"I'm a grain of truth in it," Justin said.

Her voice made him think of clear water, running over smooth stones. Gold-flecked pebble bars in the south fork of the Salmon. The fool's gold and the real stuff.

"Why a nurse and not a doctor? I mean . . . not that there's anything wrong with nursing."

"The status side of it doesn't really worry me. I don't guess it occurred to me then that I could be a doctor. I was a girl, right? You think they had women doctors up there in Zion?"

"I suppose not when I was younger," Holliwell said. One of us, he thought, has got to calm down. "I thought maybe by your time they had."

"No," she said. She sipped her beer and touched the paper

napkin to her lips, staring all the while. "You know," she said, "you look a bit spaced. Are you all right?"

"I'm perfectly well," he said very slowly. "If you don't mind my saying so, you look a little spaced yourself."

"Oh," she asked, "do I?" She tried to laugh. "Well, I am." She tried again. "Because we're moving out. And we're so busy."

"We should take things easy now. We're not working at the moment."

Holliwell called to the child for more beer.

"It's terrible beer," Justin said.

"Yes, it certainly is."

Somehow, he thought, he was going to have to tell her about the whole business—Marty Nolan, Ocampo, all of it. He would have to explain himself and that would be the hard part. His presence did not explain well. He had followed disordered circumstance, concidence, impulse and urging so heedlessly that the logic of his to-ings and fro-ings had evaporated. He made no sense. Except as an agent of Nolan's.

If he did not tell her, it might be more dangerous for her. She was in some danger already. If he did tell her, it would quite likely be dangerous for him.

"I've heard talk of you around," he said to her. "You've apparently made an impression here."

"What have you heard?"

"There are people who think you're a radical of some kind."

"Who?"

"Local people. I met a man at Playa Tate the other day after I spoke with you. He didn't seem to like you."

She seemed neither surprised nor alarmed.

"There are people here who hate my guts. They're all I have to show for being here. The local Guardia, for instance."

"That's interesting," Holliwell said. "Why's that?"

"Oh," she said, "because when the mission was open I was running some projects they didn't like. I was training women in some basic nursing and it got sort of political. There were other things too. Anything like that gets them uptight. And I was friendly with some church people who were suspected of being anti-government. I still am."

"That doesn't sound so bad."

"Maybe not to you. But it's enough for the Guardia."

"I thought it was dangerous to have misunderstandings with the Guardia."

"I'm leaving, see, so my war's over. They win. I quit."

"The man at Playa Tate was pretty nasty."

"Do you know his name?"

Holliwell thought about the question for a moment and decided to stall. It was bad business.

"Didn't catch it."

"Cuban?"

"I think so."

"I know who it was. He's a big-time hardware person. He's nice enough when I see him but I understand he has Fidel on the brain."

"I think it's all a bit frightening," Holliwell said.

"They spy on me—the Guardia do. I don't think they can do much more than that."

Suddenly, he realized that she was frightened. Fear was one of the elements composing her state that evening. What she needed was a friend. And what she has, he thought, is me.

"I hope you're being careful."

"You better be careful too, you know." He watched her glance about the room. "You don't want to be here when it goes."

"Is it imminent?"

"I only know what I hear. I hear . . . a lot."

The beer came and Justin hastened to change the subject. She was a bit frantic, manic.

"You can't drink both of those beers," she told him. "You'll be ill. I'll have to drink one."

"Sorry about that," he said. "It is sporting of you."

"You're damn right it is, this horse piss."

"You certainly don't have the manner of a nun, do you?"

"Horse piss is in Shakespeare," she said. "In *The Tempest*." And then she suddenly looked sad.

Holliwell felt she would be easier to deal with that way, although she had broken his heart with horse piss in *The Tempest*. He was more in love than he could ever remember. And the beer was truly dreadful.

"Do you feel good about your six years here? I mean have you . . ."

"Have we brought spiritual guidance to the soul and temporal health to the body of our flock?"

He checked his impulse to apologize for the question, for bringing forth her impatient scorn.

"Have you?"

"I think it was all for us," she said. "What we did we did for ourselves."

"Everyone does for themselves finally."

"Easy answer," she said.

"You expected more from being here?"

"What I expected I don't know."

I know, Holliwell thought. But he realized he could know only in part. He avoided looking her in the eyes; it was harrowing because she could conceal nothing. Along with the fear, mastering it, was a mighty pride. *More* was what drove her. Whatever the world afforded in the name of virtue, sacrifice, good works—she wanted more, wanted it all, as though she deserved it. She could be clever, she could play a little homely poker but she had never learned to trim the lights of her pride.

"What will you do when you get back to the States?" he asked her.

"First laicize. I don't belong in the church. I don't believe in it. I'm a fake nun."

"You're not a fake, ma'am, whatever you believe."

"We made a botch of it here," she said. "You wouldn't believe what a mess we made of it."

In her eyes, the hunger for absolutes. A woman incapable of compromise who had taken on compromise like a hair shirt and never forgiven herself or anyone else, and then rebelled. She could, he thought, have no idea what that look would evoke in the hearts of smaller weaker people, clinging to places of power. She was Enemy, Nemesis, Cassandra. She was in real trouble.

When he looked out of the window and saw the fishing smack steaming for its berth, two deckhands with red and green flashlights playing at being running lights, he followed the rivers of his own past. There, in an instant was Dalat, the Perfume River, its banks disgorging Marty Nolan to a second, lesser life. Holliwell had the strange notion that Nolan had found this woman out by some magic of Lazarus, had found himself a new war and an enemy. Then watching Justin eat her *charro* steak, demurely, but one would have to say hungrily, he wondered if something like the same thing was not true of him, if he had not sought out war and nemesis. But he was in love past regret. Regret, his second nature, the very fluid of his veins, and it was not there.

"You probably asked too much of yourself. I think it must be hard to make a dent down here."

"We tried. We were doing it the wrong way."

"I wonder if there's a right way," Holliwell said.

She was puzzled. "There must be," she said. Then she said: "I'm glad you stopped asking me questions. I felt on the spot."

"I'm sorry," Holliwell said. "Why do you think I was asking questions?"

She smiled a thin tense smile.

"You're seeing our part of the world, aren't you? You're an intelligent tourist and you want your money's worth. We're local color."

"You state my good intentions very coldly," Holliwell said.

"Good intentions get a going over here. Am I right more or less?"

"No, you're wrong. I'm asking you questions because I like you. And I'm an anthropologist. It's my way of communicating. It's all I know."

"You're supposed to gain people's confidence first. Even dumb missionaries know that."

"I would like very much to gain your confidence," he said.

"And why? When you're just passing through. What's my confidence worth? I'm sorry," she said. "I'm being difficult. I'm not very good company."

"Madam," Holliwell said, "you're all the company I want, believe me."

"Who, me?" she asked. She seemed genuinely incredulous.

"I like you, I told you that. I wouldn't say it if it wasn't so."

"Are you lonely?" she asked. Strange question.

He smiled. "Always. So I'm the deserving object of your attention."

She was staring at him again but her look was no longer so wild.

"It never occurred to me that someone like you could be lonely. I was thinking how interesting and full your life must always be."

"You're putting me on," he said. He was fairly certain she was not but he had to ask. There was not another soul he knew who would make such a statement without irony.

"I'm not," she said. "I most certainly am not. Do you know what fun this would be for me if it wasn't for . . . things?"

"Let's . . ." He sought words, the right words, he was desperately afraid of losing her. "Let's put things aside."

Her look was so sorrowful and so transparent that he could not bear to face it. She was shaking her head.

"They don't put aside too well," she said.

"Let's go outside," he said, "or I'll make you drink more of the beer. Is it cool to walk by the river?"

To her eyes came a smile that made them dazzle, a very small mischievous smile that she slowly gave way to. He stopped breathing.

"You mean is it safe for tourists? Yes, it's safe enough."

When they were downstairs, and Holliwell peeling out soiled Tecanecan bills to pay for dinner, it seemed to him that he saw her place her paper napkin, correctly folded, on the edge of the counter. He was too addled to take note of it at the time, but the image would come back to him later.

Beside the Gran Mura de China was a sorry little park with the warped ruin of a railing between the uncut saw grass and the riverbank. A stand selling ices was drawn up beside it. A few children played on the overgrown lawns, dodging between the sprawled bodies of three unconscious cane-juice junkies. An old black man in a Panama who looked as though he had been there all day occupied the only bench.

Holliwell and Justin walked a small *paseo* along the fence.

"The coconuts are all that's dangerous," she told him. "They never pick them off the trees."

"We'll sue."

"Good luck," Justin said.

Ahead of them, the river spread out to merge with the sea, a conjoining of darkness. The channel lights weaved restlessly between the slow current and the force of the tide.

"You're limping," she told Holliwell. "A shame about your leg."

"It was just a ploy," he said. "To get you down to the beach."

"You didn't know I was there," she said.

"No."

"I'm being simple," she said, "I'm so turned around." Then she laughed a little and he was glad she did because he felt as though he had lied and it pained him. Of course he had not lied; he had not known. "It'd be like shooting off your toe."

He knew that he was going to have to tell her. But not just now, he thought, when the weight was off her and she was trying to have fun. Wartime romance, nothing like it.

"When do you think you'll be back in the States?" he asked.

"Hard to tell. As soon as we can get it done."

"And when you laicize—what will you do then?"

"Get a job, I guess. I've got an RN. I might apply to medical school after all, if I can borrow the money." She looked at him in mild reproach. "You're asking me questions again."

"I have to," he said, "because you never ask me any. Otherwise how will we find out who we are?"

"We'll never find out," she said. They had come to the end of the railing. Beyond there was only mud and mangrove stumps and darkness.

"I hate to," she said, "but I have to go back. Can we? My God," she said, "I've forgotten your name."

"Frank. Yes, of course. We'll go back."

The road and night took them up again; they sat alone with their Furies as the jeep splashed along. Justin sat ramrod straight behind the wheel as she had on the drive in—Holliwell was halfway back to Route Three, with a sense of being caught on the road in the villes after dark, expecting a mine or an ambush and ready to dive for a ditch if there had been one.

When the jeep pulled up before the mission, they stayed in their places listening to the night sounds. Somewhere in the distance, an English-speaking voice was raised in some frenzied incantation. Neither of them remarked on it.

"God," she said, "how I hate this place and what it means."

Holliwell climbed out of the jeep. Justin stayed where she was.

"Look," he said, "let it go. It'll be your past and you'll have learned something from it. There isn't a lot you could have done differently."

"Six goddamn years," she said. She took the keys out of the ignition, climbed out of the jeep and started to walk around it. "We could have done a lot differently. We could have helped people defend themselves . . . from these American flunky thugs that run things here. Instead of dispensing APC's and holy water. Now it's too late."

He came around the jeep to her.

"Sorry," she said. "I'm blathering."

When she looked at him, he saw that she was exhausted. Her face was drawn; she was near breaking.

"Nothing is too late for you, Justin. You're young."

She bit her lip and looked at the ground, her eyes wild again, like an animal looking for a way to run. His hand went out toward her as though he could not have held it back and he took her hand. It was trembling but dry, a small fastidious hand in his large sweating palm.

"My name is May," she said suddenly. "I was born in May."

"May," he said, "I have to hold you a minute. You're shaking."

She looked up then and stared—past him, through him.

"No," she said. "You can't do that here. You don't know what you're doing to me. You can't know."

"You're in trouble," he said. "I think you're in trouble. I'm coming back tomorrow."

"You mustn't do that . . ."

"I'll come tomorrow. And if you think you have to—you'll send me away."

She only shook her head.

He forced himself away from her, walked to his rented jeep and started it up.

She was standing at the foot of the steps as he drove out. He could take his eyes from the roadway only for a moment to look at her; he tried to smile.

"Be careful," he heard her call to him. May.

When the mountains and the aircraft beacon were in sight above the horizon, Pablo cut his speed back to nine knots and watched the Loran digits roll toward what he hoped would be the figures on Mr. Callahan's line-of-sight chart. The dock

lights on the chart were dimly visible now, a single glow
below and to the right of the beacon. From time to time, he
glanced at the Fathometer. The bottom was still in its place.

Two local shrimpers showed their working lights far off
southward; the *Cloud* itself was showing no lights at all. As
Pablo watched, the mountain beacon loomed ever high above
him and through his glasses he could make out the little dock
on which the dock lights shone. He could even see lights in
the windows of the building behind the pier.

He cut his speed further; the rattle of his engines in the
quiet night was making him nervous. He was swallowing another pain pill when the Fathometer suddenly plunged to ten
feet and sloping up—he took manual control and came about;
the DF signal after so many constant hours began to waver
and wander in its tone. He turned it down. The zero-zero-zero
course meant nothing now, he was up against a wall of coral,
blundering for the Loran fix, trying for all he was worth to
line up the beacon with dock lights at the proper bearing. The
night seemed full of treachery.

He began to panic. Everywhere he turned the wheel, the
marbles were waiting for him. Instincts of mindless flight
possessed him. To turn seaward. To put out and follow the
coast to the appearance of safety. Or to Negus' promised
islands of bliss, or San Ignacio or Colombia. But he could no
longer believe in refuges, he dreaded the morning light and its
exposure and dreaded more the open sea from which he had
escaped and which was now beyond his managing. Whatever
was done would have to be done here.

Half praying, drenched in sweat, he spun the wheel. Trying
to put the light bearings where they should be, watching the
Loran digits.

Suddenly there was a voice on the open CB. The voice
sounded so close and clear that Pablo turned from his desperate work in guilty terror. It was as though someone were
there.

"Mr. Fry? Do you copy? Mr. Fry?"

In the situation he was almost tempted to call for help. At
the moment, nothing seemed worse than being where he was.

"Do you copy, Mr. Fry?"

He fought the impulse to answer and the voice desisted.

Once, when the bearings seemed right and the digital reading was square with Callahan's, the Fathometer reading was

less than fifteen feet. It was all wrong. Just before he spun her around, he saw his bottom reading fall off all the way to seventy, then eighty, then ninety feet. He laughed and swore and was cutting his engines when the terrible sound of something striking the hull shook him to his soles. He swung hard to port, knowing it would be too late—and ran to look over the side. There, in a light which was purely the illumination of God's grace, was the marker, bouncing along his starboard side like a tin can along a windy street, until its anchor held it fast and it cleaved to his hull like a puppy.

"Ave Maria purissima," Pablo said aloud.

The inshore current was already easing him toward the reef edge. Moving quickly, he released the windlass and let the chain play out. There was no extra line across the anchor crown—if it stuck fast, then he was stuck fast—he could not concern himself with that now. The current spun the vessel round so that her forepeak faced the open sea. Pablo looked at the ocean and trembled. He was sick and hurting, he wanted no more of it out there. More than anything he wanted to land.

But turning shoreward was no comfort. Behind the lights that had shone to save him was Tecan. It was all the game and there was no end to it.

He hastened to arm himself—reloaded the Remington and put another clip in his own automatic. He retrieved his shoulder holster from the lazaret and slipped it on under his dirty work shirt. There were no more slugs for the Nambu, so he pitched it overboard. Then he seated himself outside the cockpit and waited.

It was not long before he heard engines approaching in the darkness. They were strong outboards, the kind that pushed the heaviest Boston whalers, and there was more than one.

"Mr. Fry!"

It might have been the voice he had heard over the CB. The other boats had cut their engines; only one advanced toward the *Cloud* on low throttle. He raised his head over the rail. What he saw in the darkness might have been a boat with men in it. Or might not.

"Mr. Fry?" asked the voice from the ocean.

Pablo thought about it for a minute.

"That's right," Pablo called back. "That's me. Who are you, cuz?"

He was answered with silence. Then all the outboards
started up together; there were three or four. There were no
more hails from the water, they were waiting for codes.

"No sé las codas," Pablo shouted. He did not know the
Spanish word for codes, whether it was *codas* or not. "I'm just
a peon on this boat."

"Show yourself," a frightened voice called. When he came
to the rail, he was holding the shotgun. He could see their
boat now; it was in fact a whaler and there were four men in
it, all of them pointing what looked like M-16's at him. The
other boats hung on their throttles in the darkness some distance off. There would be other guns covering him there.

"The gun!" a second and even more frightened voice called.

Pablo realized that he was holding the Remington and
threw it over the side. If they'd landed as many pieces as had
gone over the side this trip, he thought, they could have
themselves a couple of revolutions. And it was a damn fine
shotgun.

Lights went on in his face and from the startled reaction he
heard from the men in the boat, he imagined he must be a
strange sight.

The friend of Mr. Fry had regained his composure.

"Everyone aboard together," he demanded. "Everyone to
show themselves."

Pablo felt very tired in spite of the speed.

"The hell of it is," Pablo shouted back, "there ain't no one
but me."

Silence again, while the unseen boats circled off somewhere
and the four men in the nearest boat watched him. Finally
they pulled alongside. As the others tried simultaneously to
hold their rifles on Pablo and steady themselves in the swell,
the main man began to clamber aboard. The artificial hull
deceived him; stepping from his own boat, he found himself
short of the rail and was forced to come in hand over hand.

The men in the boat flashed their light on Pablo and on
their leader and then turned it off again. They were plainly as
chary of lights as he was.

Pablo shrugged to show his good will. His diver's knife and
the automatic were still concealed on his person.

The man from the whaler was trying to watch Pablo and
look around at the same time. In a moment, he called his
friends aboard, and Pablo heard the other whalers draw closer.

The four men who had come aboard tied their whaler's painter around a bit. The leader, the one who spoke, had Pablo spread-eagled on the deck beside the wheelhouse. The two others made their way cautiously through the compartments. They carried lights but showed them only in closed spaces.

"*Sangre*," Pablo heard one of the men say. Perhaps for that reason the leader ripped open Pablo's shirt and found the automatic there. When there was a second man to back him, he took the whole harness, holster and all, and put it over his own shoulder.

The leader spoke to one of his men in words that Pablo could not make out and the man spoken to made a noise over the side like a soft cattle call. The other boats came in now and people began climbing over the rail. Pablo had the feeling there was another boat off somewhere, perhaps keeping watch.

They could kill him now, Pablo thought. A number of them crouched around him, keeping below the rail shining their lights on him as though he were some strange sea creature they had brought up.

Men were shoveling aside the ice covering in the hatches. When they found the weapons crates, he could tell from their cries that not all of them in fact were men. They were hauling the crates out of the hatches now; their boots crunched against the overturned plastic baskets and the shrimps' useless shells.

He turned his head to one side and between the legs of the men who guarded him saw the boat people working on the crates with their crowbars, checking their contents. A woman in a bandana knelt with them, holding a checklist, reading off contents.

"Galil. Seventy-five. Fifty-round clips. Three boxes." She read on, hesitating, as though the words must be unfamiliar to her. "TRW. Seventy-five. Five point fifty-six. Thirty-round clips. Three boxes."

They had the crates out on deck and were working on the second hold.

"You're shot," the man who was the leader said to Pablo.

"Did you figure I didn't know that?"

"I have to know what happened."

Pablo laughed. "I wish I knew," he said.

"Tell it as best you can," the man said. "We are at war here. Were you attacked?"

"Naw," Pablo said. "It was just paranoia."

The man who was questioning him laughed. None of the others did.

"In other words, you fought. And the others?"

"You figure it out."

"They were killed by you. That's how I figure it out. And their bodies thrown to the sharks. How's that, Yanqui?" the man asked him. "How's that for figuring it out?"

"I don't care what you do to me," Pablo said. "None of this was my idea."

From the forward hatchway came indiscreet cries of joy. It seemed, to Pablo's understanding, that they had discovered rockets there. The leader, the man who had been questioning Pablo, got to his feet and quieted his troops. They formed passing lines and commenced to offload the cases onto their whalers.

When he returned to question Pablo, the leader directed all but one of his men to a loading station.

"Can you walk?" the head man asked Pablo.

As they were helping him to his feet they discovered the diver's knife against his calf. Shaking their heads, they helped him into the cockpit. The boat leader and Pablo sat down in Negus and Callahan's cockpit chairs. The leader's number two stood in the hatchway, his weapon leveled at Pablo's chest.

"If our business is betrayed," the head man said, "if anyone ratted here . . . you die first."

"If I didn't think the meet was O.K., I wouldn't be here," Pablo said. Although he had no idea where it was that he might be, regardless of what he thought.

"The fight was about the money, no? Or about the guns? Maybe someone tried to stop our operation?"

Pablo was at a loss to make them understand.

"It was part personal. It was part about the money." He looked at the leader and at the man with the rifle. "Things happen that way."

"Yes, truly," the leader said. "Often in this world. And you are the winner. You must be very strong."

"What's that get me, chief? You're the boss now."

The leader wore a yellow oilskin and underneath it he carried a hand briefcase of cheap plastic. So full was it that the cloth beside its zipper bulged. Holding it under his arm, the leader went toward the *Cloud*'s CB receiver.

"I don't think I like to be your boss," he said.

He lifted the receiver off its cradle for a moment, then set it back down again.

"This isn't good," he told Pablo. "We thought we dealt with responsible people, you understand. This is trouble for us and we don't need it."

Pablo looked at the folder and said nothing. One by one he had heard the small boats taking off; the last boat was alongside now and the people in it were calling for their chief in low hisses. The armed man in the hatchway looked from Pablo to the last boat.

"*Hay que matarlo,*" he said to his chief. "We have to kill him."

"*Y la barca?*" the chief asked, watching Pablo. "What about the boat."

"Sink it."

The leader looked as though he were about to smile. From the envelope in his hand he took a roll of bills and threw it on the chart table. Pablo saw that there were hundreds. On the top at least.

"It's enough for one man. Two men in this country make less in a year. Now get yourself and your boat away from us."

Pablo's outrage made him speak without thinking.

"You see what he's doin'?" he demanded of the second-in-command. "He's grabbing money that's mine. He aims to keep it himself."

"*Hay que matarlo,*" the man with the rifle said.

"No," the leader said. "Now," he told Pablo, "go while you can."

The two men went out of the cockpit and began climbing into the last waiting whaler. Pablo hobbled out after them. The whaleboat was floating free now. Pablo leaned down over the rail.

"I can't make it," he called to them. "I'm hurting and I don't know my way out there."

Someone started up the outboard.

"Look," Pablo shouted, "that bread's no good to me now. I got no place to go. Let me join up with you guys. I'm trained, you understand. I swear to Christ, *compadre*, I'm your man!"

"Some other time, eh," the leader in the boat said. "You're tough." And the outboard disappeared into the darkness, its throttle held low.

"You stole my money, you fuck!" Pablo screamed. Probably no one heard him. There was no point trying to shoot at them; they were out of sight and shots would bring the law.

Thinking of the law, Pablo looked around quickly. The pier lights had gone out and the only light in view was the aircraft beacon on the mountaintop over the little harbor. Seaward, the breeze was as gentle as ever but a quarter moon was rising now, to show the lines of the *Cloud* against it. He looked at the ocean, lightly moonlit, and a wave of pain and exhaustion passed over him. The sight of it filled him with dread. He was afraid. He could not go back to it now.

Then the thought came to him that the town they had passed during the afternoon could not be far. A seaport—with great freighters loading up at cement piers. City lights had been going on there. He might find a billet on one of the ships. There might be buses, even an airport.

He wiped his brow, counted the money on the chart table and discovered that he had something less than fifteen hundred dollars in American bills. Fifteen hundred and a diamond—he would take his chances at sea no longer, in a boat full of blood, among reefs. He decided to set out for shore.

There was a tiny, self-righting aluminum dinghy set in davits just behind the lazaret housing. Pablo went aft for a look and found the davits and the lowering windlass wire rusted and corroded; the only piece of bad maintenance he had encountered aboard the *Cloud*. It took him the better part of an hour, using engine wrenches and even chain cutters, to get the dinghy over. When it was afloat, he secured it by a painter to the rail. For an outboard and an oil can, he forced himself to go down into the lazaret again but he found none there, nor anywhere else aboard. The lazaret had oarlocks and a set of mismated aluminum oars. Pablo put them in the dinghy.

In the cockpit chair now, he went over Callahan's Loran charts, trying to find out where he was. The aerial beacon was on all the charts and the town to the north was called Puerto Alvarado. Even on the detailed charts it didn't look like much but it would have to do. Around his boards it was Reef City. If he put the *Cloud* on almost any southerly bearing it would hit marbles; a course between two-ten and three hundred would send it into the outer reef and if it went fast and far enough it would strike hard enough to break up and sink in deep water. He saw now that he had made it to the marker buoy by sheer miracle. He would never, he was sure, have made it out.

He spent a few minutes going through the vessel, opening every hatch and porthole and watertight door that he could find. He supposed there might be sea cocks down in shaft alley—but he had no time to find them now. In the saloon he found a life jacket and a laundry bag. He put the life jacket on and tightened the Dacor knife about his good leg. He would leave the guns where they were. They were only incrimination now and excess weight. The diamond, the pills, and the fifteen hundred he wrapped in the laundry bag to stash it in the dinghy.

Pablo gave the *Cloud* just enough power to set her heading for the outer reefs and took up the anchor. The anchor came up clean, to his relief and gratitude. With the course set he untied the painter that secured his lifeboat, and as the little boat drifted shoreward, he shoved the diesel throttle forward for flank speed.

When he hit the water, he found it warm, although cool enough to make his leg hurt. His wound made him think of sharks and he paddled breathlessly for his floating dinghy, hauling himself aboard by the strength of his arms and his one good leg.

He was into his second rowing stroke when the shrimper struck. There was a double wall of coral there and it must have been just below the surface because the *Cloud* barreled over the first barrier as though she had turned amphibian, plowing over it, hardly seeming to slow, but ripping her seams fore and aft. Yet the rudder shaft and the engines had come through and not until she took the second ridge did there sound, together with the tearing of wood, the crash of suffering metal, the hopeless hissing rattle of a smashed machine.

Her guts on the reef, the *Cloud* raised her forepeak in the moonlight. Pablo, resting for a moment on his oars, watched the bow gradually sink as the weight of water billowing into the after compartments shifted forward on the fulcrum of the coral and commenced to take her down. A few small fires were burning in the after sections, there was a silent explo-

sion, a fiery puffball burst itself to cast a moment's glow on
the bland easy ocean. Then another crash, another little fire-
storm, and she turned completely over on her bow and settled,
upside down, beneath the surface. Pablo, still watching as he
rowed, could not be sure whether the white water he saw in
the faint moonlight marked the tip of the reef or some exposed part of the vessel. If she had not cleared the second wall
altogether she might be settled on a slope, in shallow water,
easily visible. He put the thought out of his mind. In time, he
hoped, all thoughts of her would pass. Things would be different.

He rested on his oars again, breathing in the sweet smell of
land, and checked the bag for his diamond, his money, his
pills. They were all in place. So, gritting his teeth, he pulled
on for the black shore behind him.

Holliwell found the restaurant hangar of the Paradise aswarm
with the people who called themselves contractors. The crowd
and the noise surprised him; he had not brought a watch and
he had supposed it was the middle of the night.

For a while he stood under the palms outside, looking in at
the party. Someone called his name and he turned to see Mr.
Soyer smiling at him. Mr. Heath was sitting beside him and
across the table from them were Olga and Buddy. They all
found him in some way amusing.

"What are you doing out in the dark, Holliwell?" the
Cuban asked good-naturedly. "Come in and have a drink."

He thought it an oddly promiscuous grouping.

Holliwell stood in the darkness where he had thought himself concealed and stared at them.

"Come and tell us how things are," Mr. Heath said. "Nun-
wise."

He walked away from them and into the bar. It was two-
deep there. A man next to Holliwell said: "That fucker needs
his hat rung." He was talking to someone else, of someone
else.

Holliwell wanted a telephone and they did not want to give
him one. The bartender was unhelpful. There were no representatives of management in view.

He persisted; the bartender led him to an office near the
kitchen where a young Spaniard was doing accounts. From

the depths of his zombie state, Holliwell summoned up the energy to represent a pain in the ass. He shouted, he could hear himself at it, bullied, threatened and begged for a phone. It developed that the Paradise possessed a radio-telephone hookup; the young Spaniard observed that he could not rely on a connection and that it would be very expensive. He was trying to call the capital and Captain Zecca.

In the end a line was brought him. He stood with his back to the clamor of the bar beyond and listened to the undersea sounds in the receiver.

To his own surprise and relief, he got through. There was a Marine guard on the other end; the connection was adequate. It was fine.

He asked the guard who answered for Captain Zecca's home telephone number and the guard asked him politely to wait. Then a young woman came on, the embassy duty officer. When he asked for the number, there was a long pause and she said she would see if it was available.

"Captain Zecca speaking," said the next voice on the line.

"Tom," Holliwell exclaimed, "you're there! It's Frank Holliwell."

"Yes, sir," Zecca said. "Yes indeed."

"I'm down on the coast near Alvarado," Holliwell said.

"I know where you are, sir."

"I need your help," Holliwell said. "There are people here who need protection. Because there's going to be trouble here."

"Would you speak carefully, Mr. Holliwell? If you don't speak carefully I won't be able to hear you."

"What?"

"Speak carefully, Holliwell."

"I have to tell you the situation here," Holliwell said. "How can I?"

"We know the situation there. This office isn't handling that."

"What do you mean, Zecca?"

"I mean we're not handling it. You'll have to talk to them. There."

"Them there? Who where?"

"Holliwell, we can't have this conversation if you won't speak carefully. I mean the people who are handling it. Surely you know whom I'm referring to."

"I don't think . . . I don't think . . . I know them."

"You know them, Holliwell. They know you."

"Oh," Holliwell said. "Yes. I know."

"You should. I'm sure you do."

"They have it wrong," Holliwell said. "That's why I'm calling."

"I can't believe we're having this conversation. If you think they've got it wrong, man—tell them."

"I don't think they'll want to hear my side of it."

"Look, old friend—it's theirs. It's not mine. It's yours and theirs."

"Can't you do anything?"

"Afterwards. Possibly."

"After what?"

"Hey, Holliwell," Captain Zecca said. "Go away, will you, pal?"

"I don't know what to do, see."

Zecca sighed at long distance. "Use your judgment. It's all going down. Talk to them."

"I understand," Holliwell said.

"Do you? I don't. I'm going to hang up."

"Yes," Holliwell said.

"See you, schemer. Hang loose." And he hung up.

When Holliwell went out to the bar, he saw that the Cuban was not at his table beside Heath. He ordered a whiskey and in a moment the man appeared from the direction of the bungalows. He wore a look of concern. Holliwell saw him look at the table where his drinking companions were and then scan the bar. When their eyes met he was waiting. When he saw Holliwell, the Cuban's worried look turned into a smile that was bright and false and layered with contempt. Holliwell gulped his drink to ease the chill of it. Then he walked past the man and into the darkness outside.

Ashore, Pablo gathered up an oilcloth and an anchor bag and left his aluminum dinghy adrift on the light surf. There was a dirt road beyond the mangrove and he crossed it into a thick wood where treetops closed out the stars and the air was heavy and still. After a while, he found a lean-to at the edge of a burnt-over clearing where melons rotted on the ground and the night's rats fled from him. He tried to sleep on a ledge of crossed sticks, wrapped in a cloth, a canvas bag under his head for a pillow. There were animals outside.

He dreamt of morning light, fiery columns that blinded. The light was of dreams only. After a while he got himself up and took some of the blue pills to contain his pain. He slipped the bottle and the folded bills in his jeans and put the diamond back in his pocket. He was hearing voices, Deedee's voice and the old Jew's. Sometimes he heard his mother's voice.

He began to feel his way through the forest. The wounded leg was steady under him; the bone was sound and that was good enough for picking it up and putting it down again. His body was functioning well enough but his mind was febrile, ablaze in the rank darkness.

Somehow he found a trail to walk along and true light to follow. Most of the time it was not the distant firelight he saw, but a succession of past darknesses, filled with doings that were lit with their own light. The light of things happening in the dark.

He felt night-sighted like a creature. Before long, it seemed his whole being would be in darkness and he would run from light. His numbed fingers sought the diamond in his shirt pocket, a tiny lamp to think by. He thought of his knife, of bullets, fists and teeth. The voices inside sang and conspired.

The path took him to another clearing where there were fires burning and people gathered around them. Hammocks were strung between boughs. The sight of humankind made him angry.

Gooks, he thought, and then he saw it was Stateside people. There were twenty, there were twice that. The place looked like the bo jungles he had seen as a child. But the people all looked young and tender.

He hung back for a moment and then stepped out among them. One by one, they took notice of him. He was the Darkness King, it was his party.

An older man at one of the campfires addressed him: "*Oye, señor.*"

A fat Anglo.

"*Oye, oye, señor,*" Pablo said in his softest voice, "*chinga su madre—hijo de la siete leches.*"

He laughed at the man's fleshy face.

"Where's your prez, fat?" The fat man's mouth fell shut, his teeth clicked. "Where's the main person here?"

The man shrugged and turned partly away. Pablo took a step to face him, tilting his head to one side, staring, his brows knit.

"There's an old fellow who lives here," a girl at the same fireside said. Pablo turned to her. "He's over there somewhere." She pointed across the clearing, to the far side of three stone slabs that stood in the center.

"Thank you," Pablo said. He held her look to see what her face would do. She looked away. As he walked toward the stone slabs someone called to him.

"Hey, your leg's bleeding."

The slabs were like tombstones the height of a man. In the flickering light of the nearer fires, Pablo examined the first one he came to. He saw the profile of a face with the features chipped away. Over the figure's head was what appeared to be a fanged cat with its mouth open wide. Below the obliterated face was another, upside down; it seemed the same face reversed like the obverse head of a one-eyed jack. Below that face were things like the rattles of a snake, feathers, a lizard.

It was a sign of the place, Pablo thought. The slabs were what everyone was there about.

Some distance beyond the three carved stones, an old man in a white shirt was feeding twigs to a small fire. There was a Bible beside him and a bottle of liquor. Pablo watched him awhile and then approached the fire.

"Say ho," he said to the old man.

Father Egan looked at him without surprise.

"Hello, son."

Pablo let himself down across the fire from Egan and leaned his back against a log. He felt, for a moment, as though he would never rise again.

"You know," he told the priest, "like, I just come out of the ocean here. I was shipwrecked."

Egan's face was blank.

"I'm not lying," Pablo said weakly. "We tucked in a reef a few miles down. I think our boat's under."

"For heaven's sake," Egan said. He poked at the fire. "Is everyone all right?"

"Yeah," Pablo said. "It was just me."

"You've hurt your leg."

Pablo nodded, reached for the priest's rum and drank.

"I need help," he said. "I need to lie down. I might need medicine."

"You're lucky," Egan said. "We can provide you with a bed and medicine."

"No shit?"

"Absolutely not," Egan said.

Pablo closed his eyes in gratitude.

"The other thing is . . . we weren't supposed to be here. We ain't supposed to fish off here, understand? Ain't got the papers for it. So we don't want any cops or coast guard or like that. We don't want them to know about us being here." He kept his eyes on the old man's face. Egan looked untroubled. "I'm asking you because you're a fellow American. You are a fellow American, ain't you?"

"More or less," Egan said. "A citizen, yes. A citizen of no mean city."

"So if you could help me out, see? I got some money. Coming to me anyways." He secretly touched the folder of bills in his pocket. "If you could put me up and leave me see to my leg. And you kept it quiet—that would be real good. I could see you got paid."

"We can do all that for you, I suppose. What's your name?"

"Pablo," Pablo said. "Goddamn, that'd be great, bro. That'd be real fine."

The priest let the fire be and looked at his guest.

"It wasn't you I was expecting, Pablo."

Pablo smiled and settled back against the log. It was too good to be true but he was too exhausted for caution. He believed.

"It's me you got, though," he said. Then he passed into unconsciousness.

When he came to himself again, he could not remember where he was. He smelled damp wood smoke and heard the night birds, sat up and saw Egan at the fire. He felt as though he were choosing one dream from among many. There were birds in all of them.

"You were angry," said the priest.

Pablo looked about the clearing and saw few other fires

burning now. The strangers had tucked themselves into shadow. Someone was playing chords on a guitar, hammocks were strung between trees.

"I wasn't anything, mister. I was asleep."

Egan's empty gaze was fixed on the fire."

"Was there a fight on your boat?" he asked Pablo.

Pablo shrugged and frowned.

"No. I mean, I couldn't say. I don't remember too well. Maybe I hit my head."

The priest looked at him thoughtfully. Pablo returned a warning smile but Father Egan went right on staring.

"Where were you coming from? Where were you going?"

Pablo hunched his shoulders as though to throw off the questions.

"Florida," he said. "You know," he told Egan after a moment, "you shouldn't ask me a whole lot of questions. Then you won't be concerned, you see what I mean? Down here, the way it is, you shouldn't be."

"Down here," Egan said. "Absolutely right. Well, I'm very discreet. I'm known for my discretion down here."

"You said you could help me out."

"Yes, I can help you out, Pablo. We have to stay here for a while, though, because I'm waiting for someone."

"Who?" Pablo demanded.

"No one you have to be afraid of. Wait and see."

Pablo bent forward to touch the knife strapped to his calf and chewed another pain pill to stay primed for uncertainty. After about ten minutes, Father Egan said: "He's coming."

Pablo followed the priest's gaze and saw a massively tall figure picked up in firelight, a man in bib overalls with a straw sombrero. When he drew nearer, they could see his broad square-boned face. He had a nose that drew attention to itself, being long almost to caricature. His eyes were blue and small and set in a web of fine wrinkles. In age he might have been anywhere between eighteen and senescence.

"His name is Weitling," Father Egan told Pablo. "I used to call him the Farmer."

"He ain't American," Pablo observed.

"No."

Pablo watched the Farmer come up to the fireside and look cautiously around. He was very big indeed, six-four or -five. His whole body bespoke physical strength.

"Who is that man?" the Farmer asked in a soft, almost womanish voice. He had reference to Pablo.

"That's Pablo, Weitling. Are you afraid of him?"

"Yes," Weitling replied. He gave his answer a faintly interrogative tone.

"Don't be. He's a friend."

"A night friend?"

"Yes, another night friend. Like you."

Pablo had bared his upper teeth, he was not pleased with Weitling. The huge man hunkered down and removed his sombrero. The fair hair on his head was so fine it seemed to reflect the firelight.

"Tell us, Weitling," Egan said, "what have you seen and heard and what have you thought about?"

"I'm not to say what I have heard," the Farmer explained to them. "It's forbidden. They are secrets." His English had a Germanic slur. "Sometimes you . . . I've thought about."

"Very good, Weitling." Father Egan nodded grave approval. "About what I said to you?"

"Yes," Weitling said. Then he turned his attention to Pablo, whose face had gradually contorted itself into a mask of hatred beyond loathing. The Farmer faced Pablo's malevolence with the unconcern of a draft horse.

"Tell me what you've decided," Egan said. He poked at the fire with a long green stick, and as he did so his hand trembled slightly.

"The world is full of devils," Weitling said. He was looking at Pablo. "He is a devil." He turned slowly toward Egan, who was looking into the fire. "You also."

Egan did not look at him. "By your fruits shall ye know them," the priest said. "Have I told you anything to make me seem a devil?"

"I have heard so," Weitling said softly. "I have heard tell."

"From the voices?"

The Farmer uttered his soft questioning affirmative.

"Ah. But of course you can't tell me what the voices said." Egan pursed his lips.

Pablo had drawn as far away from Weitling as his posture permitted. Inwardly he made a sign against the Evil Eye. The Farmer's eyes were like blue buttons. Stuffed-animal eyes.

"Let's try and remember what we talked about," said the priest. His voice was informed with a music of few tones;

Pablo recognized the calm singsong of the practiced confessor. "I told you I thought when you hurt people it was instead of loving them. That you really wanted to love. Did I not?"

The Farmer was silent.

"I suppose you thought that was nonsense. Maybe it is nonsense. Overwrought pap. Eh?" He looked at both of them in turn. "It didn't seem so at the time. It seemed vaguely true. What do you think, Pablo?"

"Hey," Pablo said, "you know, I couldn't say."

"Let's forget that then. A maudlin conceit. But, Weitling, I did tell you that the Lord likes his little creatures as they are and that's not just an emotional transport of mine. It's true, believe me. I said, I believe, that he never made anything more wonderful than a small child. You're forbidden—forbidden, Weitling—to harm a hair on the head of a child. I gave you chapter and verse, didn't I? Luke 18:16, eh? Matthew 18:6."

In the great square of Weitling's face, a turmoil was reflected.

"*Ja*," he said. "*Ja.*"

He seemed excited for a moment; he began to bounce in his squatting position, the muscles in his thighs shifted under his overalls like railway lines.

The sparks of hope were fanned in Egan's dull eyes.

"Now you've thought about all this, haven't you?"

"*Ja*," said Weitling. His hands ·gripped his knees, he was staring into some distance. "I thought and thought it over. I was in pain from it, yes. I prayed. Then they said you are the devil and you're tempting me."

Egan drew in his thin lips and raised a weak hand to his forehead.

"But you know that's not true, don't you, boy?"

Then Weitling stopped bouncing on his haunches and turned to Egan with a great glowing smile. His teeth were regular and white.

"I think," he said, "you are." And he laughed.

Pablo, to his own confusion, saw that Egan was trembling.

"Weitling," the priest said. He licked his lips and leaned forward. "Weitling, think of God's sparrows. 'Are not two sparrows sold for a farthing? and one of them shall not fall upon the ground without your Father. But the very hairs of your head are all numbered. Fear ye not therefore, for ye are of more value than many sparrows.' That's what the Almighty tells His children, Weitling. You dare not harm them."

The Farmer laughed again; the laughter came from within his body, it was unlike his thin soft voice. When he stopped laughing, he fixed the old priest with small fiery eyes. "And fear not those who kill the body! Yes? It says, nix?"

"Don't listen to the voices, Weitling! They're evil things."

"No," Weitling said. "God speaks."

"God forbids murder, Weitling. God watches over the little children. He is Who loves truly. He made the lamb."

"One day there will be a ram for sacrifice," Weitling declared, looking beyond the fire. "When things are made clean I will see a ram with his horns caught. Then sacrifice by bad monkeys will be over and it will be the ram. I am promised this."

"Ah, Weitling," Father Egan said, "we talked it out so carefully the other night. We were both so lucid. I thought you'd listened to me."

"I have to fool you," the Farmer said, and his features were illuminated by another witless smile. "I am smart. I was fooling you."

Pablo Tabor was driven toward homicidal delirium by the Farmer's manner. He had spent several secret minutes changing his position in order to have a grab at his knife when the time came. Now, Weitling's smile put him over the top. "Crazy fuck." He spat bile through his teeth. No one seemed to notice.

"Weitling, son . . ." Egan stretched a tentative bony hand toward the young man. "What kind of a thing would God be if He made you butcher His innocents?"

As Egan and Pablo, flesh acrawl, watched, Weitling threw back his head and puckered his lips to form a quivering O. From the oval space issued a shrill keening.

"Oooh, he is terrible," Weitling sang. His face was distended by fear. He folded his arms across his chest and thrust his hands under his armpits. He was in ecstasy. "He is more terrible than you can know. His face is like Indian corn, of colors. Then sometimes invisible, the worst. The hair of him is blue. He is electricity. Arms and legs are made of worms. The power. And it is like space beneath you, you are falling. I fall. I, poor myself, I fall. He crushes me. And he is terrible music, a howling. I am made to see his terrible face and to hear his horrible voice. He makes the noise of a drum. The noise of an organum. *Ein flaute,* also. Also of parrots, and sometimes is so, a parrot. He says I will fall more and I am squeezed. Poor myself. He says there is not mercy anymore. He says of Jesus Christ—hex not rex. He says that I must see the corn face. He says I am bad Weitling and I am frightened cold."

Weitling bent his great head as far backward as his neck allowed and uttered another cry.

"Oooh, he says the wine is blood! Eat flesh meat, he says this. He will make blood run out until fields are covered and he will bowl the sun to dry it. He has not mercy for Weitling. Nor for children. They are in depravity, he says. He is free. He takes them up, their bones, their gut bags. He makes rain out of them. The rain, this is him laughing at Weitling. His laughing is rain. He makes the rain of parts of children. The fish are fed with blood. When they see his face their eyes are opened, they eat their teeth. He says Weitling go down. And I go down and do it. We are shit upon the ground to him. This he tells me."

"Lamb of God who takest away the sins of the world, have mercy on us," Father Egan said softly, and struck his breast. Pablo could not take his eyes from Weitling's enraptured face.

The priest reached out with an unsteady hand to touch Farmer Weitling's shoulder.

"Weitling, the necessary sacrifice was made long ago. No one asks anything of you except that you get yourself healed."

Weitling rocked to his drummer god; Egan's hand fell away.

"He is king and I, his bad monkey. I am the bad monkey in the trees. They tell the children run from the bad monkey and the children run. But whose monkey I am, they don't know. He calls. He screams like a hungry monkey. He must make the rain. In his horrible voice he screams at Weitling."

"Stop it," Egan said in a dull voice. "Stop it now, son."

Weitling kept rocking.

"They don't know what I, Weitling, know. I make the sun to come up. I hear it come up. Without me there is no rain. When the sun is bowled and the blood is dry things so beautiful will be. *Ja,* it's so. No hungering. No wondering. Everything we must have will be."

Egan watched him for a moment, in silence.

"Well now," the priest said, "I've heard that one before."

"But if there is not blood everything is destroyed. Darkness and the sun falls and the stars and moon. The ground opens and it is all crushed like Weitling."

"But you're deluded, Weitling. It all takes care of itself. That's the beauty of it—so they say." He put his hand around the bottle of rum as though he were about to drink but after a second he took the hand away. "Don't you see that it's better that the world endures its own destruction than that you make yourself work such cruelties? Or that an innocent child is made to suffer and die?"

Weitling stopped rocking and began to stand up. The mask of celebration dissolved and his broad stolid face relaxed.

"I am small," he told Egan, looking down on him, "but I'm too big for you. He's with me and I'm strong."

"Well, you're too strong for me but that's no trick. Go, Weitling. Go back to our people, find your bishop or your elder and let them help to cure you."

"Where I go," Weitling said, "They don't find me."

He looked about him and then turned on Pablo.

"You," he told Tabor, "you're not a good boy."

Pablo snarled. "Oh yeah?" he said.

The Farmer took a step backward, turned and went his way rejoicing.

"Some big creep," Pablo said. "You ought to put a fence around this place."

"You should know," the priest explained, "that he's a killer of children. We're not sure how many he's done in. He hears voices."

"He really does that? He kills little kids?"

Egan, looking into the fire, nodded.

"If he does that, man, you got no business letting him run around."

"What should I do?"

"Well, shit, you oughta tell someone. Or just take him out—bingo."

"If I told anyone around here, Weitling would be strung up the same day."

"What's the matter with that? Then he couldn't hurt no more kids."

"Yes. But I'm not sure he's beyond help."

"Are you kidding me? You just don't have any kids, that's why you can talk like that."

"Ah," Egan said. "Maybe you're right." He was thoughtful

for a while. "You know, I've always valued children above everything else—even though I haven't any. It's always bothered me that the world hurts them. That they got lost in the bush, wandered into traps, all those terrible things. The thought of those things could always spoil the most beautiful day for me."

"Fucking-A, man. Kids are the only clean thing in this rotten fucked world. You can't give a shit about people, they bring their trouble on themselves. But kids, that's different."

"But Weitling—he's a kind of a child himself, isn't he?"

"A fucking killer ape is what he is. There's only one cure for him."

"He's very sick and his head is full of dreams and stories that went bad on him. He's not alone in that condition."

Pablo sighed and turned over to lean on his elbow. "I don't know, bro," he said wearily. "I got troubles of my own, you know."

"I've tried to get to the Mennonites about him—I've had my friends up-country get in touch. But they don't have telephones, they live in inaccessible places and some of them don't talk to strangers." Egan reached for the bottle again and this time he took a drink. "You're right, of course. I'll have to see that he's picked up. I'm as deluded as he is."

Talk of being picked up was troubling to Pablo. As he watched the old man's vacant face, cadaverous even in the firelight, his leg began to hurt and he felt cold. Things were wrong, he thought. Things were wiggy.

Egan was drinking now; he sat with his head lowered, talking softly to himself.

"Again I couldn't see," Pablo heard him say. "Could it be that because there was no concupiscence I was . . ." The priest's thin voice trailed off.

Pablo sat up.

"Hey, man, you said you could help me out. You said you'd give me a place to crash. You said you had medicine. Now I'm sick, you understand me?"

"The boat," the old man said, "you fought on the boat. That's why you're here."

"Never mind the fuckin' boat," Pablo said. The fear that had been hovering in the surrounding darkness touched him with its feathers. The place was wiggy. There were killers and the old man was stoned mad. He was one of those people—

whatever you wanted they had it, but jack shit was what they had. It was a turned-around place, a bad place. Maybe not a true place at all.

"Something's going on, Pablo," the priest said. "Something to do with the place we're in."

Pablo's throat was dry as sand; he opened his mouth to breathe.

"What do you mean?" He knew that the pills had started to poison him at last. And people had better beware then and they had better not try to turn him around.

"Did you look at the stones?"

Pablo realized he meant the inscribed upright slabs in the center of the clearing.

"Yeah. Sort of."

"Did you examine them? Did you read them?"

"It was dark. Anyway, how'm I gonna read that craziness?"

"The stones tell about human sacrifice. All the glyphs and all the figures here are about that and nothing else."

"Human sacrifice," Pablo said.

"A man came here once from the national museum. They took rubbings of those stones and they picked up everything that could be moved. They said it was for the museum's collection but of course it was for the President's family to sell. They picked up bone carvings and shards with graffiti on them. The man said he thought the graffiti might tell him something about everyday life here long ago, about how people went about life. But it turned out that he was wrong, it turned out that every single stroke represented human sacrifice—even the graffiti. It was as though there was no everyday life. Only sacrifice."

Tabor looked at him blankly.

"You understand, Pablo? There's a charge on the place. It draws people like Weitling and people like you. The field of blood. The place of the skull. They played the ball game here, you know." The old priest frowned and shook his head. "Can that be? A temple? A temple of the demiurge?"

Pablo felt as though the short hairs on the back of his neck were on end. He opened his mouth to breathe. "The ball game," he repeated.

"But why not?" Egan asked. "Whatever life is, it isn't rational. Signs and wonders, eh?"

"Now look," Pablo said, "you're tryin' to turn me around."

Something like the taste of an old bad dream stirred under Pablo's memory. Place of the skull. "What happened on that boat, man, that was the purest case of self-defense you could want. Those people were bad, man, they were wanting to kill me. I'm just lucky I'm alive."

The old man's eyes had come to life. He pursed his lips and thumped Pablo on the chest.

"Something's going on, Pablo. Always. Something taking its course."

"I don't . . ." Pablo began. "I don't . . ."

"A process." Egan took a deep breath, held it and released it in a hoarse whisper. "Measureless."

I'm in such trouble now, Pablo thought, I might as well be dead. He thought of mornings in the piney woods, of going for quail. But he had shot his dogs.

"Imagine it," Egan said. "This colossal immanent force and it's a gleam in the muck. Layer upon layer of intention, consciousness. Measureless will. Unseen and encompassing everything."

"Could I have some of your rum, bro?" Pablo asked. "See, I don't feel good." When Egan did not respond, he reached over and took it.

"It's woven in," Egan said. "Hiding in the universe. Everywhere and yet never anywhere. Always present and never available." Father Egan's bright gaze fell upon Tabor. He appeared not to recognize him. Yet he called him by name. "Pablo," he said, "what a mystery, eh?"

"No," Pablo said, "no, I don't feel so good and that's the truth. I don't like the way I feel."

"It's here after all, marking a passage, setting traps. Like insect traps among the leaves. For butterflies. We never find it. Does it ever find us?"

"It's my leg that's hurting," Pablo said. "I think it might be pretty bad." He reached with difficulty into the pockets of his jeans. "See, all I got is these pain pills and I gotta have more." He held up the little glass bottle for Egan's inspection. "And even aspirin, if I had that, see."

"Telling the dancer from dance, Pablo. That's what the poem's about, you know. That's the problem."

"You don't even give a shit," Pablo said bitterly.

"But I do," Egan said cheerfully, not looking at Pablo.

"Now, listen. A friend of mine, a Maryknoll chap, lived fifty years in Africa. He told me they had a moth there that lived in colonies. The colonies lived in the branches of a certain kind of tree, they would settle on a branch and there they would form a leaf and flower pattern unknown to nature. It was totally their own. Now that's marvelous, isn't it? But that's not the half. If you shook the branch, the moths would fly away. Then in minutes they'd settle down again and form the same leaf and flower. Hundreds, maybe thousands of moths, every one in its exact place. Each moth an exact part of the whole." He turned toward Pablo. "A jigsaw."

Desperate, Tabor rolled his eyes and ground his teeth.

"I don't even know what the fuck you're talking about, you crazy old bastard. You said you'd help me out."

Egan patted Tabor's forearm.

"Inconceivable," he said. "*Credo quia absurdum.*"

Pablo was tired of anger. His anxiety was dissolving into a gloom like that of the grave. He would have to take more speed and suffer the loss of rest, risk the terrors at the bottom of the pill bottle. There was rum and that might help. He felt as though he were cringing behind his own eyes.

"Shining," Egan said. "Shook foil."

Pablo put the pill in his mouth and tried to swallow it. His mouth seemed to be stuffed with dry straw; the stalks hurt his throat. When he closed his eyes there were small whirling lights. The Place of the Skull. I am the drug, he thought.

"Why are You so unavailable?" Egan sang to the forest. "Why must it be so?"

"Who are you talking to?" Pablo demanded.

Egan gave him a sad, reassuring smile. Both of them waited, as though for an answer.

"Pity the Weitlings of the world, Pablo. They're victims of things as they are. Some chemical in the blood, a shortage of sugar in the brain cells and they get the process whole. What they see is real enough, it's so overwhelming it must seem like God to them. You can't look on what they see and not run mad." He turned in the direction Weitling had gone, watched for a moment and then faced the fire again. "They've been elected. Priests, because they've seen it, poor bastards. That's what Satan is, Pablo. Satan is the way things are. Remember Mephistopheles, eh? 'Why this is hell nor are we out of it.' "

Pablo closed his eyes and shivered.

"We say they're deluded but reality's their problem. Unlike you and me, they see it plain—no breakdown, no story material to go with it, so they have to make up their own story. It burns out their minds and they have to call it revelation. Primitive association, sympathetic magic—whatever comes to hand. You know how it is, boy, everybody has to make suffering mean something. The other guy's firstborn, paschal lambs, sacrifice. But that's not revelation—not by a long shot. Revelation is something else." Egan was silent for a moment, then he opened his mouth as though he were about to speak.

Pablo was at the point of screaming. "What is it, for Christ's sake?"

"It's all right, Pablo, do you see? That's what it comes to. Everything is all right. In spite of appearances. There's no other conclusion."

"I don't know who you people are," Pablo said despairingly, "but you all are crazy. I thought you could help me out. I got no business in this freak show."

"Pablo, listen, it's all right. It's all right for you too. We'll take care of you. You're among friends."

The old man's eyes gave him no peace. He searched the field of vision for escape, a token of reason, a clue, the light of dawn. Things overcame him.

"Hey," he asked the priest, "what did you say this was a temple of?"

Egan looked blank for a moment.

"Oh. Oh, the demiurge. A kind of metaphor. At least I think so but who knows, eh? Another theological system." He laughed to himself.

Pablo felt the hairs on his neck rise.

"You said . . . about Satan. Didn't you say about Satan?"

"Same sort of thing."

"Jesus," Pablo said. His heart beat faster.

"These systems, Pablo . . . words for the process. It's what it comes down to that matters."

Pablo Tabor looked hard into the shadows. A numbing excitement thickened his blood.

"Holy shit," he said. "I'm in this. Me. I am."

"Of course," Egan said.

"Something is going on here," Pablo said breathlessly.

"You're right, old man. Something far out and special. Things are going on here."

"Yes, indeed," the priest told him. "You can feel it now, can't you?"

Pablo trembled, fixed between elation and terror.

"I *do* feel it," he declared, nodding furiously. "Fuckin'-A."

"It's the world moving in time," Father Egan explained to him. "One gets these little epiphenomenal jolts. Petty spookery in a way. But underneath it all—there is something." He clapped Pablo lightly on the shoulder. "It's in the moment. Take it in your hands, my boy."

Tabor stared wide-eyed into the fire. In the dancing flames he saw dragons, winged horses, a choir of demiurges and such things.

"It was meant to be," he said in a choked voice. "It was all meant to be like this." He put his hand to his face and shook his head. He felt happy.

"This is what I came down here for," Pablo told Father Egan. "This is how come I went over the hill. It was all leading up to this, see? There was a goddamn planned purpose to everything." He thought of the diamond in his pocket and touched it.

"Surely," Father Egan said.

"When I shot those dogs," Pablo explained raptly, "I started this whole thing going. I was headed here from that time."

"You were trying to get back, Pablo. Like everyone."

"Then I came down, see. I got to the *Cloud.* I was learning all the time but I didn't know it then."

Father Egan nodded.

Dizzy with recognition, Pablo stared at him in wonder.

"St. Joost, I met this old Jew. He was dying right in front of me. He was telling me stuff I couldn't understand, but I understand it now. He gave me something." Pablo reached into his pocket and took out the diamond. "I wouldn't show this to nobody down here unless I thought they were all right and I think you're all right and I'm showing it to you. That old Jew gave me this here." Egan looked at the diamond. "I ain't giving this to you, understand? The old man gave it to me for my boy. It's worth a whole lot of money—you can tell that just by looking—but it means something, I think. It's got a meaning, like."

"Let's see," Egan said, "what would it mean?" He took hold of Pablo's hand cupping the stone and held his own hand under it. " 'The jewel is in the lotus,' perhaps that's what it means. The eternal in the temporal. The Boddhisattva declining nirvana out of compassion. Contemplating the ignorance of you and me, eh? That's a metaphor of our Buddhist friends."

Pablo's eyes glazed over. "Holy shit," he said. "Santa Maria." He stared at the diamond in his palm with passion.

"Hey," he said to the priest, "diamonds are forever! You heard of that, right? That means something, don't it?"

"I have heard it," Egan said. "Perhaps it has a religious meaning."

"Listen," Pablo said, and swallowed. "Can you tell me about my past lives? That's what I'd really like to know about."

"Well," Egan said, "I'm afraid not. I don't know anything about past lives, or even if we have them."

"You kidding me?" Pablo said. "I thought you knew about this kind of stuff."

"Not about past lives. One life at a time with me."

"Somebody's gonna tell me someday," Pablo said. "I'm gonna find it all out, man, because I'm meant to. People gonna be coming to me to find it out." He yawned. The fever of revelation was a drug of its own, stronger than the Callahans' pills. It made him feel strong and calm, peaceful, as though he could not be turned around.

"Maybe so, Pablo. Maybe you're the one with the talent and energy to know about it. We hold our treasure in earthen vessels."

"Fuckin'-A," Pablo said.

The fatigue he felt was no longer threatening. He spread himself out on the coarse grass beside the fire and closed his eyes.

Egan put a hand on Pablo's forehead and saw the youth shiver. For the first time he saw the wound on Tabor's leg, and though he could not determine its gravity in the firelight, it was obviously dirty and untended.

"We can go now," the priest said. "I've been running on, I've talked too long. If you can walk, I'll help you over to our dispensary. It's not far."

Pablo opened his eyes and shook his head.

"You need looking after now. You need some antibiotics."

"No," Pablo said. "I want to wait a minute. I'm too wasted right now. What I want to do, I want to lie down here and listen to those birds and I don't give a shit." He was looking into the fire, his head turned to one side. A howler monkey screamed an alarm from the edge of the clearing. A girl's voice seemed to answer—one of the young foreigners, talking in her sleep. "I come a damn long way, you know that?"

"I'll go back and get help for you. We have a nurse with us and you'll be all right here."

Pablo seized Egan's arm and held it.

"I want you to stay, bro. I want you to tell me everything you can that I'm supposed to know becaue that's what I'm here for."

Egan settled down on the log where Pablo had rested and took a drink of Flor de Cana.

"All right," he said. So he began to tell Pablo about the Sacred Pleroma and the Incomprehensible, Inconceivable One within Whom all things were, the Master of the Silence and the Abyss. He told him about the Errant Sophia, the whore of Wisdom, who in her foredoomed passion to comprehend the Holy One underestimated the depths of the Abyss and became lost. Wandering, stricken, Father Egan told Pablo, Sophia found herself walled out from the All, the Ineffable; she encountered, for the first time, Limit. From the torment of her loss, Egan explained, Sophia brought into existence fear and grief and bewilderment and all the things which were to make up the world without Him. Then, from these things came forth the Demiurge, the force of ignorance under whose power Pablo and he himself and everyone else made their blind passage through outer dark. He told these things to Pablo not as he had written about them, but as though they were literal true things, as one might tell a story to a child. As Pablo had pointed out to him, he had never had a child. Then he thought that perhaps they were true things, real things, as real as the sun which was rising now over the clearing.

Pablo had gone to sleep, so the priest took a ground cloth and wrapped it across a sharp stick to keep the risen sun from the young man's eyes.

Tabor's fist was clenched; Egan gently pried the fingers

apart and found the diamond. He slipped it back into the shirt
pocket from which Pablo had taken it to show him. A curious
thing, he thought. He supposed the youth had stolen it. Perhaps had killed for it, on his boat. He shook his head and
picked up the bottle and drank.

In the city, in the villages of the coast, Tecan's children
were shouldering their daily burdens, prepared to endure with
ancient grace the rule of plunder and violence. Nearby, the
touring adolescents stirred at their campfires. At sea, the first
light, filtered to green and gray, would begin to penetrate the
depths where a murdered girl lay distantly mourned. Nor
would she be alone there. And in the forest, Weitling would
be looking at the sunrise and taking fire with fantasies of
sacrifice and blood. Egan thought of the hunt he would have
to set afield now, for the saving of other children.

The priest shielded his eyes and considered the Incomprehensible; he wondered if, across the awesome gulf of the
abyss, across the darkness and the silence, he might presume
to address toward It a prayer. He thought about it for some
little time; in the end, he dared not. He picked up the rum and
drank and then the exertions of the night set their weight on
him and he fell into a sleep of his own.

Holliwell did not sleep although he lay in bed until dawn. In
the slant of the new sun he drove to the mission, parked and
walked the narrow beach.

The sight of the ocean oppressed him. He was not deceived
by its exquisite sportiveness—the lacy flumes of breaking
wave, the delicate rainbows in the spray. He knew what was
spread out beneath its trivial entertainments. The ocean at its
morning business brought cognate visions to his mind's eye; a
flower-painted cart hauling corpses, a bright turban on a leper.

Beside the beach at Danang he had seen a leper with a
"Kiss Me" tee shirt. There was nothing to get angry about;
some stern wit had made a statement and the leper had got a
shirt.

For a long time Holliwell stood by the water. A few yards
away under the slate-blue rollers, the universe was being most
spontaneously itself. Its play dazzled. It beguiled temporal
flesh with promises and it promised all things from petty cheer
to cool annihilation.

Things were a lonely and dangerous business and he was tired of them. He wanted clarity and it was not to be had. It seemed to him that one could not stand in clear light for the twinkling of an eye. Each moment was immediately overrun with chemical illusion flashing up from the sea and its dependent blood, from the great steaming jakes of the mind.

So one had always to wander through vapors among phantoms, one was always just out in it and it never stopped. Illusion compounding illusion, a limitless hallucination without end or reference point—desires, fears, dread shadows and pretty lights, one's own delirium and everyone else's. It was what kept you going. It kept you going until your heart burst.

He was in love, he remembered. With May. And she was being hunted down.

He lit a cigarette and smoked and turned to see her standing by the beach road. She was waiting for a jitney bus to pass, shielding her eyes from the sun. He flicked the filtered butt into a crystalline wave.

She came to him across the litter of desiccated palm leaves and dead kelp; his heart raced. What was it then? Love? Another yearning distilled of fancy, another drug in the salt blood. Another passion to whipsaw in the wet cave of consciousness.

Then she was beside him trembling in the morning sun, honey-haired—and you wanted to be with her, of course you did. You wanted to salve the loneliness. You wanted to break down, however you might, the entombed separateness of the two selves there, yourself and May. Anyone would.

He started to speak but the look on her face silenced him. Remembering it, he would think that she looked like a vision —a figure of some other stuff, suddenly manifest. The diluvian chaos he inhabited was alien to her. He thought that she must live in some secret arrangement with the world of things; her beauty was the beauty of inward certainties. Such a woman could live, die, make choices, all those things—with a quiet heart. She could minister, heal the sick, march with apocalyptic legions. She looked like a vision to that degree.

Now, she was certainty confounded. She could not bring experience to bear and she had no guile. Through innocence, she had set herself in his quarter of things where the earth trembled underfoot and there was only seeming. The Queen of Swords betrayed. Or simply common sense at its ultimate reduction, at the end of its tether.

In this aspect, she was a challenge and a provocation to the likes of Holliwell. The impulse stripped down was to love her or destroy her. Stripped further it was toward both those ends, to subsume her in flesh and spirit. It was predatory.

But he was an honest man, known to be such. He was capable of honor and sacrifice. As a result she presented to Holliwell something he dreaded far more than a challenge. She presented a choice.

He closed his eyes and opened them. His mind was unstrung with fear, sleeplessness and booze—not for the first time. He was seeing things.

"You did come back."

"Of course I did," he said.

They walked together across the sand and up the steps to the dispensary. There was coffee simmering on the heater; she poured them out two cups.

"I wonder," he said after a moment, "if you could let me have a nip of brandy to go with this."

She rose immediately from the chair she had taken. Still shaky, her face almost blank, she brought him the miniature brandy bottle.

"I drink," he explained.

"I know you do," she said. "I can tell by your face. Where it's soft."

Holliwell drew back, amused and stung.

"Your face is hard and soft," she informed him. "It looks hard and sort of mean but in some places it's soft."

He nodded warily.

"I know your face pretty well by now. I've been thinking about you."

He wondered who it was she thought about. Who she thought she saw.

"I felt very close to you last night," she said.

"You were."

"I know. You have to understand that's a rare feeling for me. And I don't know how to handle it."

He drank the fortified coffee. Oh, May, he thought, I'm not your lost Tiger. He was the Adversary. He would not let her go now, although it was within his power. Shown flesh, the

Adversary eats; presented with inner space, he hastens to occupy it. The Adversary is a lover.

He drew up the ends of the soft net she had stepped into. He said: "I fell in love with you. That's the only way I can put it."

He put out his hand and touched her. Gratitude, joy, remorse struck him all together. There were two hungers and an illusion of fulfillment. He thought he understood hers better than his own.

She did not know the drill and this made it awkward for him but exciting as well. He told himself that he was not trifling with her but taking honorable comfort in a friendly place.

It was not one of those times when one forgot the forest for the trees. She was there, always. If he abandoned her she would intrude herself; her expectations were limitless and she pursued their satisfaction without shame. The satisfactions she pursued were innocent and had to do with her idea of earthly love. At times he thought of her as Eve.

Over and through it all was the beating of her heart. Holliwell felt it throbbing in his own body; he caressed her heartbeat as a sexual exercise. He studied its measure under the warmth of her silken skin; he wanted to hunt it down inside her, to be inside her, where its cadence ordered the scheme of her gut and bone as primum mobile. He wanted to be mastered by her heartbeat. He wanted her heart in his hands.

It was difficult to make it last, he was so inflamed. Her intrusions on his selfishness helped, and he was ready when the time came for the thing he had rather dreaded. The ram beat against the shuddering gate, echoing along the walls. Again, again. She did not hide, she was there.

He thought that he could share her pain. The stabbing aside of virginhood was as it should be—his extended flesh prodding after habitation, inching through blood and tissue after her quickening heart. They experienced it together, an enacted metaphor.

Once inside her he was free. For a moment he could make himself believe that the walls of self were melted and identity overthrown. It was all lyric for him, bloody, lubricious. Her heart kept beating faster and faster. They finished as a process of ocean.

Not for some minutes afterward did he realize that she had eluded him after all. He could not understand how it had happened. He turned to her on the mat beside him and saw that he had lost her. Her teeth were bared, biting into her upper lip. Her eyes were bright with tears. Of course he had expected too much of the act; it had been strangely naïve of him. They had both expected worlds too much.

Stupidly, he asked the tedious questions. Whether it had been all right, if she was hurting, whether she had, as he said, enjoyed it. He was pushing her away, he whose science was Other. Each tedious question, each polite reassurance put them farther apart.

He got up, drew water from the sink to wash himself and walked to one of the windows. She had closed all the shutters. He unfastened the one at the window where he stood and looked to the ocean again.

The sea on one hand, the woman on the other. Himself in between. All separate again in their loneliness and fixedness, illusions of union fled.

When he turned to face her she was sitting on the bed wrapped in the sheet. His eye fell on the bloodstains and he looked away. There was a strange smile on her face. When she spoke it was in a small somehow disembodied voice.

"A Wife—at Daybreak I shall be—" he heard her say. "Sunrise—Hast thou a flag for me?" She looked him in the eye with the cool despairing smile. "Nothing ever goes the way I think it will," she said.

He turned back toward the ocean.

"I wish you hadn't said that."

"Oh no," she said. She stood up with the sheet draped around her and came over to him. "Oh no. Please don't misunderstand me. It was pleasurable. It was very pleasurable."

When he turned his face to her, she stood on tiptoes to kiss him on the cheek.

"Very nice, sir. Very nice and new."

"It hurt," he said. "It wasn't what you expected."

"That wasn't what I meant," she said. 'I just didn't think it would happen like that."

"Neither did I." He clasped his hands round the nape of her neck and looked into her tears. "It didn't happen. We did it."

"Yes," she said.

Her body was still when he held her. She delicately stroked his shoulder with three fingers as one might pet a cat. It was an odd hit.

"Wait for me," she said, gathering the sheet round her. "I have to wash."

"I'm not going anywhere."

He leaned in the window, smoking, watching the road. He could hear her crying in the shower.

She came out wearing an unadorned light blue dress and her hair was tucked up in a matching scarf. A nurse's uniform —almost a habit.

"You really are in trouble," Holliwell told her. "Very serious and dangerous trouble. You're being watched by some very bad people."

Justin was looking down at her warped reflection in the surface of a wheeled metal table.

"I know that."

"Do you know who they are?"

"Sure. The Guardia Nacional and people who work for them."

He was silent for a moment.

"There are others," he told her. "Foreigners. They could be the local CIA station assets. They're cowboys."

"What does that mean?"

"It means no one much cares what they do. And they're after you."

She managed to smile. "Me specifically?"

"They think you're a subversive element."

"I am. But I'm not very good at it."

"Well, you've attracted their notice. They want you."

"Come on," she said, "it's not me they're really after."

He watched her slowly raise her fingers to her lips.

"Yes, it is," he said. "It's you."

He would not be able to explain it to her. She had aroused an appetite in them as she had in him. He called his hunger love, what they called theirs he had no way of knowing. It was malice, shame—the desperado's rage at innocence and grace, the villain's abhorrence of love and life and goodness. Names and words were of no account; it was an old game, older than words.

He thought of her heart beating next to his and the notion came to him of that heartbeat pulsing across silence, its brave flutter sounding in the inward ear of those men like the lateral rhythms of a lost sea creature among the reefs. Of her heart as a magical beast bringing the hunt upon itself. A unicorn.

"Let them be after me," she said, still staring at the table-top. "While they're after me, the people who are really doing something can take this country from under their noses."

"Are they wrong about you then? Aren't you involved in any real activity?"

"They're not wrong. I was involved in the fight here. Was. Formerly. I knew they were casing me. I pulled out. I've told the people concerned."

He shook his head. "It's too late," he said. "We have to get you out of here." He looked down at the road. "If you leave with me we might make it."

"Oh, Frank," she said, "I can't, you know." She shrugged her shoulders with a wan exasperated smile. "I'm responsible for Father Egan. I'm responsible for everything here."

"You have to, May. They'll hurt you."

She looked at him sharply. She was frightened and angry because of it.

"Why do you keep saying it's me?"

"It's you."

"No," she said uncertainly, "I'm nothing in this."

"You could come with me up to Miami. After that . . . I don't know."

Nor did he. He could not imagine a time beyond the moment. He felt her eyes on him.

"That would be something, wouldn't it?" she said.

"Let's try it, May."

"It would be something. But it's not possible. I can't leave a sick old man alone. I can't walk out on people who trust me." She shook her head slowly. "No, Frank. Not now. I have to tell my friends what you've told me. And then I'll think of something clever, I guess." She was staring at him wide-eyed, the way she had the night before. "How do you know all this? About these people and who they are? These cowboys?"

"I know one when I see one. I was in Vietnam once."

"Is that where you got that little scar?"

He touched his earlobe.

"That's right. In the mountains there. It's a piki scar."

"You said . . . somewhere else."

"I lied."

"It must have been bad there," she said. "Was it bad?"

You'd have liked it, he thought.

"It was all right."

"I don't know who you are," she said.

"May, for Christ's sake! Let's get it together and get out!"

"Do you think I'm too dumb to be frightened?" she asked. "I'm plenty frightened. Yes, I'd like to run. I'm scared and I'd like to run. Don't you see that it isn't possible?" She shivered and raised her upturned palms. "It's not possible. I can't do it."

She started toward him, he moved to her and held her. She stood in his arms with her shoulder to him, very stiff and frightened, facing the open window. Then he heard her say: "My God, they're here."

He released her and stepped back.

"Who?"

Going carefully to the window, he saw a young woman in braids and native dress—a Carib, he thought—walking along the road.

"Who?" he asked. "This Indian kid?"

"She isn't Indian. She's from town. She's my contact." Justin swallowed and squared her shoulders. "I sent them a note last night that I was pulling out. They wouldn't send her out here in broad daylight unless something was up."

"Can you keep her outside?"

"I don't think so." She looked at him ashamed. "You'll have to hide. Sneak out."

Like a man in a bedroom farce, Holliwell left through a window in the washroom, sliding down a hardwood buttress that anchored the dispensary wing to the overgrown hillside. He made his way through the brush to the trail that ran along the creekside and started inland. He followed the trail for about five minutes and then stopped, sat down under a coco- bolo tree on the bank and watched the water insects skim the brown surface of the creek.

He understood that she would not go. He had neither the force nor the moral authority to persuade her. He was in danger himself now; he had gone along too far. What it came to, what he had to face, was that he had somehow supposed that he could run with the hare and hunt with the hounds.

Informally of course. In the name of communication. He had imagined a place for himself in the business and then assumed that the place existed.

There would be regrets now and they would be deep and bitter. He knew vaguely that his life would be changed somehow. Whatever happened, he thought, he would not be wiser. He did not suppose that his judgment would improve.

The forest enfolded him, shutting out the mission and the sea. Drawn into its silent airless ambiance, he moved through the shady perfumed spaces like a dreamer. The trail and the river kept him from losing his way.

When he had wandered on for about a quarter of a mile, he was brought up by the prospect of an open space ahead; there were hills beyond it and then a precipitous wall of mountains. In the space were three stelae in a staggered row, quite exposed, as clear of earth and vegetation as though they were on exhibition. The one nearest him was discolored from frequent rubbings. If it was not protected, he thought, it would soon be lost altogether.

He advanced and studied the clearing. One of the hills behind it, Holliwell saw from the contour, was a pyramid covered in jungle. There might be more. It was an impressive site; the manner in which it lay half excavated and unprotected was a measure of the government's barbarity. Whoever had made the rubbings might just as easily have unearthed the entire stela and trucked it away. He was surprised that Oscar Ocampo had not got round to it; there was a fortune to be made here.

The clearing itself was curiously infertile and the meagerness of soil had helped to keep the stones exposed. The ground was sandy and covered with shells—there would be salt or brackish water only a few feet down and the limestone crust was sterile. Perhaps there was some priestly curse over it.

As Holliwell started from the cover of the forest, he saw a young man asleep on the far side of the clearing. He stayed where he was and then began to back toward the tree line.

In the shadow of the mission building, Holliwell found himself a hiding place beside the creek from which he could see the beach road. Above him, he could hear Sister Justin in conversation with her visitor; the discussion sounded businesslike and cordial.

At length he heard a light sandaled step on the porch stairs
and the girl in braids went past him on the road toward town.
He waited until she had gone some distance and then went
around to the front of the building and up to the dispensary
wing. On his way up the steps, he saw Father Egan—in
pajamas—standing at the kitchen window, blinking in the
hard sunlight. Egan saluted him with a soft disjointed wave.

He found Justin standing where he had left her, beside the
window. She watched him come in with a sad smile.

"There are people back at your ruins," Holliwell told her.
"They don't look very reasonable."

"We have everyone back there," she said. "It doesn't matter
now."

Something about the way she said it frightened him.

"What went on?"

She took a deep breath and exhaled it slowly.

"I'm . . . back in it, I guess."

"What do you mean, May?"

"It's happening tonight." Her eyes widened. "Do you know
what that means? What we've all been waiting for. The rising,
Frank. They're going out tonight."

"Good Christ," he said.

"They need me," she said. She met his fearful look. "I
asked them and they said they did. They expect me at the
company clinic at eight o'clock. They have the guns and the
people and they're going to take the coast."

"May, can't you see how crazy this is? For you?"

"Don't, Frank," she said. "I'm so happy, see. I'm happier
than I've ever been."

He turned from her and began to walk the length of the
dispensary. The bed where they had been was stripped.

"It must be that your friends don't understand the heat that
you've attracted."

"The spooks are out of luck," Justin said. "There won't
be any secrets tomorrow."

"There are agents and police all over the place," Holliwell
said. "For all you know they may be just waiting for you to
make a move so they can come down on you."

She did not answer him.

"Oh, for God's sake, May. They can have their goddamn
revolution without you. If they win, they'll expel you anyway."

"I didn't come down here to see the world or make my

fortune or be educated. I came in my simpleminded way to help people. I'm not going to pull out now."

"Ah, shit," Holliwell said.

"I don't decide what the people here need from me. They decide and I try to do it. Those are the rules. I've always accepted them."

"You're just being used."

"Damn right," she said. "At last, thank God."

He found another miniature brandy and opened it.

"I'm going to tell you something now, May, that I didn't want to tell you. I'm telling you so you can have some idea of your situation." He forced himself to look at her as he spoke. Her face still held a pale defiant smile. "When I came down here I was asked by a man I know to be in the intelligence community to check this place out. I was supposed to find out what you were up to. Do you know what that means?"

"Go on," she said.

"It means that someone's been reporting on you—all the way to Washington. Not very long ago I was sitting in a restaurant in New York talking to that man about you. Now go ahead and figure out what your chances are."

She put her hand over her eyes and leaned against the window casing.

"Well," she said after a while, "you'll have a story to tell, won't you? And a dirty joke to go with it."

"I refused him, May. I said I wouldn't do it. Then I was approached in Santiago by another agent. You again. You're public property, you and your friends." He finished the brandy and tossed the bottle into a metal GI can. It rang against the ribs of the can with an ugly sound that hung over the long room. "I refused them all. It was for my own purposes that I came here, believe it or not. Maybe I wanted to see somebody doing something they believed in. Maybe I was just curious. They came to me because I did a job for the Company in Vietnam. I don't work for them now. I'm not making any reports."

She was crying silently. She took her hand from over her eyes and walked up to him.

"You're very convincing, mister," she said. And then she punched him across the bridge of his nose, a hard stiff-armed punch that numbed him. She hit him twice more, right hooks with a windup. His nose began to bleed. He put his handker-chief to it.

"I'm telling you the truth. You can have me killed if you want to, you've got time."

"Do you know something?" she said. "I almost went with you. I almost did."

"I wish you had, May."

"You're just another one of those bastards," she said. "I can see that now. I don't care what you say."

"You're wrong. I told you I was in love with you and I meant it. I'm not sure what falling in love is. It's probably something trivial and foolish. But for what it's worth I love you, I swear."

"I thought I was dumb," she said. "You're worse than me."

"I didn't want to tell you. I wasn't going to. Apparently it wasn't necessary."

"Oh, but I'm glad you did. So we know who we are—just a little."

They stood in silence, both of them looking at the scrubbed wooden floor of the dispensary.

"There's not much I can do for you at the hotel. Just be warned. The people over there think they know why I'm here but they're not taking me into their confidence." He smiled. "I suppose they don't trust me."

"Well," she said, "you're in a bit of a spot. If you're telling me the truth." She looked at him as though she were ashamed. "I have to presume you're telling me the truth about not working for them. I wouldn't know what to do otherwise, I'm new at this."

"I'm in a bit of a spot, yes."

"We're going ahead, Frank. I'm going where I'm told. This place is going to blow up and it's *you* that better be out of it."

She went to a refrigerator in one of the closets, brought out a shard of ice wrapped in gauze and handed it to him. He held it under his nose and brushed at the congealing blood.

"God doesn't work through history, May. That's a delusion of the Western mind."

"Too metaphysical for me," she said. "I don't know how God works."

"The things people do don't add up to an edifying story.

There aren't any morals to this confusion we're living in. I mean, you can make yourself believe any sort of fable about it. They're all bullshit."

"Like love," she said.

"Yes. Like love."

Justin smiled. She was looking at the ocean.

"When I was a little girl I was riding my pony up along the wire one time—and I saw this thing coming down the road and I couldn't tell what it was. So I stopped and got down and watched and what I saw was an enormous house being pulled along by a truck. It was a big old farmhouse, Frank, it was set on a flatbed that took up the whole road and these old boys were pulling it along taking it somewhere else and all of them looking so tickled with what they were doing. Tickled at me watching them." She turned toward him and laughed; his heart rose up as he watched her. "I was so thrilled! I couldn't believe that men could move a house. It was like they were moving a mountain. It made me feel proud. It made me feel like people could do anything in the world if they put their mind and their strength to it." She looked at him amused. "You don't know what I mean, do you?"

"No," he said. He laughed himself. "I don't have a clue what you mean."

"We don't think much alike," she said. She shook her head. "God, that was crazy of us hopping into bed like that. Strangers. Like a couple of rabbits. My fault, I guess. Land, that was unconscious."

"I didn't think so," he said.

"You see, I don't have your faith in despair," Justin said. "I can't take comfort in it like you can."

He wet his handkerchief on the melting ice and threw the ice and the gauze into the GI can.

"It was a dishonest thing you did to me, Mr. Holliwell. You really ought to be ashamed." He saw her passing beyond him, out of reach, out of life.

"I'm sorry," he said. "But I'm not sorry."

"I believe everything you say," Justin told him. "I don't pretend to understand you though. Are you always going to be the way you are?"

He shrugged and she put out her hand and touched his face. He was surprised at the tenderness with which she touched him.

"I think despair and giving up are like liquor to you. You get high on it. But it's not for me, Frank. I don't have the temperament. I don't have the sophistication to bring it off."

When he started toward the door she came with him. She took hold of his hand for a moment and then let it go.

"We'll both have to explain your being here if anyone saw," she said. "We'll both have to think of lies."

"So you won't denounce me to the revolution?"

"No," she said. "I won't denounce you. I want you to come back when we're finished. I guarantee you won't know the place." She stopped and he stopped with her. "I'm trusting you now. Please tell me I'm doing right."

"You're doing right to trust me," he said. "I love you, don't I? I told you that."

"What a funny word," she said.

Holliwell learned that the Río de la Fe would bear no passengers that day. The boats had not come through from the city on the lake and in the tin-roofed offices of the steamship company there were not two who would agree as to the reason. A clerk from the offshore islands said the problem was paperwork. An Indian from the mountains said the river was bad that day. It was all in the hands of God, the Indian said.

The Vietnamese woman at the airlines office told Holliwell that there were no planes. She invited him to imagine there might be one on Thursday. He drove his jeep back to the hotel and found its precincts quiet; the spies and the contractors were in cover. He bought a bottle of light rum at the bar, went to his bungalow and drank himself insensible.

Sometime after dark a group of men came into his room to awaken him. There were three of them; they turned on his bedside lamp and shook him. In the warm lamplight he recognized Mr. Heath and Soyer. There was a Guardia officer with them, a short, broad-shouldered man with soft eyes.

"Hello, Holliwell," Mr. Heath said. "Sorry, but we've some work to do."

Holliwell swung his feet onto the floor. The three men who had come into his room watched him as he sat, blinking and nauseated, on the edge of his sweated mattress.

"Dress, will you?" Heath said. "We're going out."

Holliwell helped himself to some water from the pitcher on the night table and stood up. The Cuban took a tin of Anacin from his own pocket and offered the pills around. Holliwell took two.

"What's the difficulty?" he asked them as he put his shirt on. "Just," Heath said, "that the job's over where you're concerned."

"I don't know what you mean by the job."

"I should pack if I were you," Mr. Heath told him. "You won't be coming back here."

Holliwell discovered that he was still fairly drunk.

"Am I being turned out of the country?" he asked.

The Cuban answered him.

"You're in danger. We protect our friends. You are our friend, sir."

When he had packed his bag, he followed them outside; the clamor of night creatures was almost alarming. There was a Guardia jeep at the door.

"What about my bill?"

"Let's make it quick, Holliwell," Heath said. "There's a good fella."

Holliwell climbed into the rear seat; Heath got in beside him. The Cuban and the Guardia officer sat in front, the officer at the wheel. As they rolled past the main building, Holliwell saw that it was darkened, the tables stacked, the bar closed. When they made the road, a second Guardia jeep fell in behind them, carrying three men in helmets and camouflage fatigues. It carried a mount with a 7.62 machine gun.

"What's going on?" Holliwell asked Mr. Heath.

"Treason," Mr. Heath said, in a mock-heroic manner.

"I'm not sure what it has to do with me."

"Well, you'll have to be debriefed before you leave. Then we'll find out, won't we?"

On the way to town, they passed a Guardia roadblock which had established itself behind two wooden sawhorses and an *Aduana* sign. Two lines of young Guardia troopers crouched Indian fashion along the edges of the road, squinting into the jeep's headlights as it approached them. Seaward, a helicopter with a spotlight dodged between the beach and the reef line in figure-of-eight patterns, its light sweeping like a tentacle.

Along the riverfront of Puerto Alvarado there were half a dozen LCVMs tied up at the docks. The town itself appeared to be going dark although it was only just after seven; the Syrians were locking fast their shutters and the few small neon signs around the plaza were dimmed and the shops closed. The square itself was jammed with soldiers turned out for combat, standing in loose ranks or crouching on the grass. Above them, the cathedral was dark and unavailable behind its great oak door.

At the west end of the plaza, upwards of twenty trucks were parked in rows, and as Holliwell watched, new ones would pull up carrying yet more Guardia. The trucks would be coming from the airport or from some disembarkation point upriver. There were very few civilians on the street.

The jeep in which Holliwell rode pulled up in front of the Municipalidad, escorting jeep behind. As he stepped out, he saw that a crowd of women had gathered in front of the doors of the police station; a Guardia sergeant was addressing them in a low voice. Heath got out after Holliwell, then the Guardia officer and Mr. Soyer. A trooper ran across the street from the square, got behind the wheel of their jeep and drove it out of traffic. The escort jeep pulled out after him. It was all peculiarly efficient.

The crowd of women was blocking the doors of the police station and the sentries began, fairly gently, to clear a way for Holliwell and his party. The sergeant was telling the women that the people they inquired after were not to be found. They were town women of mixed blood for the most part and though it was hard to tell, they appeared to be mainly over thirty. Holliwell glanced over the crowd and recognized among them the young woman who had visited Justin that morning and whom he had taken for a Carib. She was staring at him and her stare was intense, its informing emotion uncertain. As far as he knew she had never seen him before but the look she gave him betrayed recognition. It was a troubled stare and trouble, he thought, was what it portended. The company he was in would not recommend him to associates of Justin.

There were more men on guard inside the police station; its spare outer office looked readied for a siege. Sandbags were stacked around the barred shuttered windows and the Guardia detachment on duty were in jungle fatigues and carried grenades on their belts. The noncom in charge saluted as Holliwell and his acquaintances came in. Holliwell reflected that he had taken a few too many Guardia salutes to be altogether uninvolved in Tecanecan history. The door to the street remained open behind them; their Guardia lieutenant was in a state of some agitation over someone he had seen outside. Holliwell thought it must be the young girl in braids.

Heath went back to see what the trouble was and the Guardia lieutenant pulled him outside.

"Happen to see anyone you know out here?" the Englishman called to Holliwell. Holliwell walked to the door and looked over the sentries' helmets at the dispersing group of women. He did not see her any longer. "No. I don't know many people here," he said.

"No?" Heath asked.

The Guardia officer jogged across the street to the square and out of Holliwell's sight. The sentries held the door open until he came back in, then bolted it down.

Holliwell followed them through the barricaded outer office and into a strange windowless room in the center of the building. The oddness of the room was disorienting and it made him even more uneasy. It had stone floors and damp walls of whitewashed brick, the roof was of corrugated metal over a netting of barbed wire that made it feel like a cage. There were two overbright institutional lights in green-painted housings at the center of the metal ceiling such as one might see on factory fences or prison yards. In one shadowed corner was a litter of what appeared to be electrical equipment—extension wires, hand generators and disused batteries lay in a cluster on the slimy floor. Looking more closely at the walls, he saw that there had once been windows along the two longer walls, but the window space and casements had been plastered over. Blackened chips of spackle lined the edges of the floor. There were two desks in the middle of the room—on one was a telephone.

The odd room smelled of mildew and disinfectant and of other things as well, familiar but unpleasant things which he could not quite identify. As soon as it struck him that the room was in fact the central patio of the building nailed down and sealed off from air and light, he realized that the dark stains on the stone floor were bloodstains.

Soyer had Holliwell's suitcase on one of the desks. He thrust a hand toward Holliwell's face and rubbed his fingers together.

"He'd like the key," Heath said helpfully.

"I hate to spoil his number," Holliwell said, "but he'll find it's open if he tries it." Holliwell was drunk and disgruntled but he was growing more and more fearful.

The Cuban looked at Holliwell and then at Heath. Heath had a soothing half smile.

His suitcase was indeed open and Mr. Soyer examined the contents deliberately. The contents were innocent enough; there were only toiletries, cigarettes and clothes. The clean clothes were neatly folded, the soiled ones in their hotel laundry bag. But Mr. Soyer took his time.

"You're impatient with us," Mr. Soyer said. "Anxious to be on your way. We understand."

"He's a bit pissed in the bargain," Heath said.

"Yes," Soyer said, affecting to sound the suitcase for false bottoms, feeling the lining, messing about with the laundry bag. "There is something—about our part of the world—that makes the North Americans—reach for a glass. Isn't there, Holliwell?"

"Could we have it straight, Soyer? Without the flourishes and games?"

Soyer closed the suitcase.

"Straight?" he asked. "Straight is how you would like it?" The man's eyes drifted to a point behind Holliwell's head. Holliwell remembered that the Guardia lieutenant was behind him.

"I don't think I want to talk to this man," Soyer said to Heath. "I find him crude and insolent." Heath grinned.

"In technology they are giants," the Guardia officer behind Holliwell said in Spanish, "but in culture—pygmies."

Mr. Heath spoke.

"Know what happened to Ocampo, Holliwell?"

"What?"

"He's dead."

"He was a friend of mine," Holliwell said after a moment. "I was very fond of him."

"This chap Cole you came into the country with—he's dead as well."

"Cole was just a reporter. There was no reason for anyone to kill him."

"Think not?"

"I told him not to go up to Tapa by himself," Holliwell said. "The guy was sort of unsound."

"Was he?" Heath asked. "He's sound enough now. But dead. We think someone may have mistaken him for you."

"There isn't," Holliwell said, "a reason for anyone to kill me either."

"I'm sure you're right," Heath said. "Eh, Miguel?"

"Next to certain," Soyer said.

"But the thing is, Holliwell—with Ocampo dead and Cole dead and you messing about with Mistress Feeney down coast —what the fuck is going on?"

"There's no mystery," Holliwell said. "Marty Nolan asked me to have a look at that mission when I came down here."

"You declined. Remember?"

"I declined. But I got curious. I'm an anthropologist, after all."

"And this was a field trip, was it, Professor? A sabbatical adventure?"

"Call it what you like," Holliwell said.

Soyer rendered his dull smile.

"Be careful, Professor," he said. "Be careful of what you allow us to call it. We may call it something you don't like."

"Ocampo also asked you to come down here," Heath said. "Do you mean to say he didn't tell you why?"

"He told me it was enough that I be seen to go. Those were his words. I was curious and I wanted to do him a favor to that extent."

Heath grunted unhappily.

"Damn it," Holliwell said, "I don't know quite why I came." He looked into Heath's wine-dark face. "Come on, Heath! People do such things, you know. You may live in a world of absolute calculation but I don't. For one thing I didn't expect to get down here for the goddamn . . ." But by the time he cut the word off it was too late. He became afraid, really afraid— for the first time. It seemed to him that he had nearly talked his way out of it and then lost it all at the very last. He was drunk and he had vainly imagined that truth was on his side—but of course there was no truth. There were only circumstances.

"The goddamn revolution," Heath said. "But you did. Sorry. And what you've been up to here, Holliwell—uncharitably interpreted—smacks of a double game."

The Guardia lieutenant came forward and stood in front of Holliwell; there was a look on his face that suggested acute physical pain, manfully subdued. He lit a cigar and tossed the match, almost by accident it seemed, at Holliwell's shirtfront. The extinguished match stayed there, resting in a crease. Holliwell did not brush it away.

"We're not in a position to extend charity," Soyer told him. "We interpret actions strictly. We're trying to be serious."

"It's like this, Holliwell," said Mr. Heath patiently. "While you're observing the situ-a-shon actu-well and thinking deep thoughts, people are fighting quite desperately over things they believe in. I hope you won't think I'm sentimental. But with you having all these moral adventures you can dine out on in the States—it's really very difficult to wish you well."

"But we do," Mr. Soyer said, "because you are North American and all the world loves you. We try to understand."

"And do we succeed?" Mr. Heath asked.

"*Claro que sí*," the Cuban said. "Indeed we do. We know our good neighbors the North American people who are allied with us for progress. We know their profound concern for international morality. Their sense of brotherhood. Their dedication to human rights. Sometimes we find them difficult to understand, we who are only what we are. But understand we must."

As Mr. Soyer concluded, he was unable to keep smiling.

"If you expected me to work with you," Holliwell said, "you should have taken me into your confidence."

"We couldn't, you see." Mr. Heath had a small metal flask half covered with worn leather. He took it from the side pocket of his dark lightweight jacket, shook it and drank from it. "We've had our fingers burned. They send some of you chaps down here—well honestly, it's frustrating. You speak with two voices, frankly. Makes it very hard going for us. I mean—whose side do you think we're on after all?"

"So," Soyer said, "we couldn't take you into our confidence. However, others did, am I right to think so? Sister Justin? We believe you know something about what she and her friends are doing tonight."

"I don't know anything about their plans," Holliwell said.

Mr. Soyer's jaw seemed to tighten with a little tremor. He turned to Heath. Heath sniffed and drummed his fingers on the desk top.

"Really, Holliwell, that's very difficult to believe."

Soyer moved closer to where Holliwell stood.

"Because we're so ready to understand, Professor—that's why we don't believe you. But I assure you, sir, that you'll tell us what you know."

The Guardia lieutenant spoke for the first time.

"We have to know where the nun will be," he said in Spanish. His air of stolid resolution was impressive, even daunting.

"I can't give you the answers you want," Holliwell said. "I don't know them."

Heath's eyes went out of focus and he looked away. Soyer was tapping his knuckles against his own forehead.

"Holliwell," he said, "not everyone will be alive in the morning. In Yanquiland it's true that no one dies. Here life is sordid."

"Sorry," Holliwell said.

"Sorry," Mr. Soyer repeated. "Sorry?" His pistol was out and he put the barrel gently against Holliwell's lips. "The next thing out of your mouth, you overfed son of seven tits, will be God's truth or I'm going to tear it out of your throat."

When Soyer withdrew the pistol, Holliwell took a cigarette out of his pocket and put it in his mouth. He realized from the taste that the cigarette was in backwards, filtered end out.

"Don't be a bloody fool, Holliwell," Heath shouted at him. "Get that fag out!"

Holliwell was glad to oblige as though that were the only problem.

"He thinks he's a hero," Heath said. "He thinks he's at the fucking matinee." He shook his head in disappointment. "Leave us together, Miguel, there's a good fella."

"He's going to tell me about that hole he puts it into," Soyer said.

"In the interests of time," Heath said to Soyer. "As a favor."

Soyer wiped his forehead, swallowed hard and went out of the peculiar room. The lieutenant followed him.

When he was alone with Holliwell, Heath took out his flask, shook it and put it on the desk with the phone.

"Give it up, chum," he said. "Everybody talks."

"Do you really think I'm party to all the other side's secrets?" Holliwell asked. "Do you think she gave me their order of battle?"

"You don't understand the situation," Heath said, "so I'll explain. I'll do it clearly if I can but I'll only do it once. Soyer is going to kill you if you don't help him. The only reason he hasn't already is that he's afraid he'll get in trouble with his higher-ups and his higher-ups are basically your government. Plus he doesn't trust me not to tell what I see—but he's wrong about that. I'd cover for him absolutely. Clear so far?"

"Yes," Holliwell said.

"Good. You, Holliwell—so far as we're concerned—are a source. Soyer is for practical purposes your case agent. He has a request from the authorities of the host country—namely Lieutenant Campos—concerning the activities of Sister Whatsit and he wants to comply with it. Understand, please, that no one is in any doubt about what she's up to or the people she's tied in with. Nor are we wondering where to find her—I'm sure she'll be at the mission wrapping bandages for the boyos and looking marvelous. However, since she and the priest are U.S. citizens and the mission is an American entity, Soyer is involved directly and so are you. With all you Yankees involved we have to approach the situation in a rather cumbersome bureaucratic fashion. You are paying attention, aren't you, Holliwell?"

"I'm paying attention."

"War is hell as I'm sure you know. Things have their own momentum. In the face of all this promiscuity we need a coherent version of events that may someday find its way into someone's files. Some bloody politician or other asks what happened in Tecan at such and such a time. We say what happened is this—blah blah blah. We say what happened is: Soyer debriefed Holliwell. Holliwell fingered Justin and her mission. Soyer passed the information as requested to the friendly service of the host country. Follow? Soyer needs this chain of circumstance. He wants, as you say, to *be seen* to do it this way. Appearances if you like. It's part of his job."

"It's supposed to be me that tells him what he already knows, is that it?"

"That's it. To his mind that's what you're here for, and as we know, he hates your guts. He wants to see you shop her."

"It's foolish of him to push people that far," Holliwell said.

"That may be, cock, but don't tell me. And for Christ's sake don't tell him." Heath shook the flask again and, this time, drank.

"What happens to her then?"

"She'll be expelled. At least she will if we can get to her before Campos does. She's better off with us, you know."

"Are you telling me you'll protect her from Campos?"

"Why not? Soyer works for your government. I should think they'd rather not have a dead nun on their hands after the fact. And from our point of view we'd be well pleased to talk to her. We're trying to get the big picture pieced together and it's not easy from here. We don't have to tell the Tecs everything we find out."

"What if she doesn't want to talk to you? I don't think it's likely she will."

"Think I'm going to put a sister of mercy to the third degree at the risk of my immortal soul? Why, Holliwell, I wouldn't know how to start."

"I think you would. So would your friend."

"We won't harm her, Holliwell. Come on, man, it's her best bet. And it's your only bet because you won't leave here alive if you don't do it. You're ours now."

"How do I know you won't feed her to the lieutenant?"

"It would be more convenient not to. Anyhow it won't matter much to you if you're pushing up daisies. Look, Holliwell," Heath said, "we're just asking you to do a little more of what you've been doing all along. Preserve the forms, eh?"

"Will you give me your word that she won't be harmed?"

"My word?" Mr. Heath asked. He laughed a little but he looked rather sad. "No one's ever asked me for *my word* before. But if you want to put it like that—sure, Holliwell. We'll look after her."

"All right," Holliwell said.

"Ah," Heath said. "Good lad."

He offered Holliwell a drink from his flask and Holliwell was happy to have it.

Then Heath summoned Soyer and Campos back into the room and Holliwell explained to Soyer that he had discussed local political issues with Sister Justin Feeney of the Devotionist mission at Las Ruinas and that she had admitted to him her involvement in a conspiracy against the stability and integrity of the Republic.

Soyer listened cheerfully; his eyes were moist and his questions were soft and polite. He translated the answers for Lieutenant Campos, who listened impatiently.

"What else can you tell me, Professor?" Soyer asked after Holliwell had made his deposition. "Surely she's told you her hopes and dreams? What does she understand will happen in the country as a whole?"

"She doesn't know any of that," Holliwell said. "She's only a nurse. She wants to be where she's needed."

Having said that much, he glanced uneasily at Campos. The lieutenant's lips were rolled back over his white teeth.

"Pure," Soyer said. "Eh, Holliwell?"

"Yes," Holliwell said.

Soyer smiled broadly.

"That's good, Professor. And it's very good of you to share with us. I think your only problem in life is that you can't recognize your friends. We are your friends here—and you betray us."

Holliwell took a cigarette from the pack and put it in his mouth, correctly this time. Soyer lit it for him.

"We do your dirty work here, gringo. When you go through attacks of cowardice and remorse, it's we who pay, not you. One day if you keep up this way your enemies will put your entire fatuous country to sleep and there won't be many tears, believe me."

Holliwell looked at the cigarette between his fingers.

"Rest assured," Soyer said, "that it's not for you I'm fighting. I'm not such a fool as that. It's for my country—and the bad of it is that we have to depend on you. A nation of betrayers," he said to Heath. "Without pride. Whiners. I hate them all."

Heath finished off the contents of his flask. He winced afterwards as though the liquor hurt him inside.

"I don't know about that," he said. "All kinds in every country. All the same, I do remember that a chap I knew in the army used to say—When you've heard what a Yank has to say in the first five minutes, you've heard everything he'll say the rest of his life."

Soyer was only half listening; he snorted happily.

"Garrulous. Like this professor." He stood in front of Holliwell; he was about an inch shorter, a tall man. "So, Professor, want to give me an *abrazo* now? The Americans," he told Heath, "love most of all to give *abrazos*. They—" Holliwell threw his cigarette in Soyer's face and struck him above the mouth with a straight-armed right. In a second, Heath and the lieutenant had pinned him. The lieutenant had the strength of a weight lifter; Holliwell's arm went numb in his grasp but the shoulder to which it was joined hurt quite a lot.

He was pleased to see that Mr. Soyer had stopped smiling. Mr. Soyer was several feet away now, his lip bloody and his face pale. But he held a gun in his hand that was pointed at Holliwell.

"Steady on, Miguel," Heath said.

Holliwell immediately regretted his rashness. He watched the gun in the Cuban's hand as the man walked toward him again. If he was not shot, he thought, he would be struck across the face with the gun, and hitting Soyer was not nearly satisfying enough to buy that. But Soyer did not hit him.

"He wants to act like a man," the Cuban explained. "Too late, Holliwell," he said, putting the gun away. He touched his swollen lip. "Too late for that."

"By Christ," Heath said disgustedly, "you're a bloody fool, Prof. You're asking for it, you know." They let go of him.

"I'm not offended by his bad temper," Soyer said. "He's going to take a ride with me. That's right, Holliwell," he said. "We're going out to the mission, you and I together, and we'll bring in Sister Justin. Then you can explain yourself to her as you have to me."

Soyer and Campos went out again—Campos to communicate with his force at the mission, Soyer to clean up. Mr. Heath looked morose.

"Very foolish of you, Holliwell. Mind you, he was provoking. But very foolish all the same."

"Of course," Holliwell said.

"You're in luck, you know. We may get your friend out of the shit. Suppose you hadn't run into us?"

"Then who knows," Holliwell said.

"The evening's business won't be pleasant for either of you. But you'll really be better off."

"Maybe I should be grateful."

"You should," Heath said. "One day you will be."

There was a small dry food stain on the sleeve of his dark cotton jacket. He began to chip it away with his fingernail.

"Miguel can't help feeling the way he does, you know. He's lived out some bad history and he's bitter. Actually he's not bad as these fellas go."

"What about you?"

Heath smiled.

"Oh me. I'm just standing my lonely vigil. The watch on the Rhine."

"This is a bit far-flung for Six, isn't it?"

"Six? I'm not Six, Holliwell. Well, not really. Not that I mind making my services available to the British taxpayer. Or the U.S. taxpayer. But I work for Investors Security International. We in turn work for the corporations that own land here. It's a very large investment that's under consideration on this coast, converting to tourism and so forth. Lot of money's been paid out. They want to know what's going on, eh? If we can help them maintain a favorable environment for their business, we do it. Nothing wrong with that, is there?"

"You enjoy it so much," Holliwell said, "it must be all right."

"That's exactly the way I see it. I do like my work, you know. Now and again I can right a few wrongs. Make a little dent in our far from perfect old world."

"Tell me about your friends Buddy and Olga. Are they helping you straighten things out?"

Heath laughed silently, in the way of someone caught out in guilty pleasure.

"Oh, they're a project of mine. My next project—after you and the sister. They're in the way of business for me because they've got themselves a local partner and bought a thousand hectares just north of here. That sort of people always has money, eh, Holliwell?" He shook his head and his faded flannel eyes came alive slightly. "But I'd go after them on my own time, if I had to. They'll come to grief with me, don't worry. I won't have people like that about, chum—not in my bailiwick. Not running free."

"It's an interesting life you lead."

Heath slipped away from the desk where he had been leaning and walked toward the door to the outer office. "I was never for the quiet life," he said. "Life in the stockbroker belt was not for the likes of me. But never mind." He stood in the open doorway looking out; the noise of cartridge clips being loaded and the cackle of a shortwave sounded from the adjoining space. "They'll want you shortly," he told Holliwell.

Holliwell stayed by the desk looking down at the black unmarked telephone that rested on it.

"You see," Heath said, "I'm the wrath of God in my tiny way. I don't go seeking out the misguided and the perverse, not at all. Those afflicted find me. I'm the shark on the bottom of the lagoon. You have to sink a damn long way before you get to me. When you do, I'm waiting."

"That's very good," Holliwell said. "But don't you think your clients may be out of luck with their investment here?"

"Very possibly. Still, they can't say we didn't try, can they?"

"No, they can't."

"It's a war, Holliwell. Goes on all over the world. And, I suppose, in the long run the other side will win it. When they do, like all winners, they'll find that things aren't the way they'd planned and it didn't turn out quite right. Then in a thousand years it'll all be ancient history if there's anyone to read it." Mr. Heath pulled a long face. "But," he said, "am I downhearted? No! The wicked flee when no man pursueth but the righteous are bold, Holliwell."

He stood with Soyer on the colonnaded sidewalk in front of the Municipalidad, waiting for the dispatch of a jeep to take them up the coast. Military runners went back and forth between the Guardia station and the troop formations drawn up in the darkness of the square. The only lights to be seen in town now were the headlights of military vehicles and the yellow-faced flashlights of the Guardia MPs who were directing the traffic.

Around the plaza itself, the troops awaited their orders in an uncanny silence that was broken only by the shouted instructions of an officer or the sullen, deep-throated *uno-dos-tres* of a platoon sounding off by number. From time to time one could hear the rhythmic tramp of a rifle squad moving at the double, as units separated themselves from the main body of troops to take their places in one of the trucks that were parked by the dozen in front of the cathedral steps. There were mounted troops as well; Holliwell could not see them but he could hear the clatter of shod horses' hooves on the stones of Alvarado's single paved street. Officers in braided high-crowned caps were appearing now, exchanging *abrazos* in the street—and a few civilians in *guayaberas* who looked like heroin dealers from the Bronx. The officers and their civilian associates seemed elated. None of them paid any attention to Soyer or Holliwell.

This tight deployment of many soldiers in a small closed space made Holliwell uneasy; his uneasiness was the result of previous conditioning. For the moment the fortunes of the Guardia Nacional were Holliwell's fortunes—he had a side at last. He was fairly certain that from somewhere in the darkness beyond the occupied square he was being watched. He thought of the girl with braided hair and of the stare she had fixed upon him. From time to time he would see the same stare quicken in the eyes of a passing Guardia private; always it would fade when he met it, to be replaced by blankness, *nada*—or a guilty smile.

Presently two jeeps pulled up at the sidewalk where Holliwell and Soyer waited. Campos was in the lead jeep beside the driver; the escort carried four troopers and a 7.62. When Holliwell climbed into the rear seat, Soyer walked around to the passenger side for a minute's guarded conversation with the lieutenant, then swung in beside Holliwell.

"Your nun is in her nunnery," Soyer told him. "Campos has the place surrounded by Guardia but they'll wait for us in deference to your nationality." He took an automatic rifle from the rack behind the front seat and cradled the stock on his knee.

"You're responsible for her," Holliwell said.

"No," said Soyer. "You are."

The jeeps started up; a few deserted corners turned and they were climbing the tangled hill over the river. The road narrowed and descended into mangrove swamp and they could hear the sound of the ocean over their engines. Clear of the swamp they hit the beach strip. The darkness beyond their headlights was scented and absolute.

When they had driven for about twenty minutes, Holliwell found himself listening to the sound of a motorcycle somewhere ahead of them. The machine seemed to be holding a constant distance, leading them at their own speed. He began to sense the phantoms of Route Three, that paragon of war trails through night's jungle. The escort jeep behind them followed close. Too close, Holliwell thought. At night in the jungle one always had a side to be on.

The report of the first mortar was so inevitable that Holliwell failed, in the first seconds, to take note of it. It had struck a good distance inland, far enough so that the charge echoed in the folds of the mountain wall. There was a second, then another, then the rattle of a machine gun—three long bursts. From a different quarter altogether came the single-minded *wack wack wack* of a rifleman with a target. The firing came in waves of varying frequency but once it started it did not stop. None of it was very close by. Through it all, Holliwell could hear the steady drone of the motorcycle ahead.

He turned toward Soyer but could not see his face for the darkness, only that the Cuban had drawn his rifle closer and that his right hand rested over the trigger housing. Lieutenant Campos turned around in the front seat as though he were about to consult with Soyer, but then turned back again to face the road in silence. Holliwell, behind the driver, had sobered to a state of tortured alert. The dreadful visit they were about had receded from his mind; he stared into the shifting dark beside the road as though he could force its secrets to his senses. He noticed that the motorcycle preceding them was no longer to be heard.

As soon as he saw the mangrove log loom across the road at the extent of the headlights' scan he knew exactly what would come. The log blocked the road at the neck of a curve; it had never been there before. Thinking back on it just afterwards, he would convulse in horror at the time he allowed to pass between his first sighting of the barrier and his leap into darkness. But in fact there had not been much; he was rolling on the packed sand and crawling for cover well before the two jeeps pulled up short and the machine guns opened up from the bend and from the inland side of the road approaching it.

The ambush had the form of an L, as he had somehow known it would. The L's short horizontal bar enclosed the turn parallel with the barricade, the vertical bar lined the dozen feet or so in which the vehicles would have to decelerate. The gunners had nothing but time, Holliwell thought, frantically elbowing his way over the soft sand. They would have opened up before the tires stopped rolling; before them, two excellent Detroit jeeps, packed together immobile and neatly defined in their own light like a pair of squid cooked in the ink.

There was fuck-all cover on the open beach. Pressing himself into the contours of the sand he listened wild-eyed to the devouring enfilade, the shells ringing on metal, the screams. There was no moon, the stars were faint and cold in a sky ablaze with lights and colors from behind his own eyes. In that hallucinatory darkness, he could not tell sea from shoreline or even distinguish the outline of palm groves. It seemed to him, when he thought over the instants just past, that at least one other passenger had jumped for it—it would have been seconds after his own dive. Whoever it was, if he had escaped, would be with him in the darkness now, out between the ocean and the hostiles.

The shooting on the road had stopped and he raised his head to look over his shoulder. One of the jeeps was burning; he saw a figure outlined for a moment against the flames. Men were laughing, speaking in excited voices. Two short bursts sounded—they were not taking prisoners that evening. Then the voices grew fainter as the ambush party retired, inland, toward the higher ground.

Holliwell crawled a little farther from the road and then stood up cautiously. He was about fifteen yards from the water's edge. For a moment he stood still and listened hard— but he could hear no movement nearby, only the small waves laving the shore and the intermittent gunfire. He was alone and lost, in utter darkness without friend or faction. It was a frightening place—the point he had been working toward since the day he had come south. It was his natural, self-appointed place.

He hunkered down by the water's edge and tried to decide on a course. He could not go back to town, both sides would be hunting him there, and now that there was blood upon the ground, explanations would not be suffered nor bargains struck. He might try to hide in the bush, where there were tiny plantation villages. But that would be unwise, he thought. They would know him for a survivor of the ambush. He would go the way of Cole.

At last he decided that he would walk to the mission. It

seemed to him he had some claim on companionship there. He would tell her what had happened if he reached her in time, and if she could not or would not help him and he remained free—he might somehow lose himself among the other foreigners scavenging in the ruins there. He struck out along the shoreline.

He would not remember how long he walked before he came to the buildings at Las Ruinas. They had arranged hurricane lamps on the front steps in the form of a cross and these lights were the first he had seen since leaving Alvarado. He had followed the faint broiling glow of the tame surf, wetting his shoes, sinking, at places, to the calf in soft sand. On his left, the dark ocean played out its infinity of time; inland, men played out their lives in a less patient darkness. Where he walked was no-man's-land. Sometimes he felt free; at other times fear overcame him, waves of fear, congruous with the rise and fall of firing. He stopped only once—to watch two helicopters swing in tandem along the mountain slope, made visible for a moment in their searchlights.

In the cover of the mission boathouse, he stopped and tried to spy out the state of things. Thin lines of light showed behind the fastened shutters of the dispensary wing but the rest of the building was dark beyond the span of lamps along the stairs. He could hear voices and laboring footsteps on the veranda. The arc of a tossed cigarette appeared for a second at the window of the priest's apartment. There were two dark pickup trucks parked along the road out front.

He moved away from the boathouse and had started to advance along the beach when he saw two dead men at the water's edge. One lay face up with his arms outstretched as though he had rolled off the dock; his chest was destroyed. The other was on his knees, a bloodied face half buried in sand. The two dead men wore the helmets and camouflage fatigues of the Guardia. Holliwell paused for a moment and then walked on. He would be visible from the building now. He took the chance.

Shadows appeared suddenly from the tree line by the mission garden. Someone shouted. A burst of machine-gun fire exploded from the edge of the veranda and he threw himself to the sand. The firing was in his direction but aimed high. Armed men were advancing from the woods around the garden, but they were civilians, he saw, not Guardia.

"May!" he shouted. He could feel a line of guns turn on him.

A lone man in dark slacks walked from the road and across the beach toward him.

"That you, Holliwell?" the man asked. It was Father Egan.

"Yes, it's me."

"You shouldn't be here," the priest said.

Holliwell stood up and brushed the sand from his shirt.

"Want to talk with the boss?" Egan asked. "Come on."

As he walked with Egan to the mission steps, sentries tracked him with their weapons. On the steps themselves, men in Guardia uniforms emerged from the darkness of the veranda, carrying cardboard boxes. They were unarmed and without helmets; thus dispossessed, they did not seem to be Guardia any longer but only frightened young Indians. They carried their burdens in silence, moving carefully through the cruciform arrangement of lamps to stack the cardboard boxes in the parked trucks.

Holliwell looked up through the lamps' glare and saw Justin at the top of the steps. Her hands were thrust in the pockets of her white smock; he could not quite see her face. For the first time since he had met her she seemed at ease. After a moment she came down to him.

"What happened?"

"They took me out of the hotel about seven o'clock. To the *justicia*. They have thousands of troops in Alvarado." He brushed a loose hand toward the invisible mountains. "They've got choppers."

"I know," she said. She turned partly away, pivoting on a hip, her hands still in her pockets. He understood that she would not want to face him now and be undone, and have her pride of battle spoiled by intimacy with him, thoughts of the morning. "How did you get away?"

"We were coming . . . they were coming out to get you. We were ambushed."

"Campos?" she asked.

"He was there. I think they got him."

She gave a whispered gasp. There was a roll of automatic fire from the direction of town.

"I tried to get out," Holliwell said. "Alvarado was closed down by noon. They just took me in."

"You talked to them."

"I was under some compulsion. I tried to make a deal with them. They told me you wouldn't be hurt."

"You talked to them." There were men with guns watching them from both sides of the building as they spoke. Justin sighed and put her foot on the bottom step. "Oh, Frank. You betrayed me then, didn't you?"

"I don't know," Holliwell said. "I didn't think so."

"But you did," she said calmly. "Imagine not knowing."

"If you'd been there you might think better of me. Of course, it hardly matters now."

"Doesn't it matter to you?"

"What matters to me isn't important," he said.

He was suddenly impatient with her. Watching her stand cool and brave amid her war, he had been awed and moved at the measure of her courage and her delusion. He felt envy and admiration and love for her. He considered the tremor of concern he detected in her voice as she asked after his conscience unworthy of the moment.

"When I decide what happened," he said, "I'll decide to live with it."

Apparently it was his fate to witness popular wars; Vietnam had been a popular war among his radical friends. As a witness to that popular war he had seen people on both sides act bravely and have their moments. Popular wars, thrilling as they might be to radicals, were quite as shitty as everything else but like certain thrilling, unperfected operas—like everything else, in fact—they had their moments. People's moments did not last long.

"You can't stay here," she told him. "We're pulling out of here when we get the trucks loaded."

"I can't go back. I was seen at the *justicia* by your friends."

"My friends," she said, "my friends will be where we're going."

"I hope so, May, for your sake. The government's out in force here and you may not win this round. They claim you're surrounded."

She had started up the steps, Holliwell following. As she stooped to pick up one of the hurricane lamps she glanced at him over her shoulder; on her face in the flickering light was the immanence of a smile.

"We were never surrounded. We disarmed the Guardia force that came out." She raised her chin toward the defanged troopers loading the trucks. "We killed some," she said when she had turned away.

In the dispensary, the lights were on behind the shutters. Beds had been crowded to one end of the room; against two of the walls sat a dozen or so more men in Guardia fatigues. Across the long room, two black Caribs in sport shirts and Guardia helmets watched the prisoners with Uzis across their knees.

The bed in which Holliwell and Justin had made their gesture at love was occupied by a dark, hard-faced young man who was sitting up in it, smoking. His leg was wrapped in clean bandages, there was an anchor tattoo on his left arm. Father Egan, who had followed them up, sat down on the foot of the young man's bed. Holliwell looked about the room and his gaze fell on two small bottles of the medicinal brandy which were under the bed behind Egan's feet. Happily and without ceremony, he reached down past the priest's soiled, sandaled feet to grab them. Father Egan sighed.

He opened one of the brandy bottles and put the second in his trousers pocket. Justin watched him drink. He looked back at her, thinking to see her look away. He remembered now how her eyes had no edge to them, behind them she was naked.

"Well," he said, when he had finished drinking, "a terrible beauty is born."

She held his look steadily, then her sober fateful expression broke into a bright young smile, unexpected and unashamed.

"Isn't it something?" she said.

"Yes, it is."

"What am I supposed to do with you now?" she asked. "You're in it."

"I guess that's not your problem. I'm not in it with you."

"You'll just have to keep talking, won't you? Explaining yourself."

"If I had explanations left," Holliwell said, "I would make all of them to you. If it mattered."

"And I would believe them, Frank. You could get me to believe them all, if it mattered. But I'm the only one who would."

"I'm going to lose another war all by myself," he said. "This is the second."

Justin looked at the floor while he emptied the brandy
bottle. Seconds passed before she spoke.

"You're a good loser," she said. "You're a lucky man.
You'll live longer than you deserve if you help me out."

"So now we're tough guys."

"That's right," she said, and smiled a little. Her smiles were
like mercy. "We have to be tough guys now. I'm going to give
you the mission's boat. This kid"—she nodded toward the
wounded young man—"is named Pablo and he's American."
Pablo in the bed mumbled something inaudible and tried to
smile. "I want you to get him down to the boat and get the
two of you out to sea. Get clear of the coast before daylight."

Holliwell looked at the young man on the bed and back at
Justin.

"Would we really have a chance?"

"I think you'd have a very good chance," she said.

Pablo stirred himself.

"That's the truth," he said. "The weather's nothing but
beautiful. I could get a good sound boat mostly to Florida."

"Inside of a day," Justin said, "you should run across one
of the steamers coming up from the canal. We can see them
right off the beach here every day of the week. If you meet
rough weather you can turn south and if you still have
enough gas you might make Limón in Costa Rica."

"I don't have much choice, do I?"

"I don't think so, Frank. You're lucky. You'll make it."

"Me, too," Pablo said. "Always been."

"Christ," Holliwell said. He glanced at the priest at the foot
of Pablo's bed. "What about you, Father?"

"I'm not as lucky as you two. Anyway I'm staying here."

"It's the best thing, Frank. I was going to leave Pablo with
Charlie but it'll be better for both of them if he goes with
you."

"All right," Holliwell said. "Let's do it."

While the Caribs stared their prisoners down, Justin and
Holliwell set about gathering such supplies as would be
needed for the passage out to sea. In the kitchen they loaded a
crate with fruit: pineapples, papayas, a few dozen lemons.
Half the canned food left in the larders went in with it,
mainly the corned beef and beans on which Egan subsisted.
They took turns laboring over the kitchen pump, bringing up

enough water to fill a fifty-liter drum. When they had enough of everything, they pressed two of the captured troopers into service to help them carry the lot to the boathouse; one of the rebel gunmen posted on the road went along as escort. The small procession marched across the beach, past the corpses of the slain Guardia men and onto the small dock. With Holliwell standing in the whaler, they passed the provisions along hand to hand, feeling out each load from each other's arms in nearly complete darkness. From the open boathouse, they took the last half-filled drum of gasoline, some kerosene, a plastic funnel.

When they got back to the road, the two pickup trucks stood loaded and the insurrectionist commander was bringing his men in from the surrounding woods to gather along the road. The commander was a bookkeeper in the employ of an Alvarado brothel and he was still in shock as a result of his earlier successful skirmish with the Guardia. His eyes were glazed with nervous fatigue, he continually ran his hand across his face in the manner of one disoriented. In fact his sense of reality had been subverted by the action; his upbringing had been gentle by the standards of Tecan and his only prior experience of massed weaponry and its effects had been at the cinema. He did not know what to make of Holliwell and consequently ignored him. The bookkeeper was a short heavy young man with a jowly spoiled-child's face. Holliwell found him sympathetic.

As Holliwell stood by, he told Justin that there was not room in the trucks for his men, the medical supplies and the prisoners together. Justin suggested that the prisoners would have to walk. This made the bookkeeper unhappy; he had spoken eloquently to them and they had listened to him and enlisted under his command and he did not want to lose them. Nothing of the sort had ever happened to him before. Listening in, Holliwell envied him too. He had had a moment.

Justin and the bookkeeper agreed that it was necessary to abandon the mission now. The volume of fire from the direction of town seemed to have decreased but it was heavier in the hills behind them. And there was heavy firing now to the south, where there had been little before. It was the direction in which they were headed.

They went upstairs to the dispensary and the bookkeeper

began to address his huddled prisoners. He told them what his job had been until the day before and how never before had he known who he was, but in the revolution he had found his freedom as they would find theirs. He hoped that they would keep faith with him and take their place in the revolution even though it meant they would have to walk to it and surrender all over again. If he were an evil man like their officers, he told them, he might simply have killed them. If he had been captured by them, he pointed out, they would certainly have been ordered to kill him and would have done so under compulsion. Saying so much, the bookkeeper seemed hardly to believe it, although it was true enough. He was an eloquent young man. He had been overqualified as a brothel's bookkeeper but one often met overqualified people in that part of the world.

While Justin went off to get a reserve of clean bandages and some antibiotics for Pablo, Holliwell walked to the young man's bedside to see who it was he would be sharing an open boat with. Father Egan was still sitting at the foot of the bed.

"You two haven't really met, have you? This is Holliwell, Pablo. He's an anthropologist. And this is Pablo."

"How're you feeling, Pablo?" Holliwell asked.

"Could be better," Pablo said. Holliwell came to the disturbing conclusion that he was being sized up for a mark. It occurred to him that Pablo might not even realize what he was about, that it was simply his manner. "What you doin' in this here shithole, cousin?"

"I was doing a study," Holliwell said.

Pablo laughed, after a fashion. "Yeah?"

Holliwell walked away and met Justin halfway across the room, carrying Pablo's medicine.

"Who is this kid?" he asked her.

"Nobody exactly knows. Charlie Egan says the law's after him and that's good enough for me. He's probably off a boat."

Holliwell said nothing.

He and Justin lifted the young man out of bed and stood him on his feet as the Indian prisoners and the bookkeeper watched. When he was upright, the young man turned to Father Egan.

"You think it's gonna be all right?" he asked the priest. Holliwell was touched.

"Yes, it'll be all right, Pablo. It'll always be all right for you."

Pablo smiled; he looked at Justin and Holliwell with what Holliwell would have sworn was triumphant malice. Then his features clouded.

"Where's my knife?" he demanded.

Father Egan reached under the bedclothes to withdraw a huge diver's knife in a plastic sheath.

Pablo took it from him.

"You gotta have a knife, right? To cut stuff with."

"Want me to carry it?" Holliwell asked.

"That's all right," Pablo said, and took it.

The three of them walked down to the boat. From time to time, Pablo put his hand on Holliwell's shoulder and leaned his weight on it. Behind them, the trucks started their engines. The bookkeeper and his prisoners descended from the dispensary, picking up the hurricane lamps as they came.

Holliwell and Justin helped Pablo down into the whaler. He crawled to the bow and worked the forward seat out of the bulkheads and lay down on a damp tarp.

"Can you . . . run it?" Justin asked Holliwell.

"Sure."

"There's a compass in it for what that's worth. Keep to the right going out. There are reefs."

"Do you think I betrayed you?" Holliwell asked her. "I didn't mean it to be like that."

"I'm sure you didn't. I know you didn't. Like you said, it doesn't matter." She touched him very lightly on the arm. "Who knows where we're both going?"

"Ill met," he said.

"I have no regrets now. Not now."

"Goodbye. Love."

"Oh, Frank," she said quickly, as though she were embarrassed. She turned away and he could hardly hear her. "Sure. Goodbye, Frank."

When he started up the engine, he tried to watch her walk off, but the darkness swallowed her at once. Someone called to her, the headlights of the pickup trucks went on.

As he nosed the boat away from the dock, he thought of the reefs and swallowed hard. He could feel the young man, Pablo, watching him from the bow, seeing, somehow, through the darkness.

In the gathering heat of day, they brought May Feeney to the *justicia*. She rode beside a Guardia lieutenant with fair, freckled skin, light blue eyes and a tweedy brown moustache. The lieutenant said not a word to her but for the whole dreadful length of the ride he kept his hand under her skirt. Poking, idling there. She could only sit as far away from him as there was space in the seat and she kept her eyes down, from shame and so as not to see him.

In the square where everyone had come to see the waxen Christ, the vultures had come down from the treetops and were hopping delicately about the walks and lawns. There was a long line of them on the roof of the Municipalidad. They moved their necks from side to side like mechanical creatures to fix their bright bead eyes in turn on every aspect of the scene below. But the streets and the square were deserted now.

The blue-eyed lieutenant conducted her past the ocher columns and under the flattened arch surmounted with the seal of the Republic. His demeanor was formal; his hand on her arm was different, his touch neither gallant nor brutal but strangely correct. It was as though to touch her any place but where he had in the car was distasteful to him.

Inside the Guardia's building, a half dozen corporals in fatigues were listening to the radio. An actor was addressing the nation, encouraging its continuing struggle for liberty. The Communist aggressor was defeated, he assured it, and was fleeing before the Guardia's victorious arms, wielded in the name of civilization and Christianity. The Guardia corporals watched May come in; all of them had moustaches, which in the mountains were an emblem of white blood. Some smiled, others seemed uninterested.

They went beyond the outer office into a long room with bricked-over windows and a bad smell. Campos was there. She had known when they took her that he would be waiting somewhere.

"You shudder," he said.

It was true. Her knees trembled. She could feel the blood leave her face. Her heart turned.

"I had her up the ass, so you're too late," the blue-eyed officer said. He was merry. He did a business with his finger, flourishing it under his nose, thrusting it before Campos. He laughed and May thought it odd to hear a human laugh and to be so utterly outside the laughter, as excluded from the impulse that quickened it as the lizards on the wall.

Then Campos touched her under the elbow, rather as the other officer had done, and drew her to an unpainted door that opened to a shed and a courtyard. Before her were lines of coffined dead in the uniform of the Guardia and beyond them, in the courtyard, the bodies of peasants stacked in piles, swelling in the sun, stinking and beset with flies. One of the bodies was that of the bookkeeper who had commanded for a while. She turned away.

"The dead," he told her. "On account of you."

As hard as she could, she tried to make herself speak, to shout, to answer, to give him the lie. But at the sight of the corpses she was so undone and her fear of him so great that she could not utter a sound at first. When she tried too hard, a sob broke from her throat and echoed in the stone room. She hated to hear it. It dishonored her. Yet she needed to hear it—a token of herself, a sound—even if it was her own crying. It was all of her that was there. The rest was Enemy. The blue-eyed officer threw back his head and softly made the howl of a wolf, in mockery of her. Then he went out and she was alone with Campos.

The sound of the radio carried through, very faintly, from the outer office. It seemed to catch Campos' attention for a moment; he walked to the door that led to that office and opened it, standing with his head cocked to hear an exalted female voice complete an announcement. Then he closed the door and walked back to where she stood. She saw now what he plainly was and why she had always been so afraid of him. She saw that she would be spared nothing and that she must try to be ready.

When he began, she thought: I must do this, I must finish this, not him. She cast the compassing of her mind as high and wide as she could reach toward strength and mercy. She cried because, at first, there was nothing at all. Only the blows falling.

Though he beat her beyond fear, she kept trying. Until she was awash in all the shameful juices of living and she still kept on. Though she forgot in time who he was and what the pain was about she was able to think of the tears, the blood, and mucus and loose teeth in her mouth: these are not bad things, these are just me and I'm all right.

His electricity was shaking her loose of her bones. She never worried about screaming. The shocks blinded her, they were going to kill her.

"My dad would fix you, you sucker," she said.

He had hurt her head somehow and closed off light. She knew it would not get better and that she would never come back. She reached out as she had to the unresponding sea in the empty afternoons of the past months and still there was nothing and she cried. She could only live between shocks and the time was so precious. She was no hero.

Sometimes the best I'm capable of, she told him, is a little quiet probity. Tried to tell him.

Once she saw her fingers moving and she knew the electricity must be moving them. Her ring was gone. Then something began to come and she did not recognize it. She asked herself what it was when she had the time, in between. Whether it was inside or out there. Whatever it was, there was hardly anything else. It was greater than electricity and electricity was strong. It was stronger than the strong, stronger than love. It seemed as though it might be love. She was too weak to bear it. Too tired for it.

You after all? Outside, outside, round and about. Disappearing stranger, trickster. Christ, she thought, so far. Far from where?

But why always so far?

"Por qué?" she asked. There was a guy yelling.

Always so far away. You. Always so hard on the kid here, making me be me right down the line. You old destiny. You of Jacob, you of Isaac, of Esau.

Let it be you after all. Whose after all I am. For whom I was nailed.

So she said to Campos: "Behold the handmaid of the Lord."

* * *

At dawn Tecan was only a wall of richly green mountains. Holliwell had never seen her in that aspect. The sight aroused in him something that was, against reason, like desire.

Lighted ships had been passing in sight of them all during the night, but never close enough to threaten or tempt them to shout in hope of rescue. Holliwell had found a flashlight in a gear locker beside the fuel tank and tried to signal; there had been no result. He supposed that the beam was too weak or that it appeared to be a coastal light. Now, under the radiant dawn, there was plenty of shipping about. Three small freighters were steaming northward, outlined against rosy clouds; none of them was more than a few miles away. In daylight, it seemed unlikely to Holliwell that one would stop, even if a lookout saw the whaler.

His companion, Pablo, seemed untroubled by their situation. Some private emotion was aboil in him. He lay spread out in the bow while Holliwell steered, his eyes fixed on the sky. Holliwell watched the young man for a while, then looked away.

The sea's surface had turned a gentle aqua green; within minutes it would be the mirror of a burning sky. Holliwell felt for his sunglasses and found them in his shirt pocket. Miraculously, absurdly, he had preserved them unbroken.

"There's so much stuff," Pablo said. There was a small vial in his hand; he was preparing to take another of his pills. The pills had made him talkative during the night and Holliwell had pretended sleep. But he had listened well enough to be disturbed by Pablo's talk and eventually to be frightened. Pablo, whoever he was, appeared to be crazy, constantly stoned and fired with indiscriminate violence.

"More stuff in the world than anybody could imagine, brother."

"Indeed," Holliwell said.

Pablo unfurled a daft threatening smile.

The morning sun came down on them like a blow. The wind and the ocean were gentle; a mild offshore zephyr kept them rolling slowly north by east without benefit of the engine. Holliwell turned from Pablo's jeering face to scan the horizon for signs of shifting weather. By any auguries he knew, the sky portended nothing sinister.

"What do you think, Pablo?" Holliwell asked. "Good weather hold?"

He kept trying to start useful conversations with the youth, trying to discover an aspect in which Pablo did not seem demented and dangerous. He had not been having much luck.

"Yeah," Pablo said carelessly. "Weather's fine."

He leaned back against the boards and let his eyes roll heavenward.

"I mean there's more stuff, man . . . nobody knows."

Holliwell shivered in spite of the heat. He took a Dramamine from his own pill bottle.

"Well," he told Pablo after a while, "I'm going to start the engine up. Maybe we can get ourselves out in the shipping lane. If they see us that close up, maybe they'll stop."

Pablo nodded, smiling ambiguously. How mad can he be? Holliwell wondered. Doesn't he care?

The engine declined to turn over. For nearly a quarter of an hour Holliwell labored over it without effect, then, covered with sweat, he sank back against the side of the boat. Pablo crawled aft, removed the engine cover and wiped the inside with the edge of a tarp. He checked the hose connections, squeezed the pump and returned to his space in the bow.

"Try it now, Doc."

"Holliwell pulled the cord; the Evinrude roared to life.

"Points were wet," Pablo said. "That's all."

"Thanks," Holliwell said. He felt as though his bad luck with the engine would make him seem more vulnerable and quicken Pablo's madness. They exchanged looks. Pablo had never stopped smiling. Holliwell was learning to hate him.

"You know about those Indian carvings, right?"

"No one understands them completely. Only a few things about them."

"Tell me," Pablo said.

"Well," Holliwell said with a thin smile, "a lot of them are about a rain god we call God Seven."

"God Seven? That's all?"

"We don't know how to say his name."

"Not even you?"

"No."

Pablo looked thoughtful.

"That old man back there," he said, "I bet you he knows."

"There's a king on some of the stones—well, maybe he's a god too—but we think he's a king. Somebody had it in for him because everywhere he's represented they've chipped away his face. Nobody knows who he really was. We call him Stormy Sky."

"Stormy Sky," Pablo said, and then repeated the words under his breath. "Hey, tell me about those human sacrifices. What were they about?"

"Whatever they're always about. The Indians didn't invent human sacrifice."

"I understand why they did it," Pablo told Holliwell. "I can feel inside me why. I think it's in my blood."

Holliwell watched the young man and said nothing.

"You know about the magic they got there?" Pablo asked.

Holliwell reached for the jug and took a swallow of water. "What magic?"

"I don't mean the old-time stuff," Pablo said. "I mean the bad shit that goes on now. The sacrifices."

"I'm not sure I follow you," Holliwell said.

Pablo shrugged. "You don't have to tell me anything you don't want to, mister. But you might as well know the old man talked to me. I know what goes on in that place. The Demiurge and that."

"I'm afraid you've lost me," Holliwell said. He had come to realize that Pablo affected to regard him as party to some free-masonry of his own imagining. He could not decide whether the wiser course was to let him continue in that impression or to try and set him straight.

"I guess you'll talk to me when you're ready," Pablo said. "When the time comes. We could be a long time in this boat."

Holliwell interpreted Pablo's statement as threat. He figured the young man's weight at about a hundred and fifty pounds —but a hard case, sinewy and mean with enough concentrated malice and nervous energy to make him more than difficult. Moreover he was young and crazy and Holliwell growing weak with the sun and the lack of sleep. Holliwell avoided looking at him, trying to be ready and to hope for the best. They might yet be picked up.

Surely, he thought, they must have known at the mission that this boy was mad and dangerous? It might be that he was not as deranged as he seemed. He could not be sure; they were do-gooders there, *bien pensants*. There was a terrible justice in it that he was not in the mood to savor.

A small freighter had come up on the southern horizon, taking what seemed to be an inshore course. Holliwell licked his lips and fixed his concentration on the ship, holding the throttle on full.

"They say what you don't know can't hurt you," Pablo said, "but that's not so. You get turned around when you don't know anything."

"Right," Holliwell said.

"Man, I'll tell you, I found out so much since I come down this way I can't believe it. The world ain't anything like I thought it was."

Holliwell was intrigued. "Is it better or worse?"

Pablo's face broke into an adolescent smile.

"Uh . . . let's see." He thought about it for a moment. "Better *and* worse, I guess. There's more to it. For me, better."

"Good," Holliwell said.

"I see what you're doing," Pablo said slyly. "You're playing me along. I'm supposed to learn from you."

Holliwell looked at him then, studied the spare contours of his brown face, his overheated eyes. It was like looking into some visceral nastiness, something foul. And somehow familiar.

"You know a hell of a lot more than you're letting on, mister. I can tell that by now."

As the sun's force flattened out over the subject ocean, Pablo took off his shirt and pants, dipped the shirt in sea water and wrapped it around his head like a turban. He stretched himself out across the forward part of the boat and it seemed as though he were enjoying himself, enjoying the sun. Holliwell saw that the diver's knife was strapped to his leg.

The freighter Holliwell had singled out was still coming on. He fixed his eyes on its black hull now, trying to capture the ship with his will. He could see the faint diesel smoke above her funnel. His hand ached as he gripped the engine's throttle; he was trying to wrestle the boat beyond flank speed.

Pablo was watching him.

"We're gonna be O.K.," he told Holliwell.

"That's what I like to hear," Holliwell said.

"I'm tellin' you, man, you got nothing to worry about. We're going home. At least I am."

For more than an hour, Holliwell fixed his concentration on the freighter, trying to get some measure of its bearing and speed. Only when his eyes flooded with sweat did he turn away, steadying the throttle with the crook of his arm, to clean his sunglasses and wet his face with a little fresh water. Fresh water afforded only the briefest relief. He could feel his face swelling, heat and salt were marinating his exposed flesh. Lifting the jug, he drank sparingly, thinking of the wasted water. He felt sick and afraid.

Pablo had gone into something like a sleep. His yellow eyes were blank, half covered by twitching lids and shaded by the fold of the shirt tied over his brow. Though Holliwell tried his best to put Pablo's presence from his mind, it was hard for him not to look at the knife that was secured to the young man's calf. The knife had a plastic hilt and handle and a wide heavy blade. To Holliwell's mind, there was something of Pablo himself about it.

In the depths of his sun-stricken panic, a monster image began to form compounded of Pablo and his blood-guttered, Day-Glo knife. For hours he had been hearing the slurred slow speech, trying to read the murky hooded eyes, watching the muscles tense and relax in his companion's lean brown face. It was as though he had been cornered after a lifelong chase by his personal devil. All his life, he thought, from childhood, the likes of Pablo had been in pursuit of him. But he had not come so far to be trapped like this, at noon, in a lonely place. He resolved that although the ocean might get him, the sun, thirst or starvation, Pablo would not. He would see them both dead first. The resolution gave him a bitter satisfaction that was, after hope, his only comfort; he knew he would hold to it.

The distant ship was still miles away and hardly any bigger on the horizon. He felt like shouting.

"You ain't gonna make it," Pablo said to him.

The words froze his blood but he kept his eye on the ship.

"What do you mean by that, Pablo?"

"He changed course is what I mean," Pablo said. He was

looking past Holliwell at the freighter. "You won't cut across him now."

Holliwell could almost make out the company signature painted in yellow letters across the sky-blue superstructure. She was such a pretty thing, he thought.

"Maybe he can see us," Holliwell said.

"If he can, he's not stopping."

"He must see us."

"Well, it's funny down here," Pablo said. "Anywhere at sea these days. Just because a man sees you don't mean he's gonna come your way. And if he does, that ain't always good."

Holliwell kept watching the ship; her angle had shifted so that the letters under the fantail that spelled out her name and port of origin were partly visible. In desperation, he looked to other quarters. There were two other ships in view but they were very far away. He looked at his watch; the hands showed half past noon. The watch seemed a foolish thing, a little tin register of the immensities that surrounded them. And there was only so much daylight. So much fuel, so much water.

Pablo was peeling an orange. Holliwell watched him, mastering his own anger and revulsion.

"We're in a spot, Pablo, don't you think?"

Pablo passed him half of the peeled orange and nodded toward the east.

"Look there."

"What is it?" Holliwell was aware of the faint quaver in his voice. "Is the weather changing?"

Pablo smiled comfortably.

"Islands," he said. "If we don't see one today, we will tomorrow. Real pretty islands, too."

Holliwell made one last attempt to persuade himself of Pablo's rationality; it failed. He could see nothing but delusion and menace in the animal eyes.

"Well," he said after a minute, "I'll take us out for another hour. Then we better wait and see." He had the sense that Pablo found his firm reasonableness amusing. "If we don't get any help by four o'clock, I'll head north and see if we can get a start toward the coast of Compostela."

"That's against the wind," Pablo said. "We'll never get up there. We're going to the islands."

Holliwell put the orange section in his mouth, chewed the pulp and spat it out.

"I don't understand why you're so sure of that."

"Because it's meant to be," Pablo told him. "That's why."

He made no reply but Pablo seemed disappointed in his response.

"You better take it easy, Doc. A man as smart as you, you oughtn't to be so antsy."

"I'm fine," Holliwell said. "You take it easy."

Pablo's eyes went cold. A little ripple of anger flashed across their surface, a knife glint.

"Maybe you ain't who I thought you were," he said to Holliwell.

"I'm the other guy in your boat," Holliwell said. "That's got to be good enough."

Pablo watched him unhappily for a while and then eased himself aft.

"Take a break," he told Holliwell. "I'll steer for a while."

Holliwell could not bring himself to let go of the throttle.

"What the hell's the matter?" Pablo said. "Afraid I'll run us off the road?"

Holliwell gave over and let Pablo replace him in the stern. When they had crossed he spread his shirt over his face and lay back, resting his head on the tarp. He was exhausted but afraid to sleep.

"I thought you were one of those people," Pablo was saying to him. "I figured you were all right."

"What people?"

"One of those people from that place there. I thought you were part of it."

"Just passing through," Holliwell said.

"You got to understand something, Holliwell. There's a process and I'm in the middle of it. A lot of stuff I do is meant to be."

Holliwell was not surprised by this declaration; he had been expecting something of the sort and he was ready. The loathing he felt braced his blood like an antitoxin. He would stay ready. In spite of the sun and the heat he would not lose consciousness. He lifted the shirt from his face and, turning on his side, looked across the bow. Another ship had passed them by, gone north.

"You know what I'm talking about," Pablo said. "I know fucking well you do." Then he cut the engine and lapsed into silence.

Gradually, Holliwell gave in to his weariness and let his mind spin out of focus. His dreams, if dreams they were, came as salted and sun-drenched as the waking world around him. He saw ships where there were none. One seemed to loom above them less than an arm's span away; he saw it in the clearest detail, red lead on the rails, rust under the water-line when she rolled, paintwork and polished brass on the flying bridge.

When he came out of it, some of the heat and light had ebbed from the day. Heavy ridges of cloud were forming ahead and a steady wind had come up that drove the boat before it, misting them with spray at every fifth wave and hurrying them ever farther from the coast. There were no more ships in sight.

Pablo made a sea anchor of a bucket to hold the stern out of the wind and dry his clothes for the coming night. Without speaking, he took Holliwell's shirt and spread it out beside his own.

"You faked me out, mister," he said. "If you ain't part of it you better not fuck it up. You fuck it up—that's turning me around and I don't permit that."

"You have to trust me," Holliwell said. "We need each other out here."

"I don't need anybody," Pablo told him. "Not no more. Boy, I could tell you the shit trusting people has got me into. I don't even like to think about it."

"I'm on your side," Holliwell said. "Where else could I be?"

As the sun declined, color returned to the sky. A thin green haze seemed to float over the surface of the ocean.

"I don't feel good," Pablo said suddenly. "My leg . . . I got fever, I think."

Holliwell took heart; he was all concern. He wet his hand-kerchief in the fresh water and gave it to Pablo for a salve. They traded places and Holliwell took back the tiller. The wind was noticeably cooler now. Pablo put his shirt on and lay back in the bow, resting on the tarp and his folded trousers.

"You've got penicillin there," Holliwell told his shipmate. "You ought to take it."

Pablo found the pills and Holliwell observed that his fingers trembled as he lifted the plastic top from the tube. He followed the penicillin with one of his other pills, the ones that made him talkative.

"I'm hurting for sure," Pablo said.

Glancing at the boat compass, Holliwell saw that their drift was dead east. Pablo was probably right then, Compostela would not be for them. Whatever was in store would reveal itself in unbounded ocean.

Pablo struggled up and propped himself on an elbow.

"You wouldn't try and turn me around, would you, Doc?"

"Of course not," Holliwell said.

" 'Cause that'd be the last goddamn thing you ever tried, Jim. You better believe it."

"Just take it easy, Pablo." Holliwell's chest was spongy with fear. The wind chilled him and he began to shiver. Pablo sank back down to his rest and seemed to sleep. Holliwell eyed the knife strapped to his leg; it was held in the sheath by a rubber noose that circled the handle. Getting it loose would be a delicate and extremely dangerous operation. And the little bastard never properly slept, Holliwell thought. His eyes stayed open.

He was no better than an animal. He was an animal.

The lower hemisphere of the sun was almost touching the line when Tabor roused himself again.

"You said you betrayed her."

For a moment, Holliwell had no idea what he was speaking of.

"You said to her: 'I betrayed you.' What'd you mean?"

"Nothing serious," Holliwell told him. "It was a bet we had."

Pablo's eyes were vacant and confused.

"You know," he said, "I'm part of the process and you ain't."

"That's my loss I'm sure," Holliwell said.

"I thought I was just anybody." Pablo spoke in a febrile whisper. "I thought I was this loser."

"But instead you're part of the process."

"Everything," Pablo insisted, "everything that happened,

man, happened for a purpose. To teach me. So I could learn. Everything that happened. Everybody I met."

"Except me," Holliwell said.

"I ain't saying that, Holliwell. I ain't sure of that. Maybe you too. You know, he told me—that old man told me—the eye you look at it with, well, that's the eye it sees *you* with. That's what he told me."

Holliwell was moved to recall an experiment he had once read about; he had clipped the report of it for his class. An experimenter endeavoring to observe chimpanzee behavior had fashioned a spy hole in the door of the animals' chamber through which he might watch them unobserved. Putting his eye to it, he had seen nothing more than what he finally identified as the eye of a chimpanzee on the other side of the door. Ape stuff. Another spasm of trembling overcame him; his teeth chattered.

"I think I might be part of the process too," he said, when he had recovered. "I learned a few things down here."

Wrapping his shirt around his blistered body, he turned back toward the coast of Tecan, little more than a green line now on the misty horizon. He had learned what empty places were in him. He had undertaken a little assay at the good fight and found that neither good nor fight was left to him. Instead of quitting while he was ahead, he had gone after life again and they had shown him life and made him eat it.

He turned away from Tecan and faced his fellow traveler. The prospect was death now, after all, sudden or slow, neither earned nor undeserved. And he would have to face it listening to the voice of this pill-brained jackdaw, this jabbering shitbird with his pig sticker and his foul little eyes.

"Me, I was so turned around," Pablo was saying. "I was so fucked up. I mean I'm sick now but I'm a lot better off than I was." He looked over his shoulder and then back to Holliwell. "I'll be glad to get home," he said. "Things gonna be a lot different for me."

Holliwell, shivering in a burst of spray, only nodded.

"I don't know what you're gonna do, Holliwell, but I'm goin' home, goddamn right. I'm goin' home and its gonna be all different. Because I scored, you know what I mean?" He grinned; his teeth were white and regular, the only healthy part of his face, Holliwell thought. "I got regular material things to take back with me. Plenty, Holliwell—never mind asking. And I got spiritual things." Holliwell watched him repeat the words "spiritual things" under his breath. "And I got a little lady up there, yes sir. And I got a boy and he's a good boy, too."

Then a look of alarm came over his face and he touched the breast pocket of his shirt. Whatever he was feeling for was in its place.

"You just keep looking for that island, Holliwell. You're gonna see it!"

Holliwell again studied the mean contours of his companion's face and found himself beset by scruple. From sentiment, conscience, a debilitated failure of will, he suddenly recoiled from the thing he had intended. The hope flared up in him that they might survive together. He was thinking now that the boy on the boat with him was no more than a crazy kid, than whom he was older, harder, tougher, that for all Pablo's bloody prattle he did not really seem bent on murder, that he might even be seen as well-intentioned in his foolish paranoid way. Then too, she had trusted Pablo and taken him in, had given him into Holliwell's care. Perhaps, Holliwell thought, he owned her. He had an impulse to turn again toward the distant green coast but he did not. Everything there was lost now.

The act itself, the doing of it, repelled him. There might be a ship. Or even, absurdity of absurdities, an island. He decided he would keep his head and a close watch on Pablo and endure the oncoming night.

The colors of dusk shaded the sky. The sun was tame again, fixed to the textured horizon. Steady, Holliwell thought. Live in hope.

"You hear them?" Pablo Tabor asked him.

"Hear what?"

Holliwell listened hard. There were the waves, flumes of spray striking the fiber-glass. Nothing else.

"Sure you do," Pablo insisted. "The hell you don't."

"I don't know what you're talking about."

"It's for me," Pablo said. "They belong to me now." He forced himself up again. "That's just the same as me you're hearing."

"What are you hearing, Pablo?" He himself listened again, half hoping that there would be something to hear. "Are they . . . voices?"

"You're a card," Pablo said. "You're a shrewd son of a bitch." He grinned. Holliwell's heart sank.

"They're nothing but beautiful," Pablo said. "Beautiful is what they are."

Holliwell, nodding, despaired and agreed.

"We're buddies now," Pablo declared. "We're brothers."

"Absolutely," Holliwell said. He was trying to convince himself that the wound and infection had rendered Pablo too weak to be threatening. But as he looked at Pablo sitting upright across from him, charged with deluded passion, he knew that he himself was the weaker, with his chill, his burn, his sentimentality.

"I was gonna kill you, Holliwell. No shit."

"Now, now," Holliwell said. "Aren't you sorry?"

"I ain't ever sorry," Pablo told him. "You know why?"

"No," Holliwell said.

Pablo laughed. "Because I got nothing to be sorry about."

"Aha," Holliwell said.

Pablo's lean brown face was all youth and strength and chemical good nature. In time, Holliwell knew, the chemistry would turn, the creature in there would turn on him and require, as such creatures always required, an external victim. Then it would be his role to speak softly, to mouth little smiles in solicitation of pity which would not be forthcoming. With all the goodwill in the world, Holliwell thought, he was not up to it.

"I killed people," Pablo declared. "I don't give a shit. They were turning me around. They asked for it."

"I'm not turning you around."

"No," Pablo said. "And I been looking for it. Don't think I ain't been."

Evening brought forth the wind without remission. The power of Pablo's madness and the chill on his braised body laid Holliwell low. He steadied himself on the side of the boat; he could not stop shaking.

I know you now, he thought, watching Pablo. Should have known you. Know you of old.

He felt the force he had encountered over the reef.

The stuff was aqueous, waterborne like cholera or schisto-somiasis. He had been around; he had seen it many times before. Among swarms of quivering fish, in rice paddies, shining in gutters. It was as strong as anything in the world.

Stronger perhaps, when the illusions were stripped away. It glistened in a billion pairs of eyes. Comforting to think of it as some aberration, a perversion of nature. But it was the real thing, he thought. The thing itself.

"What's the matter with you?" Pablo asked.

"I guess it's the sunburn," Holliwell said. "The chill."

Pablo drew up the tarp on which he had been resting and handed it to Holliwell. He started undoing the top button of his work shirt.

"Hey, you want to wear my shirt on top of yours? I don't need it. I'm fine."

"Thanks. Keep your shirt."

The failing sun glowed like an ingot plunged in clear liquid, casting its refracted light on them. Pablo sat facing it.

"Your regular run of people," Pablo said, "I don't care about them. They're no goddamn good."

Tabor closed his eyes for a moment and opened them.

"Nothing can stop me now, Holliwell. I got it all together. Like there are ten million people think they got it all together but I'm the one who has. That's how it was meant."

"Good," Holliwell said. "Good."

"We're gonna stick together, us two. You're gonna tell me what you're supposed to—I'll make you. And then," he said, "I'll do the same for you."

He leaned forward and took Holliwell by the arm.

"When you got the mojo, brother—when you're on the inside—the world is fantastic." He surveyed the empty sea, the sky, the violet clouds, with a look of triumph. "It's mellow, it's all a high. It's wonderful."

"Good," Holliwell said.

He was not seeing Pablo any longer; it could have been anyone there. His heart beat faster. An old anger was quickening it. If we could get them all together in one place, he thought, all these inspired, these bright-eyed ones, they might no longer make us tired of living.

When Pablo sank back to his rest, Holliwell watched the knife in its sheath as he had watched the ship that passed them in the afternoon. Then, his eyes on Pablo's flickering lids, he reached down, and as gently as he could, lifted the rubber noose that held the hilt and drew the knife out of its bright plastic sheath. The blade shone, in the last of the sunlight. When he had it, he put it behind him, on his belt.

Within minutes, Pablo roused himself. Holliwell waited for him to notice the missing weapon but he never did.

"You know anything about people's past lives?" Pablo asked him.

"Not me," Holliwell said.

Something about Holliwell's look disturbed Pablo. His eyes narrowed.

"You O.K., brother?"

"I have a dream," Holliwell said. He shuddered, not with the chill but with fear and revulsion. He laughed. "I mean I keep having this dream. It recurs."

"What dream?" Pablo pulled himself upright along the thwart.

"In my dream," Holliwell explained, "I'm different from everyone else. Maybe I'm on the subway, understand, and everyone in the car is black except me. Something really lousy is about to happen to me—only nobody cares. Everybody's laughing because they're not like me." He was trembling and dry-mouthed, his heart beat so hard that he felt he could barely contain it. "Or else I'm on a ship. The crew are Chinese or Malays, Indians, anything, something that I'm not. That thing's about to happen. No one cares. It's funny to them. I'm different from what they are."

Pablo nodded, wide-eyed.

"Oh, you got it," he said. "You got your finger on it."

"Do I?"

"Because that's me," Pablo said excitedly. "That's what I been running into all my life."

"That's what things are like," Holliwell said.

"I'm Spanish, see? Or my mother was. She was . . . I don't know, Indian, Spanish blood. So I never been what anybody else was. And down inside me, I never been. That's why all these people turn me around."

"A terrible thing," Holliwell said.

"It's the worst thing in the world when people turn you around because you're something else than them. It hurts you. It fucks you up so bad. You just go round and round."

"There's a story about how people are," Holliwell told Pablo. "You hear it a lot of places. You used to hear it in Vietnam. They probably tell it in Tecan as well."

"I'm free and clear," Pablo said, looking at the ridge of violet cloud ahead of them. "Free, man."

"It's about a buffalo and a scorpion. I'm sure you've heard it."

Pablo turned his attention back to Holliwell and he shook his head absently.

"What is it?"

Holliwell put his hand behind his back to touch the knife. His arms tensed. He took a deep breath.

"A scorpion comes up to a buffalo on a riverbank. Please, sir, says the scorpion—could you give us a ride across? No way, says the buffalo. You'll sting me and I'll drown. But the scorpion swears he won't. Why would I, he asks the buffalo, when if I did, I'd drown along with you? So off they go. Halfway across the scorpion stings the buffalo. And the poor buffalo says, you bastard, you killed us both. Before they go under, the scorpion says—it's my nature."

Pablo looked blank and nodded.

"You get it, don't you, Pablo? That's how it is, right?"

"It don't have to be like that," Pablo said.

Holliwell licked his rope-dry lips.

"I'll tell you what, Pablo, I think you're right after all. I think each of us has something to offer the other."

"Damn right," Pablo said.

"But what you offer, Pablo—I'm not having any, understand? Because in my lifetime, boy, I've had fucking enough of it. So let me offer *you* something while you're still in the mood to learn."

Pablo was perplexed. "Say what?"

"Call it," Holliwell said, "the abridgment of hope." He braced his legs against the stern.

After a moment, Holliwell saw Pablo's lips move. He was repeating the phrase silently. The abridgment of hope.

Holliwell sprang forward from the brace; his left hand clutched at Pablo's throat, his right, bent at the elbow, held the knife. In the next second, he made the thrust and felt the horizontal blade strike resisting bone. He shoved harder and the tip worked free of the rib and went in. He pushed until the hilt was against Pablo's shirt. He was shouting; exhausted, he leaned his full weight on Pablo, forcing him back against the side. Pablo's hand was gripping his left arm, twisting it numb. When the hand relaxed, he drew back and then he met Pablo's eyes. In their look was surprise and also disappointment, yet beyond all that something expectant, as though there might be a good part yet to come. Holliwell pulled the knife out and Pablo grunted. There was no good part to come and Holliwell felt sorry.

"Sorry," he said. Then he punched Pablo across the face to turn away the wrenching accusatory stare, and in a long straining wrestler's roll, he heaved Pablo out of the boat and into the darkening water. One of Pablo's hands was reaching for the side; he had an impulse to strike it away but he could not bring himself to do so. He was spent, in shock. Scarcely able to breathe, he watched Pablo's head and struggling shoulders drift away from the stern. If there was blood he could not see it against the color of the sea.

The last of the sun shone on Pablo Tabor. He brought his arms up once—but only once—in a single feathery stroke, trying to tread water. Then he threw his head back, keeping his open mouth above the surface.

Against his will, Holliwell looked at Pablo's face. He was at a loss now to find the shimmering evil he had seen in it before. The stricken features were like a child's distorted with pain and fear yet still marked with that inexplicable flicker of expectation. It was a brother's face, a son's, one's own. Anybody's face, just another victim of ignorance and fear. Just another one of us, Holliwell thought.

I get the joke now, he said to himself. We're all the joke. We're the joke on one another. It's our nature. In the same moment, he thought of May. What a misfortune, he thought, that we have only each other.

The boat drifted further and Pablo was gone. Small swells, borne on the offshore breeze, closed the tiny rent in the seam of ocean where he had been suspended.

When the sun was down, a thin stream of low clouds moved north across its azimuth and were lit to red and gold beyond imagining. Holliwell had started the engine out of an impulse to escape; he held the throttle at full, riding the breeze eastward. When he saw the illuminated clouds he began to recite.

"See, see," he said aloud, "where Christ's blood streams in the firmament!

"One drop of blood will save me."

In Vietnam he had recited the lines in company to amuse and they became a little sunset superstition, a formula in times of stress, never remotely a prayer. He said them now, over and over until the words were purged of meaning. There was blood on his shirt. He took it off and, shivering, scrubbed the wet stains in sea water. Then he saw that there was blood in the boat as well; he cleaned it up with more salt water, using Pablo's trousers and the bilge pump and the bailing can. After dark, he was still looking for blood; he cut the engine, took a flashlight from the gearbox and inspected the deck for traces of it. Under the bow, he found a small sparkling stone. It appeared to be a rhinestone when he examined it in the beam of his light. He threw it overboard, together with Pablo's bloodstained pants.

Half an hour later, the lights of a passing ship came in sight and Holliwell signaled S O S with his light until it was apparent that there would be no result. He was feeling very cold and sick now; even the warm drinking water in the jug made him shiver. He lay across the tarpaulin and tried to sleep.

During the night, things overtook him. There was music that had somehow to do with the passage of the stars overhead and there were jokes. In one of the jokes a shark passed near the boat, on his way to a feeding frenzy.

"What is there?" the shark asked a companion.

"Just us," the other shark said.

Holliwell laughed in his thin sleep.

"She's dead," Lieutenant Campos told Father Egan, "your nun." In the surrounding woods ramon nuts were falling from the higher boughs, an unceasing rain that rustled the leaves softly.

"I knew it," Egan said.

Campos had come weaving into the clearing where the stelae stood, thrown himself upon his knees and demanded Penance. He was pointing his service revolver at the priest; it was a sacramental hijacking. He had not made it to Miami like the President, so he was forcing Jacob's ladder.

"The Lord who loves tricks," he said bitterly, "has played a trick on me."

Campos was wearing a jaunty lemon-colored yachting cap with crossed anchors, badly soiled above the visor. It was the kind of cap that street-corner sports in Alvarado favored. His white shirt and trousers were caked with red mud. All that remained of the former official Campos were the one-way sunglasses. When he removed them to wipe his face, Egan saw that the pupils of his eyes were dilated. He would have taken Justin's bag for the drugs, the priest thought.

The lieutenant's pit-centered lustrous eyes rolled under his brows.

"Such a thing as you—how can you understand? A coward is degenerate. I am a man that knows who he is and you want to make me ridiculous. A man of stern formality with a responsibility for order. You're not worthy to kiss my prick but I'm on my knees to you."

Egan was bemused.

"You did kill her, didn't you?"

"I killed her. She was a dilettante." He sniffed ferociously and spat on the ground. "How many deaths were caused by her? Hundreds? Thousands? She herself didn't know how evil she was."

"Oh, Campos," Egan said.

"Confess me!" Campos shouted, waving the pistol loosely. "It's my right."

Egan drew a benediction on the air. You who love tricks, he prayed silently, who made Leviathan—why will you confront us in these monstrous aspects? Who made the lamb?

It was His way of not listening, the priest thought. On the field of folk He is never at home, never available. Reach out a hand and there's only the terrifying touch of flesh, nothing firmer or finer. Ask questions and the answers are veiled in illusion, words from a fever dream.

"She was tortured, I presume?"

"In the Guardia we're serious. It wasn't a birthday party."

Egan bent forward over the flat stone on which he sat and leaned his forehead on his fist.

"Why confess, Campos? I'm not your judge."

"For my peace," Campos said thickly. "You see what's happened, priest? I was what I was and now I'm poorer than the poorest Negro. My life is in danger. My soul also. The church exists for people like me."

"Oh, the church," Egan said, and smiled. "Of course."

"Before she died, she said, 'Behold the handmaid of the Lord.' "

Egan raised his head. "Justin did? Good heavens. How about that, eh?"

Campos curled his moustache and looked at the ground.

"She said that, did she? You beat her lifeless and you did your business with the cow prods and she said that? Good girl." Egan wiped his eyes. "She *was* special, young Justin. "Well," he said to Campos, "I guess that showed you, eh?"

"It showed me up," Campos admitted. "It put me in the wrong. Then I knew that God had played a trick on me."

"Maybe you're just being superstitious."

"I?" said Campos, outraged. "It was a sign from God!" he shouted. "Don't dare deny it! A sign from God to me."

"Of what?"

"You don't even know how to be a priest, you *maricón!* A sign that I would have to ask forgiveness."

"Oh, I see." Egan found himself looking at the purple flowers growing from the vine on one of the pyramids. "I suppose Justin would forgive you if she could. She's all right now. But you have a debt to discharge to her."

"I'll swear," Campos said.

"If you want Justin to forgive you, you'll have to stop murdering young women. They may be well out of it, see, but it's very hurtful to their families. That kid you had in the freezer couldn't have been more than twenty and that's awfully young to be terrified and murdered."

"It happens everywhere," Campos said.

"All the same, Lieutenant."

Campos crossed himself and squinted ardently at the flawless sky.

"But I must have comfort," he said when he had sworn.

"If you want comfort along with Justin's forgiveness you'll have to embrace a vision. Could you?"

"With ease," Campos said. "That's the sort of man I am."

"You must concentrate as hard as you can and imagine a world in which you don't exist. A world in which there is no trace of you whatsoever."

Campos crossed himself again and closed his eyes.

"Just a moment," he said. "I don't understand this."

Egan, looking at the flowers, was impatient. "Oh," he said. He thought he had been clear.

"I must know that God forgives me," Campos insisted. "I've come. I've humiliated myself before a *maricón* of a priest. Now it's up to Him."

"Campos, God doesn't care what you do."

"Not care?"

"Of course not. Why should he?"

"Don't tell me God doesn't care what I do," Campos said indignantly. "He must. He must or . . . there can be no mercy."

Egan turned to the lieutenant and smiled.

"There is no mercy. Not the kind you're talking about. Not in this place. We can't bestow it and we can't receive it. It's just not available at this level."

"But I believe in it," Campos said. "I believe in mercy."

"One as experienced as you should know better."

"What is there, then?"

"Oh," Egan said with a shrug, "you know, don't you, Campos? Half moments. Glintings. A little rising of the heart, eh? It's dappled."

Dappled, he thought, looking at the web of vine and flowers. Good.

"But mercy in that sense? Oh, no, I don't think so. One does what one can."

Campos stared at him and struggled to his feet.

"I'm on my knees before a devil," he said. A shudder seized him. Breathing hard, he backed away from the rock on which Egan sat and leveled his service pistol. A convulsive giggle rattled in his throat and he pulled the trigger. The weapon clicked in a businesslike manner. He pulled the trigger again with the same result.

"Holy Mother," he said, "my cartridges are gone." He lowered the gun and felt the pockets of his shirt. "I'm disarmed," he told Egan in a tone of apology. "I have no more cartridges."

"Well," Egan said, "I haven't any."

Campos put the pistol in his belt and looked about in despair.

"Look," he exclaimed in a stricken whisper, "there's someone there!"

Egan turned to see. A few hundred yards away, at the base of an unexcavated pyramid, two men were digging with pick-axes and shovels. The men had arrived immediately after the battles, while the shooting was still going on, and commenced to circle the overgrown structure with a trench. They worked with great single-mindedness; from time to time one of them would climb the wall of red earth their digging had thrown up to put a pot or a piece of copal jewelry in the flour sack they kept nearby. They had been hostile to Egan at first, they had threatened him. Now they ignored him. They had not seen Campos yet. Both of them wore holstered pistols.

"They're *huaqueros*," Egan told the lieutenant. "Robbers."

"Ah," Lieutenant Campos said. He began to back silently away in the direction from which he had come. His eyes, fixed on the laboring *huaqueros,* were wet with rage and desire.

Egan watched him go. By the time the *huaqueros* spotted him he was passing into the cover of the trees. The two men stood motionless for a moment, hands on their weapons. Then one gathered up the half-filled flour sack, and they dodged out of the clearing.

When they were gone, the priest's attention returned to the net of flowers enclosing the ancient stones. In the days since the battle, the flowers had seemed to spring from their pods almost as he watched. Their odor was heavy and sweet; it hung like a Mystery over the clearing and the surrounding forest.

He had seen the tracer bullets in the distance on the night the company's plant was stormed by the Guardia. Justin had been there and they had captured her. Then, during the next day, there had been more shooting, and when it stopped the motif of a Schubert trio had settled on his inner hearing and stayed. He could not think where he had heard it first; long before, in another place. It was just a little jig of a thing, a ditty, but its particles of sound were so wondrously conjoined that the sensing of it was delicious, an ineffable pleasure. Egan wondered what made him feel so happy at times.

"Never a dull moment," he said to himself.

It was true. His moments were never dull since he had come to occupy them one by one. Something was always happening and he passed many of the daylight hours without a drink. But happy as so many moments might be, he was not yet proof against sadness. It was not the same consuming soreness of heart that had poisoned his life before, but it came and he had to endure it. He was able to examine it now.

Oppressed, he would consider the quickening decomposition of his body and its attendant faculties. He could hardly recognize his own image in a glass. His hands shook constantly, his fingers were numb, his heart fluttered. All the keepers of the house were trembling. This relentless failing of life was comforting in its way. It reminded him that however desperate and alone one single creature might feel, creation looked after its own and brought everything round full circle.

He had been elected to awareness, and while awareness had its satisfactions, it was not easy to watch all the world's deluded wandering across the battlefield of a long-ago lost war. One had to close the heart to pity—if one could. The truth was a fine thing, but it had to be its own reward.

Much later the edges of the world came alight and Holliwell was relieved at first, but soon he realized that there was much to dread. Fearfully he looked eastward, knowing the sun would rise there. He felt afraid of sunrise.

When the first burning sliver came out of the sea, he knew that he would see the eye of the world, and the knowledge made him tremble more violently than he had throughout the long imprisoned night. He turned his back on it.

In the core of the risen sun, it would be there for him to see—the eye of things. Blue, yes. Boiled clear. A guileless stare. He would be transfixed before the eye and every cell of his identity would rise up in recognition of itself. He, Holliwell, was things. There was nothing better. The absence of evil was the greatest horror.

Then out of the sky suddenly blue as the eye of things there came in dogged laboring flight, heavy-winged, a pelican with a spot of blood at its breast. His head snapped back to follow it, but he dared not turn full round and face the eye in the sun.

A little later, a yellow bird, a tiny thing, came and stood on the edge of his boat. It took a few hopping steps, inches from his face, and cast its eye, the size of a flower seed, on him. In the trifling lizard glance, the world's eye was fleetingly reflected. Yet, he could confront it there, he thought. It was only a little yellow bird.

Keeping his flayed back to eastward, he turned in a crouch and saw with astonishment that there was an island close by. There were low sandy bluffs and above them low hills covered with bright green and yellow vines. There were cacti and sea palms. Coconut trees. Light surf rolled gently toward a leeward shore and he was drifting in. He looked over the side and saw coral heads only a few feet beneath his keel. It was the island Pablo had promised him.

He reached out and groped about him for the water jug, still afraid to see the sun. When he had drunk and put the jug by, there was another sight to amaze him.

A hundred feet away swung a boat, scarcely larger than his own whaler but with a forward superstructure and two fishing chairs mounted aft, fast to the deck. Between the chairs and a cooler in the stern three people stood watching him, mute and motionless.

A black man in a blue captain's hat held the wheel. Beside him was a middle-aged white American, very tall and balding, in steel-rimmed glasses and wearing a long-sleeved white shirt. A tourist—a visitor to the island out fishing.

The third person in the boat was a child, a boy of eleven or twelve. The boy held a red Coca-Cola can in one hand and a long sport rod in the other. He was staring straight at Holliwell and his expression was beyond surprise, the expression of someone seeing such a sight as he had never seen or thought to see. His face reflected the sun; the look of its eye was in the boy's eye.

A trick, Holliwell thought. In desperation he turned at last to face down the sun and it was only a glare, a blind star.

Holliwell began to laugh until the spasms froze his jaw and he clenched and ground his teeth.

"Ho," he called across the water.

The helmsman kept the fishing boat well off, as though he were afraid that Holliwell would try to board them.

"It's just us kid," Holliwell said. He looked into the boy's fearful eyes and it was all there—all of it. We look at us. The thing looks at itself. It's as innocent as daylight.

What is a good word, he wondered, to say to them?

"American," he called out. That was a good enough word for his purpose.

"Hey, brother"—he directed his question at the boy's father "—know the one about the three monkeys?" He was only mumbling.

Know the one about the Demiurge and the Abridgment of Hope?

They all went on staring. The eye you see it with, he told them, is the one that sees you back.

Nor, he thought, am I going to tell them stories about murder. This is another day.

"I'm glad to see you well," Holliwell called. "I require rescue here."

The helmsman gunned his engine and hung back. They were floating a little fiber-glass minuet. Holliwell tried to stand but the sun beat him down.

"Why is he looking at me like that?" Holliwell asked.

As though I should be something else. Because it's not as if I haven't tried.

She has her sunrise, he thought, and I have mine.

Holliwell knew that he was home; he had nothing to fear from the sun. A man has nothing to fear, he thought to himself, who understands history.